UNDER COLD MOONS

THE CROWNS OF TALAM

LE VAN VEEN

storied stars

First edition December 2023

Published by Storied Stars Books

Cover Design by Kelly Ritchie

Copy and Developmental Editing by Becky Wallace

Proofreading by Noah Sky

Map by Alyssa Hurlbert

Author Photo by Marigold Visuals Photography

ISBN 979-8-9892243-0-2 (ebook)

ISBN 979-8-9892243-1-9 (paperback)

ISBN 979-8-9892243-2-6 (hardcover)

www.LEVanVeen.com

To the dreamers and the believers.
To the younger me who longed for this feeling.

TAISTEALAI

The way the three ancient beings billowed about the room never failed to raise the fur along Taistealai's spine.

The small squirrel peered from the shadows at the baby nestled against her mother's heaving chest. The ornate bed was silent, and Taistealai could taste the fear of the new parents on his tongue while the norns held the room in suspense.

Aisling, Aisling, Aisling.

Three feminine voices echoed through the air as though coming from no source at all. They hummed their chorus that declared the fate of each elf upon their birth, and this birth was no ordinary one.

Taistealai held his breath while he awaited their next words, resisting the urge to tap his claws nervously on the wooden floor in order to avoid detection. The scent of childbirth mingled with the unique stench of life and death that followed the norns wherever they went.

A dream. A vision. A blessing or a curse.

The messenger of the gods watched as the father cradled the mother's hands and traced nervous circles on her pale skin with his thumb. He knew the words that rested on the tips of their tongues

—the question they wanted answered above all else. It was the question only he and the norns held the answer to. The answer would be the true prophecy, the correct and faithful whisper of the norns from nine generations ago that would remain their secret until the elf's nineteenth naming day.

The elf born into the ninth generation. The elf born of the richest bloodline. The elf to deliver or destroy the realms. The elf born into a prophecy you cannot yet know lies before us.

The words settled like dust in a forgotten nook, and the air grew heavier with each passing moment. Taistealai swallowed as he watched a single tear roll down the mother's cheek. It brought their fears and their most dreaded truth to fruition through the chilling song of the norns.

While Taistealai could not see the faces of the norns from where he crouched beneath the rocking chair, he knew they would show no emotion. They had long known this day would arrive, long before the mother and the father were even of this world. And Taistealai had known too.

Taistealai watched through watery eyes while the most ancient of the norns pulled a shining golden thread out of thin air and gently pressed one end into the bottom of the infant's left foot. It stayed there as the norn pulled the other end up into the air, where it shot through the ceiling and into the skies—out of sight.

The golden glint of the thread lingered there for one beat . . . two beats . . . three beats before disappearing into thin air. The norns faded away along with it, leaving the family of three in the elegant and desolate room.

Taistealai hung his head low as he readied his aching paws for the long journey back to the home of the gods.

PART ONE
SWARM OF OMENS

I

AISLA

The ash trees of the Tus Forest swayed in a way that seemed to taunt Aisla Iarkis from where she peered beyond the emerald scales of her wyvern's wing.

The sound of rustling leaves echoed in her ears, even from their distance away. Her ears strained to take it all in with the deep breath that filled her chest. Dead branches littered the tree line from the passing winter, as other branches flourished with the green of coming spring.

But that was the Tus Forest.

When she directed her gaze towards the southern tip of their continent, there was no hint of the vibrant greens. Her throat constricted as the evidence of the lofa ravaging her home became harder to ignore with every flight atop Muinin.

"You okay, Ash?" Ruairi Vilulf called out to her from her right.

Ruairi, who never let anything slip past him. He was one of the two people closest to her, and the other flew to her left. Ruairi was always the first to pick up on what she was feeling without her needing to say the words. He had just returned from a scouting trip where they sailed along the southern coast to investigate the mysterious plague that first appeared just over three moons ago. There was no known source, and civilizations along the southern coast had moved north, where they could sustain growing populations.

The communities had been happy to help those fleeing the devastation until lofa became a viral disease infecting living beings. Then, uncertainty and panic became the next thing to level their continent.

"All good," she called back to him with a forced smile, and she wondered why she even bothered lying to him.

Ruairi pressed his lips into a thin line. His brilliant red hair shone in the light of the rising sun. A sense of longing filled her as he held her gaze, trying to read her, but she turned back to look out at the sky as Muinin flew through thin, wispy clouds.

"Of course she's not okay," Eire grumbled from their left. Her voice was hoarse, as though she had spent the night shouting. "It looks worse out there each sunrise, doesn't it?"

Aisla could only nod, but she knew Eire had not been expecting an answer. Eire was nothing if not honest. The liveliest and most energetic of the three of them, Eire had been vocal with her thoughts on the lofa. While Ruairi scouted out food sources and explanations, Eire turned to the gods, as her family always had. And Aisla—she was forced to stay out of it all. Her grandmother kept her nearby under claims of protection, but Aisla knew her skills would be of better use spent out with Ruairi. She matched him, if not bested him, in every training course in scoil, save for esos. Aisla still lacked the control necessary to harness the magic coursing through her veins, and her grandmother never failed to remind her of that.

Esos wasn't necessary on the scouting missions, though, and they both knew that. Dwarves and humans joined in too, despite not having esos at all. Aisla would give anything to finally be permitted to take part in making a change, but as their mathair, her grandmother would always have the last word.

"It definitely isn't getting any better," Ruairi bit back.

"The gods won't turn a blind eye to us," Eire spoke under her breath.

Aisla sensed that each time Eire said it—each time she insisted it —she believed it a little less herself. Aisla couldn't blame her. She had always admired Eire's commitment to her faith. Sometimes, she wished she felt the same; but that faith had started to feel more like naivety.

"It appears as though they already have," Ruairi said.

Aisla winced.

She tightened her grip on the leather reins that harnessed Muinin. The tension in the air was palpable, and while Aisla agreed with Ruairi, she stayed as neutral as she could. Any time she hinted towards Ruairi's side, Eire would just blame it on the feelings she swore she saw between them—feelings Aisla had held on to for longer than she would ever tell Eire.

"There!" Aisla shouted, thankful for the reprieve as bright purple flowers came into view.

Aisla steered Muinin towards the patch of them. She had been searching for the rare plant for weeks now, hoping to add it to the collection pressed between pages on her bedside table. It was a silly hobby, given everything else going on in Eilean, but she was limited in where and how she could help. Collecting the flowers, herbs, and foliage of her continent gave her something to do and something to preserve. She became obsessed with adding each species to her collection and recording all that she knew about them in hopes it would one day prove useful. Aisla had no desire to become an herbalist or a farmer, but she enjoyed the knowledge that came with her expeditions.

Most of the time, she went alone with Muinin, but on mornings like this, when Ruairi was home and Eire had the time, Aisla was thankful for the comfort of their presence and that they humored her mission. Ruairi often brought her home new plants from his scouting trips, too. Some of her favorites were ones he had returned with.

The grassy earth came flying towards them as Muinin hit the ground with a thud that Aisla had long grown accustomed to. She stroked the scales along his neck as she heard two more heavy thuds sound behind them. Then there was a third, softer thud. A feminine yelp followed.

Aisla whirled to look over her left shoulder and watched Eire's head fall back to follow her body that had fallen from her wyvern, Combha.

Confusion muddled her brain, but Aisla wasted no time sliding down Muinin's side as she sprinted to Eire where she lay on the ground. She was clawing at her own neck as she gasped for air.

She coughed, choked by an invisible source.

Shock rattled Aisla, and her hands trembled. She dropped to her knees beside Eire just as Ruairi knelt to her other side. Aisla cradled her neck to lift her head up in an attempt to get air down her airway again. Eire continued to gasp as her eyes locked onto Aisla. The gentle blueness of them shone with desperation and the urgency settled into Aisla, warring with her helplessness.

Aisla fought to calm a roaring wave of her esos that came to life with the overwhelming feeling rising inside of her. The uncontrollable force threatened to break free, but Aisla knew she could not let it.

"It's okay," Aisla breathed out through clenched teeth. "It's okay. Take a deep breath."

Ruairi's warm arms wrapped around Eire as he lifted her higher without a word. He gently pounded on her back to help with the choking as Aisla leaned back onto her heels and took in the graying of Eire's skin. Her mouth dried as she recognized it in the death of the crops along the south. She shook her head as though she could lose the thought as easily as it had entered her mind.

Foreboding stirred in her chest.

Eire fell still in Ruairi's arms. Aisla watched as he used two fingers to check her pulse beneath her jaw.

"Ru," she whispered. "You don't think. . ."

Her voice trailed off and she would not allow herself to finish the sentence.

"We have to get her to the infirmary," Ruairi responded.

Aisla nodded in agreement, slowly bringing herself to stand again as she pushed past the fear threatening to keep her kneeling there. Ruairi lifted Eire with ease and walked her over to his wyvern, Gaotha. A pang of sympathy shot through Aisla as Combha groaned with the ache of watching the pain of her rider. Combha had seen enough pain as it was, having lost her previous rider, Aisla's mother.

"I'll take Muinin and Combha back to the wyvern caves," Aisla directed. "You get Eire to the infirmary and I'll be right there."

Aisla's heart raced as she mounted Muinin with not flowers, but a fear seated deep within her as she refused to look at Ruairi and Eire. She kept her gaze ahead while tears burned the corners of her eyes.

Not Eire, she pleaded with gods that had never heard her. *Please, not Eire.*

2

AISLA

Eire's dark curls fell limp, as though they had lost all of their
life.

Aisla knelt by her side, her chest tight with emotion as
she untangled knots of sweat-dampened hair. Her tawny skin had
paled to a sickly shade. Her lively, outgoing best friend was hardly
recognizable, tucked beneath a heavy floral quilt pulled all the way
up to her chin. Her body was visibly trembling underneath.

Ruairi stood behind Aisla, ever the protector. She could practically feel his heart fracturing along with her own.

They were permitted into the infirmary so long as they wore
cloth tied around their mouths. The infectious nature of the virus
was still unknown, as was so much about it.

It was one thing to fall ill. Plenty of sicknesses were common in
the city, especially during the shift from winter to spring, but this
was different. This was new. Eire was hardly breathing, and all of it
had happened so quickly.

The rapid decline is what scared Aisla the most.

Aisla hardly noticed the tear that rolled down her cheek and
landed on the quilt as a sort of emptiness settled within her. She

stopped untangling the knots and gently took Eire's hand in between her own. It was icy cold, despite the sweat beading along her forehead. If Aisla had better mastery over her esos, she would have used the warmth of her fire esos to warm Eire, but it was far too much of a risk.

"We attempted mending," the nurse said gently from the doorway. "Even the life esos has no effect. The menders have never seen anything like it."

The room followed her statement with silence. Aisla found her words stuck in her throat.

"What is to be done?" Ruairi spoke for them and she silently thanked him for it. "There must be some way to heal her."

"We are working on it," the nurse insisted. "I promise we are doing everything we can. We have menders and world tellers alike looking into it already. It's the first we have seen of lofa this far north."

Aisla's stomach churned, and she pushed herself up from the ground. The world seemed to be closing in around her. A suffocating feeling originated in her core and pushed itself outwards. The whispering rush in her veins came to life in response.

A ringing sounded in her elongated ears.

She needed to get out.

Aisla said nothing when she pushed past Ruairi and the nurse, her tears flowing freely. She refused to acknowledge any of the sympathetic glances that were cast her way as she broke into a jog to escape the building.

She made her way out of the infirmary—a blur of gray walls breezing past in her peripheral vision, and found herself behind the building, facing the woods as she stumbled to the earth. An audible sob racked her trembling body as the ringing grew louder, and dark shadows curled around her shaking frame. They swirled in circular formations, enclosing her within. Aisla was caught in the middle of her shadows, the dark esos, and hardly seemed to notice.

It was a comfort and a peace inside her esos. A place for her to escape.

Her mind was lost. Terror consumed her thoughts, while every worst-case scenario raced through her vision in a dizzying manner. Her stomach clenched as though she would vomit at any moment. She could not breathe. The air was stuck inside of her lungs even as she reached for it. Her hands grasped at her throat in desperation.

She would drown in the shadows.

Aisla, a feminine voice spoke from inside of her head. *Aisla come back. Come back to your esos.*

The voice was soft and beautiful. Insistent, yet patient. But Aisla could not come back.

"Aisla!" It was a male voice this time. A male voice that she knew, and it was not coming from inside of her head. "Aisla, please."

Ruairi's hand gripped her shoulder, shaking her gently. He was not afraid.

His other hand rested gently atop hers. She brought her focus to his touch and grounded herself there in the way his skin felt against hers. She gasped and inhaled, then exhaled slowly, drawing out each breath to slow her spinning thoughts and her racing heart. She opened her eyes and looked down at her hands, digging into the cool earth. She gently released it, and took several more deep breaths. Her esos released its hold on her.

Ruairi traced soft circles on the back of her hand. The warmth of his touch ignited a flicker of that fire within her.

The ringing stopped.

The shadows fell to the ground and dissipated. Exhaustion racked her body, and she slumped backwards. Ruairi pulled her against him, gently rocking back and forth, tightening his grip. She leaned into his warmth.

He was the one person who could pull her free of the darkness, and she found a safety in his arms. She felt it when he rested his chin atop her head, as he often did, and the familiarity continued to slow her rapid breaths.

"It's okay, Ash," he murmured. "She'll be okay."

She wanted to ask how he could know that. How he could look at Eire's unconscious body, the way she seemed to have left them already, and he could still promise that. With all the fear already instilled in them surrounding the lofa, how could he be so sure?

Eire, who had been there through it all. Eire, who knew Aisla better than she knew herself. Eire, who was always the first to lighten the mood. Eire, who was a light in dark times.

Aisla couldn't bear the pain in her chest when she thought of a life without Eire in it.

Anger, sorrow, and frustration coursed through her. Each emotion pulling on different threads of her soul.

She felt so many things, but she forced a numbness within herself—within her esos, that was wholly uncontrollable most of the time.

"I'm here," Ruairi murmured over and over like a prayer until she realized that his reassurance had to be enough. And it could be.

Aisla nestled deeper into him. Her breathing fell into a steady rhythm, and the tightness in her chest loosened. She allowed herself to stay silent until she could taste the air in her lungs once again.

"Thank you," she whispered, and his muscles relaxed.

They stayed there for a moment that could have been a lifetime until Aisla mustered the strength to stand up. She gently pushed away from Ruairi and pulled herself to her feet before turning around to offer him her hand, which he took.

They exchanged a look that said more than words ever could. They were in this together. His gaze held hers for a beat too long in the silence. The way his green eyes held her there sent a shiver down her spine.

"Ready to walk back?" Ruairi asked, cutting through the emptiness and the tension, and Aisla looked away.

"I'm going back to Muinin. I never got those flowers," she muttered with a half-smile.

They both knew it was an excuse to get away, and Aisla had always been more comfortable with her wyvern, far away from the bustle of the city.

"I understand," Ruairi nodded. "Eitilt go maith."

Ruairi spoke the term of old for *fly well*—a common phrase used when taking flight.

"Thank you."

Ruairi opened his mouth and closed it again, as if there was more he wanted to say, but instead he turned away from her and disappeared around the infirmary. Aisla longed to reach out to him, too. There were words she could not find the voice to speak as he turned away.

Despite asking for the space, Aisla felt a loneliness creep in with each step he took away from her.

———

Aisla made her way back to the wyvern caves, climbing over a small range of green hills. The caves were massive and ancient, their gaping mouths serving as a home to the wyverns of Eilean—the last wyverns of Talam.

All elves in Eilean either inherited a wyvern or were granted a young wyvern upon their first year of flight training in scoil.

Aisla's own wyvern, Muinin, approached with a shake of his massive wings. He had been waiting on the outskirts of the mass of caves for her. She knew he would be restless and eager to see her again after the way she had left him that morning, but had long been trained not to come unless called upon. If wyverns were able to go to their riders any time they sensed distress, it would create chaos. The wyverns were intelligent beasts blessed with the esos of flames from the gods. They could sense their rider's call from anywhere within the nine realms, and nothing could stop them from responding to that call.

Muinin had been her father's wyvern. After he'd passed on, Muinin waited until Aisla was of age to take him as her own. Her mother's wyvern, Comhba, had been granted to Eire, as they had always shared a close connection.

On one of Eire's flights with Comhba, they hit a bad storm, far from Caillte, their home, and Comhba had a rough landing, which knocked several of her teeth out on the western shore. Eire retrieved her teeth and brought them back to Caillte. A dwarf jeweler crafted bits of the teeth into a necklace for Aisla so she would always have a part of her mother's wyvern.

The necklace was a beautiful gift, and her favorite. Dark twine knots held nine carved pieces of wyvern tooth, and Aisla wore it every waking moment. She found herself touching it now, thinking of Eire and wishing to bring her closer.

Muinin was among the wisest of the wyverns. He and Aisla shared a special connection, and Aisla spent more time within the caves than many elves did. She found peace among their kind, and the presence of Muinin was a peace she needed right now.

She held out her hand to Muinin, who nuzzled his emerald-scaled head into it with a deep purr. They touched foreheads, and Aisla loosed a shaky breath.

Aisla walked around to Muinin's left side and mounted the wondrous beast. Muinin's wings flared out from his body.

"Let's fly," Aisla said to him.

Muinin released a low roar in response and began to beat his wings in a rhythmic pattern. He took a few steps forward and then they were airborne, taking off again into the wispy clouds of the late morning sky.

The wind snaked through Aisla's unbound hair, and she came back to life above the mountain peaks.

Flight was permitted across all of Eilean, but ever since the Siege of Arden, wyverns were not allowed on the main continent, Iomlan.

Flying a wyvern to Iomlan had been declared an act of war.

Aisla let her head fall back and her eyes flutter shut, and her legs squeezed tightly behind Muinin's shoulders. She inhaled deeply and opened her eyes again, catching a glimpse of the dual moons that had nearly disappeared to give way to the morning sun. The dual moons, Sneachta and Braon, lit the nights in Talam as a gift from the gods at the creation of the nine realms, so that its inhabitants may never know true darkness.

There was a tranquility in the skies that Aisla never felt on the ground. She felt the pressures of a prophecy and the weight of her inheritance slip from her shoulders until she was not the Mathair Apparent or the *Gheall Ceann*—the promised one born in nine generations of waiting—but just Aisla. No more and no less. She often found herself wishing that was all she was ever expected to be.

Muinin soared from the east coast to the west of their small continent, and then down through the southern tip of Eilean, where Aisla made a conscious effort not to look down. They flew over rocky mountain ranges and the many forested lands. She saw the waking villages—the humans, elves, and dwarves that she would never meet. They would not know her from any other female elf, but they knew her name, and she would one day be their Mathair.

As they looped back up towards the north, Aisla guided Muinin back towards the patches of purple flowers she had been seeking earlier. Muinin glided into a gentle landing. Muinin lowered his body to the ground, and Aisla dismounted.

Aisla trotted up to the lush bushes of flowers that had not yet been touched by the lofa. She ran her fingers along the soft leaves before plucking a few to bring home to her journal. She hurried back to Muinin, not wanting to linger where the memories of Eire falling from her wyvern were still so fresh.

A full day of teaching combat awaited her, and she knew Ruairi would be counting on her to be there. If nothing else, she hoped it would provide a distraction.

While there was nothing in her own power that Aisla could do for Eire, she would keep herself busy. Ruairi had promised they would get through this, and Aisla trusted him.

And Aisla also knew the only way they could get through was with Eire by their side.

3
WEYLIN

Weylin Myrkor walked in a way that radiated power.

Bloodline aside, it was hard work that had forged Weylin into the beast of a man he had become. With skill honed by rigorous training under the strict and watchful gaze of his father, the Udar of Talam, Weylin was a threat to any that may cross his path, even at the young age of twenty.

Weylin squared his shoulders as he stood outside the gates of Castle Tromlui, of the realm of Briongloid. He admired the grandeur of the castle—its haunting beauty. The duality of it, as it could have been a thing of dreams or a thing of nightmares, nestled between massive green hills. The walls were a smooth white stone, and the roof was a brick-red color. It was one of the largest castles of the realms—the tallest towers reaching up into the clouds.

Weylin's midnight black mare, Eolas, chuffed at his side as though she was anticipating this visit as much as Weylin himself was. Weylin knew the following sunrises would forever change his life, and he could feel his duties weighing heavier on him than they had in a long time. Sometimes he cursed the norns for the golden thread that had set his fate. Other times, he praised them for the power coursing through his veins. No matter how out of reach it was.

How out of reach it would always be.

It would all be worth it when he sat the Arden Throne.

Weylin gave a curt nod to the guard that stood to his left, waiting for him to give the signal to call upon Brendan Dorcas, Lord of Briongloid. It had been many years since Weylin and his father had visited the realm, despite it being just northwest of their border.

Briongloid was known to have tense relations with the Udar. During the War for Descendants, Briongloid had backed Eilean, only switching sides when the tide turned in a way that could not be undone, which made this journey all the more important to Weylin and the future of the nine realms.

The gate shuddered as it opened. Brendan appeared before Weylin. His hazel eyes narrowed as he studied him. His features were sharp and none too welcoming, but he gave a bow of respect to Weylin. Weylin nodded his approval and looked the elf over. He appeared older than Weylin remembered, worn down.

"And what brings us the pleasure of the company of our Udar Apparent? Weylin Myrkor, the Young Wolf." Brendan's voice boomed when he used the name which the realms often called him.

"I wish to spend time in the realm of Briongloid," Weylin responded with authority in his voice. "It has been far too long since our families shared the same space. Unfortunately, my father has other matters to attend to, but I insisted on making the journey alone. It felt long overdue."

Traveling alone was a risk. A risk especially for the Udar Apparent, but it showed good faith and presented a trust to the Dorcases from the Myrkors—a trust Weylin was hoping to build upon.

And even aside from good faith, Weylin had no such need for guards. He would love to see anyone dare to try to harm him. It would make for an eventful visit, and Weylin was always itching for a fight. He had no doubts he would come out on top every time.

"Aye," Brendan said. "It has indeed been a while. We welcome you into our company, Lord Weylin."

"Just Weylin will do," Weylin said with a grin.

Brendan gave a nod of acknowledgment.

Weylin turned his attention to the three elves who had accompanied Brendan to the front gates. The other three members of the Dorcas dynasty were two females and one male. The older of the two females Weylin knew to be Brigid Dorcas. She was Brendan's mate, and had pale blue eyes and stark white hair that matched his. It was a common trait among the elves of Briongloid. The younger male was their son, and heir to their realm, Oisin. He had the same white hair and Brendan's hazel eyes.

Last, was their daughter, Rania. Rania was a striking elf with long, braided white hair and brilliant blue eyes. She wore a slight smirk as she caught Weylin's gaze and did not look away.

"I'm sure you remember my mate, Brigid," Brendan spoke up. "And my son and heir, Oisin."

They both stooped low in a formal bow, Brigid, with a friendly smile on her face. Weylin dipped his head in greeting.

"It is good to see you again, milady. And you, Oisin."

"And you might not remember my daughter," Brendan spoke again. "She was very young during your last visit, and spent most of her time in her rooms."

Rania Dorcas was only a year younger than Weylin. On his last visit, she did stay mostly to herself, while her brother, who was four years older than Weylin, spent much more time with the Udar Apparent, showing him around their castle and its grounds.

She stepped forward with a confidence and grace that Weylin rarely saw amongst the females his age. Weylin held out his hand to her, and she gently placed her own in his. He brought it to his lips, keeping his eyes fixed on hers the whole time. Her skin was cold and soft in his calloused palm. Her blue eyes danced with mischief and she gave him a small, courteous bow.

"Of course I remember the Lady Rania," he spoke softly.

"Well, allow me to show you to your rooms for the duration of your stay," Brendan said with a grunt, as his eyes locked on Weylin. "Oisin can take your horse to our stables."

"Thank you," Weylin replied, shouldering the weight of his pack that he was more than ready to lay down after his journey.

Weylin made his way out of the Dorcas's private dining room after dinner.

Brendan had talked about everything from weather to food, blatantly avoiding any hint of political conversation. Brigid listened, occasionally interjecting to agree with something either of them had said.

It was pleasant enough, Weylin thought. If all went according to plan, this would be the first of many visits to Briongloid for him, and they would have more time to dive into such matters.

The halls were crowded and busy as Weylin made his way through them. He had no intention of going straight back to his rooms, and Brendan had given him full permission to make himself at home.

Not that he needed it.

He walked through the ornately decorated corridor, avoiding the darting, curious eyes of passersby who could not possibly recognize him, but knew the Udar Apparent was visiting. He was a stranger in their midst.

He kept his eyes open for *her* while he turned corner after corner, wondering just how big Tromlui Castle was. He was about to give in and call it a night when he caught sight of her elegantly braided, cloud-white hair.

He meandered towards her, hearing other female voices in conversation, discussing something he couldn't care less about.

"Oh! My apologies, milady," Weylin said with an apologetic dip of his chin after conveniently bumping into her from behind. He cocked his head as he pretended to realize who he had crossed paths with. "What a pleasant surprise, Lady Rania. So we meet again."

"Indeed, we do," she said.

Weylin realized it was the first time he had heard her voice as an adult. It was soft and lilting with a hint of mystery. It might have been the most pleasing voice he'd ever heard.

Weylin watched her icy-blue eyes look him once over, amusement glimmering while she worked to discern how accidental this truly was. A small smile played at the corners of her lips.

"We should leave you to it," one of the young females she was talking to said and cleared her throat, trying to stifle a giggle.

"Oh, no," Weylin shook his head. "I would hate to interrupt."

"I was just about to take my leave," Rania spoke. "Perhaps our Udar Apparent would be so kind as to escort me?"

Weylin could not have planned this better if he had tried to. "It would be my pleasure."

Weylin held out his arm for her to hold on to. Her grip was soft, but confident as she took hold of him and he stood a little straighter. They both nodded farewell to Rania's companions. They were hardly ten steps away from them when Rania spoke up.

"I know why you're here," she stated abruptly, not turning to look at him.

Weylin nearly missed a step, but he kept his composure. Her claim took him off guard, and the way she spoke to him was not the way he was typically addressed as the Udar Apparent. All formalities seemed to have dissipated now that they were alone and walking towards the western wing of the castle.

"To visit one of the world's most intriguing realms because it has been far too long," he answered confidently.

"I am not ignorant. My father might be blind to your motives, but I have grown up in court and have observed the game for far too long. Care to try again?"

"Hmm," Weylin hummed aloud. "I am here to visit a beautiful female who I have not had the pleasure of meeting since we were both children. And I felt it was about time to change that."

"Closer," Rania said, with the slightest hint of annoyance. "Must I say it for you? I don't think this is how these matters are usually handled."

"What matters?"

Rania's head snapped towards him with an incredulous expression on her face. Weylin loosed a chuckle.

"I didn't exactly plan to broach this topic on the first night of my visit—"

"But why dance around it?" Rania interrupted.

"But," Weylin continued, shooting her a pointed look. "I think it is long overdue that our dynasties put the past behind us and come together. There is still unresolved tension across the realms for the choices our ancestors made. With the ninth generation upon us, I feel it is more important than ever to stand united on Iomlan against whatever may arise. The Dorcas dynasty is a powerful bloodline, and it would be my honor to join our two houses. With your brother being heir to the seat in Briongloid, I should ask you to join me in Samhradh."

Rania smirked with a victory that said none of this surprised nor flattered her. In a way, it both irked and intrigued Weylin. He had thought over her many possible reactions in his mind, but her rather arrogant indifference was not an outcome he had predicted.

"In what capacity?" she implored. "As your handmaiden? Or perhaps the kitchen help? I'm excellent with a blade if you seek a tutor in that regard."

"Word travels fast around here when a man is in need of new help, doesn't it?" Weylin quipped, playing into her game.

Rania let out an indignant gasp, but she was grinning all the same. Her teeth shone white and Weylin noted her natural beauty.

"Rania Dorcas," Weylin stopped walking as they entered a dark, empty corridor of the castle. He gently took both of her hands in his and they faced each other. "I would ask that you join me in Samhradh as my mate. I would ask for your hand in union."

4

AISLA

"Relax, Aisla," Cliona Iarkis instructed.

Aisla bit back a retort as she forced her shoulders to relax. She took a deep breath and squeezed her eyes shut while she wordlessly willed the rush in her veins to the surface of her skin. Her budding esos was just beyond her reach. They had been at it for longer than her patience could manage, the sunrise after bringing Eire to the infirmary. Aisla hated the way her grandmother went about, as though nothing had happened at all.

"Aye!" Aisla exclaimed with a startled jump when a stick thumped the back of her knees, nearly causing her to lose her balance.

"I said to *relax*," Cliona hissed. "It appears you somehow managed to grow even more tense."

Again, Aisla chose silence over the quip resting on the tip of her tongue.

She cricked her neck to the left and to the right, then shook out her hands while she loosed a breath. Her mind focused on the mantra taught in scoil when she first learned to wield her esos: *Feel,*

*but still your heart. Think, but ease your mind. Endure, but find your
peace.*

She repeated these words over again until she fell into a steady
rhythm of breathing. The words curled about her mind and
through her veins, calming her and speaking to the energy she
needed to harness. She had spent far too long out of control.

Aisla slowly raised her arms to her waist and held her palms
towards the sky.

A burning sensation tickled her palms. Her eyes blinked open to
a sphere of the esos of flames dancing in her left palm. She gently
twitched each of her fingers as she watched the green flames jump in
response.

Her right arm fell to her side, and a smile tugged her lips
upwards. She noted the way the shadows that were cast by the
glowing green light of her esos flickered around the clearing. Aisla
looked to Cliona, victory gleaming in her yellow-green eyes.

Aisla could wield any weapon with the skill of the best laochs.
She could loose an arrow with an accuracy that would take anyone's
breath away. She could defend herself against the toughest of oppo-
nents, but her esos did not come naturally to her. Cliona knew that
better than anyone else.

"Now, strike that tree," Cliona spoke.

Her long, crooked staff crept over Aisla's shoulder and pointed
towards a tree across the clearing.

Aisla assessed the target before her. It was not an overly challenging one. Cliona could have chosen something harder, but she
also could have chosen something easier. Aisla squared her shoulders and narrowed her eyes at the tree.

The burning energy in her hand encouraged her as she took one
step forward and felt her power surge. She curled her fingertips to
prepare for release. She pushed her hand forward to propel it, but
the flames sputtered out before her eyes.

Disappointment sank through her and she slowly faced her

grandmother, her chin tilted downwards in defeat. She always lost that spark of courage and confidence she carried with Ruairi and Eire when she was around her grandmother. Cliona's disappointment wore on her like a burden that tugged her down towards the core of the earth.

"This time, my dear," Cliona spoke with a small smile, "it was overconfidence. You can never be too sure of the path forward. You must focus your mind towards your esos, and not only your own will and strength. Always be conscious that this fragile thing which you wield is its own entity."

"Just moments ago, I was too unsure, and now I am too confident," Aisla retorted, not bothering to hide her irritation. "It's impossible."

Aisla watched a rare glimpse of sympathy in eyes that were the same color as her own. Cliona gently laid a hand on her arm.

"Treat your esos like an infant, Aisla," she said. "Nurture it, attend to it, be gentle with it, and understand the pace at which it must grow. Not the pace at which *you* wish it to grow. All in good time, Aisla. I know you will find your way."

Aisla could only nod as words escaped her. She felt like she had heard these words over and over before, only phrased slightly differently each time. Eire was already a master tsuna, sending storms of water esos down upon whoever she pleased. And Ruairi could move entire tables as a zephys with the esos of winds.

"You have a different source of esos than your peers." Cliona spoke as if reading the thoughts circulating in her granddaughter's head. And she very well may have, given her nature as a pryer with the esos of mind manipulation, but Aisla was careful to always have her walls up, so she doubted it. That was one lesson in scoil that Aisla had known to pay close attention to, as an attack on the mind was the worst kind of attack. "You must not compare."

"I understand," Aisla lied.

Cliona looked her over from head to toe with a glance that

said she did not believe her. "I think you have earned your dinner. Let's go back." Cliona put an arm around her granddaughter's shoulders before they began the short hike towards the village center.

From atop the hill, Aisla observed the bustling of her village. The people of Caillte were always moving. The humans, elves, and dwarves hurried about their business, only stopping to chat with a neighbor before moving on to another task.

As they descended the hill, Aisla straightened her shoulders and lifted her chin a little higher in an attempt to stand taller. It took a conscious effort to walk as the Mathair would. She thought of all that the title would encompass when passed to her. She would strive to lead her lost realm with grace and humility, as the Mathair should.

"All will happen as it is meant to, Aisla," Cliona said when they reached the path where they would part ways. "Do not fret over things that have yet to pass."

"Thank you, grandmother." Aisla dipped her head in response. She took a deep breath, gathering the courage to ask the question that had been stirring in her heart all morning. "What is to be done for Eire?"

Cliona turned to her, but she did not look surprised. She had been expecting the question.

"I have a plan," she replied in the tone Aisla and Ruairi often referred to as her *Mathair* tone. All business, no trace of the grandmother Aisla had grown up with. "You need not worry about it. Your friend will be a priority and we are doing what we can for now."

"*I* want to help," Aisla declared with a firm set of her jaw. "You cannot keep me sheltered forever."

"You can help when you are not a danger to everyone around you," she snarled back, the tension in the air quickly shifting as her eyes darkened. "Just yesterday you lost yourself, *girl*. Until you can get a hold of the gift the norns have blessed you with, stay far away from trying to give aid."

The words hit just how they were meant to. They stung and burned and riled up the esos, just as Cliona had intended.

"I didn't ask for this," Aisla spat. She felt her anger and her pain warring inside of her.

"Neither did we. Neither did any of us—any of your *people*, Aisla. The least you can do is learn to use it to fix what has been broken." Cliona's eyes darted back and forth between her own with an intensity that forced Aisla to look away. She gazed beyond her grandmother to the thriving ash trees of the Tus Forest.

The words lingered in the air, echoing through Aisla's scattered brain until Cliona turned her back on her and headed towards Castle Farraige, where she resided. Aisla's parents had lived there too, and her father had grown up there with Cliona. Aisla knew she would one day move there—one day when she could walk the halls and not feel as though she were brushing up against the ghosts of her parents.

In the meantime, she had chosen to live in a baile near Eire and Ruairi, who also lived on their own. The independence had given Aisla the breath of normalcy that she needed, despite Cliona's protests to keep her close.

When Aisla reached the stoop of her baile, she pushed through the heavy wooden door into the small building that was her home. The space was large enough for her washroom, a decent-sized bed, her desk and a chair, and a small sitting area with a bookshelf and two armchairs. It was a tight fit, but cozy in a way that suited her.

She stumbled wearily into the washroom and caught a glance of herself in the mirror. Hollow eyes stared back at her, and strands of mousy brown hair were slipping out of her braid. She tucked the loose bits behind her elongated ears, heaved a frustrated sigh, and splashed cold water over her face before changing into clean clothes. She always left training with her grandmother feeling like a shell of herself, but this time was worse than ever. Aisla was well aware of her shortcomings, and was presented with them every day and everywhere she looked. The way her grandmother wielded them like a weapon was too much to bear most days.

She tucked her dagger, *Oidhe*, into her waistband. It was the one thing she could never leave home without. The dagger was a beautiful iron blade forged by the dwarves with a larimer crystal handle and silver engravings that crawled along the edges of the blade to form a pair of wyvern wings. Ruairi had gifted it to her when they finished their final year in scoil together.

A knock sounded at her door. Aisla yanked it open, expecting to see Cliona, but a rush of relief flooded her as bright green eyes met hers.

Ruairi took a half-step back, startled, but Aisla threw her arms around him. It only took a moment for him to wrap his arms around her lower back. He squeezed tight; his familiar scent of ash wood and mint flooded her. Aisla held onto him as though he could disappear from her grasp.

"I just came to check on you," he murmured into her hair and a chill traveled down her spine.

Aisla tightened her grip in response, balling the fabric of his shirt in her fists.

"Thank you," she said softly. She knew Ruairi could not know how much his presence meant right now after the morning with their Mathair.

Aisla released herself from the embrace and immediately felt the absence of his warmth.

"You doing alright?" He asked.

Again, she could not help but notice the way his eyes softened when he held her gaze. The way the gentleness of it felt like a caress against her skin.

"Honest answer, or the one I've been telling myself since

yesterday morning?" Aisla said with a half-smile before sitting at the edge of her bed.

Ruairi moved to sit down next to her before replying, "Always honest with me, Ash."

"No," she said. "But it's not like you are either. Or anyone else in the city now that Iofa has reached us. I didn't think it was anywhere close."

"I don't think anyone did," he said with a sigh. "Has your grandmother said anything about it?"

Just the mention of her caused Aisla to shift uncomfortably beside him.

"Only that I am not to be involved in whatever plan she is concocting. I'm still too unpredictable, she says, and a part of me knows she's right, but a part of me wonders how long this can go on for. I can't stay in her clutches forever—I need to be out there doing something."

"I know, and you know I agree with you," he said. He gently reached out to rest his hand on top of hers where it lay on top of her quilt. The warmth of his touch reddened her cheeks, but he did not pull away. "How *is* your esos coming along?"

"Not good enough. I was able to hold flames this morning, but then failed to actually do anything with it. And you saw what happened behind the infirmary." She lowered her voice as she finished.

"Train with me," he blurted.

"I—I don't know. She is pretty specific about our training."

"She doesn't need to know," Ruairi replied, and Aisla could see in his eyes that his mind was already made. "It would be beneficial to me, too. I'd like to train other young zephys soon."

"If you insist," Aisla replied with hesitancy.

She could already feel the embarrassment of failing in front of Ruairi. It was one thing to fail to grasp her esos in front of her own kin. It was another thing entirely to do so in front of *him*.

"I do," he said with a smile. "We both need something to occupy our minds anyway. I'd been hoping we'd be able to spend more time together after finally getting back from scouting, so this is the perfect reason to. I missed you."

"I missed you too, Ru," she said as she leaned into him, allowing her head to rest on his shoulder.

It hadn't fully settled in with her yet that he was back. He had only been home two sunrises before Eire had fallen ill.

"Tomorrow then? Before classes start," he asked with a quirk of his brow.

"Fine," Aisla agreed with a genuine smile.

She didn't have time to overthink the shame of failing as she urged the kernel of herself that was never afraid of failure to return. Those confident and brash pieces of herself were the pieces that had been lost with the death of her parents.

5

WEYLIN

t was a struggle to keep the anticipation out of his expression, even for the Young Wolf. The next words from her lips, the next words to break this silence, would change his future.

They would change the future of all nine realms.

Rania's pale blue eyes flitted back and forth between his, a smirk pulling the corner of her lips up as danger danced in the depths of her irises. His frustration built. She seemed amused more than anything else, and he did not know what that would mean for him.

"Weylin Myrkor," she said, and Weylin found himself leaning in closer. Tension brewed through the air in the waiting. She seemed to feed off of the feeling. "I accept," Rania whispered her answer so soft, he could barely hear the words that left her lips. "I will become your betrothed until air turns to fire."

The world moved in slow motion while the words echoed inside of Weylin's skull. He tried to pin down his feelings that felt scattered in the wind. It was the answer he had wanted, but it all felt final. It would not be concrete until vows were shared, but he was now betrothed to a female he hardly knew. He had seen his father's plan to fruition, just as he had done his whole life, but yet there was always more to be done and never approval to be won. His father would never give him that satisfaction.

Weylin felt her expectant gaze and forced a grin.

He gently took her hand in his and lifted it to his lips, and placed a kiss on her icy fingers.

"You bestow a great honor upon me, Rania," Weylin said, holding her gaze. "The norns have entangled our threads from here until our passing on. May the gods bless our journey forward."

The words left his dry throat as though they'd been rehearsed.

"Until our passing on or until the misty sky splits open," Rania spoke vaguely.

Weylin furrowed his brows. He puzzled at her meaning, but did not question it. He merely nodded. "I was planning to speak to your father," Weylin said and cleared his throat uncomfortably.

Her eyes went wide with understanding. "I assumed you already had?"

"I felt it was important to speak to you first."

Weylin swore he caught a glimmer of approval in her eyes, but it was quickly washed away by concern.

"Tomorrow," Rania decided with a dramatic yawn. "Tonight, I grow weary. I wish to retire to my rooms."

"Of course," Weylin replied.

Her lack of enthusiasm did not upset him, but it did unnerve him. Females back home would throw themselves at him for a chance to be the mate of the Udar Apparent. Anything to further their social standing and bring their own offspring into his bloodline.

"Well," she said as she looked around the corridor, but no one was in sight. "Good night! I shall see you when the sun is in the sky again."

She half-smiled before striding down the corridor and disappearing out of sight. Weylin watched as her snow-white hair vanished.

He did not know how he should feel after making his betrothal official. He supposed he should feel fortunate, maybe moved, but it felt more like crossing an item off a never-ending list.

Weylin straightened his neck and dropped his shoulders before heading back to his own rooms, ready to lie in the unfamiliar bed and put his mind to rest.

Weylin awoke to the sun shining in through the giant windows that littered Castle Tromlui. He stretched his arms above his head and pulled himself to a sitting position. His sleep had been restless as he grappled with the events of the previous night.

He had yet to figure out how he would broach the subject with Brendan Dorcas, but he couldn't imagine his reaction being anything but positive. Their betrothal would guarantee the Dorcas' bloodline protection and power. Their descendants would be rulers of Talam for generations to come. A heavy duty, but the highest of honors.

For as far back as was recorded, the Myrkors had always mated within the realm of Samhradh. Sometimes love matches formed between neighbors of the same realm, but generally matches were made to ensure a strong and united front. The rare pairing of *searc* —true mates as declared by the stars and the norns—had never been recorded in the Myrkor line. And Weylin would never concern himself with such things.

To publicly declare such close ties with Briongloid would be risky, but they could only hope that it would guarantee them a strong ally across their northwestern border.

They already had strong allies in Earrach, Bitu, and Geimhrigh since their dynasties had all fought side by side in the War for Descendants when they brought the Arden throne to Iomlan. This left them with questionable relationships with Briongloid and Fomhar.

Weylin felt fairly secure in their relationship with Briongloid after his arrangement, and Fomhar would fall into line shortly afterwards. He had no doubt. The two realms had been the only ones to back Eilean in the war, giving their support to the Iarkis dynasty, who had long been dealt with and left to exile on their own continent across the Tusnua Sea.

Weylin found himself sneering at the thought of that cursed family. The family that wrecked centuries of peace and drained the continent of all esos. Weylin would never see the full potential of the power coursing through his veins as his ancestors had. He would never learn which source of esos he had been blessed with.

Anger stirred in his chest.

Weylin stormed to his washroom and splashed his face with cold water. He looked up at the mirror and into his own amber eyes and the darkness writhing in his irises. He recognized his father's sharp jaw, but his mother's gaunt eyes. He took a deep breath, preparing for the day of politicking ahead.

He exited the corridor outside of his room, and admired the sprawling marble floors beneath his feet. The walls were a deep teal with linear golden patterns traced across them. Briongloid was known as the Realm of Dreams, and the decor definitely lived up to the title. The Dorcas dynasty revered stags as their house animal, and there were golden statues of them scattered about the interior of the castle.

He made his way to the terrace outside around the back of the castle, hoping to get fresh air.

The doors opened to the morning sun pushing through the towering fir trees that surrounded Tromlui Castle. Weylin glanced about the gardens and recognized the profile of Brendan Dorcas. He sat on an iron bench looking out into the garden of statues, a Dorcas tradition of memorializing members of their dynasty.

Weylin debated turning around and finding somewhere to venture that was anywhere but there, but he decided it would be better to get the conversation over with.

Another task checked off his list.

"Good morning, Lord Dorcas," Weylin greeted when he approached the older man.

Brendan looked over his shoulder at him, surprise crossing his features that faded into exhaustion.

"And good morning to you," he said and dipped his head in respect to Weylin. "I hope you found your rooms to your comfort?"

"Of course," Weylin replied curtly. "Thank you for your hospitality."

"It is our honor to host the Udar Apparent."

There was a cautious edge to his voice, as if he wasn't entirely sure how this conversation would play out. Everyone had been so on edge lately, given the timing of it all. All interactions felt like coded pieces of a larger political game, and Weylin was not blind to it.

"I need to speak with you regarding a matter of importance," Weylin said.

"I am open to listening," Brendan responded slowly, careful not to promise anything, even a conversation. He rose from the bench. "I prefer discussing important matters outside of my castle when possible. It releases some of those formal pressures."

"I respect that."

"Thank you. Now what important matters do you have to discuss with me, Weylin Myrkor?" Brendan asked. He began to walk towards the courtyard.

"Just Weylin," Weylin insisted before continuing. "As you are well aware, the ninth generation is upon us. It is more pertinent than ever for Iomlan to find strength within and lean on each other should our preventative measures not be enough. Briongloid has always been a powerful force in Talam, and Samhradh does not forget the way you played a role in helping us forge this new realm."

Brendan paused next to a statue a few rows into the courtyard. There was hesitation in his movement as he recognized the duality of the words and the slight threat in the undertone. But he expected no less of the Young Wolf. Weylin noted the nameplate of the bearded male elf whose marble statue they stood beside.

Padraig Dorcas—the Lord of Briongloid during the War for Descendants. Weylin had read his name in the world tellers' books. He was a male of valor and bravery who stood by his friends across the sea until the very last moments. Despite his position, Weylin could respect the loyalty shown. He could only hope that Brendan and Rania would maintain the same devotion to his realm all these years later.

Brendan waited for Weylin to continue.

"I think it is past time that we formally unite our families. I should ask for your daughter's hand in union. I should ask that she stand by my side when the day comes that I sit the Arden Throne and wear the Speartha crown. I could think of no worthier female for such a position," Weylin spoke while they continued their walk through the statues.

Brendan's face did not so much as flinch.

Weylin could not discern if the proposition took him by surprise, or if he had been expecting it. Again, Weylin felt irritation at the lack of appreciation for his offer. He could have made the same offer to any powerful family in any of the realms and it would have been received with countless thanks and blessings.

"I assume you've already spoken with her," Brendan spoke at last.

Weylin paused at the final row of statues that was speckled by white rose bushes in full bloom. He wondered if this was some kind of trick. It was old tradition to speak to the father before the daughter when it came to betrothals, but Weylin found he did not care enough to lie.

"We spoke last night."

"And her answer?" Brendan averted his gaze as he reached out to caress a white rose on the bush nearest them.

"She accepted."

"Then it is settled. That shall be my answer as well." Brendan nodded as his fingers left the petals of the rose and his hand fell to his side. "I admire a man who values a woman's right to give herself away. My answer would have been different had you come to me first."

The answer to such a proposition should have been yes, no matter the circumstance, Weylin thought to himself. *It should not even need a second thought.*

"I look forward to the union," Weylin said.

"As do my family and my realm," Brendan replied, gazing straight ahead.

The conversation left an odd feeling in the pit of Weylin's stomach. It was a mixture of irritation and confusion, and he felt it building the longer he stood there, but he gave a forced nod to the father of his betrothed.

"We will celebrate this news tonight," Brendan decided. "A feast will be prepared in the honor of this new age. The colors of both our houses will fly."

The finality of it all hit Weylin like a wave crashing on the seashore.

6

AISLA

"Rise and shine, Ash."

Aisla shot upright, instinctively reaching for the dagger under her pillow. She slipped off the side of her bed while she regained her footing.

"Shhh, it's just me," the voice said with a chuckle.

Aisla dropped her dagger to the floor once she recognized the deep voice as Ruairi's.

"A knock would have been nice," she muttered, ignoring the flutter in her stomach.

She had often dreamed of waking up next to Ruairi, but this wasn't quite the situation she had envisioned.

Aisla went to her bedside and lit a candle with a match, silently cursing herself for not being able to do it with her esos as any skilled asher would. The light illuminated Ruairi's messy bed hair and his sly grin, and she softened at the sight.

"What are you doing here before the sun is even in the sky?" she said as she picked up her dagger and laid it on her nightstand before sitting on the edge of her bed.

He opened his mouth as though to say something, but closed it

again without a word. He rubbed his thumb against his forefinger
—a nervous tick that Aisla picked up on long ago. The air tightened
in her small baile while she waited for him to reply to her question.

"Training. Don't get too comfortable, we've got no time to
waste. And don't bother changing, we won't run into anyone at this
time of the morning anyway," he spoke at last, diverting his gaze to
the floor.

"You're completely mental." She looked up at him and saw the
seriousness in his gaze.

"Up, up, up!" He held out a hand to pull her up. "Training in
the bailes is greatly frowned upon. And I'm sure our neighbors
wouldn't appreciate any house fires that might blow their
direction."

"What about Eire? We should go to see her first."

At the mention of their neighbor, Aisla immediately thought of
her friend. All daydreams of Ruairi appearing in her baile in the
early hours of the morning dissipated with the thought, quickly
replaced by a panic rising within her.

Ruairi's hand dropped.

"I already went," he said after a moment's hesitation. "They
won't let us in, Ash. They aren't letting anyone in right now—not
for any visitors."

"No," she shook her head. "No, no, no."

"The menders are concerned about the contagious nature of
lofa. They took in four more patients overnight with similar conditions," he said. "It is strange, though. None of them had been in
direct contact with Eire in the past few days. It could be contagious,
or it could not be. But for now, they're prohibiting guests, and if we
start feeling ill we are to admit ourselves right away."

"Did they say anything regarding her condition? Is she okay?"

Ruairi hesitated before responding. "She has not woken up, but
she is still breathing. Her fever has yet to break."

Aisla had a feeling that it was worse. She knew Ruairi too well, and the way he avoided meeting her eyes, the way his voice was slightly strained, and the lack of hope in his eyes. There had to be more that he wasn't saying.

Whatever it was, he would not admit it to her, and maybe not even to himself.

"I hate this," Aisla breathed out. She decided not to push, at least not now.

A sort of numbness crept into her body, beginning at her fingertips. Ruairi reached out and wrapped his arms around her. She allowed herself to lean into his comfort, and she felt selfish for the peace she found there, for feeling this togetherness with Ruairi while Eire was lying alone on that cot, suffering.

Neither of them spoke for a long moment. Neither of them needed to.

"Come on," he said, offering his hand once again. "I think we could both use a distraction."

With a sigh, Aisla slipped her hand in his.

"Atta girl," he said with a grin.

"I'd like to at least put some real pants on," Aisla replied with a sigh, gesturing to the night shorts she had worn to bed.

"Fine." Ruairi said. He dropped onto her bed, lying flat on his back as he waited. She watched the way his loose red curls tumbled around his head.

"It's good to have you back," she said softly, before pulling the washroom door shut behind her.

Ruairi took Aisla to the same clearing she and Cliona had gone to the day before. He dropped to the ground and sat cross-legged. Aisla watched him curiously, tilting her head.

"Aren't you going to join me?" he asked. He looked up at her, his eyes sparkling with a playfulness she had missed.

"Why do I want to sit on this forest floor in the middle of the night?"

"To train," he replied. "Or I could just say, because I am your instructor and I told you to do so."

"Your ego can hardly fit in this forest," Aisla murmured before lowering herself to the ground beside him, mimicking his posture. The cool earth was wet with morning mist. "What are we doing down here, exactly?"

"We're concentrating," Ruairi said. He closed his eyes, so Aisla did too. "Where is the source of our esos?"

"The ash trees," Aisla answered.

"Exactly. So what better way to master it than to bring yourself closer to the source? Tus Forest is known for its abundance of ash trees, and all those roots below us have helped the elves of Caillte remain strong since our creation. We were always meant to remember the source."

Aisla nodded as her shoulders dropped, working to shake the tenseness from them.

"Now here we never have to worry about draining our esos. The ash trees keep our esos replenished and ready for use, but out there —outside of what we know—you'll always want to be aware of the nearest source for your esos."

"And what happens if you can't locate a source?" Aisla asked, keeping her eyes closed.

This was all knowledge that was taught in scoil, and Aisla recalled it all at least vaguely, but her grandmother never used it during training. She focused more on the action of creating the esos, rather than the sources behind it. Aisla usually thought of it as drawing from herself, not drawing from the true source. She never had to worry about it, given the popularity of ash trees throughout Eilean.

"If you cannot locate a source, you might deplete your esos. If you find yourself in a region that lacks ash trees, you only have what is stored within you—and that is a very limited source. As you know, wielding esos is draining to your body and your mind. But depleting it entirely can also deplete your body and mind." Ruairi's voice dropped to a near whisper as he continued. "Some elves have passed on after depleting their esos. Others can never get *back* to their esos. I would not recommend dancing along that line."

Aisla nodded again, even though her eyes were still shut. She nearly jumped out of her skin as Ruairi took her hand and turned it so her palm faced the pre-dawn sky. He traced small circles in the center of her palm. She kept her focus on her own steady breathing, but couldn't stop the chill that ran down her spine. Lightning rushed through her at the touch of his skin.

"Focus your core into this space, the very center of this circle," Ruairi instructed softly. "If you can focus all of your esos into this point, you'll be a step closer to being able to call it out at will."

Aisla drew in a long inhale as she followed his instructions. She focused on pulling the rush of esos into the small point at the center of her palm. He was no longer tracing the circles there, but his touch still lingered. She listened to the call of her blood and allowed it to choose its own shape. She heard the rush of wind in her ears before she felt the breeze and her eyes opened.

She blinked and looked up in disbelief. She met Ruairi's gaze and he grinned back at her, his eyes shining with pride.

"See, you can do it," he encouraged.

Aisla gently lifted her other palm and made a conscious effort to think of the esos, and not of herself. She nuzzled the ball of wind into her other palm. She floated it back and forth between her hands and a laugh of joy escaped her. She felt giddy, like a child—the opposite of what it was like to train with Cliona.

"I've only summoned fire and water before," she said.

"Maybe your esos is speaking to mine," he said with a shrug. "I don't know what it's like to have an arsenal of esos at my disposal, but I'm sure you'll come to know them each."

"What do I do with it now?" Aisla asked, hardly daring to take her eyes off the esos for fear it would flicker away into nothing if she did.

"What do you *want* to do with it?"

She'd never considered that before. Cliona had always given her an objective. Aisla never chose her own next move—then again, rarely did she get to follow through with a next move.

Without giving a verbal response, Aisla sent the wind skyward.

Aisla held the esos in her right palm and gently tilted her wrist to flick it upwards. The esos hovered slightly higher, then dropped. Aisla loosed a breath of relief when it did not flicker out. She set her mind on the tangled roots below her crossed legs, and pushed a little harder towards the esos. Glee filled her as she watched the wind shoot above the tree line. She waited for it to come back down, worried it had disappeared altogether. It came plummeting back, only slowing when it hovered over her palm.

She flicked her wrist to send it back above the trees, willing it to expand as it went. She watched the sphere of air grow as her mind envisioned it, and then she released. It burst into the sky, nearly out of view, and sent twigs and leaves raining down on them. It was the first time she had allowed it to disperse rather than flickering out on its own.

Power coursed through her veins as she dwelled in the ecstasy of her esos. It was not much compared to others her age. This was something they had learned even years ago, but it was an enormous leap for Aisla, and that was enough.

"Did you see that?" she asked with a laugh of disbelief, turning to Ruairi.

It was like they were children again.

"I did," Ruairi grinned. "You're incredible, Ash. Truly, you don't give yourself enough credit."

"Well, I've got to give you credit here, too," Aisla said,

dismissing his praise. "I haven't been able to do anything like that before."

"Seems to me like we might have to make this a regular thing, yeah?" He asked with a raised eyebrow.

Aisla nodded. "I can't wait to tell Cliona of my progress."

Aisla caught Ruairi's smile, faltering slightly.

"What's up with you and the Mathair?"

"It's nothing, really. I just don't think we always see eye to eye," Ruairi said, as he stood and held out his hand to help her up.

Aisla allowed him to pull her to her feet, and they began the trek down the hill back towards the village center.

"On what matters?" Aisla pushed.

"On most matters." Ruairi scoffed as Aisla furrowed her brows. "Look, it's not a big deal. I know she's our Mathair, and your grandmother, and I respect that. I just think I would do things differently, and it is what it is."

His dismissive tone rubbed Aisla the wrong way. She bit her tongue, deciding whether or not to continue.

"She must respect you enough if she chose you to be in her inner council, especially so young."

"I will never understand why she did that. And honestly, I don't think she knows either." Ruairi shook his head. "I think she did it more as a favor to you than anything."

"A favor to me?"

"We both know you can't sit on her inner council until it is time for you to take over as Mathair, so by giving me a seat it's as though she is giving you representation."

"She could have chosen Eire. They don't seem to butt heads nearly as much, and we are just as close."

Ruairi looked at her with amusement glimmering in his eyes. "Eire's pursuits don't lie in politics, you know that. She'd sooner become a priestess than step foot anywhere near the council chamber."

"Fair enough," Aisla replied.

The Trygg dynasty was long regarded for their allegiance and loyalty to the gods, sometimes blindly.

The sun was rising when they arrived back to the bailes. The dual moons of Talam faded away as the red glow of the morning sun peeked above the mountain range that surrounded Caillte on the west. Patches of snow still lingered on the tallest of the peaks.

"After classes, I'm going to go to the library," Aisla said decidedly. "Surely there's something to be found in those stacks of books that can help Eire. Are you in?"

"I wish," Ruairi said with a frown. "I can't. I've got a meeting with the Mathair and the inner council after classes. But we can meet up after and regroup?"

"What are those meetings even about?" Aisla asked, ignoring his suggestion.

"Typically, resource gathering and planning for our next scouting trips. Getting the crew organized and planned," Ruairi said. He watched Aisla's eyes light up with concern. "Don't worry, she won't send me out so soon after our last trip. They try to rotate us. I'm not going anywhere."

Aisla nodded, but doubt and worry still clouded her yellow-green eyes.

"Let's go get these classes over with," she said with a sigh. "Sounds like we've both got a long night ahead of us."

7

RUAIRI

Ruairi glanced around the massive elm table in the center of the inner council chamber in Castle Farraige. He caught glimpses of the stoic expressions on the other inner council members' faces as Cliona stood at the head, both hands flat on the tabletop, while she leaned in towards them. Her yellow-green eyes were cold and calculating, unlike Aisla's which were wide and warm.

Ruairi had never liked Cliona, and he never understood how he had come to be appointed to her inner council of most trusted advisors. He was the youngest in the room and could not help feeling out of place when he looked at his fellow council members. He would not question it, though. He preferred to be in the know when it came to decisions regarding the future of his realm.

"We must be proactive in this situation," Linus, a dwarf who was one of the eldest members of the council, growled from Ruairi's side.

"We are doing all that we can," Cliona responded smoothly.

She radiated authority in a way that made Ruairi's skin crawl.

"What happens when that is no longer enough?" Ruairi spoke up, something he rarely did in meetings.

Cliona turned a steely gaze to him, but Ruairi did not flinch under her stare.

"Do you have any suggestions, Vilulf?" She asked, laying a trap.

"Is there any chance of negotiation with Iomlan?" He questioned and watched a shadow pass over her eyes.

"You truly believe the Udar would work with us? At this time—the time of the ninth generation?" Cliona seethed. "You, of all people, should know better than that."

Ruairi pressed his lips in a tight line, holding back the words he wanted to say. The urgency in the room was even more palpable than it usually was, with lofa ailing their people.

Cliona dragged her gaze from his.

"We could give him what he wants. Then he would listen." Linus spoke again, and Ruairi felt his mouth drying. This is not what he had meant when he interjected. "We all know *who* the problem is—the reason for our exile. It is for fear of one person and one person only. I think with her out of the way, the Udar would be more than willing to listen to us, and our demands."

Ruairi felt rage blossoming in his chest as the dwarf spoke the words. His esos roared to life, filling his ears with the familiar rush of wind. He knew exactly what Linus implied—they all did. He kept his mouth shut, trusting Cliona to protect her granddaughter.

"He's not wrong." Conor, a human, and the second youngest member of Cliona's inner council, spoke up. Ruairi slowly moved to face him. The man's brown eyes gleamed viciously. "Besides, she lacks the control that is absolutely necessary to handle the abilities the norns have granted her. We all heard what happened behind the infirmary. She cannot be trusted."

Ruairi's hands shook. He fought to sit by and watch the scene unfold. His throat constricted with a thousand words he wished to speak, to shout, to scream, but he knew making an emotional argument would not be taken seriously by anyone here. And he knew himself well enough to know he was not capable of any other argument in that moment.

"And you would suggest I *murder* my own kin?" Cliona seethed through bared teeth, and Ruairi felt the weight on his chest lift ever so slightly.

"If it is the only way," Conor said as he stood from his seat, an obvious challenge to the Mathair. "I offer my blade if you are unable to."

Ruairi lunged across the table in one swift movement. His wind esos knocked Conor to the ground and then Ruairi was on top of him, landing a swift blow to his right cheek as Conor struggled to push him off. Ruairi swung again and blood spurted from Conor's nose. Conor spit more of the red liquid from his mouth. Ruairi felt his esos rush beneath his skin. He forgot everyone else in the room. The sound of the other members of the council standing did not register to him. He grabbed Conor by the collar of his shirt and pulled him off of the ground, closer to his face.

"If you *ever* speak of her again . . ." He dropped Conor back to the ground before swinging his fist one last time. He let his final blow finish his threat. Hands grabbed at him, pulling him off of Conor.

Ruairi shook them off and stood up on his own, taking a few steps back to watch through narrowed eyes as Conor struggled to his feet. He was grinning sadistically, his white teeth coated in dark, red blood.

"That's the first time I've seen you stand for anything in your life, Vilulf," Conor sneered. "I'm sure your little *Gheall Ceann* would be so proud of you if she could see you now."

Wind rushed in his ears and Ruairi lunged again, hands stretched before him, reaching for Conor's throat.

Stop.

The word sounded in his mind, and Ruairi's skin crawled as his hands fell limply to his sides. Cliona's voice was in his head as she used her esos as a pryer. Ruairi could only blame himself for being too distracted to keep his mental shields up.

Ruairi dragged his gaze from Conor to Cliona. He saw red, fighting to build his shields back into place.

"Outside. Now!" Cliona demanded with sheer authority.

Ruairi refused to look back at Conor and the others, who knew she'd used her esos on him—that it was the only thing that stopped him from escalating further. He headed straight for the door, keeping his focus directly ahead of him. He exited and let the door slam shut behind him. Half of him debated leaving the castle all together rather than waiting for Cliona, but the better part of him wanted to hear how she could justify his removal for defending Aisla, while Conor was allowed to remain.

The door opened several long moments later and Cliona entered the corridor, which seemed to darken with her presence. Her eyes looked weary, and she appeared to drop her intensity as the door closed behind her. He saw her vulnerability in the way her shoulders slumped forward, weighed down by being the Mathair of Eilean and the last kin of Aisla Iarkis.

"I cannot stand for outbursts like that," Cliona said with a long sigh, meeting his gaze. "You know this—"

"It was so obviously provoked. You cannot—"

"I did not finish," she hissed, and Ruairi closed his mouth. "As the leader of this realm, it would set a poor example to keep you in the council after such aggressive actions. I will not condemn you or punish you, but I cannot stand by what you've done."

Ruairi set his jaw and did not utter a word.

"Now," Cliona continued, almost cautiously. "I have a request for you."

"Go on." Ruairi was well aware that such disrespect towards his Mathair should be punished, but he could not find it within himself to rein his emotions in.

"Linus and Conor were correct in saying that we need to broker a peace. What our people are not yet aware of is that a total of fifteen people are now showing signs of Iofa." She paused, as if thinking how she should phrase the next words. "Two of them have already passed on, despite every effort on behalf of the medics. Not Eire. She is still fighting."

Ruairi felt relief and pain and fear all at the same time. He had not known how quickly it spread, or how fatal it could be.

"You saw how aggressive they were today. You can only imagine how tensions will rise as things grow worse and more urgent. There is a cure." She watched for his reaction, and Ruairi fought to keep his face blank, but the tension in his shoulders eased. "Our contacts on Iomlan have reason to believe it is in the Udar's possession. And it has been, ever since Iofa struck Iomlan before even the prophecy existed. Go to him on behalf of our menders and beg him for it. We will not push for any other resources or peace. My hope is that if we start small, if our desperation is obvious enough, the Udar might have mercy on us, at least enough to give us the cure, gods be willing. You will go with Mona to Samhradh with this package in your possession, and it will be our peace offering."

She held out a small parcel to him. He let it stay there, waiting in the air between them while he mentally assessed her words. He kept his eyes on the package and his stomach twisted and tightened.

"If either of you were to open this package before it gets to the Udar, execution would be your punishment and I, personally, would be the one to drop the blade. Do you understand?" Cliona said with a deadly gleam in her eyes. "This package is the only hope we have of obtaining the cure, and if it is altered before it gets to him, it will do us no favors. If we do not stop Iofa now, Eilean will not survive the year."

"I never said I would accept," Ruairi said at last.

"Perhaps I should send Conor to broker our peace instead?"

Ruairi bristled at her threat. He thought of Aisla and how angry she would be with him if he left her now. But he knew for Eire, she would understand.

Fear and hope battled internally within him before he gave his response: "Fine."

"You will set sail tomorrow first thing in the morning. I will pray that Muir will grant you safe waters and guide you to the shores with ease. When you get to Briongloid, one of our contacts will meet you at the Briseadhceo Inn. I haven't had time to get her reply, but I have sent a message to her, and she will have an updated map to help you on your way to Samhradh. After that, you'll be on your own until you get to the capital. Another contact will meet you in a home in the city. He will arrange for you to gain audience with the Udar. I have marked both locations on your map, so keep that one with you. Our contacts will know you when they see you. We know little about Iomlan, as you know how risky communication is there, even with the few willing to try. Your airgead will be good there and they speak the same tongue, but laws on esos are unknown and I would suggest you tread with caution. There is no time to waste, and I am sure you would agree," she said.

Tomorrow. The finality of it rested within him like a boulder.

"I'll let you be the one to talk to Aisla about it," Cliona said, and he finally took the small package and folded map from her outstretched hand.

He tucked them in his back pocket and shivers traveled down his spine. Despite its light weight, the gravity of the package pulled him down below the soil.

"Thank you for your service." Cliona ducked her head to him before disappearing back into the inner council room without another word.

Ruairi stared after her for several beats, unable to do anything else. His fist ached at his side. His nostrils flared and sweat beaded along his forehead. A hollow feeling entered him. He knew he would never be able to find the right words to talk to Aisla, not after he just promised her he would not leave her again so soon. And even more than that, he could hardly bear the thought of leaving her here —in a home that was no longer safe for her from what he could see. Even with the terrifying and mysterious nature of Iofa aside, Ruairi did not trust Cliona to defend her from the likes of Linus and Conor, who would sooner see her dead than give her the chance to grow and harness the power she had been blessed with.

Ruairi would not know a moment of peace in a world where he left her alone here. She had lost her parents, and Eire would not be able to help her. If he left too, who would fight for her? He was well aware she didn't need him to fight her battles—she never had—but she was only one elf, with only one voice.

He took a deep breath and felt his esos slowing in his veins; the whisper quieting down until he could finally hear his own thoughts again.

Ruairi was already sitting at a table outside the tavern when Aisla arrived and plopped down next to him with her plate of rations that tasted worse by the day.

"I hope you've got news because I've got nothing," she said with a sigh.

She dropped her bag on the bench and settled in, lifting her fork to her full plate. Her eyes looked weary, but he could see a hope in them.

Ruairi's stomach sank as it twisted with guilt.

"You first," Ruairi spoke quickly, before she could ask him to divulge his own updates.

She looked at him curiously but took his small smile as answer enough before replying.

"I spent *hours* at the library and wasn't able to find a single useful thing," she said with exasperation. "I haven't been able to find the existence of lofa *ever*. There's one book I didn't get to, so I took that one along for some bedtime reading. It's called *The Dawn of Talam*, so I am not very hopeful it has any relevant information for us."

She took the book from her bag to show him. He gently lifted the forest green book from her hands and studied the engraved silver title. It was plain and worn. It did not look like it would have the answers they needed—that Eire needed. He handed it back to her with a frown.

"I know," Aisla agreed with his silent sentiment. "Hopefully you have something from the inner council meeting? What are they doing about the situation?"

"I—" he started and then thought better of it. "Can we take a walk, Ash?"

"I haven't finished my food," she pointed out.

"I know," he said. "I just feel this conversation is better had in private."

Ruairi could see her mind turning as she worked to come up with what he could be priming her for. He watched her beautiful yellow-green eyes flicker, and she pursed her lips. Worry furrowed her brows and she let her fork clatter to her plate.

"It's not . . ." She paused to take a shaky breath. "Eire—is she okay?"

"Yes—I mean as okay as she can be. It's not about Eire, well not directly," Ruairi fumbled for words.

"And suddenly my appetite is lost," she muttered as she stood. "Let's go."

They took their plates and emptied the leftover contents into the waste bin before leaving them at the counter for the dishwashers —a job Ruairi was glad to have aged out of.

Ruairi felt his guilt growing with each step they took away from the village.

"Go ahead," Aisla snapped, her fear and concern turning to irritation.

Ruairi watched his feet walking the same path he had walked with Aisla so many times before. It was a winding, scenic trail that led from the village tavern to the coast of the Tusnua Sea. He and Aisla and Eire had stumbled along its course more times than he could recall.

"Aisla," he began and took a deep inhale. "I don't know how to even go about this. It's the one thing I was not expecting to come back and tell you. At the inner council meeting today, there was, of course, a lot of talk about Iofa and the damage it is doing. This led to talk of peace negotiations and the like, which is an ongoing conversation, but the Mathair informed us she suspects the Udar has a cure for Iofa, from when Iomlan dealt with it long ago. There is no other remedy for it that we are aware of."

"There has to be," Aisla cut in, shaking her head.

"I wish there was. You know how I feel about Iomlan, about the Udar. Your grandmother has asked me to go and—"

"No." Aisla stopped in her tracks and faced him. Her eyes writhed with flames that were almost frightening. "No. You promised we would get through this together. You promised it wouldn't be you this time. You were *just* gone. *You promised me.*" She held his gaze, and he felt every word like a knife in his gut. "It already feels like I'm losing Eire. I can't bear to lose you."

She spoke with rage in her heart, but gentle tears fell down her reddening cheeks. Ruairi's heart fractured into pieces as he looked into the eyes of the one person he never wanted to let down.

"I have to, Ash," he said, taking a step towards her. Pain blossomed in his chest as she recoiled away. "We need that cure. Fifteen new cases have been found in Caillte, and Eire isn't getting any better."

"Why can't someone else do it?" Her voice broke.

"I don't trust the inner council. They don't all have the best intentions, and I would rather be at the helm of that ship than anyone else," he explained, slowly.

He avoided mentioning the threats made against her. It would do no good for anyone—the last thing he wanted to do was begin tearing Eilean apart internally.

"It's a suicide mission," she insisted. "You won't make it past the blockade. Cliona *knows* that."

Ruairi wanted to close this distance between them. He yearned to pull her closer, to feel her familiar warmth and let that be enough to replace the answers he did not have. The look in her eyes told him that now was not the time.

"She seems hopeful," he replied around a tight throat. "She gave me a package for the Udar. She is confident that if we ask for the cure, and nothing more, he might hear us out."

"What could we possibly have that the Udar is so desperate to get his hands on? They took everything they wanted during the Siege of Arden. Ruairi, it's a trap."

"I don't know. I'm forbidden from opening the package. It is meant for the Udar's eyes only. The Mathair emphasized that." Ruairi chose to leave out the part where Aisla's grandmother threatened to end his life herself. "It might be a trap, but what other choice do we have? We have to act."

"Will you be alone?" She asked, and he felt both relief and sorrow as he heard the defeat entering her voice.

"Mona will go with me. She's a capable fighter and an expert mender. She'll be able to heal me if I need it."

Aisla nodded slowly, and she dropped her gaze to the ground beneath him, and he could physically see her guards dropping with the slump of her shoulders.

"Hey," Ruairi said, as he took another step forward and reached out to hold her arms at the elbows. "Look at me."

Aisla did not fight him, but looked up at him from under long lashes and watery eyes. His hands shook.

"I'll be back before you know it." Ruairi pulled her into his chest and she allowed herself to be led there. After a moment, she wrapped her arms around him. Her body quivered. He rested his chin on her head. "I'll come home and we'll have the cure, and Eire will be okay. The three of us can go back to life as it was. We will be stronger from this, and I'll be able to tell you everything I saw on Iomlan. I'll bring you back every new flower I see. We'll be together and never separated again—don't worry about that."

Ruairi chased the doubt that followed his words from his mind. He fought away his own fears, careful not to let her feel them. For her sake, he would pretend he believed them to be true.

"I cannot lose you," she rasped.

"You won't."

He placed a kiss on top of her head as a single tear slipped down his own cheek.

Ruairi had never prayed to the gods before.

He had not grown up in a home that felt any allegiance to them, after all that had been done to Eilean. But in that moment—in that moment he prayed to each of the nine gods that this would not be the last time he held Aisla Iarkis in his arms.

8

AISLA

Aisla stormed towards Castle Farraige with anger in her heart. Her esos brewed in a wild storm just below the surface of her skin, and she could feel it gnawing at her, begging for release. Her skin itched with the need to free it.

She burst through the oak doors that lead into the foyer of the ancient castle. She passed through familiar emerald-green corridors, her feet gliding over dark wooden flooring.

At last, she reached the door to Cliona's office, and was thankful to find she had not locked it as she pushed it open.

Cliona slowly looked up from the papers in her hands where she sat hunched over her desk. Her eyes were tired, but alert as they met Aisla's.

"I need to speak to you," Aisla demanded as she dropped into the armchair across from her grandmother.

Aisla met her gaze with ferocity, fire dancing in the depths of her eyes. Cliona's own turned steely and cold the longer she looked at her. Aisla pushed her shoulders back and crossed her hands in her lap to maintain control over her esos as anxious energy flooded through her. The confidence she had entered the room with faded under the frosty glare of the Mathair.

"Go on," Cliona spoke with authority. "I can imagine you are displeased with me."

"That's an understatement," Aisla snapped. There were an infinite number of questions swirling through Aisla's mind, but one stood out above them all. One was bold and clear while the others were white noise that she would need the time to sort through. "Why *him*?"

She asked that most pressing question. The one that tore at her heart every time it crossed her mind. She felt sorrow clenching at her throat as she asked it—as she looked her grandmother in the eyes and said the words aloud.

"Ruairi is a strong laoch, and a level-headed male. He has good morals and I know you are aware of that," she said, not breaking eye contact for even a moment. "We might have our differences, but if we can trust anyone on Eilean on this quest for diplomacy, it is him. We need the Udar to hear our case if we ever want a cure for Iofa. Ruairi loves Eire the same as you do. He has the motivation to push him forward, and Mona will be there to aid him. She comes with her own valuable skill set that will complement his."

Aisla heard the cold calculation, and it made her stomach turn.

"It's a suicide mission," Aisla hissed. "I know you know that." Her voice betrayed her as it cracked.

"I've heard rumors that the new Udar is a reasonable man. He—"

"The Myrkors have imprisoned us here like animals in a cage." Aisla could hardly recognize her own voice as it rang, harsh in her ears. "You'd be *ignorant* to think otherwise."

"I would be cautious of the way you speak to your Mathair, *girl*." The words were a guttural growl from Cliona's throat that sent a chill down Aisla's spine. "You might be my blood, but I will not tolerate this disrespect. Speak out of turn again, and there will be consequences. You are not above the order of things."

Aisla bit the inside of her lip as an animalistic force roared within her, begging to be set free. Her esos was loud and angry and impatient and bursting at the seams. It was a physical ache.

"There has to be a time for change. A time for peace. Arriving in good graces to request the cure is a start. We will show them a confident front and they can see that we hold no grudges—"

"Hold no grudges?" Aisla scoffed. "You seem to forget the legions of souls that family has ripped from the earth. You seem to forget that Eilean has been a dying kingdom long before this plague, because of them."

Aisla knew she was far beyond overstepping, but the power and her rage made her unable to hold back.

"Trust me, Aisling," Cliona said, and surprise dropped Aisla's guard at the sound of her birth name. A name she had not heard since her parents had passed on. "I know the pain he has wreaked upon us better than any other. And this is why I know we must find a way forward. Our current conditions cannot sustain us. This is a step in the right direction, and Ruairi would not have accepted my request if he did not agree with that. You seem to forget that he had a choice in this as well."

"Hardly," Aisla snapped back, even as she felt her walls beginning to crack.

"My dear," Cliona said. "Ruairi Vilulf would do anything to protect the future of this realm. To protect *your* future. And that is why I know he is the right choice for this. Do you not trust him?"

Aisla's heart sank. She felt nausea creep in. She knew her grandmother was not waiting for an answer.

"What's in the parcel?" Aisla asked after a few beats of silence passed between them.

"I cannot tell you. The contents must be for the Udar's eyes only. The norns will it so. Interference could be catastrophic to our cause."

Aisla fought the urge to roll her eyes at the threat of the norns. She found it harder every day to believe in the norns and the gods alike.

"I will answer any questions you have, but not this one," Cliona said firmly. "Aisla, one day, these tough decisions will fall upon your shoulders, and you will have to face the reactions of *your* people. You will be responsible for the outcome as well. The Mathair is not a title for the weak-willed, nor those who make decisions rooted in emotion. You have to learn to remove yourself from the position and focus on the needs of your people, of your realm."

Aisla averted her gaze to the floor. She fought back the tears that stung the corners of her eyes.

"I have no doubt you will be one of the greatest Mathairs the realm has seen," her voice dropped to a calmer level. "The prophecy has foreshadowed your great power."

Words escaped Aisla, lost in her anger and frustration that had not subsided.

"If I could take your burden, my dear, I would."

"Would you?" Aisla breathed out. A tear fell as she looked up again to meet Cliona's eyes. "Would you really?"

Cliona did not reply, but Aisla had not expected her to. It hurt all the same.

Aisla stood from the chair and made her way to the door of Cliona's office. She flung it open and listened to it slam shut behind her without a glance back.

The room was dark, besides the faint flicker of her nearly melted candle as Aisla lay awake in her bed. She found herself praying to gods she had long lost hope in. She wished she had the faith of Eire, but she felt the silence from them echoing through her core.

Everything was quiet and hollow as Aisla was forced to lie there with nothing but the company of her own mind, which was the last voice she wanted to hear. She felt numb as she stared up at her sloped ceiling.

She had crawled into her bed fully clothed after she left Castle Farraige, unable to find the energy to do anything else. Her esos had gone from angry and stirring to unnervingly still and quiet. It settled within her in an icy sort of emptiness, that she had a feeling she would need to get used to with Eire absent and Ruairi soon to follow.

She flipped over and lay on top of her covers on her side. She curled into herself, giving into the despair that purred deep within her. She squeezed her eyes shut as she willed her mind to rest.

9

WEYLIN

The dining hall was decorated with intermittent banners of maroon and marigold, and lilac and teal. The colors of the realm of Samhradh and the realm of Briongloid. It was the first time since before the War for Descendants that their colors had flown together.

Pride filled Weylin's chest as he strode into the room with his head held high and his face set in stone. He wore the iron Myrkor crown he would one day trade for his father's crown, the Speartha crown made of gold and set with stones of onyx.

Four long tables were set up in the center of the room, and seats filled quickly with citizens of Scamall, the capital of Briongloid. Glances were thrown his way and whispers erupted when they realized who he was. He kept his gaze ahead towards the fifth table that was set horizontally where the rest were set vertically.

His betrothed sat at the head table, facing out towards her people. Her gaze found him from across the room. The pale blue dress she wore matched her eyes, enhancing her beauty in an enchanting way. Her hair was half braided back while the rest of it fell in loose curls over her bare shoulders. She sat tall, poised, and proud. She looked like the royalty she would become, but she wore an expression of boredom as she watched him approach. Weylin knew it would take a long time to figure Rania Dorcas out, but gods be willing, they would have plenty of time to do just that.

Weylin knew she would make a suitable mate for him from the way she held herself. Being the daughter of one of the realms' reigning dynasties had long prepared her for the position she would one day occupy.

He reached the table and bowed first to Brendan and Brigid. Brendan looked stoic as ever, but Weylin was not intimidated. He had gotten what he came here for, Brendan's blessing and their realms united, and Weylin would require no more of him. The betrothal was publicly celebrated, and there would be no going back.

Brigid was beaming. Pride shone in her glistening eyes as she looked to Weylin. She had gotten what every mother dreamt of. When it came to her children, Brigid had won by all societal standards. Her son would take a mate and be the Lord of Briongloid, while her daughter took to Castle Eagla, the highest honor of all.

Weylin turned to Rania, who was already looking at him.

"You look regal, my lady." He bowed to her and her lips curved up in a cunning smile.

He reached for her hand and placed his lips gently upon it before taking the empty seat next to her.

"We meet again, Lord Weylin," she said, almost playfully.

"I think we are past such formalities," he responded and took his seat beside her.

Her gaze was piercing, and he had noticed how there always seemed to be something within the depths of her blue irises that he could not read. It was as if she held a joke that he was not privy to.

"What are you looking at?" she asked, quirking her head to one side.

"Just you," he replied.

Rania rolled her eyes. "Is that what you say to all the ladies?"

Weylin nearly choked at that. That she would ask such a question or make such an implication. And even though they were speaking quietly enough that no one else could hear them, they were still in a public setting.

"Of course not, Rania," he responded with the slightest hint of a scold in his voice.

"I like the way you say my name," she said softly, almost absent-mindedly. "You remembered it too, I noticed. Before my father even mentioned it, you remembered from your last visit over a decade ago."

"How could I forget?"

"I suppose men do often remember my name," she smirked and averted her gaze. "Although you were only a boy then."

Weylin's eyes grew wide as he wrote her comments off as simple banter. He'd be lying to himself if he said Rania Dorcas did not intrigue him. He was not sure whether to take offense at her words or laugh along with this game that she played. The thought struck him that the feeling might be exactly what she was going for.

"You look stunning tonight," he spoke up after a few beats of silence, ignoring her previous implications.

"As do you, Weylin," she spoke his name with intention, finally dropping his formal title.

"Ah-hem," Brendan called the room to attention.

Weylin noted how informal things in Briongloid must be if all it took was a grunt to garner the attention of his people. Weylin could never imagine his father doing such a thing in his own hall. The people here looked to Brendan expectantly, some eagerly and some hesitantly. Weylin knew the majority of them would not know what to think of this union, of this public declaration of allyship.

"I would like to make a toast and plead with the gods for their blessing of the betrothal between my daughter and the Udar Apparent," Brendan continued in his gruff and authoritative voice.

Roars of celebration erupted throughout the room, yet others remained silent, cautiously looking to their neighbors. Weylin scanned the room, carefully noting the faces and matching them with their reactions. Some people stood from the table, stomping their feet, and slamming their mugs down.

"To Rania Dorcas and Weylin Myrkor. To the Gem of Dreams and the Young Wolf in the South. May their union be fruitful, blessed, and strong. May it lead us towards a more united Talam!"

By the end of his toast, Brendan was shouting over the crowd.

The room exploded with applause and shouts and whoops of joy that outweighed the silent minority Weylin was still assessing. He kept his face calm as he snuck a glance at Rania, who had a placid, mischievous look on her own face as she gazed at the room of her people. The room of the people that she knew and had grown up with. The people of dreams and a mild climate that she would soon trade for the house of wolves and hot summers.

Weylin smiled.

The feast was followed by a celebration that Weylin had not been prepared for.

They pushed the long dining tables against the edges of the great hall as it transformed into a ballroom. In a corner near the head table, which remained where it was, a band had convened and begun a cheery tune that had been around far longer than anyone alive here, even the eldest of the elves.

Everyone flocked to the center of the room, some grabbing partners, while others elected to dance alone to the music—kicking their feet out and swaying their hips to the sound of the strings.

Weylin was never one for these kinds of grand celebrations and dances. They had long lost their appeal to him, having grown up in court. He was thankful, at least, that the focus was no longer on him and his presence or Rania and their betrothal. He found himself glad he had chosen to make this journey alone. It was a brief time to himself. No one else to answer to or a strict timeline to follow.

He felt Rania steal an expectant glance towards him and he let out an internal groan. He fixed a charming smile to his face before turning to her.

"May I have this dance?" he asked, as he knew he was meant to.

He could've sworn he saw a curt nod of approval from Brendan Dorcas over Rania's shoulder.

"And every one hereafter."

Weylin held out his hand to her, and she placed her small, pale, cold hand in his. He felt his warmth spread to combat the coolness of her. She stood and allowed him to guide her. He pulled her closer as they found a space along the outskirts and then moved to face her. The music slowed, drifting into a new romantic song.

Nervousness was not a feeling Weylin Myrkor was accustomed to, but looking into her eyes, he could feel it creeping in. He supposed his days of attending endless balls at Castle Eagla might finally pay off in his favor.

He kept hold of her hand and pressed the other to her back. She moved closer until their chests were touching. She was at least a head shorter than him, and she craned her neck to look up at him from under dark lashes. It was the closest he had been to his betrothed.

She smelled of cedar and lily blossoms.

"You're quite handsome," she murmured, as though realizing it for the first time.

Weylin chuckled. "I should hope my mate-to-be would think so. You don't look so bad yourself."

Rania let out an indignant huff but smiled nonetheless, and this time felt more genuine than all of her other grins shared in front of her parents or while accepting his proposal.

They swayed to the sound of the lyre. Rania continued to hold on to him as he guided their feet in the patterns he had memorized. The way her hair occasionally flicked against his arms brought him leaning in closer to her, and for a moment he felt as though they were alone in the room, even though he knew they were the most observed couple.

The sound of the strings heightened and he led her into a small twirl and then dipped her low to the ground. She let out a small gasp as she opened her eyes to look at him. He leaned closer until their foreheads touched, heavy breaths mingling.

Her eyes flitted between his, playful and confident, yet he could see a faint cautiousness there as well. In a moment, she bridged the distance between them as she pressed her lips to his with an initial softness that transformed into eagerness as he held her there, pulling her closer. He felt her smile on his lips as they both pulled away, slowly.

"I could get used to you," she said with a breathiness to her voice while he pulled her back to her feet and they resumed their dance.

"I could say the same," he leaned in closer to her ear, "*mate.*"

He didn't miss the chill that traveled down her spine when he leaned back again. For once, she was the one at a loss for words, but he could see the cunning gleam in her eyes while they continued to sway with the music. When they resumed their dance, they were even closer and even more in tune with the other's movements. Any remaining awkwardness between them had dissipated with their kiss.

A commotion of yelps and voices sounded from behind him as Rania's eyes grew wide. Weylin dropped her hands and moved to stand in front of her, turning to face the disruption.

Two white doves had appeared and were flying around the head table, cooing noisily. Those still left at the table were jumping out of their seats with shouts and cries as they swatted at the winged creatures, who dove at the plates, ripping at the food on the table. The usually peaceful birds cried angrily and their wings flapped madly. Brendan and Brigid hurried to escape the table. Weylin made his way towards them. He could feel Rania following behind him.

Weylin stared helplessly as one of the birds dove towards Brigid. Her eyes widened with utter horror and Weylin would never be able to erase what happened next from his mind.

The dove's outstretched talons aimed straight for her left eye before digging in. The scream she released made Weylin's ears ring. Brendan roared as he lunged for the creature, but it was too late. The dove yanked away from her and blood burst from Brigid's empty eye socket, and the dove's white feathers were coated in the red liquid as it flew away with Brigid's missing eye. The blood flicked down on the white tablecloths as both birds disappeared through the highest glass window.

Rania let out a piercing cry and dashed towards her mother, who clutched her face with trembling hands and her mouth gaped open wide. Silent sobs of terror wracked Brigid's body. Brendan's arms wrapped around her and caught her before she could fall. Oisin and Rania stood by to keep their mother from the gawking stares of the people passing the gruesome scene.

Blood stained the floor around them.

"Everyone out!" Brendan's voice boomed even while tight with grief.

The people poured from the hall, careful to avoid the Udar Apparent who made his way towards the noble family while Brendan gently moved Brigid to sit down at one of the long tables.

"My eye," she whimpered as she continued to cover her face, blood seeping between her shaking fingers. "I can't see. I can't see. *I can't see.*"

The words fell from her lips as a chill ran down Weylin's spine. He could feel the anger and the sorrow radiating from the two

Dorcas children while the room emptied, and they could do nothing but place a comforting hand on their mother.

"Get us a medic," Brendan snapped to Rania, who nodded obediently.

Weylin felt a sting of pain for the poor female as she straightened her shoulders. Her hands were visibly trembling as silent tears rolled down her powdered face.

"And *you*," Brendan narrowed his eyes on Weylin. "Leave my hall!"

Under any other circumstance, Weylin would have had the male's head on a platter for daring to speak to him in such a way. He would have not hesitated to lift the blade himself to do it.

But as he looked at the rage filling Brendan's hazel eyes, at the helplessness that was all too evident, as he knew they were both wondering how differently this might have gone if menders gifted with the esos of healing still existed on this continent, Weylin deigned to bite his tongue.

"I should remind you who exactly you are speaking to, my lord," Weylin said coldly, refusing to ignore the disrespect all together. "Call upon me if there is any way I can assist your family."

Brendan's nostrils flared. Weylin could practically see him hold back his own words, and Weylin was thankful he did, as he felt no desire to further heighten tensions with Brigid's cries still filling the hall.

He turned around to follow Rania as she darted from the room, intent on her task to bring a medic back to her mother.

"I am so sorry, Rania," Weylin spoke after a few quick steps to close the distance between them while they exited the hall that reeked of fear and anger.

"It is a bad omen," she whispered, holding her quick pace.

Weylin glanced to her and saw her eyes widen as her lower lip quivered.

"What do you mean?"

"The two doves—the doves of Eabha, they haven't been seen since before the War for Descendants."

"How can you know?"

"I—I just recognized them. I don't know how to explain it," she stuttered. "You should leave. My father will want time alone with our family after this."

"I can't leave like this," he protested.

"He won't change his mind about our union," Rania said, and Weylin almost felt guilty when relief flooded him. "It would bring too much shame upon our name to denounce it just after declaring it publicly. He will ensure word of this event does not leave our castle walls. Our people are good people, loyal people, and they will protect our family however my father tells them to, even if it means their silence. But I know him, and he will not want to see your face once they leave that hall."

Weylin searched his mind to find the words to argue with her. Searched for something to say amongst the chaos while trying not to push his betrothed further than she had already been pushed.

"*Leave Weylin,*" she ordered it coldly. "My father is a male of his word. And I am a female of mine. I will see you again soon, in Samhradh."

She cast one glance at him—one concerned glance, and Weylin could read the terror in her eyes. Without a word further, she dashed off ahead of him, leaving him alone in the corridor outside of his rooms. He stopped walking as he felt the vacancy of her presence.

A silence echoed through him as he took a step towards his room and fought the urge to run after Rania Dorcas.

10

RUAIRI

"*Ru!*" a voice hissed.

Ruairi's eyes snapped open to a beautiful face hovering over him. Aisla was standing over his bed, a wildfire alight in her gaze. He blinked again, and she leaned back and away from him. He fought the urge to pull her closer—to savor these last hours before his departure.

"Ru, wake up," she spoke again, urgency lacing her whisper.

"I am up," he grumbled.

"So," she began as she made herself comfortable on his bed. Ruairi pushed himself up, so he was sitting up, facing her. "I have an idea."

"And this idea couldn't have waited until the morning?" he replied around an exaggerated yawn.

"No. No, it could not actually."

Ruairi raised an eyebrow at her, a wordless request for her to continue.

"I'm going with you," she said, with no hint of playfulness. "I have thought it through. You already have the parcel, and the ship that *you* know how to sail. I am just as skilled in combat as Mona, if not more skilled if we are being honest, and you can teach me how to sail. We've worked well together for practically our whole lives. We would be the perfect team for this. Besides, you helped me begin to finally crack my esos problem. We can't stop now."

"Ash . . ." he said slowly, suddenly wide awake. "Surely you are not serious. You cannot go to Iomlan. You're *you*. You'd be walking right into the Udar's open arms and giving him everything *they* have wanted for nine generations."

"He doesn't know my face," she snapped defensively. "I've already considered it all, trust me. No one on that damned continent knows anything about me besides my last name. I won't use my esos there, and I'll just pretend to be Mona. No one we encounter would know any different."

"You would have to know your esos well enough to control it and ensure it doesn't slip," Ruairi muttered. "Any form of random outburst would be too risky. If they see that you have more than one form, it's a dead giveaway."

"And we'll have the whole sail over for you to train me!" she chirped.

"Except there are no ash trees in the middle of the Tusnua Sea, as far as I am aware."

Aisla pressed her lips into a thin line.

Ruairi leaned his head back and closed his eyes.

His mind scrambled with thoughts that he was in no clear state of mind to truly mull over. He inhaled a deep breath, Conor's words replaying in his mind. There were threats made against Aisla's life mere hours ago. There were people on this continent—people in proper positions of power—who wanted her dead. As though that would fix all of their problems.

He had never considered taking her an option. He hadn't had the time to, given Cliona's quick timeline. Iomlan held dangers of its own for Aisla, but Eilean hardly looked any better for her.

Would she be safer with him than home, where enemies lurked

in the shadows behind the guise of politics? If she were with him, he could at least know she was safe. If she remained home, as she was meant to, once he left the continent it was out of his hands completely.

Ruairi could not help but wonder if Cliona was aware of this too—if sending him away amongst the threats made on her granddaughter's life was all a tactical scheme.

He couldn't let that thought go any further. Ruairi shook his head and opened his eyes to find Aisla looking at him expectantly.

"Aisla, you would be risking much more than your own life," he breathed out. "You realize that?"

He did not miss the way she winced at his words.

"I know. I know how it sounds, but I need to do something. I'm strong enough to hold my own, and we both know that. I won't get caught. I know what is at stake. If I stay here, I won't have you. And I cannot bear the thought of that, Ru. I would just sit here, waiting, while you go save Eire's life. I need to do something, too. I would pass on before I let the Udar take me alive."

"Don't say that," Ruairi snapped, sitting up to meet her gaze again. "Never say that."

"I just want you to know it's something I've already thought about," she said as she leaned in closer. "I am well aware of my place in the norns' golden threads."

Ruairi breathed in the scent of her, of iris and sea spray.

"What if Eire recovers? Shouldn't you be home to be with her?"

"You can look me in the eye and honestly say you think she'll just fall into some miraculous recovery?"

"Well, with the way she worships those silent gods—"

"You cannot be serious, Ruairi Vilulf. You don't believe that for one second. Do not start pretending you do now."

"You have left little room for me to debate with you," he sighed and ran a hand through his unruly red hair.

His heartbeat quickened as he battled internally for the right solution. The solution that would keep Aisla alive.

"Because you aren't changing my mind."

Ruairi looked into her eyes and saw the steely resolve there. He knew whether or not he gave his approval, she would be on that ship with him.

"You are making it impossible to say no."

"Then don't," she breathed out, an almost pleading edge to her voice.

He knew only the norns could know where this path would take them.

"Are you packed?" he asked with a sigh of defeat.

Aisla's eyes lit up as she leaned over the edge of his bed to pull up her already stuffed pack. He noticed she was already dressed for the journey as well.

"Just waiting on you," she said with a grin.

Ruairi rolled his eyes, pulling himself out from under his heavy covers. He sat at the edge of his bed, and her arms wrapped around him before he could stand up. He tensed at her sudden embrace, and she planted a soft and swift kiss on his cheek. Surprise reddened them.

"Thank you," she breathed out.

She released him and he stood, not able to find a reply, so he nodded and disappeared into his washroom to prepare for the journey ahead.

Ruairi's head ached as he thought of all he had just agreed to. He thought of Cliona's inevitable rage when she realized they were both gone, along with the ship *Stoirme*. He wondered if Mona would feel relief when she saw the missing ship and realized she no longer had to venture to Iomlan.

While the details of the prophecy from nine generations ago were blurry given that no one had ever laid eyes on it except for one man who was long dead, it was a well-known fact that the subject of the prophecy would be the son or daughter born in the Iarkis line in the ninth generation, and that elf was Aisla. The norns had shared just enough details all those years ago to incite suspicions, fear, anger, and ambition among the continents, but not enough for anyone to feel confident in a solution. Given Aisla's role as a key player in the threads of the norns, Ruairi knew he could be risking the fate of all nine realms by bringing her into the same land as the Udar.

But he also knew his drive to protect her could be enough.

He made a silent vow, there in his washroom, that he would not let it get that far. She would wait somewhere outside the capital for him, and he would go in alone. Any other way would be too risky. All of this was, but selfishly and perhaps foolishly, he could not turn her down.

Not that he had ever in his life been able to tell Aisla Iarkis what to do. He would have to trust her like she trusted him, and he could only hope they would not live to regret it.

There was one thing that Ruairi was absolutely certain of: prophecies, fate, and responsibilities to the realms aside, he would give his life for hers without hesitation. It would be an honor if he passed on so she could live.

"What's taking so long in there?" Aisla groaned from the other side of the washroom door.

"Maybe if I stall in here long enough, you'll grow bored and fall asleep so I can sneak away," he teased.

"You are not getting rid of me that easily, Vilulf," she shot back.

Her heavy footsteps approached, and she threw open the door. Ruairi was thankful he had already finished changing into his travel clothes. Her gaze met his and her eyes widened slightly with an emotion he could not quite place. The air around them tightened as they filled the small washroom.

"Your pack is still empty," she stated, glancing down at his bag on the floor.

"Thank you, oh wise one," he said.

Aisla shook her head with a small laugh and went back to sit on his bed. Ruairi picked his bag up from the floor and moved about his room as he packed clothes, food, soaps, his blade, *For*, and whatever else he could squeeze inside. His palms began to sweat with each item, anxiety creeping through his veins and riling his esos into a flurry. Finally, he pulled the small package and the map out from beneath his mattress.

Again it felt heavy, so heavy when he held it in his hand. He felt Aisla's eyes on him as he stashed it in the bottom of his bag, feeling the relief of its pressure like a weight off of his shoulders. He suppressed a shudder as he tied his pack closed and slung it over his back.

"Are we ready?" Aisla asked softly, and there was more than words could say in her question.

"Ready as we'll ever be."

He held out his hand, and she gave him a gentle smile, a smile that gave him a flicker of hope. She used his hand to pull herself to her feet, and he stepped back to allow her to lead the way out of his baile.

Once the door was shut behind them, they shared a silent glance of understanding and took off into the night towards the eastern shores of Eilean where *Stoirme* awaited them.

Adrenaline coursed through his veins. His esos brewed in a swirling wind beneath his skin. They trekked through the city center, thankful that no one was out in the dead of the night. Ruairi was grateful this path did not lead them past the infirmary. The last thing they needed was that reminder.

The woods outside of Caillte flew by in a blur. The scent of ash trees and cool spring earth mingled with ocean air that filled Ruairi's nostrils. He took it all in and tried to stop himself from wondering when he would next see his home.

The inlet of the Tusnua Sea roared ahead of them. They slowed when they neared the flat coastal land that edged the seashores. Ruairi could see the small wooden cutter sailboat that he had become familiar with over his many scouting adventures for Cliona.

Aisla looked nervously to him as their shoes brushed through the sandy terrain of the shore. She had never sailed before, and it would be the crucial difference between having her and Mona, one of the best sailors in the realm, on this journey.

"You'll learn," he said, a deep fear that they would be caught still seated in his chest.

They climbed aboard *Stoirme* under the cover of the night and the light of the moons. The moons had watched the creation of the nine realms, and watched as they ripped each other apart from the inside.

Aisla grabbed Ruairi's pack while he went about preparing the cutter. He checked the lines for tangles to ensure they were separated. He followed each end to its stopper knot and tugged to ensure it would not slip through. He didn't have to check the direction of the wind. He knew it like an extra sense. He knew the way the boat would have to face to begin their journey eastward. He worked quickly to hoist the sail. The sound of the white sheet billowing with the wind sent a chill along his arms. At last, he trimmed the mainsail and took a deep breath.

He looked over at Aisla, who stood by for any directions since she was in completely new and unfamiliar territory. He gently wrapped a comforting arm around her shoulders.

They watched their home disappear and Ruairi could feel the unspoken fears between them as he knew they both wondered if they would ever see it again.

I I

AISLA

Aisla did not sleep the night she and Ruairi set sail across the Tusnua Sea aboard the small wooden cutter.

Guilt gnawed at her until it physically hurt. In the cramped, pitch-dark cabin she lay in bed, pulling her knees into her chest and squeezing her eyes shut. The silence ate at her, threatening to swallow her whole. Ruairi had insisted she should sleep during the night, and then he would teach her to sail in the daylight so he could rest once she was comfortable taking over on her own.

She had agreed, but soon after regretted not staying out there with him beneath the light of the stars.

Aisla toyed with the necklace Eire had given her, and she wished more than anything that she could be here with them. Her fingers found the familiar knots of twine and brushed along each smooth tooth piece, looking to find comfort there. She forced herself to lie there, to get the rest she desperately needed, until she couldn't take it any longer.

She padded out of the cabin and approached the deck. The first thing that caught her eye was the way the rising sun made Ruairi's brilliant red hair look like wildfire. She paused for a moment, and thought about how natural he must feel here, how in his element this was. From where he sat on the deck, he looked at home.

Aisla found herself wondering, for not the first time, what a life with Ruairi would look like. In a different world, a different time, she thought they could live like this. They would travel the realms on a small boat, seeing all that there was to see, and he would be content. And so would she.

She took another step, and he looked in her direction. A smile lit his face, and it loosened a tightness in her chest.

"Morning, you look like you didn't get a wink of sleep," he teased, and she sat down next to him on the bench that lined the edge of the sailboat.

"You sure know how to charm 'em," she grumbled back and rubbed at her eyes. "Couldn't sleep."

"Cabin not comfortable enough for you?" He bumped her playfully with his shoulder.

"No, it's not that." She took a deep breath. "It's just a lot, you know?"

"I know. Why do you think I let you take the first night shift?"

"Maybe because I don't have the first idea how to sail a ship?"

"Well, that too," he said with a chuckle. "I suppose we will fix that today."

Aisla nodded silently.

"We also need to talk about what it'll take to reach the shores of Iomlan," he said and averted his gaze. The hairs along Aisla's arms stood on end at the foreboding tone of his voice. Her ears tilted forward to listen to the words that followed. "As you know, the Myrkor navy keeps the coast well guarded, and our first challenge will be running their blockade. *Stoirme* has the sail power needed to do it—gods know she's outrun her fair share of storms scouting around Eilean—but it won't be easy. I'll look for an opening as soon as their ships come into view. Once we get past them, we'll have to make our way as quickly as we can to Briseadhceo, where a contact of Eilean will provide us an updated map. I don't expect them to be forthcoming with us, but the fact that we can at least get a map will go a long way. Then, we just need to get to Samhradh and a second contact will meet us inside the capital to get us to the Udar. They're both marked on our current map, so we'll need to hang onto that one, too."

Aisla wrinkled her brows as she processed the information. She hadn't even thought about getting past the navy. Her naivety stood out to her and shame stung her cheeks.

"Is this what the inner council meets about all the time?" Aisla asked. "I didn't even realize we had contacts left on Iomlan."

"Sometimes," he replied, and his eyes locked onto hers once again. "It's in our best interest to stay in the know where we can. Unfortunately, there is still much more unknown."

"The blockade. . . should we be worried about that?"

"Yes, and no. It's a risk, but it's the only way through. We can't take to the skies while the return of the wyverns on Iomlan is still considered an act of war. Even if we went further north, then made our way down into Briongloid, the Myrkors have ships all the way in Geimhrigh. We'll tread as cautiously as we are able until we can't. Then we move quickly, and we'll be okay, Ash."

"I trust you," she replied.

Aisla pulled her legs up onto the bench and shifted her body to lie with her head in Ruairi's lap. She looked up and caught the glint of his green eyes as he smiled with a warmth that radiated through her core. There was a flurry of nerves in her stomach that she rarely felt around Ruairi. She wondered if he felt it, too.

She let her eyelids fall shut and focused on the sound of the waves as they crashed against the ship and tried not to think of all the creatures lurking below them. She smelled the salty sea, and the wind breezed around them. She was thankful that the rocking sea had not upset her stomach, as she was not sure what to expect. She adjusted quickly to the steady back and forth of the waves, occasionally interrupted by a bump. She supposed Ruairi hardly noticed them.

"I wonder how Eire would take to sailing," Ruairi pondered as he brushed a lock of hair off of Aisla's forehead.

"I think she would prefer the land," Aisla said with a small laugh. "I can't imagine her with sea legs. Although, I suppose given her esos is of the waters, she should feel more at home out here than anywhere else."

"That's a fair point," Ruairi nodded. "Maybe for a brief trip, nothing long term."

"What's the longest you've been out at sea without stopping?"

"Longest without stopping? Probably thirteen sunrises with Conor. It was miserable, not because of the journey, but because of the company. That man is a real ass," Ruairi said with a snort. "If it weren't for him, I don't think it would have felt that long."

"I never really got a good read on him," Aisla said. "Haven't spent much time around him."

"Consider yourself lucky."

Aisla noted the disgust in his voice—the edge of hatred.

They lay there for a while longer, passing the afternoon with a calmness she knew could not last. But Aisla did not want to move. Ruairi's gentle fingers playing in her windblown hair while the comfort of his familiar scent held her in place felt a lot like safety.

"Ash?" Ruairi's voice called her from the daydream she had lost herself in. "Want to learn the basics to sail while it's still light out? It's not as hard as it looks."

She looked at the looming mast, the abundance of rope, and the great sheet blowing in the breezy morning. She had a hard time believing it could be easy.

"I promise," he said in response to her skeptical glances.

"If you say so," she grumbled.

She sat up from the bench and followed him around the sailboat while he pointed to different parts, naming them with ease, and she repeated them back, determined to master the skill before they reached Iomlan. He showed her the hull, cleats, boom, bow, mast, rudders, and winches. He taught her how to use each, and how they all operated in coordination with one another to make the beautiful ship glide through the seas.

He walked her through tacking, gybing, and luffing, allowed her to move through the motions of it until she could do it without his guiding hand. Although they were already sailing and would not be stopping anytime soon, he gave her the steps for running through a check before setting sail to ensure everything was clear.

"And you never want to sail directly into the wind," he explained as the afternoon sun beamed down on them. "You'll always want to go in at an angle to keep moving forward. And while wind direction is instinctual for me because of my esos, it's important to do your own check before setting sail."

"Got it," she said, nodding.

"When teaching opportunities come up, I can hand it over to you and put these terms into action," he said. "But for now, it should be enough for you to be comfortable sailing on your own while I rest."

"And that's good enough for me," Aisla chirped before dropping onto the wooden bench. She was mentally exhausted from all the new words and maneuvers she was trying to hold in her brain. "I'm starving."

"It is about that time."

Ruairi laughed as he rummaged through his pack for some of the food he had brought for them. He retrieved a block of cheese and dried-out meat with some bread. They broke off pieces of it and shared the meal.

"I remember the first time I ever saw you," Ruairi said softly as her eyes found his. "It was our first day of scoil. You were tenacious even at seven years old. Everyone had been waiting for you to show up, since the rumors were already rampant. Your arm was hooked through Eire's when you walked in those doors. She smiled big and proud, and you wore a grin that was nearly the opposite. It was cunning, and it said *eat shit* where a seven-year-old could never say it aloud. You walked in with something to prove, that fire burning in the depths of your irises, even then. You looked through the crowd of first years, careful to make eye contact with each elf in the room, and held their gaze for just long enough for them to remember the look. I remember when your eyes finally found mine, I laughed. It was so comical, the way you waltzed in with cheerful Eire and you looked so cross."

Aisla rolled her eyes, knowing what came next. She grinned despite the blush creeping into her cheeks.

"And when I laughed, you dropped Eire's arm and marched right up to me, until our noses were nearly touching. I remember the childish gasps erupting, and the instructor stepped towards us, but she stopped like she was also curious to see what you would do next," Ruairi continued, his grin growing wider. "You got right up in front of me and you said, 'What's your name?' and, of course, I replied 'Ruairi Vilulf' and then you said 'Well, Ru, I think we'll make great rivals' and then you stuck your hand out to me and I shook it. I can still remember suppressing the urge to laugh again as I watched your eyes narrow in a way that said you meant it. And oh, were you right. Took me a couple of years to even like you, but we were always competing for something."

Aisla burst into laughter as she remembered it all, exactly the way he described it. She didn't even try to fight the embarrassed flush in her cheeks as Ruairi roared with laughter beside her.

That was her before her parents passed on. She had changed so much and she found herself missing that fiery spark that her seven-year-old self had displayed so well on her first day of scoil.

"I don't know how you ever became my friend after that," Aisla said when she could finally find her words again.

"I don't know how I could resist," he grinned. "You've always been special, and not because of any gods or any golden threads. You're special to me."

His words lingered in the air and felt like a gentle caress against her skin.

"You're special to me too, Ru," she said back. "I wouldn't want a life without you in it."

"Then let's survive this. It won't be easy, but it will be worth it."

Aisla nodded in agreement, and moved to close the distance between them. She leaned her head on his shoulder.

Ruairi pressed his cheek against her hair, and wrapped a strong, comforting arm around her, pulling her closer into him.

Aisla closed her eyes as the sun set over them.

12

RUAIRI

Ruairi put up a fight, but Aisla insisted she would take the early night shift so he could rest since he had not had the chance to. He went down into the cabin shortly after the sun had set, and was surprised when he fell into a deep and restful sleep. Halfway through the night, he woke up and found Aisla to trade off. Thankfully, she had not run into any complications during her watch and was able to fall into a steady rhythm with the night winds.

He sat alone, watching the waves as they passed, the sound of them quieting the constant anxiety in his heart. He let his head fall back while he fought not to think about all that they were approaching, the more distance they put in between themselves and home.

He was eager to get within view of the Myrkor blockade so he could start planning a way to break through it. He knew they would land on the western coast of Briongloid, which was the realm to the northwest of Samhradh, the home of the Udar. Briseadhceo was not far from the shore. Once they made it there to talk to Cliona's contact, he would feel better.

Ruairi pulled the map out from his pack to study it again. He had memorized many landmarks and cities, but would feel more comfortable once they had an updated map. When they were on Iomlan, they would each create an alias with enough of a background story to be convincing. Ruairi knew they would also need to get a read on the use of esos in Iomlan to blend in as best as they could.

They had heard rumors of a strict regime under the current Udar, Faolan Myrkor, but none of their contacts had mentioned specific restrictions on esos. Their job would be to lie as low as possible and attract as little attention as they could. When they reached Omra, Ruairi would go in alone and use his parcel as the bargaining chip Cliona had claimed it would be, while Aisla waited outside the capital. This part of his plan, he had not shared with her yet.

He already knew she would protest.

Ruairi sighed as he traced the path from their estimated docking point to Castle Eagla. He'd done it so many times the paper was growing thin along the path. He folded the map along its worn creases and gently tucked it into the pack at his feet. He could feel the weight of how unprepared they were in each breath that he took.

His eyes grew heavy in the pre-dawn darkness despite his rest. The sounds of the sea lulled him into a state of drowsiness as he let his eyes shut. A sort of peace enveloped him as he leaned into the steady rock of *Stoirme*.

Ruairiiiiii, a female voice rang out and his eyes snapped open.

He half-wondered if he imagined the sound when he listened and heard nothing but the crash of waves for a long moment. He leaned forward, straining his ears as his heart pounded.

Silence again settled over the deck, and Ruairi leaned back again, shoulders still tense.

Ruairiiiiii, the voice sang. It was lilting and beautiful, and this time it came clear and crisp to his ears on the wind.

It almost sounded like Aisla, but he knew in his heart that it was not her. It was some sort of imitation of her.

Ruairi glanced to the lines as though there was something he should be doing with them, even though the ship had been sailing on its own for some time now. He was just awake for precautionary measures.

Ruairiiiiii. A third time.

Ruairi could feel his mind growing cloudy, the edges of his vision blurred, and his tongue felt heavy in his mouth. He tried to shake his mind of the fog, but he was only pushed deeper into it. He took a deep, shaky breath and blinked.

Ruairiiiiii, the voice crooned once more; the sound carried to him on the wind until it caressed his cheek and whispered along his neck, sending a chill down his spine. *Help me!*

Ruairi stood and grabbed his blade from his pack and clasped it in his right hand, his palms growing sweaty. The voice stirred something within his chest, something he could not place as his feet dragged him forward of their own accord and a figure appeared before him, standing on the other side of the deck. He didn't know when she had gotten there, or how she had appeared without him noticing, but there she stood.

His eyes widened in shock. Before him stood a bare woman with long, sandy blonde hair that covered her breasts. Her sea-green eyes gazed at him with a longing he had never felt before. Her pale skin shone in the moonlight and Ruairi averted his eyes to the deck, but he did not miss the way she smiled at him. How she grinned with a warmth that reached out to him where he stood.

Ruairi, I have been waiting for you. Her voice hummed as an invisible force tugged on his chin, begging him to look up again.

His mind grew cloudier with every passing moment.

"What do you want?" he mumbled, his voice not coming out nearly as strong as he had meant for it to.

Isn't that obvious? She laughed and the sound of her laugh stirred something deep within his chest. Her very essence hit him like the waves surrounding them. *I want you, Ruairi.*

At that, his chin snapped up in a way that made him stumble back a step, dizzy, but she was there to catch him. Her arm wrapped around his back as she held him on his feet, her skin pressed against the fabric of his clothes.

Everything in Ruairi screamed at him to pull out of her grasp— to push her away—but as he looked down into her imploring gaze, he heard his blade clatter to the ground and his muscles loosened as his own arms reached out to hold her. His fingertips brushed her skin and bumps rose along his arms. He opened his mouth to speak, but no words came out.

An alarm rang out in the back of his brain—a warning that came out muted and hard to reach.

She smiled shyly as her hand moved to rest against his cheek, gentle and smooth, almost cautious, and he found himself leaning into her touch as his heavy eyes blinked slowly.

Her other hand lifted to his face, her thumb ran along his lower lip and he could hear his heart in his ears above the roar of the waves and above his instinct to run.

"I—"

Ruairi began to speak, began to say something that might have been a protest, but her lips crashed into his as both of her hands held him in place, pulling him in. He tried to push her away, but she did not budge. His arms fell limply to his side as he gave in and kissed her back.

A deep purr of approval loosed from the woman, and he felt it in his own chest. She bit his lower lip, tugged on his hair, and clawed at his back until he was lost in it—lost in her. He could no longer remember where he was or what he was doing or why he had ever wanted to fight this feeling. His arms wrapped around her tightly.

He could not recall his name, nor hers, nor anything besides the feel of her. Her touch, her lips, her breath, her smell, her skin on his. They kissed greedily, never breaking apart. It was as beautiful as it was torturous, but he knew nothing else. He wasn't sure he could pull away, but he had no desire to.

The woman released the embrace and the absence of her took his breath away. He leaned in for more. His eyes fluttered open to familiar yellow-green eyes looking up at him, and he could not find the words to speak. He shook his head, vaguely trying to free something in his mind, but he wasn't sure what.

Come with me, Ruairi. Her voice hummed, and he smelled lilac and sea breeze. *Follow me to a place where only I know. A place where you will know nothing but the taste of my lips until your very last breath.*

Ruairi felt a scream from deep within, a scream of protest, but he pushed it further down. He knew her. Her smell and her eyes and the light brown hair that fell down to her exposed waist. He would follow her anywhere she asked and beyond.

She reached out and took his hand, gently but firmly, and he felt a peace. Peace he had never felt before as she led him towards the edge of the boat with a smile that chilled his blood.

"I'm yours," he spoke at last, his thumb tracing a small circle on her hand and a strange feeling of familiarity washed over him.

13

AISLA

The sound of beating wings and boisterous coos awoke Aisla from her deep slumber aboard *Stoirme*. She squeezed her eyes shut and buried her head beneath her pillow as she tried to ignore the agitating sounds, but they were relentless.

She threw the pillow off in defeat and opened her eyes to two white doves flying about her room, nearly grazing her face.

"Damn birds," she grumbled a curse while she swatted at them.

They backed off of her enough for her to sit up in the bed, then they circled her with intent. She tilted her head back to look up at them, and it was as though they were trying to communicate with her. They wanted her to *move*. She rose on weary feet and rubbed at the sleep, blurring her vision before following the birds herding her out of the cabin.

They continued their frenzied pattern until she was out on the main deck of the ship. The waves overpowered the sound of the birds' wings, and the salty sea air engulfed her. The winds were stronger than they had been when she had traded shifts with Ruairi, blowing her hair all around her. Aisla squinted through the flying strands as she watched the birds disappear into the sky. She recalled the legends of Eabha and her two doves, Smaoinigh and Intinn, that were ever-present on her quest for wisdom. Aisla wondered if the mother goddess was watching over them now.

The thought left her mind as quickly as it arrived when she shifted her attention back to the deck and took in the scene before her.

Aisla's mouth fell open in disbelief. Her chest constricted with an emotion she could not name. She reached for *Oidhe*, sheathed at her waist. Her cheeks heated with anger.

A nude woman was kissing Ruairi. He held her close, and she gazed into his eyes. It made Aisla sick. The woman's hands trailed along his back, then into brilliant red hair. Aisla was stuck, frozen to the deck.

Rage and esos coalesced into a violent urge, pleading for release. The woman moved to the railing, Ruairi's hand still in hers. He was going to follow her over the side.

Something in Aisla snapped.

She took two heavy steps forward, drawing the attention of both the woman and Ruairi. The woman turned to her with a wicked, toothy grin. Her lips curled back to reveal sharpened teeth that made Aisla shudder as she imagined them sinking into her flesh. Ruairi looked to Aisla for only a second, but a second was long enough to see his swollen, red lips and the lovesick look in his green eyes.

Another burst of urgency flared through her. Her palms burned and flames burst from them. She held them towards the sky. The flickering light cast dancing shadows across the wooden boat. The green flames grew as she rushed forward and gripped Ruairi by the shoulder, yanking him out of that *creature's* grasp. Her esos singed his shirt, but did not touch his skin. He stumbled backwards with a yelp of surprise.

Aisla stood face to face with the sneering undine, a creature from her legends courses in scoil. They were one of the countless races of the seas and children of Muir, god of waters. The undine was just as beautiful as they were rumored to be, but Aisla saw through its seductive guise.

Flames danced on her palms as she pulled on the power inside her until she realized she was no longer among ash trees. And no matter what type of tree this boat was made of, her esos could only derive from a living source.

In a panic, Aisla shook her hands out, allowing the flames to dissipate, quickly drawing *Oidhe* from her waistband. She would not risk depleting her esos out here.

What's wrong, little mallaithe? The feminine voice crooned, trying to enrapture Aisla. It used the term of old for *cursed*. The magic of her voice wrapped around Aisla's hands and her legs and sent shivers across her skin as it worked to calm and lull her, but Aisla's determination only grew. *Can't use your own esos?*

"Go to Hel," Aisla spat and drove her dagger towards the undine.

The creature lunged to the side, but not quick enough to avoid Aisla's blade. Blood seeped from a deep cut on her upper arm.

The undine snarled and her nails grew into sharp points as she leapt on top of Aisla. Her talons dug into Aisla's shoulders as they fell onto the deck. Aisla ignored her pain and tried to throw the creature off of her. The undine gripped Aisla's wrist, drawing blood as she worked to force Aisla to drop the dagger. Aisla held on with all of her strength, gritting her teeth.

Give up, Gheall Ceann, she said, her hot breath fanning across Aisla's face. She used the title often used when people discussed the prophecy, the term of old for *chosen one*. It made Aisla's stomach turn. *Your journey is cursed from every angle. You will never survive Iomlan alone. Give up and give in and I can take you to a better place. A place beneath the waves and into the waters.*

Aisla shoved harder, fighting the power of the undine's song. She kicked with all of her might. Pain seared through her arm and she struggled to get enough control of her dagger to drive it through the wretched creature's beating heart.

The undine snapped her teeth in Aisla's face with a haunting laugh. Aisla strained to put as much distance as she could between her throat and the undine's gnashing teeth, when suddenly the undine's eyes rolled back into her head and the pressure on Aisla's arm released. The undine fell atop her, a weight holding her down. Sobs wracked through Aisla as she fought to free herself. Alarm quickly followed her relief as a metallic scent filled her nostrils.

Warm liquid pooled between their bodies, and then the weight was rolled off of her and onto the deck. Aisla gasped for air as she scrambled to her feet, dagger in hand, but the creature had already passed on.

Ruairi stood over the creature.

His blade, *Fior,* dripped with blood and the undine's corpse oozed the red liquid all over *Stoirme's* deck. Aisla was drenched in it.

Aisla closed the distance between them, throwing her arms around Ruairi's shaking body. She tightened her grip, and he wrapped his arms around her lower back as he nuzzled his face into the crook of her neck. It was a relief to feel him—to hold him when she had nearly lost him.

Their breaths fell into a steady rhythm of relief in the silence.

The jealousy that had consumed her when she stepped out on the deck faded with the feeling of his warmth enveloping her. As uncomfortable as it was for her to see, she knew enough about undines to know that her enchantment was not his fault. She could not hold that against him, no matter what feelings it had aroused in her.

"You scared me," she said at last.

"I know, and I'm sorry," he said, and she knew he meant it.

"You could've died," she whispered the worst part of it all. The words scraped her throat like a knife blade. "I'm so glad I woke up."

"Me too." His hot breath warmed her neck, and she gave him another squeeze before releasing the embrace.

Ruairi still trembled. In that moment, Aisla realized how much he meant to her. The idea of losing him was a pain she could not bring herself to imagine. Eire and Ruairi had been her best friends for so long and through so much, but it was different with Ruairi.

And the look in his eyes as she pulled away told her he felt it, too.

She gently took his hand and wove her fingers through his. She led him to sit on the bench. They would deal with the body of the undine later.

"Are you okay?" She said and settled in next to him.

"I am." He glanced down at their hands before looking up to meet her gaze. "Are you?"

"Yes. Ru, it was—there were two doves that woke me up. They brought me to find you before it was too late."

"Doves?"

She nodded her head and watched the realization cross his green eyes.

"You don't think. . . like in the legends of Eabha?"

"I don't know," Aisla replied as she averted her gaze to the red of the rising sun. "It just seems like an odd coincidence. It was so intentional, too. I tried to ignore them, but they were relentless until I got out onto the deck."

Ruairi remained in silent contemplation for a few moments, and she knew he was thinking exactly what she was. Something so terrifying to hope for, and so outside of both of them to even believe in.

"I'm not sure what to make of it, Ash," he said at last. "All I know is I wouldn't be here if they didn't."

A chill travelled down Aisla's spine as tears stung the corners of her eyes. She could only press closer into him and hold his hand tighter. She could only thank the gods and hope that they were listening. She would grip that ember of hope with everything that she had left as they entered lands she was wholly unprepared for.

14

AISLA

"Ru!" Aisla said as she jostled Ruairi awake from an afternoon nap beside her on the wooden bench. "Ru, I can see the blockade."

Ruairi jolted up. Any sign of drowsiness disappeared as he walked towards the bow to get as close as he could to the steadily approaching ships. He stood wordlessly for a moment, and ran his fingers through his hair. Aisla could feel the anxiousness radiating off of him. She walked over to him, wincing as she passed over the bloodstain left by the undine.

"We'll figure it out," she murmured, and he only nodded. She wasn't entirely sure if she was saying it to convince him or herself. "We always do."

"We've never been up against anything like this before," he said, and Aisla's throat tightened.

She nodded in agreement because she could not find the words to speak. He was not wrong, but now was not the time to give up hope.

The first thing Aisla noticed about the ships was just how massive some of them were. They were a mix, and the larger ones were closer to them while the smaller ones were farther in near the shore. Most of them were larger than *Stoirme*. The blockade was fairly sparse, a few ships clumped near each other in one area and then an enormous gap before a few more.

They must be surrounding the ports, Aisla thought to herself.

Beyond the ships, Aisla could see a land mass that was lined with swaths of dense forest beyond the sandy shores. There were tall pine trees and shorter oak trees with long, winding branches. She could hear the branches scraping together.

She reached out and placed her hand on top of Ruairi's, where it rested on the wooden railing of *Stoirme*. She held it with a confidence that she did not feel, and he gently squeezed hers in response. Each passing moment brought the blockade closer to them, and there was nothing they could do to stop it. Aisla felt the pressure more than ever as her palms sweat and her chest grew heavy.

"Well," Ruairi broke the silence. "This is it. We've made it this far, First Mate Iarkis."

Pressure in her chest released with the humor in his tone.

"I never really stopped to think about what this moment would feel like," Aisla breathed out. "But I don't think I could have prepared myself for this feeling."

"I don't really think anyone or anything could," Ruairi said, nodding in agreement.

A knot grew in her throat as she slowly released Ruairi's hand and walked towards the starboard side of the boat—the side that faced the enemy ships and Briongloid.

As she gazed upon the continent that had caused so much destruction, her eyes stung with grief for all her ancestors had lost. It festered within her like a physical thing. She leaned forward, breathing in the salty air that was the same salty air that lingered on the coast of Eilean, and allowed it to anchor her to the boat and to her promise to bring home a cure for her people—for Eire.

Her mind lingered on Eire's beautiful blue eyes, her soft laugh, her gentle touch, and her sharp wit, as it often did. She wondered how she was and wordlessly hoped for a miraculous recovery while they were away. Aisla knew in her gut that she was still alive. She knew Eire was fighting for each breath she took, because she knew that if Eire stopped breathing, she would feel it. She had no doubt of that.

She could feel Ruairi's eyes on her back, and knew he was thinking of her, too.

"What's the plan now?" She said in a whispered tone.

Without a word, Ruairi pulled their map from his pocket and held it up so he could look at it as he observed the shore. His eyes darted back and forth from the map to the ships until he lowered it and faced Aisla.

"We'll shoot through the blockade there, in between ports," he said and pointed a little to the north of where *Stoirme* was aimed. "Then we'll weigh anchor and swim to the shore. We'll be about a day's journey from Briseadhceo where our first contact will be waiting for us. It'll be a long day, but I think the quicker we can get through it and get the map, the better."

Aisla nodded in agreement. She had little to add to the plan since Ruairi had been given all the information. This would be her chance to finally prove herself. She could show her grandmother that she was more than capable of joining in their cause to protect Eilean and their population from Iofa and come back stronger than before.

"I'm going to use a bit of my esos to give *Stoirme* the advantage she'll need," he said with hesitancy. "Thankfully, *Stoirme* was designed with a need for a quick getaway. We've had our fair share of trouble with children of Muir in the seas, and needed a boat that could get out swiftly."

Aisla trusted Ruairi enough to know he had weighed the benefits of putting his esos in use before finding ash trees.

"How can I help?" She asked.

"Be ready to toss down the anchor and swim when I tell you."

She nodded again even as she felt the sting of the reminder of her lack of skill. She knew he had not meant it that way.

Aisla moved to stand near the anchor and Ruairi positioned himself near the line that lead up the mast. She felt his esos enter the atmosphere, and a chill ran down her spine. He did not need to aim his palms at the sky or work himself up to it. His esos emanated from him as naturally as walking as it wound up into the sheets. Aisla's stomach lurched as they were suddenly hurling faster towards the shore. She braced her feet on the deck as they sped straight into the blockade.

A loud horn sounded from the ships, and Aisla's eyes grew wide as she looked to Ruairi, whose lips were pressed into a thin line.

Her palms were sweating, but she remained silent, allowing Ruairi the space to focus and get them out of danger. They had been spotted.

Their speed picked up even more, and Aisla had to cling to the side of the boat to keep from falling. They were soaring along the waves. Splashes of water flew up to wet her clothes while his winds propelled them along. She could imagine that familiar tug of draining energy that came with the use of esos. That tug would grow stronger and stronger as an elf neared depletion.

They broke through the ships exactly where Ruairi had planned. They were far enough between the two ports surrounded by ships that none of them were close to reaching *Stoirme*. Aisla knew that would not be where the danger ended, though.

Their small cutter slowed when they neared the shore and Ruairi prepared the ship to be anchored.

"Now, Ash," he spoke with urgency.

Aisla hauled the heavy anchor over the side of the boat and listened to the crawl of the chain until it hit the ground below them. *Not too deep*, she noted to herself.

Aisla grabbed her pack, pulling the string tight around the top before tying the flap down over it. She silently thanked the dwarves, who had mastered the art of waterproofing canvas. She hoped it would prove effective and save what little food they had brought with them, as well as their clothes.

"We'll be back soon," Aisla whispered to the boat, hoping that the words were true.

She looked over as Ruairi shouldered his own pack on. His gaze held hers with a thousand words they could not speak.

"It'll be okay," he said.

"I know," she said before taking a deep breath and diving over the edge of the boat.

She heard a splash from Ruairi following behind her. Aisla worked her arms quickly, pulling the water behind her and kicking her feet, coming up every few strokes for a breath.

When they finally reached the shore, they darted into the cover of the trees before Ruairi pulled his map out from the bottom of his pack, which thankfully had remained dry.

"It looks like we're just outside of Trasnu," Ruairi said, looking over the map one last time before tucking it away into his pack. "We'll head eastward and go as far as we can tonight, then put up a tent and rest for the morning. Then, we should get to Briseadhceo tomorrow in the early afternoon."

Aisla nodded. Meeting his gaze, she saw her own fears reflected in his eyes. She swallowed and looked away.

"A journey of endless sunrises begins with the very first step," Ruairi murmured, and Aisla smiled.

"When did you get so wise?"

"I've always been wise. It's just taken you ages to notice," he teased. "Let's get moving."

Ruairi took off into the forest just as a heavy rain started to beat down upon them. Aisla cursed under her breath as she pulled the hood of her cloak over her head, and Ruairi did the same. She followed him silently into the woods, staying a few paces behind while they moved with hurried and careful footsteps.

They agreed they would stop in small cities when necessary for supplies in between their contacts, but otherwise they would mostly stick to themselves as an extra measure of precaution. No one would recognize them, but it had been too long since anyone had ventured onto Iomlan from Eilean to know what to expect. There were too many conversations that could go wrong and mark them as outsiders, and the last thing they needed was to draw attention to themselves.

The earth muddied beneath their feet as it mixed with the rainwater. They passed through a dense forest that opened up into a large clearing before becoming forest once more. The air smelled of rain and pines, and Aisla noted the familiar traces of the sea, as it remained not far away. To the east, Aisla caught glimpses of a vast mountain range. The moons above them lit their way in the dark of the night.

Neither of them had said a word since they had left *Stoirme*. Whether it was from fear, conserving energy, or both, Aisla could not say. They continued on until Aisla felt her legs might give out beneath her. She struggled to keep up, but she would not be the first to give up, so she gritted her teeth and kept up Ruairi's pace as the rain soaked through her clothes and onto her skin.

Finally, she noticed Ruairi slowing when they neared a small clearing between patches of forest and her chest loosened.

"Here for the night?" He asked, speaking over the rain that seemed to grow louder.

Aisla nodded in agreement and tucked her pack beneath a tree to keep it out of the worst of the mud, and helped Ruairi set up their tent. Aisla and Ruairi had plenty of practice setting such tents up from adventures on Eilean, and made quick work of getting it set up under the shelter of a large pine.

They crawled in through the narrow opening and sealed it shut behind them, glad to be out of the pouring rain.

"What a night," Ruairi muttered as they unrolled their sleeping mats and pulled out their thin blankets.

Aisla nodded, fumbling through her pack for the dioluine herb she had packed for them. She handed a piece to Ruairi, who looked to her with gratitude.

"Aisla Iarkis, have I ever told you what a genius you are?"

"Not nearly enough," she quipped as she ground the sweet herb between her teeth.

"I hadn't thought of bringing the immunity herb," he said. "Good call, especially given the terrible weather."

"That's what I'm here for," she said with a shrug of her shoulders.

Dioluine was known for enhancing health and immune systems. Aisla had known it would come in handy.

"This is our grand welcome back to Iomlan, I suppose," Aisla said after taking a swig of water from her canteen to wash the rest of the herb down. "It almost seems fitting."

Aisla settled into her makeshift bed, which was considerably less comfortable than the cabin of *Stoirme*.

"At least we're used to these bed mats from camping back at home," he said with a humorless chuckle. "But we do usually try to plan around the weather. It smells like wet rat in here."

"Eire would hate this," Aisla said with a snort as she looked up at the top of the tent.

"You're so right. She only likes the rain when she controls it, and I think this would have been a bit beyond her grasp."

"She would have been roaring complaints since the moment we got off the ship," Aisla added. "'You guys picked the *worst* time to get off this thing. The gods clearly don't want us here, let's turn her around.'"

Ruairi chuckled beside her and nodded in agreement.

"She would definitely have had a lot to say about your run-in with the undine," Asla said, but she regretted the words the moment they left her lips.

They had not spoken of the incident since the morning after it happened. The sight of Ruairi with that creature still nagged at the back of her mind. And maybe that was why she found herself bringing it up now, in their tent under rainy skies.

Ruairi turned on his side to face her where she was already facing him. Their noses were just inches apart and the air around them seemed to grow tighter. His eyebrows furrowed as if deep in thought, but he said nothing as he looked at her. Aisla's gaze flitted between his deep green eyes which looked like they were holding countless secrets beneath their surface. Aisla did not like it. She was used to being able to read him like a book.

"What is it?" Aisla asked, searching his eyes for answers instead of questions.

His gaze softened, and Aisla felt a familiar flutter in her stomach.

"I'm just sorry," Ruairi replied. "I wish that had never happened."

"Me too," she whispered. "I'm just glad you're alive."

Ruairi's brow creased as he sat in thought.

"That was my first kiss," he said so quietly, it took Aisla a moment to know that she heard him correctly.

"Oh," she replied.

Her chest filled with relief to hear that there had not been someone back home. He was gone often enough that it would not shock her if he had been with someone before. She knew he wouldn't have brought it up with her, so she had decided to never ask. She knew it wasn't her place to.

"I think," he said and took a deep breath. "I thought it would be different."

"How so?" She asked.

"I always thought, well hoped, that it would be *you*."

The words lingered in the air between them. Aisla's heart leaped into her throat. She was not prepared for this, not in the least. Her lips parted with words that would not come to her.

He reached out a gentle hand to caress her cheek, and she leaned into it. He felt like home—a time and a place she longed for with her whole being. His thumb brushed her cheekbone, and he opened his mouth to say something more. Before he could, Aisla leaned forward, closing the distance between them. She couldn't stand the space between them that made her skin itch with need and her chest tighten with longing. She didn't know when exactly she had started to see Ruairi as more than just a friend, but she knew Eire would say she saw it long before either of them had.

Ruairi's lips met hers with a faint groan of relief. His arms wrapped around her, pulling her close, and a shiver ran down her spine. He was warm and welcoming and firm and stable.

They pulled away at the same time. Her eyes fluttered open to see him gazing back at her under heavy lids. They'd found a cautious peace.

Aisla nuzzled into his chest, and he held her tighter as though she could slip away at any moment. She listened to the steady rhythms of his breaths, matching her own to his.

"I've been wanting that for longer than you could ever know," he said.

"Then what were you waiting for?"

"I—I never knew how you felt. If it would ruin what we had as friends, or if it would make it even better than before," Ruairi stuttered. "It scared the Hel out of me, but I knew I couldn't lose you, so I guess I played it safe."

"Ruairi Vilulf, play it safe?" She pulled away to look up at him and saw the amusement glimmering in his eyes. "That's not my Ru."

"I know," he said. "If I had known it would feel like this, I would have done it ages ago. Now I feel like we've lost all this time."

"It's not lost time." She shook her head. "We still had each other in the ways we needed each other. And we've still got time."

The last words were almost hard to say. Aisla clung to him, feeling as though she had so much more to lose now. Everything had changed in that kiss. They were still Aisla and Ruairi, but now there was more than that. And it scared her as much as it excited her.

"Mmmm," Ruairi murmured in agreement. His hand held the back of her neck and once again pulled her into him.

Their exhaustion filled the tent like a fog. She found solitude in his strong arms and safety in the scent of him as her mind drifted away and a heavy sleep engulfed her.

15

WEYLIN

Weylin Myrkor trotted away from Castle Tromlui and his betrothed in the midst of chaos. He pulled his hood over his head as they carried onward.

Weylin had never been one for superstitions, especially given the silence of the gods following the War for Descendants, but he was no ignorant male.

The doves of Eabha were the clearest sign the gods could have given to the realms. His union to Rania Dorcas was not favored by the mother of the gods, the most powerful force to ever exist. The thought did not scare Weylin Myrkor as much as it angered him. He had done everything as he was instructed. His forefathers had done everything they could to prevent the downfall of Talam, yet they were endlessly punished for it. He would not bow to their will any longer.

The gods had now broken two centuries of silence to condemn him, but it would not stop Weylin. He would wed Rania and they would lead the realms of Talam into a golden age not seen since before the days of that cursed prophecy.

The last omen they had sent the realms was the removal of ash trees from Iomlan.

Weylin felt that ancient power in his veins. The ancient power that ached and groaned within. He ignored it as he always did—as he had no other choice. He set his sights on the path that would lead him home to Castle Eagla. Weylin knew his father would be pleased to hear that his betrothal was finalized, and he knew the news would reach him before Weylin could make it home. The word would spread through the realms at a faster rate than he and his horse could travel.

He was thankful for Eolas beneath him, and knew the road would be lonely without her. He had originally intended to take the captain of his personal guard and closest friend, Callum Ronan, with him. But his father had assigned Callum to settle a dispute in a different region of Briongloid, where matters were seemingly getting worse. Weylin had considered meeting up with him to celebrate, but Weylin did not care to travel in a group with the others.

It was hard to make companions in a position of power like the one Weylin held, but Callum had never seen him as the Udar Apparent unless they were in a situation where that was the only acceptable way to see him. Outside of that, Callum only saw him as a rival, an equal. It was a pleasant change of pace for Weylin.

Despite being a human, Callum sparred with Weylin with the same force and strength he would any other opponent, unlike others who held back knowing his status. They had grown up together, training side by side until Weylin was forced into his political position and then he declared Callum his right-hand man as captain of his own guard. It was hard for anyone to claim it was nepotism when Callum had long proven he deserved the highest rank available to a laoch.

Eolas released a sharp huff, calling Weylin back to the present as she noticed the storm clouds rapidly rolling in. Weylin groaned.

Massive gray clouds loomed above them, and the air grew quiet in an almost palpable anticipation of the brewing storm.

"Come on, Eolas," Weylin's voice broke the surrounding silence. "We can outrun it. It's coming from the north."

With that, Weylin jerked the reins he was holding and Eolas broke into a run, chasing the lighter skies in the distance.

The wind blew the dark hood of Weylin's cloak off of his head, leaving him exposed and chilled. The cold air felt refreshing. This rare glimpse of freedom shredded through his chest with a power that elated him. He felt lighter than he had in a long time.

He refused to think about his father, the ninth generation, the norns spinning their golden threads, or Rania and her strange comments about recognizing the doves of a god who had been dormant for far longer than either of them had been alive. He thought instead of a world where his life was simpler. A life where he was in no rush to wed. A life where he lived amongst villagers in Samhradh or even Earrach and lived in a baile rather than a castle. A life where his father sat at the head of the family dining table rather than on the Arden Throne. A life where he was Weylin Myrkor, not the Young Wolf of the South.

A roar of frustration ripped from his throat as the rain pounded down on himself and Eolas. Eolas reared on her hind legs, nearly dropping Weylin from her back.

"By the wyrd, Eolas!" Weylin cursed. "We'll stop at the first village we come across, I promise."

Eolas calmed with a small chuff, and Weylin pulled his hood back over his head. Eolas's hooves squished in the quickly muddying earth as they carried on at a steady pace. The woods were dense outside of Castle Tromlui. The air smelled thick with rain and moss. For a while, there was nothing to see around them except the pine and oak trees. No lights or buildings or even tents in sight. Usually that was exactly what Weylin was looking for when traveling alone, but now he would do anything for a roof over his head and a place to rest.

It became harder to see through the rain as they carried on, but finally Weylin could make out buildings in the distance. Eolas must have noticed, too. She picked up her pace and darted between trees towards the entrance of a small city.

The woods gave way to a cleared path that led into the city, and Weylin dismounted to follow it on foot. He held the wet leather reins in his hand and kept his hood up, glancing from side to side for anyone approaching. He passed a cluster of bailes and two pubs. He noticed a few different food vendors that were currently vacant as he kept his eye out for somewhere to stay. The buildings here were made of clay and cobblestone. They looked old but sturdy, and reminded him of the outskirts of Omra. At last, they came across an inn with a stable attached deeper into the city.

Weylin removed his pack from Eolas and gently stroked the beautiful beast's nose before heading towards the entrance of the Briseadhceo Inn, which he took to be the city's name, although he had never heard of it before.

"Aye," the man behind the front desk spoke with a thick western accent when Weylin walked in. "Here for the bar or for a room?"

"A room," Weylin responded, lowering his hood. "Add a horse stable to my tab as well."

"How many sunrises are you booking for?" The man asked, and scribbled with charcoal on a page in front of him.

"We're waiting out the storm. Heading south. Hopefully, no more than a sunrise or two."

"We'll start with one and go from there, eh?"

"That will do," Weylin said dismissively, reaching to take the key from the innkeeper.

"And what might I be calling you?"

"Fenian Daro," Weylin said, giving the alias he had prepared for his journey back.

The man ducked his head in acknowledgement and muttered a polite, yet gruff, "Enjoy your stay."

It was typical for Weylin to use an alias when traveling, especially when traveling alone. He would change it up each journey so it could not easily be traced back to him, and this was his first time with that particular alias. He always thought through enough of a backstory to get himself out of any sticky situations. Fenian Daro was a male visiting his aunt in Fomhar after his uncle had passed away and was helping his aunt with the funeral, as they had no children. He was now making his way back to his hometown of Phoghrian, a small city outside of Omra where he lived the life of a harvester.

After settling Eolas into her stable, Weylin laid down long enough to get bored with staring at the ceiling. He wandered downstairs to the bar. He took an empty seat at the counter and ordered a pint to add to his tab at the inn.

The downstairs pub was busy and loud. The sounds of voices both deep and high, elves and humans and dwarves, and laughter and shouts alike filled Weylin's ears as he worked to pick up bits of the conversations going on around him.

He sipped the stout and listened to two men argue about naming a new farming tool one of them had taken to using and then averted his attention to a dwarf groaning to a few others about broken tools at his shop. He overheard a new couple discussing their plans to reveal a surprise pregnancy to her parents. Weylin winced and finished his glass before ordering another.

As the bartender handed him back his full glass, a young female elf sat next to him.

"You're not from around here," the female said as the bartender handed her a full glass without her having to ask for one.

Must be a local, Weylin noted.

"That would be correct," Weylin responded curtly. "Headed south."

"Interesting," she said with a nod, and took a swig of the dark amber liquid.

Weylin turned his attention back to his own drink, hoping that would be the end of their conversation. But he could feel her curious dark brown eyes on him still.

"What's your name?" she asked.

"Fenian."

"Mine is Sinead," she continued, "Sinead Bracken."

"Okay."

He was considering going back to his room, but then she was talking again.

"I'm not technically from here either, but I'm practically a local now. My family lives in the capital, not far from Castle Tromlui actually, but the big city wasn't for me. I'm not about all the politicking that goes about there. So, I packed up at fourteen and found work here and finished my education on my own. I prefer to enjoy drinks amongst strangers who get in a tiff over the proper way to skin a fish, than the constant babble of alliances, uprisings, and family agenda."

"Fair enough," Weylin grunted.

He noted her sharp features—pale skin and her long, jet-black hair that stood out among all the lighter shades more common in Briongloid. He assumed her family must have migrated here since she looked like someone from the Bitu realm.

"And gods, the women here are so much better, too. The women in the capital city only care about your family name and the money weighing down your pockets. It's impossible to find any form of sincerity in that bunch," she muttered.

Weylin almost found it ironic that his betrothed was from the very place she was berating. He understood her, though, more than he could begin to tell her. Weylin Myrkor grew up never knowing who was talking to him to get to know Weylin or who was trying to get closer to the Udar Apparent. But Fenian Daro was from a small town, and he could not relate to such political frustrations.

"How far south are you headed?" she spoke up after a moment of silence had passed between them.

"Phoghrian," Weylin lied. "Small village outside of Omra."

Weylin knew she would recognize Omra as the home of Castle Eagla and the Udar.

"So you have the pleasure of being neighbors with the tyrant, eh?" she said, taking another gulp from her glass.

Weylin kept any reaction to her words off of his face, gazing blankly back at her. He knew well that the people did not always have a pleasant response to his father, but he had never heard of a ruler whom all people loved. He was surprised, though, that she would speak so openly with a stranger. He supposed Briongloid had long been known for their tense relations with Samhradh.

"Never met him," Weylin replied with a shrug of his shoulders and the slightest bite to his tone. "I like the heat and I like the coast, so regardless of who neighbors my city, I would never leave Samhradh."

"Fair enough," she said with a smirk as she repeated his words back to him. "What brings you this way?"

"I have family in Briongloid. My mother's brother passed on recently. My parents sent me to aid his family, as they have no children of their own to help my aunt with funeral arrangements."

"Sorry to hear it."

"Don't be." He brushed off her sentiment. "Never knew him."

"I'd like to visit Samhradh. In fact, I think visiting all the worldly realms is something I'd like to do before I pass on myself. There's so much out there to see."

"A female who hates the city, and prefers the presence of drunks, who wants to travel the six worldly realms? Not what I would have guessed," he said with a sneer.

"A female can dream," she said with a drawn-out sigh. "And I would love to make it to all *seven* worldly realms, but I fear no one will ever set foot in Eilean again. That realm is doomed to collapse on itself. Maybe once all its inhabitants are long passed on and gone, the tyrant will allow adventurers such as myself to see the shores where the wyverns live. I suppose I'll likely be passed on by then, though."

Weylin felt an instinctual bile rise to the back of his throat at the mention of that exiled realm, and he had to work to maintain a neutral expression. He mentally noted what side of the conflict Sinead was on, and decided her policy of avoiding politics was probably best applied to their conversations as well. He was far too tired to stir up any trouble.

"If you look over there," Sinead pointed towards two men hunched over a small table in the corner of the room. "Those are two of the laochs of the Dorcases. They have them planted in every city, always listening. It kind of gives me the creeps."

"Why are they here?" Weylin asked curiously, noting the way the two men looked him over.

"Gods know," Sinead replied, averting her attention back to the bar in front of them. "To keep us on edge, I suppose. Can never be too comfortable, especially during these times."

Weylin nodded, staring down at his nearly empty glass.

"I'm a bartender here, by the way," she said, changing the subject. "I hear and know all that goes on around here. It's my night off."

"Not a bad gig."

"I suppose the unlimited free drinks make up for the pervs that like to follow me around after hours, and the mated men who like to get handsy after too many drinks," she muttered in response, clearly not in agreement with Weylin's statement.

"Why not leave, then?"

Sinead bristled. She finished the drink she was holding in one long swig and slammed it back on the countertop.

"Not everyone has the privilege of having a way out of their circumstances, Fenian," she said bitterly and stood. "I'll be around to fill your glass tomorrow. Good night."

Weylin did not say another word as Sinead bounded up the stairs to the rooms. He had a feeling this would not be the last he saw of Sinead Bracken.

He felt two pairs of eyes on his back. He turned around to find that the two laochs were again looking at him through narrowed eyes, as if they were suspicious of him. Weylin held their gaze until they looked away.

He took his time finishing his drink and savored each sip as the hints of barley sourced straight from the local fields warmed him. He would show the laochs that even as Fenian Daro, they would not intimidate him. He stayed down in the bar drinking until the two men exited the inn, then pushed away his glass and stumbled his way to the quiet of his room.

16

RUAIRI

Ruairi was up before the dawn light had filtered through the tent. His nerves were higher than they had ever been as he lay beside Aisla's sleeping form. He watched the steady rise and fall of her chest as he fought to calm his heart.

Aisla. Beautiful Aisla.

Aisla, who had stolen his heart long before she would ever know, and Aisla, who he would breathe every breath for if she would have him. Everything seemed to fit into place last night when their lips met. Everything he had longed for in one perfect moment, and he could still feel the ghost of her touch. His heart ached for her more than he could put into words, but he would spend the rest of his life trying.

There was this feeling now, in the core of him, that despite all the nerves and anxiety and fears, if they were together, it would all work out.

Ruairi rolled onto his back to stare up at the sloped black canvas above them. He could still hear the rain coming down and dreaded the day of travel ahead. His bones ached and his mind was tired, but he had hoped they would at least have clear skies to accompany them on their first full day on Iomlan.

The sound of heavy hooves punctuated the constant rain. Ruairi held his breath. His heart raced as he strained to listen. He sat up slowly, careful not to wake Aisla.

The voices weren't quite close enough to be distinguishable from their tent, but they were close enough to be concerning. He couldn't make out all of what they were saying, but he caught enough to gather the words *ship, blockade,* and *trespassers.*

And that was enough.

Ruairi's stomach twisted, and his palms began to sweat.

"Shit, shit, shit," he cursed under his breath. He jostled Aisla awake.

Her eyes blinked open, and he immediately put a finger to her lips to quiet her. She looked afraid when she sat up.

Ruairi was thankful when she didn't ask the questions that her eyes were pleading for answers to. She was alert right away, the fog of sleep quickly fading from her eyes. Ruari pointed to his ears, indicating for her to listen. He watched the faint twitch of her ears as they strained. Her face fell as she heard the traces of a conversation that was nothing but bad news for them.

She mouthed the words to him, the question that had been racing through his mind since the voices had first drifted towards him: *what do we do?*

Ruairi cursed himself for not putting more distance between themselves and *Stoirme* before stopping for the night. For not waking up early to get a head start to the day. There was nothing Ruairi could think of that was a guaranteed safe move. They could come out and explain themselves, but how could they explain away their ship rushing through the blockade? They could lie and say they were from a different realm, but the unmarked ship and suspicious nature of their maneuver would be hard to explain. They could fight, but Ruairi didn't have any way of knowing what kind of forces they were dealing with. The only option he found himself coming back to, even as it made his throat dry, was to *run*.

They could escape, put as much distance as possible between themselves and the beings behind the voices, and then gather themselves and their strategy before moving forward.

"We run," Ruairi breathed out, barely audible.

Aisla nodded in response, tucking *Oidhe* away in her waistband. Her face set with determination.

They packed up their belongings inside of the tent as quickly and quietly as they could. The urgency was a tangible thing in the air around him. It felt so dense he could nearly choke on it. They were ready to move, but there was one last thing weighing heavily on Ruairi. He withdrew the small parcel from Cliona from his pack, the heaviness of it pressing upon him until his chest constricted. That familiar sense of foreboding filled him.

"Ash," he whispered. Her eyes met his, almost refusing to look at the parcel in his hands. "I need you to take this." Aisla was already shaking her head back and forth, the rejection clear in her eyes. "If this goes wrong, I need you to get back to the *Stoirme*. I need you to take this parcel back to Cliona and tell her what happened here. I don't trust it, and if we are taken forcefully, they'll have no reason to bargain with us. They'll have all that they need already and *this*, whatever it is, would just be the icing on the cake for them. I'm not letting it fall into the Udar's hands without the payment from him. It seems to be the only thing Cliona thinks we have as leverage, so *he* will only get it once *we* have a cure. You're a strong laoch. You know how to sail now. I trust you to make the journey back home if you need to."

He knew she understood his meaning. The words that he could not bring himself to voice to her. If they ended him here—if they couldn't make it past the first enemies to cross their path—she would need to have the parcel and she would need to leave.

"I can't," she continued, shaking her head furiously. "What about you?"

"Aisla, you know I hate to ask this of you. This is only worst-case scenario," he said. "But you can't think of me. You must think of your people, of our realm, Eire, and our continent. Of all the promises we have made, that cannot end here."

"I cannot make any more promises," she breathed out shakily.

"Just one more," he pleaded, his eyes searching hers. "Just this one, Ash. We are running out of time."

Wordlessly, and without breaking eye contact, she took the package from his outstretched hand. She shoved it to the bottom of her pack, and that was acceptance enough for him.

"We'll leave the tent behind," he said, his throat strained. "It's not worth the risk. We'll buy another in a city when it's safe."

Aisla nodded even as Ruairi winced at the rain continuing to pound down just outside of the tent flaps.

Ruairi leaned forward and placed a gentle kiss on Aisla's forehead, his hand resting against her cheek for a moment that passed far too quickly. He memorized the feel of her skin, the warmth that radiated off of her.

He took her hand and led her out of the tent.

They crouched outside of it, listening for the shuffling hooves or nearby voices, until Ruairi felt it was safe enough to move. He threw a glance to Aisla, and she gave him a knowing look before he took off to the east, her shaking hand still clutched in his. He scanned the ground for any stray rocks or jutting roots as he moved swiftly between the trees. Their feet squished through the muddied forest floor. There would have been no way to hide their footsteps in this muck, so Ruairi was thankful for the rain as it continued to pour, and it would quickly wash them away.

The rush of the rain dimmed his senses as he strained to listen when the beat of hooves sounded in his ears. His heart pounded in his chest until he could feel it in every inch of himself. He considered every path forward.

He heard them nearing. He plunged forward, quickening his pace. Dragging Aisla along behind him. She did not slow.

With every step, it became more and more obvious to Ruairi that the horses and whatever men were riding them were now in pursuit.

Ruairi assessed the facts. They could not outrun a horse. The approaching forces outnumbered them. He would not risk Aisla. She was never meant to go all the way to the capital.

He raced on. One foot in front of the other. Never missing a beat.

His breaths grew quick and heavy, partly from the effort and partly from the decision weighing on him.

This could all go wrong—so, so wrong.

Aisla's hand in his served as an anchor. It tied him to that vow to protect her at all costs. To protect what mattered most to Talam. What mattered most to him.

He slowed to a stop. Mud seeped into his thin boots, wetting his socks beneath. His hair was soaking wet, and he felt chilled to the bone. He stopped to face her.

"Ash, you have to keep running," he said, nodding his head to reinforce the words. "If I don't find you, you go on. If you encounter anyone, anyone at all, don't tell them anything. Lie. Do whatever you must to get back to Eilean. I need to get them off of our trail, and they cannot know that there are two of us."

Shadows flickered across Aisla's eyes. Shadows of fear. Anger. Doubt. Hurt.

"Please," he squeezed her hand. "It's the only way."

An acceptance seemed to settle over her. She did not say a word or give any indication that she heard him at all. He could hear his heart tearing.

"I'll find you," he muttered and gave her hand one last squeeze.

With that, Ruairi took off in the direction of their pursuers and could only hope that Aisla had listened, and that she would get that parcel and herself back to Eilean if he did not return to her soon.

It didn't take long for Ruairi to encounter them.

There were seven of them. Two females and five males, both humans and elves, but no dwarves. Each of them sat atop a massive horse, glistening in the falling rain. Ruairi did not get a good look at their faces. They each wore dark maroon cloaks pulled down over their faces, adding to the haunting feeling in the pit of Ruairi's gut.

Maroon—the color of the Myrkor dynasty.

A feeling of relief washed through Ruairi in confirmation that he'd made the right choice, but it was quickly replaced with dread as he faced seven of the Udar's laochs alone with pieces of a rapidly failing plan.

Weapons glinted in the few beams of morning sunlight that shone through the stormy clouds.

Ruairi held his hands up in the worldly sign of surrender, and his jaw set with resolve. The two elves nearest him dismounted, hands on the weapons at their sides.

"Was that your ship, *boy?*" The female elf approaching him sneered.

She was tall and muscular. He noted the signet of a howling wolf pinned to her chest.

Ruairi did not say a word. He kept his arms held up.

"Are you deaf or dumb?"

"Maybe both," quipped the male to her right.

"I said," the female came so close to him that he could feel her breath. Her voice drowned out the downpour around them. "Is that *your* ship we found?"

"I have a message for your Udar," he replied once he found the voice to speak the words.

Everything was happening quickly—too quickly. He could hardly parse through all the thoughts circling his mind.

"A message from an elf who runs our blockade and attempts to evade when we approach?" She continued taking one step closer. "What reason do we have to waste the Udar's time with your presence?"

"It's a message from Eilean. For your Udar's ears only."

"Aye, Deirdre," the youngest of the laochs, a handsome man who rode behind the rest, interrupted. "Stand down."

"What are you going to do about this?" The female called Deirdre said with a sneer.

Ruairi noted the tension amongst the laochs as the young man dismounted and approached. He noticed the way Deirdre's glare faltered, and had the feeling the young man held authority here.

"Best to mind your place, Dee," the tone of the man had shifted to one of pure authority as Deirdre finally stepped down and away from Ruairi, giving the young man a straight line to him.

The young man's light green eyes were unreadable as he assessed Ruairi, looking him up and down. Ruairi stood with his chin tilted up, refusing to be intimidated.

"We'll take him to the Udar," the man declared.

The words hit Ruairi like a wind that nearly took the breath from his lungs. He felt himself struggling for that next breath as he fought to keep any reaction off of his face. His muscles tensed, ready for action, but he knew he could take none.

"But Callum, is the Young Wolf not just at the castle? In this very realm?" Someone spoke up from atop the horses. "Why not bring the elf to him? Make it his problem."

"This is the time of betrothal celebrations for our Udar Apparent," the young man, Callum, replied and turned on his heel. "No need to interrupt such a thing when we are already headed back to Omra. I'll explain everything to him upon his return to Eagla."

"Aye," the voice grunted in response.

Deirdre grabbed Ruairi's hands and bound them with a thick rope. She was not gentle, and Ruairi gritted his teeth as she shoved him towards her horse and forced him to mount before she settled in behind him.

Fear expanded until his chest felt too tight, his heart pulsing with anxiety at the thought of what was to come. As they trotted through the ongoing storm and the horses' hooves sunk a little deeper with each step, the laochs remained silent. It was eerie and did nothing to help the nerves rousing the esos within Ruairi's veins.

Ruairi closed his eyes, focusing on the sound of the rain. He searched through his esos for any peace he could hang onto.

In that moment, Ruairi Vilulf took a vow of silence. A vow that no matter the circumstances to come his way, he would not utter a word that could put Aisla at risk among these people. Not until he reached the Udar, and then his words would be minimal—carefully chosen and cautious. He would have the entire journey there to plan them.

A journey of endless sunrises begins with the very first step.

He repeated the line he had given to Aisla. He repeated it until it became a loop in his mind that served to ground him, as he knew this was all for something bigger than himself. And he knew his journey—his life—would not be for nothing.

PART TWO
JOURNEY OF ALIASES

17

AISLA

The absence of his voice. The absence of his warmth. The absence of his scent. The absence of *him*.

Guilt wracked Aisla like the storm raging around her, until her hands were shaking so hard she could barely maintain her grip on *Oidhe* as she dashed through the woods of Briongloid. She couldn't tell if there were pursuers following her over the sound of the rain.

Mud splattered her linen pants all the way to her knees. The rain had soaked her boots through and her hair was sopping wet even under the hood of her cloak, pulled nearly over her eyes. They should have planned better. She shouldn't have inserted herself where she did not belong, as she wondered how this might have played out had Mona come instead of herself.

She never promised to go home and take the parcel with her.

She couldn't because it was a promise she couldn't keep. She'd never make a promise that would damn him.

The guilt of his absence swallowed her whole.

It roared louder than the storm around her and she felt the power in her veins rushing with a force that felt like she would explode. It was painful, this power. It ached and burned, and she used every ounce of her will to keep it subdued. She wished it could have been her who made the sacrifice, not him. She wished she did not carry the weight of her birthright, and it would have been possible to let Ruairi escape while she ran to confront the strange voices.

But it could have never been her, and that fact was an unimaginable pain that burned like a knife wound.

She focused her attention on putting one foot in front of the other as her legs carried her faster and faster through the muddying forest. She could not allow herself the time to feel such things. She knew she would feel them for a long, long time, until her eyes met his again, but right now she had to push it away. Had to keep the guilt at bay long enough to continue getting further and further from the *Stoirme*.

The great pine trees swayed above her head and the sound of their bristles rubbing together echoed in her ears. She strained for any sounds that might be out of place. Every cracking branch made her jump as she couldn't help but wonder what creatures lurked in these woods. What malicious spirits could be waiting for her to let her guard down for even a moment. Aisla tried to make distance her only thought as she ran towards Briseadhceo. She would still need to get the new map from their contact, then she would make her way to the capital, where she knew Ruairi would be taken.

She kicked up mud, running faster despite her exhaustion. She held onto *Oidhe* as though her life depended on it and her pack grew heavier with every step. She would get this parcel to the Udar and save Ruairi and take him and the cure back to Eilean if it was the last thing she did. Her neck burned where her necklace sat, and she thought of Eire and all that was at stake for her. She wished Eire was here with her now.

Her guilt grew into a physical pain, writhing in her core until she could no longer take it. She paused, resting her hand against a tree, and the world spun around her. She steadied herself, panicked breaths coming in sharp pants until she vomited on the forest floor. Her stomach lurched as she dry heaved over and over, having no more food to lose.

She breathed in and out, slowly gathering her strength and stood tall, swallowing down air. She forced herself to slow down, closing her eyes, tucking *Oidhe* away in her waistband. She shook out her trembling hands and worked up the energy to carry on. To push forward, as she knew she had not yet traveled far enough. She slowed her run to a brisk walk, finding a pace she knew she could keep up until sunset, when she would look for somewhere to settle for the night.

Ruairi was counting on her. Eire was counting on her. The two people she cared for most in this world—she would not let them down.

Aisla repeated their names over and over, ignoring the ache in her muscles and the cramp in her gut. She found herself praying to Eabha, the mother goddess. She didn't know what she was praying for, but she held onto a faint hope that Eabha was watching over them ever since her encounter with the two doves.

It had to mean something.

Underneath the rainwater that soaked every inch of Aisla, she was sweaty and caked with mud. As the day drew to its close, her lungs felt heavy with the wet air and her body groaned with each step.

She had the map of Iomlan. The compass. No tent, but that was doable. She was nearly out of food, but had enough to make it through the night and the next sunrise. She had airgead to spend on replenishing her supplies at a local market if she ran into one in a village. Ruairi had reassured her that airgead was still the accepted form of currency from the bits and pieces their contacts had shared throughout the years.

Ruairi had ensured she had everything she would need. As he always had.

Once the sun was no longer in the sky and had been chased away by the pale moons. Once Aisla could no longer muster the energy to shuffle forward, she scoped out a place to rest for the night.

Everything was wet and unpleasant, but it would have to do with no tent.

Aisla crawled under an ancient oak tree with a massive trunk whose branches shielded her from the rain. She settled in against it, relief flooding her sore and exhausted body. She pulled her thin blanket from her pack, wrapping it around herself, knowing she would regret it in the morning when she would have to shove it back in sopping wet.

She took a deep breath and reached her hand down into the bottom of the pack, where she had shoved the parcel. Her breath hitched as she saw it was soaking wet and realized it must have gotten drenched in their exchange. They had been too focused on the looming danger to notice. A shiver travelled down her already frigid spine. Her fingers danced along the edges as something in her began to twist and turn in foreboding, but yearning too. She strained her ears to ensure that no footsteps were nearby and held her breath before tearing through the wax seal of her family and there was no undoing it.

Ruairi may have promised Cliona that he would not open the package, but she had done no such thing. There was little her grandmother could do to punish her.

The first thing that caught her eyes was a glint of silver and she pulled a thin-banded ring with a rectangular emerald gem nestled into the center out from the corner of the envelope. It felt strange in her fingers. It was foreign, but familiar at the same time. She turned it over, admiring the daintiness and elegance of it. She slid it onto one of her fingers and could've sworn she saw it glow under the night sky. She splayed out her fingers, swollen from the rain, and felt something inside of her come to life at the touch of the ring. It was warm and comforting on her finger, but its glint seemed to whisper of danger. Something in it called to her, it spoke seductions that felt like it was for her and her alone.

She quickly took it off and shoved it into her pants pocket on the side where she always kept *Oidhe*. She knew it was something to be protected.

Her attention shifted back to the envelope resting in her lap, and she pulled out the letter tucked neatly inside. As she unfolded it, her hands trembled with dread. The scrawled charcoal marks on the inside unfurled into view, and it immediately became apparent that Aisla could not read any of the symbols. She knew enough from scoil to know that these runic figures were from before even the ancient tongue, Aosta, was spoken. These symbols were from the time the gods and goddesses walked the earth and dwelled among elves, humans, and dwarves alike.

Some of the world tellers in Eilean spoke and read Aosta, but she did not know of anyone who would understand this runic language. She ran her fingers over the marks as she wished it could speak its contents aloud for her. She traced them mindlessly, careful to protect it from the raindrops coming down overhead. Aisla wondered how the Udar would be able to make any sense of it. She tucked the curious letter back into its envelope before shoving it into the bottom of her pack.

Something about it, holding it, made her feel sick. It was not like when she held the silver ring between her fingers.

Gods knew what content lay on the page that Cliona had given Ruairi as a bargaining chip.

Aisla relaxed against her pack, feeling more exhausted than ever. Her body was sore and ached all over. She longed for her warm bed in her baile and the covering of her roof over her head.

She closed her eyes for a moment when a whispering sound

rattled through the branches of the trees. The air around her came to life and the atmosphere changed entirely. Alarm flooded her. Her hand reached for *Oidhe*, but she made no move to stand and show herself. She stayed rooted to her spot, perking her ears to listen.

You are not alone, Gheall Ceann. A female voice reached Aisla's ears on the wind. *The path is right at your feet, young elf. Rest. Your journey is only beginning.*

Something about the voice soothed Aisla rather than frightened her. The words eased her tense muscles and comforted her with each syllable. She tucked *Oidhe* into her waistband again. She caught a glimpse of home in this foreign land, carried on the scent of this new wind and in this disembodied voice.

Aisla felt the weight of the ring in her pocket warm as a heavy sleep crept in. She closed her eyes to the soothing sound of the voice on the wind that hummed a lullaby long forgotten.

18

AISLA

Aisla awoke with the sunrise, and her stomach was already groaning.

She slept soundly, despite the storm continuing on through the night and finally ending sometime in the early hours of the morning. Her muscles didn't ache the way they had after that first night in the tent. She stretched out her arms and squinted into the faint red sunrise coming through the dissipating gray clouds. She felt a renewed sense of energy. She only wished she could satiate her growing hunger, but refused to deplete her very limited food sources so early in the day.

Aisla rose and pulled her pack onto her back. It felt lighter than it had last night now that the contents of that parcel were less mysterious to her.

Oidhe was in her waistband, the ring nestled in her pocket, and Eire's necklace fit snugly against the middle of her throat.

She pushed away her hunger pains as she moved away from the coast, further from *Stoirme* and her home. With no ship to trace back to her, she could be anyone from any realm, and then she could survive alone and go wherever she needed to get the supplies for her journey. She would make her way to their contact in Brisead-hceo to get the map Ruairi referenced, and after that, she would arrive at the capital as quickly as she could.

Aisla walked until sunset, when her stomach pains were nearly unbearable. She considered delving into her pack and eating the last scraps of cheese and bread she had, but decided it might be better to catch this meal while she had some energy. She was thankful the rain had stopped, and although the ground was still muddy and continued to soak her boots, it was far better than the conditions she had endured since stepping foot off of *Stoirme*.

She pulled her bow and arrow from her pack and started off in a low crouch. If she managed to catch a bird or a rabbit, she could start a fire and have a decent meal. She did not care if anyone was drawn to the fire at this point. She was far enough removed from the shores to begin to weave her alias and lies.

Aisla sent a muttered prayer to Leighis, goddess of medicine, harvest, and the hunt. She prayed for a small prey to come wandering into the line of her bow, anything that would not eat her first. As she had never been to Iomlan, she had not a clue what to expect in this new and foreign terrain. It was frightening, but a part of her suppressed a thrill of excitement. She had always been an adventurer at heart.

She stalked forward, careful to keep her steps soft and stealthy, moving with her bow knocked and pointed at the ground. She was top of her class in archery and there was comfort in the feel of the wood of her bow in her hand. She had excelled in all of her classes, save for esos.

Just at the thought of it, she could feel her esos rising in response. It stirred within her bloodstream, calling for release, but now, of all times, she would not even dare to attempt it. Not only did she lack the control necessary for such a risk, but she had yet to locate any ash trees that would restore her source if depleted.

Aisla inhaled and shook her head, knowing that this line of

thought would get her nowhere good and surely no closer to her next meal.

Rustling leaves sounded to the west, and she dropped into a deeper crouch, instinctively raising her bow to eye level. A small brown bird hopped through the fallen leaves, sticking its short beak into the ground searching for its own dinner. Aisla drew the arrow back and just before she released, the bird flew away with a slew of chirps, causing nearby birds to scatter to the skies.

The arrow struck empty air and sunk into the wet forest floor.

Aisla's stomach lurched, but not because she had lost her prey. She took a step backwards, her heart in her throat, as she knew something was amiss in the woods. There was no way her arrow had startled the bird. It flew away before she had even loosed it. Another step back and her eyes were darting around the clearing until she saw the dark mass standing on the other side of where her arrow had landed.

It was a nasty brute with fangs the size of Aisla's hands, dripping with slobber. It had shaggy dark gray, nearly black fur, with glowing golden eyes, and looked like the larger, more lethal cousin of a wolf. Its massive paws thumped against the forest floor as it paced in a frustrated circle before sniffing at her arrow. Its ears flattened and its lips pulled back, giving her a better look at its row of deadly, yellowed teeth as it realized it may have lost the bird to an even greater prey. She recognized the beast from myths class in scoil, a barghest.

Aisla's heart pounded in her throat. Her hands trembled. Her raging appetite disappeared entirely. She took another slow step backwards. The smallest of twigs cracked beneath her boot, but it felt like the loudest sound she had ever heard. Sweat beaded along the back of her neck. Her mind spun to come up with a plan, any way out.

Its demonic golden eyes snapped to hers and she saw a horrifying hunger there. This creature was from the underworld, the realm of Hel, a child of Ifreann. She thought she caught a glimpse of that realm of dead souls in its eyes.

It took a moment before Aisla turned and ran as fast as her tired legs could drag her body. Adrenaline kicked in and she raced through the trees, quickly falling into a full-fledged sprint, deeper into Briongloid, no longer having any sense of direction as instinct took over. She heard the snarling beast take the chase and cursed under her breath. Its chomping maw and deep guttural growls echoed in her ears. It was a sound she would not soon wipe from her memory if she managed to live through this.

She dropped her bow and withdrew *Oidhe* from her waistband in one swift movement. Aisla gripped the familiar blade so tightly in her hand she could feel her knuckles straining. She heard a stream not far away and the flow of the water echoed in her ears. She felt damned by the gods despite the mysterious voice that had visited her under the light of the moons of Talam. Damned by them, despite Eabha's doves dropping in to save Ruairi's life. Too many moments like this made her feel damned at every turn she took.

The barghest was closing the distance between them. She would have to face the creature. She could not outrun it.

She listened for the creature to come up on her side, just close enough to close its jaws around her, then she lunged, hoping to use the element of surprise to her advantage. Her dagger struck its hide. She dragged it down with all of her force, sinking it deeper as she pulled, creating a gaping wound that gushed dark blood and stained her hand. She jumped back, creating distance between them again. The beast howled so loudly she saw the surrounding trees sway. A shadow of rage crossed its glare as they danced around each other in a vicious circle. Power coursed through Aisla's veins.

She lunged again, and the barghest carved deep scratches down her forearm, ripping a shout of pain from her dry throat. Aisla gritted her teeth against the pain and used the moment to her advantage, slashing *Oidhe* across its throat. Blood sprayed from the wound and Aisla leaped away as flecks blurred her vision. Her insides churned and her chest tightened, but she forced her eyes open and watched as the beast's eyes rolled back. It collapsed with a thud that shook the ground beneath her feet.

Aisla did not have time to feel relief, or revel in her victory. A sharp bark echoed through the trees, followed by another, and another. She couldn't outrun a pack of barghests. She had no time to think.

Aisla darted into the clearing and grabbed her bow from the forest floor before running to a nearby tree, using it for cover. She knocked the bow and held it at the ready, waiting for the beasts to come into view. She fought to steady her hands and focused on calming her racing heart.

Everything seemed to move in slow motion as the next beast bounded into the clearing, right into her line of vision. She breathed out as she released and struck the creature's beating heart. With a cry of both surprise and pain, it fell to the ground. Aisla could not celebrate her successful shot as another pair of beasts hurtled into view. Their snarls grew louder and more vicious when they took in their felled brothers.

Aisla loosed another arrow, but this one was not so lucky. It lodged in the beast's shoulder.

They both whirled in her direction and her hands shook so hard she struggled to control her weapon. She quickly nocked another arrow and released it into the same beast's eye. But the shot didn't kill it, only succeeded in making it angrier.

Both beasts charged her, and she only had time to release one more arrow. It lodged in a barghest's front leg. Aisla dropped her bow and arrow, pulling her dagger from her waist. She steadied her stance and bared her teeth at the creature, a growl emerging from her throat. She would not go down without a fight.

The nearer barghest flew towards her without hesitation. She sidestepped its charge and plunged towards the other one, who was not prepared for her attack. She lodged her dagger in its shoulder, but it changed course, leaving a wound hardly deeper than a skin puncture. Aisla cursed as they both closed in. She could not fathom how she could take on the two of them at once and alone.

She was in far over her head.

Aisla sprinted into the woods, hoping to use the trees to her advantage while the beasts trailed in pursuit. She whipped a sharp half-circle around one tree, using the momentum to fling her behind one beast. She drove *Oidhe* into its back, pulling her dagger all the way to the base of its tail. It turned around, maw snapping at her. She jumped to the side as its enormous mouth opened and closed around her arm. She was not quick enough.

Aisla screamed so loud it reverberated through the trees. She yanked her arm away and clutched it to her chest before diving forward again. Her vision blurred red with pain and rage.

Aisla prayed out to the gods.

To anyone who would listen, who would hear her.

She prayed they would not allow it to end here.

To end like this.

19

WEYLIN

The storm finally let up just before Weylin's second sunrise at the Briseadhceo Inn.

The day dragged on as he spent most of it reading an old history book in his room. He went to the bar again at night, and just like she said, Sinead was there to fill his mug. She was as talkative and bubbly as the previous night, but stayed busy enough to keep out of his hair. He enjoyed the silence as he sipped on the amber liquid.

The next morning, Weylin packed his bag, ready to leave the inn and never return. He ambled down the rickety stairs when Sinead's jet-black hair caught his eye. She was seated at a bar stool, drinking out of a wooden mug. She looked over and gave him a wry grin.

"Bit early for a drink, eh?" he muttered as he came up beside her.

"Mind your business, Daro," she said and rolled her eyes. "Headed out?"

"Aye."

"If you ever find yourself in these parts again, you've got a friend in Briseadhceo," Sinead called after him.

Weylin ducked his head in thanks and silently handed over the keys and enough airgead to cover his bill. He made his way to Eolas in the stables. She nodded her head joyfully at the return of her rider. Weylin ran a hand along her beautiful black coat before attaching his pack and leading Eolas out of the city.

They trotted along at a leisurely pace. Weylin felt no urgency to return to Castle Eagla and begin the mental work of politicking and preparing for his union officially. They continued on until the skies were turning pink and he knew Eolas would need a rest. He stopped near a small stream and led Eolas to it, allowing the horse to drink from the cool waters.

While he waited, Weylin rested against an oak tree, leaning his head back and closing his eyes as the fading sunshine beat down on his face. The air still smelled of the storm, but he was thankful the ground had dried enough around the tree for him to sit. The water level of the stream looked higher than typical for the small body of water. Several branches were scattered about in the storm's wake.

Weylin's head snapped up as a blood-curdling scream sounded through the trees, sending the birds scattering. Eolas stomped her feet in response and Weylin stood up, grabbing her reins.

"Calm down, calm down," he muttered as Eolas bucked her head.

Weylin strained his ears, listening for where the feminine cry had originated. A familiar, vicious snarl reached his ears. *A barghest.* He had encountered his fair share. Weylin heard their roars, but no more noise from the female. He shook his head in dismissal and moved to mount Eolas, but a second cry stopped him and Eolas gave a loud neigh.

The sound wasn't very far away at all, and there was only one voice. No one, male or female, laoch or not, elf or human or dwarf, could stand against a barghest, let alone a pack. Whoever had been caught in the grip of them would not make it out alive. That much Weylin was sure of.

He mounted Eolas with a sigh and headed toward Castle Eagla. He fully intended to leave, to go on as if he had never heard any of the commotion at all, but something tugged at his chest. Something pulled him towards those sounds until his hands were guiding Eolas's reins of their own accord.

He trotted onward with an urgency he couldn't explain until they arrived at the scene.

He noted the two felled barghests. One with an arrow through its heart, and another had its neck slashed open. The clearing was covered in the black blood of the beasts. Red blood mingled with their black blood.

Weylin dismounted Eolas in an effortless movement and withdrew his blade, *Uamhan* from its sheath. It didn't take long to locate the final two barghests as they closed in on the petite figure he could not make out from his angle.

Each of the remaining barghests had at least one arrow stuck in their hides. If this figure truly was alone, that would have been an impressive feat, even for any of his laochs who had trained in combat all of their lives.

Weylin let out a low whistle and stalked forward, blade at the ready. The two barghests shifted to face him, golden eyes gleaming with the intent to kill. Weylin's heart did not falter as he faced the great beasts.

He dashed forward, moving between the beasts, swiping while he moved. He cut the nearer barghest's head clean off. It was still falling as he whirled to watch the female who he now deemed to be elven, burying her dagger into the last barghest's side. It whirled on her with a snarl, but she did not balk. The female *bared her teeth* and dropped into a crouch, holding her dagger out in front of her.

Weylin took advantage of the moment to run up on the beast from its blind spot and stabbed it clean through the heart. Weylin withdrew his blade, and it fell to the ground with a final massive thud.

Weylin froze when his gaze met the female's. She was a dichotomy of ferality and grace. Nothing about the female was ordinary. Her yellow-green eyes sparked with fire. Her light brown hair was matted and dampened with dark blood. A necklace of carved bone nestled against her throat, adding to her wild appearance. Her focus reminded him of a shark's—flat and menacing. A deep wound on her forearm rushed with red blood, and she pulled it protectively against her chest.

Her eyes shifted ever so slightly, forecasting her next move, but Weylin read her like a book. He lunged towards her and quickly knocked the dagger from her hand. Rather than shock at being disarmed, the female ducked away from him, but it was a trap.

Weylin swept her legs out and pinned her to the ground with his blade against her throat.

The stench of blood and mildewy cloth filled Weylin's nostrils and made him want to gag as he leaned into the female.

She went still. "Release me," the female hissed in a voice that was rough like the sand along the coast.

"And why would I do that?" He responded coolly, increasing the pressure of his blade enough to make her squirm.

She flinched at the feeling of his breath on the side of her face and blood beaded along her neck.

"Why would you save my life only to take it?" She spat back.

Weylin paused to ponder the question.

"I'd be cautious of the kindness you assume from strangers, *banphrionsa*," he murmured in her ear and got a thrill out of the way he felt her fear take hold of her.

"I was handling it myself," her voice came out strangled as her grit gave way with the pressure of *Uamhan*.

"I won't lie. I was impressed you were able to fell two of the beasts on your own," Weylin crooned. "That is no minor victory. But your arm would not have been the only thing those mutts were chewing on had I not shown up to save your life."

"Kill me then," she seethed. "Or do you enjoy toying with your prey?"

"It's quite tempting when you give in to the bait so easily."

She said nothing. Her silence was answer enough. He had won, and she was now in his debt.

He released her with a shove, and she winced in pain. Weylin took that moment to look around the clearing. Pools of black blood and splatters marred the trees. Red elf blood stained the earth. One solo female elf had created an impressive mess, as there were no other bodies lying around.

"Any spare cloth in that bag?" Weylin nodded to the pack on the ground across the clearing, not far off from a discarded bow.

"Why?" she snarled.

"Okay. I'll be on my way then," he shrugged, standing to his own feet. "Good luck with *that*." He indicated her arm.

The female's lip twitched with a retort, but she made her way over to the pack, withdrawing a spare top and tossing it to him. He approached her, and she took a cautious step back. He let out a sigh and snatched her hand. She hissed in pain, trying to pull away, but he held firm.

He could see bone in the deepest part of the bite. It was a nasty wound and her flesh showed where each sharp tooth had sunk in and dragged its way out. He could only imagine the pain she must be in. Weylin ripped the shirt into one long piece and made quick work of wrapping it tightly around the wound. He tied it in a knot, applying as much pressure as he could. She hugged her arm against her chest the moment he loosened his grip on it. Not so much as a *thank you* from her lips.

"You're going to need a medic," Weylin stated.

"No shit," she growled.

Weylin considered turning away then. He'd saved her life, and he owed her nothing further—in fact, she now owed him if anything.

"We're near a village," Weylin said with a sigh. "They'll have an infirmary."

The female eyed him curiously, as if trying to decide if she trusted his words.

"I don't see anyone else trotting along to offer you a solution. If I were you, I would accept aid when it is offered."

She scowled at him, crinkling her bloodied nose with distaste.

"Follow me." Hesitancy flickered across her fiery yellow-green eyes, but she followed him, injured arm clutched to her chest. He led her to the clearing, where Eolas awaited him dutifully. Weylin noted the concern in her thoughtful gaze and the effort it took her to stand straight.

Weylin took Eolas's reins and decided to travel to the nearby village on foot.

"What's your name, Slayer of Ifreann's Mutts?" Weylin asked, voice dripping with condescension.

"And why should I tell you?" she snapped back.

Weylin whipped toward her, and she stopped in her tracks, surprised to now be facing him. They were hardly an arm's length apart, but she did not back away as her shock became a raging flame once again.

"Being a *bitch* isn't typically how we thank strangers who go out of their way to not only save our lives but also escort you to a medic," he snarled with an intensity that made her flinch. "So, I'll ask again, *banphrionsa,* what. Is. Your. *Name?*"

Her defiance brought his power roaring to just below the surface of his skin. His chest flared with aggravation.

"Ellora," she bit back. "Ellora Morlee."

"What a lovely name," Weylin said with a smirk before turning toward Eolas.

"And yours?" she asked, a question he was already prepared for.

And he would give the same answer he had given everyone he had encountered on this journey back so far.

"Fenian," he said. "I take it you aren't from around here, given your willingness to follow me to a medic rather than going back to your own."

"No," she replied with a slight hesitation. "I am from Fomhar."

"What brings you to these parts?"

"I wanted to visit my brother in Briongloid before taking my journey south."

"And what calls you south?" He asked.

"I seek to train as a laoch. I tire of my days as a housemaid and think my skills would be of better use for our Udar," she said straightening her shoulders, standing a little taller.

This girl sought to be a laoch?

There were plenty of female laochs in his father's ranks, but they usually did not look like Ellora. She was far too beautiful to spend her life collecting scars.

This would mean they had the same end destination. If she ever encountered him in Samhradh, she would discover his lie and realize that he was the Udar Apparent. For now, though, he would be Fenian Daro to her. It was too risky to be anything but that.

"I imagine the Udar himself would be impressed with your performance with the barghests," he said, truthfully. "Although, I would not be surprised if you were turned away at first glance with that scrawny build. You don't look like you could intimidate a child, let alone a true laoch trained in combat."

"Looks aren't everything," she said, visibly bristling.

"But a first impression is."

"My business in the south is no business of yours," she snapped. "I didn't ask for your opinion *or* your advice."

"Fair enough."

They continued on in silence, the wind whispering through the trees the only sound between them. Occasionally, he would catch Ellora's pained panting as she dealt with the wound on her arm. She was fortunate that barghests didn't have any venom in their bites, as other creatures of these parts often did.

Weylin caught the tops of tall stone buildings over the peaks of the pine trees. They were close.

The city, Speir, was not as large as the Briongloid's capital, Scamall, but it was close. Weylin had never visited it before, but he remembered the directions on the map and had heard about it from travelers in Samhradh. It was a popular destination and had great medical facilities as well as a massive library. Having never visited before, he would be able to maintain his alias.

They entered the city on foot, Eolas trailing behind until they encountered a passerby shortly after entering the gravel path into the village. Weylin ducked his head towards the man in a nod of greeting.

"Where is your infirmary?" Weylin asked, not wasting any time.

The stranger's eyes widened at the blood-soaked top Weylin had wrapped around Ellora's arm.

"That building," the man said, pointing them toward a taller building further down the main city path.

"Thank you," Weylin dipped his head, and the man nodded in response.

"Gods be with you," he murmured, directing his words to Ellora, who gave a tight smile in response.

They hurried down the road, Ellora's gasps growing louder and more pained with each step until they reached the front door to the Speir infirmary. Weylin yanked open the large wooden door and heard Ellora catch it.

A medic sat at a desk near the door where she looked up at them from the parchment laid out before her.

"Oh wyrd," she breathed out upon her first look at Ellora. "Let's get you into a room."

Ellora nodded wordlessly as she followed the female down a corridor and into an empty room. Weylin wasn't sure if he should follow or not, but his feet trailed after her. Ellora looked at him with irritation and confusion when he took the empty seat in the corner of the small room. Her expression screamed, *what are you still doing here?* And that was a question he did not have an answer to. So, he focused on the medic across from her.

"How did this happen?" The medic asked as she reached for Ellora's arm across the wooden table between them and started undoing the makeshift bandaging.

"Barghest attack," Weylin said just as Ellora opened her mouth to speak.

Her jaw remained open as she glared at him. If looks could kill, he would be dead on the spot. Even the medic looked over her shoulder at him in surprise before averting her gaze back to Ellora.

"I was out hunting birds in the woods, and four of the beasts appeared to be after the same bird that I was," Ellora said. "I got rid of two of them quickly enough, and then one of the last two bit my arm while I was trying to hold them off."

"And then I swooped in and handled the rest for her," Weylin said with a smirk that made Ellora's eyes go wide.

He leaned back in his chair as he looked at the medic, perfectly amused.

"Not soon enough to save her from this nasty wound apparently," the medic murmured to herself, slowly turning her arm over to look at the brutal marring from different angles.

"I didn't need saving," Ellora seethed from between clenched teeth.

"I would beg to differ," Weylin responded.

"It's going to need stitches," the medic interrupted them before they could get into it.

The medic released a foreboding breath before grabbing an assortment of tools from the tall cabinet in the room's opposite corner. She laid them out on the table and mixed a concoction in a small cup before handing it to Ellora.

"Take this," she instructed.

Ellora's nose wrinkled as she knocked the painkiller back with one swift gulp. The medic twisted her arm to get at the base of the bite.

"You can leave now," Ellora shot a sideways glance at Weylin.

"I think I would prefer to stay and watch," he responded coolly and watched Ellora's brows furrow with anger, but he knew she would not make a scene in front of the medic. He knew she would sit back and bite her tongue.

The medic paused uncomfortably before leaning back in and beginning to work on Ellora's wound.

Weylin settled into his seat, and he folded his arms over his chest. He watched Ellora squeeze her eyes shut, partially from the pain and, he thought, partially to block him out. To pretend he wasn't there as the medic worked carefully and quickly with her nimble fingers.

20

AISLA

ake up. Wake up. Wake up. Wake up!

Aisla jolted up with a gasp and frantically clawed at her throat, gasping for air. The eerie chanting grew more urgent with each syllable and scraped the sides of her mind. She had forgotten how to breathe. The walls closed in and terror erupted within her as she looked about the unfamiliar room, taking in gulps of air to fight the feeling of drowning. She reached out around her and the fabric on the bed was not her own.

Her eyes darted back and forth.

Not home. Not Eilean.

Aisla closed her eyes and inhaled as it all rushed back in a wave that threatened to take her under once again. She focused on the whisper of power in her veins, the response to her call for security, and the way it danced just below the surface of her skin. She was not home.

Ruairi was not here. He had not returned.

She took another deep breath and rubbed at her tired eyes. Then she remembered *him*.

Fenian.

Fenian, who had insisted on buying two rooms at the local inn because the sun had long set by the time they left the infirmary. Aisla did not realize how much time had passed between when she first pulled her bow and arrow out and when the nurse tied off her final stitch. She had left haggard and half-asleep, but fully prepared to part ways with Fenian, which was long overdue. She would be lying if she said she wasn't a little relieved when he got two rooms at the inn and paid for them, too. But she also hated the idea of owing him any more than she already did.

She was in that foreign inn somewhere in Briongloid now.

Not home.

Aisla Iarkis did not trust Fenian for even a moment.

The male was a brute disguised as a shockingly handsome elf. With his light brown skin, black hair, and sharp jaw, he was the type of handsome that knew it. The very worst kind.

His every movement radiated a power she couldn't grasp. He terrified her, angered her, and drew her in all at the same time. His amber eyes held more secrets than she thought any one soul could unpack. When he was near her, she felt her esos rising to the surface, and she did not know whether it was in defense or in eager greeting. Something in him felt familiar, but she had never met anyone like him before.

And the way he sliced through those final two barghests like butter on a roll was enough of a warning for her to know to run the other way.

His presence set her on edge, and the way he spoke as if the entire world should bow to his every word rubbed her the entirely wrong way. She wished he had not insisted on remaining in the room with the medic after escorting her there. She wished she didn't have to meet his lazy gaze over the medic's shoulder every time she looked away from the needle sewing her skin back together. She wished she had not stood helplessly while he bandaged her wound.

He was not gentle by any means, but he had thought to do it when she had not.

But most of all, she wished she did not feel as though she now owed him.

She was losing Eire.

Ruairi had been taken from her.

She was on her own in this ruthless realm that would not hesitate to sever her head from her body if her identity were discovered. And now, she was indebted to the first person she encountered. Anger grew within her as she clenched her teeth and stood.

Her legs were shaky, and her mind still felt foggy. She rubbed her hands on her pants and then shoved her few scattered belongings back into her pack. She double-checked the emerald ring was still in the pocket of her pants, and fastened her necklace from Eire at her throat. Finally, she sheathed *Oidhe* in her waistband and snuck out of the room on quiet feet.

This was her chance to lose the male elf, who had no concept of boundaries.

She was alone in the hallway before sunrise. The other guests of the inn were still in their beds, enjoying their rest. Aisla wished she could.

She crept down the stairs, careful not to jostle her injured arm too much. It was still sensitive from the stitches, and it ached with each slight movement.

At the bottom floor, she glanced around and saw the innkeeper dozing off with his feet kicked up and his head lolled to the side. She tiptoed to the door and relief filled her chest as she pushed through it, but it did not last long.

"You're up early," his voice rumbled as he leaned against the stables next to the inn.

"What are you doing?" she hissed, her heart sinking when he stood up and walked towards her.

"I heard you wake up," he replied coolly. "I figured I would get a head start on preparing to depart."

"Are you out of your mind?" she snapped. "Our time together ends here. In fact, it should have ended in that clearing next to the bodies of the beasts. This goes no further."

"I'm headed south and I have a horse," he continued on, ignoring everything she had just said. "You seem like you could use the help getting there. In the spirit of *atruach*, it is my duty to ensure you reach your destination safely."

Aisla recognized the Aosta term for an honor-bound task. She hadn't known that Iomlan took such things so seriously, but questioning it could make her appear as more of an outsider than she already did. She supposed she would no longer need to reach their contact in Briongloid if she had an escort who knew the land. Aisla could go without the updated map and save time if she was traveling with Fenian under the guise of his honor-bound duty.

"Well, contrary to how it may seem," she took a step towards him, glaring up at him from where he stood nearly two heads taller than her. "I do *not*."

"I did not ask. I am telling."

Aisla bit her cheek at his audacity. Her temper flared and her esos roared inside of her ears.

"You seem terribly used to telling people rather than asking," she fumed. It irritated her to find nothing but boredom and a trace of amusement glinting in his eyes. They stood toe to toe, and Aisla's fists clenched until her knuckles ached. "But you will *not* be bossing me around or even thinking you have any authority to tell me what to do. Should you *insist* on traveling alongside me, we need some ground rules—"

"I could not agree more," Fenian interrupted, and Aisla's jaw nearly dropped to the ground. "The first is that you need better hygiene. You smell like something straight out of a swamp."

Aisla bit back all the words that she wanted to scream. She ground her teeth and balled her fists even tighter.

"I'll work on my hygiene when you work on your manners," she snarled.

"Looks like we're stuck being smelly and snarky then," he quipped as Aisla folded her arms over her chest. "Come on, *banphrionsa*. You'll only waste your energy fighting, and gods know you haven't got much to waste."

She stiffened as he used that term again. It was the Aosta word for *princess*. She recognized it from scoil. The realms had once been structured differently—long before the Udar and Mathair. It was an obvious dig at her, but she did not know where he had gotten such an idea.

"Let's head out then," he said when she remained silent.

He gathered his horse and started off towards the outside of the city. Aisla followed him, one foot in front of the other. She couldn't completely understand why, but she also knew that if she turned around and headed in the opposite direction, she would not be able to walk away.

For whatever reason, the ancient norns had woven her thread with Fenian's, and she was not getting out of it until they reached the south. Once they made it there, he would return to his home and get out of her hair, and she could make her way to their contact marked on the map Ruairi left behind. She would save Ruairi and bring the cure home to Eire and all of her people. She just wasn't sure of all the steps in between yet.

Aisla took a deep breath, and they made their way out of the village.

A journey of endless sunrises begins with the very first step.

21

RUAIRI

The air grew warmer the further south that Ruairi and his companions ventured into Briongloid.

He had not spoken a word. And he did not plan to. Not until he was face to face with the Udar.

The thought sent a chill down his spine.

They had stopped for the night after a full day of travel. He was thankful the rain had quit in the middle of the previous night, but that didn't relieve the feeling of doom that increased with each passing moment.

Ruairi glanced about the dark clearing, lit by the flickering light of the fire. Two of the laochs had caught squirrels to roast for dinner. Looming pine trees and shorter oak trees littered the forest. It felt as though this forest was never-ending, and he knew they had cleared quite a bit of distance atop the horses. Ruairi had never ridden a horse before. Back in Eilean, he always walked or flew with Gaotha. There wasn't much to learn, though, as he was merely a passenger to Deirdre, who guided her speckled gray mare.

His boots were caked with mud, and his socks were still slightly damp. Everything hurt. He dreamed of a hot bath where he could wash all the grime away. His skin felt buried under layers of foreign soil, sweat, and rainwater. He would give anything to rinse off the dirt and feel like himself again.

The air smelled of smoke and damp soil, and he longed for the salty shores of home. He longed for the scent of iris in Aisla's long light brown hair.

He flexed his fingers and closed his eyes as he sat on the uncomfortable wooden log. He was nearest to the laoch they called Callum Ronan, a handsome human man with curly brown hair and dark green eyes. It was clear to Ruairi that Callum was the highest ranking in their group. He commanded with a quiet confidence, and almost everyone fell into place, save for Deirdre, who tended to challenge him.

"Here," a gruff voice called him from his thoughts. Ruairi looked towards the captain, who held out a chunk of roasted squirrel to him. "Eat."

Ruairi took the meat with a curt nod of thanks and hunched over as he ate it. It was an effort to eat slowly as the taste of the smoked meat made his mouth water and warmed him from the inside. He knew this portion would not be enough to satiate his growing hunger pains, but he savored every bite. Letting his tongue soak in all the flavors. Despite every effort of making the squirrel last forever, it seemed to disappear. Ruairi wiped his hands on his stiff pants and leaned back once again, easing his tense shoulders.

"You could speak, you know," Callum grumbled, quiet enough for only Ruairi to hear. The other laochs chattered amongst themselves, sharing ale and squirrel and stories told far too loudly.

Ruairi said nothing.

"It would make this easier on everyone if you would just talk," he continued, turning his piercing gaze on Ruairi. "You could tell me anything, but maybe start by explaining why your ship ran our blockade. Why it came in along the coast closest to *Eilean*?"

He spoke the name of Ruairi's home continent like a filthy

curse. Ruairi's heart pounded as his throat tightened. There was no suitable answer, no way to cover his tracks, and more importantly, Aisla's tracks. He remained silent, as he had vowed that he would until he was able to speak directly with the Udar.

"That's well enough," Callum said with a sigh. He looked back towards the slowly simmering fire once again. "But you're not doing yourself any favors. I am extending my hand to you, but if you'd prefer to go it on your own, that's your decision."

The male sounded genuine. Ruari thought in another world, in a time where there was not so much at risk and they had met in a different way, they might have been friends. But in this world, Callum was bringing Ruairi to the Udar himself, Faolan Myrkor. The name caused bile to rise in the back of Ruairi's throat. It was Faolan's forefathers who had exiled Eilean to a fate they knew would drive the smaller continent to extinction in time. The torture the Myrkors had thrived on, the souls they had ended both directly and indirectly, the families ripped apart—all for the sake of power and fear of a prophecy that had no real backing. Its words had been twisted and contorted through the generations, with no written record of it to be found.

It made Ruairi sick. It made him angry, and he yearned for vengeance by his own blade.

Ruairi could not linger there, not on these thoughts. His anger made his esos rise to the surface of his blood and it created a physical ache in his chest. This was the longest he had ever gone without using his esos since he had learned to wield it, and the absence of it was taking its toll on him. Ruairi had also noticed that they had not passed by a single ash tree. He wouldn't be stupid enough to use esos even if they had, but he kept a careful eye out for it along their journey and had yet to catch sight of the esos source. He wondered at this lack of source within this realm, and he thought it could be under order of the Udar, or perhaps a punishment from gods who had long fallen silent. Ruairi refused to believe they would serve such justice, but he could not help but find a hint of victory in the prospect.

Eire would surely have many thoughts on it. It would probably further ignite her blind allegiance to the gods who had let Eilean fall. The Trygg family had a history full of priests and religious leaders. Eire herself had no such interest in these positions, but that did not dampen her beliefs.

Ruairi gazed straight ahead, refusing to give Callum so much as a glance. He held onto his silence because it was the last thing left in his own control.

The air between them tightened. The words Callum wanted to speak lingered, though he said nothing. Instead, he stood up and went into his tent on the other side of the fire pit. Ruairi elected to stay on the log. He sat there while each laoch disappeared into their own tent until only one male was left—the male assigned to be his watch for the night—to ensure he did not run or escape.

Ruairi closed his eyes again and let his neck muscles loosen. Glimpses of Eire's bright smile and flashes of Aisla's lilting laugh played on repeat as he clung to the thread of them. He held on to it desperately because he knew if it slipped away, he would lose the willpower that had gotten him this far.

22

AISLA

It didn't take long for Aisla to adjust to the silence that had settled between her and Fenian as they advanced their travels south.

She desperately wished for Muinin, and her feet ached with every step. It wasn't just the convenience of transportation that made her heart ache for her wyvern, although her feet were covered in blisters she feared might never go away. The bottoms of her boots were bloodstained and her arches burned. She knew this pace was not entirely sustainable, but memories of Ruairi's parting words and Eire's lifeless form in the infirmary kept her motivation high.

"Do you ride?" Fenian spoke up as if he could read her thoughts.

"I haven't before," she replied.

"It's easy to pick up," he said. "Especially when you're not the one holding the reins."

Aisla was silent for a moment. She had never had to learn how to ride a horse because she had always had Muinin, but this was not something she could explain to Fenian since wyverns were not permitted on Iomlan.

"Fine," she spoke up, and they both stopped walking.

"Her name is Eolas," Fenian said, and Aisla gently stroked the mare's nose. She gave a low huff in response, leaning into her touch. She was rough and soft at the same time, her hair coarse and short. "The best horse there ever was."

Aisla smiled as she ran her hand along the horse's long snout. She smoothed Eolas's mane and patted her back, growing more and more comfortable with the beast that would hopefully bring her closer to completing her journey.

"Here," Fenian offered her a hand, which Aisla took reluctantly.

His hand was hard and calloused in hers. It was the hand of a male who knew hard work and long days. She knew hers would feel similar as he helped her onto Eolas's back. She tossed her leg over Eolas's side, bracing her core and clenching her legs when she tipped to the side. The horse remained still, despite Aisla's struggle to find her balance. It was an unfamiliar feeling, a new feeling. It was not unlike mounting Muinin, but Muinin felt like an extension of Aisla herself. This creature was foreign. She was stiffer and narrower than Muinin. Aisla rested her hands on the saddle, getting comfortable with the feeling of the horse beneath her.

"Good girl," Fenian murmured and Aisla's head snapped towards him, her jaw open. "I was not talking to you," he said with a dark chuckle and a sly grin that made Aisla's stomach clench. "I was talking to Eolas," he finished with a *tsk* of his tongue.

Aisla felt her cheeks reddening as she narrowed her eyes at him.

Without hesitation, Fenian swung himself up to be seated behind her. His legs wrapped around her, squeezing gently to secure his own balance atop the mare. She wondered if Eolas felt as natural to him as Muinin did to her.

Aisla pushed her shoulders back and held her chin higher, trying not to react to the way his arms snaked around her waist to grab the reins. A warmth radiated from the rude man, and she could not help but inhale the scent of sea salt and oak.

"Much easier this way," Fenian said. "Wouldn't you say, *banphrionsa*?"

"I have a name, you know?" She hissed back. "And that's not it."

"Yes, Ellora," her alias rolled off his tongue. "I know your name. The other just feels more fitting."

"I cannot imagine why," she snapped.

"Do you miss Fomhar?" He asked her abruptly, and she nearly forgot the story she had originated for herself in this strange land.

"I prefer the cool climate there and the color of the leaves," Aisla said without missing a beat.

Aisla pulled from her memories of the realm in scoil. She kept it both specific but vague enough to not get caught in any kind of lie. She'd had plenty of practice lying while growing up under the watchful eye of Cliona.

"It is a pleasant realm," Fenian responded. "I can understand the draw."

"So you have been before?"

"I have," he said, offering no further explanation, and Aisla decided she did not care enough to ask.

She merely nodded in response.

"Why do you wish to become a laoch?" Fenian asked, and Aisla could've sworn she heard genuine curiosity in his gruff voice. It felt like it was a question he had been waiting to ask her.

Aisla was glad it was one she was prepared to answer.

"I'm naturally gifted in combat, as you saw," she said. "All of my instructors in scoil noticed it at a young age and continued to train me well past what is mandatory in Fomhar. Studying was never for me. I enjoy reading, but not textbooks. I'll be damned if I end up in a village kitchen, and I think everyone else would avoid my cooking like the plague, anyway. Iron smithing isn't my calling either. As you can imagine, there is not much for someone with my skill set to do in Fomhar, so I would rather offer my services to our capital. I would rather be there, preparing to fight for our continent if the time arises, especially during the ninth generation."

The words *burned* as they left Aisla's lips. She could have gagged on each one when it slipped her tongue. It was an effort to keep the disgust from her tone. It was essential to her lie, to the persona she had created. To the believability of it. While there was truth to her skill set, the capital did not deserve her or her skills. It was the very last place she would fight for and the thought of it had her seeing red. She dug her fingernails into the palms of her hands and focused on the crunch of the leaves beneath Eolas's hooves.

"If what I saw was your gift, you might want to turn right around," he quipped, and she felt her irritation deepen.

"I did more damage to that pack of them than the average laoch could," she seethed.

"Hmm," he murmured, and she felt the reverberation of the sound through her pack on her back. "It's not easy."

At the very least, this declaration confirmed that he bought her every word. His tone held little interest or genuine concern. It felt more like he was trying to imply that she could not handle it, but she supposed she had expected as much from him.

"Neither is anything about this world," she replied, allowing the fire in her veins to cool as she pulled at the water esos she knew she possessed to combat the esos of flames that was ready for any hint of an opening to release.

She felt Fenian stiffen behind her, as if surprised by her response.

Good, she thought to herself. *Let him lose this* princess *image he has of me. Gods know where he got that idea in the first place.*

"And what do you know of this *world*?" His tone was condescending in the worst of ways.

"Surely more than you," she fired back.

She felt his legs tighten around her, reminding her who was holding the reins—who was in charge—and it drove her mad.

"You seem to me like a spoiled prick who is far too used to getting what he wants when he wants it," she continued. His legs tightened further. "I'd hate to meet whatever pathetic souls have groveled at your feet long enough to make you think you can treat people the way that you do."

"You know *nothing* about me," he replied in an icy tone.

The surrounding air shifted and the hair along her arms stood on end as a sense of danger hung between them.

"No, I don't. But I am better at reading people than most."

"So you think, little *banphrionsa*," he leaned in close, his hot breath grazing her neck as she sat straight as an arrow. She took deep breaths in and out through her nose, fighting to maintain the control that was hanging on by a thread as thin as the norns' golden spool. "*So you think.*"

Aisla clenched her teeth and worked to slow her racing heart. The whispering rush of her esos was a roar in her ears that she feared Fenian would be able to hear, but he made no indication. She paused for a moment to wonder what esos flowed in his veins. What power this cruel male could wield, but she would not ask. For the conditions of esos on this continent were unfamiliar to her and not worth any risk. She knew, though, that whatever esos Fenian possessed, it was a power that could rival her own. It radiated beneath his skin, calling out to her in challenge. She could not help but wonder if he felt that call from her as well.

"Don't underestimate me, Fenian," she tilted her head slightly, and their lips were nearly touching. Aisla pushed her own legs outwards on his, relieving the pressure he had been putting on her. She spoke with a threat hanging on her every syllable as the sun beat down on them. She was desperate to take back some of the control that he so clearly felt he now owned. "Not for a *moment*."

Aisla could feel his surprise in the way his legs tensed and the way he sat back away from her as she adjusted to face the road ahead. She focused on the steady rhythm of Eolas's steps that did not falter even with their intense exchange of words. She felt a small grin rise to her lips at his lack of response.

"You know, Ellora," he spoke up after a few moments, causing Aisla's irritation to rebuild. "I find I enjoy it when you act feisty. Keep it coming."

Aisla's breath hitched in her throat as the words arose like a purr from Fenian. She whirled around with her fist closed, already swinging at his face—consequences of doing so atop a horse be damned. He caught her flying hand as though he had been expecting it. As though he had intentionally goaded her into it, and the smirk plastered on his lips was enough to make her want to scream.

"You're such an ass," she seethed between clenched teeth as she tried—and failed—to yank her fist free.

The elf's amber eyes were hazy with unreadable emotions.

"It wouldn't be the first time I've heard that."

"And it certainly won't be the last," she snarled, and he released her fist, nearly sending her off the side of Eolas.

He eyed her curiously as if awaiting her next move. All amusement had disappeared.

Aisla gritted her teeth before turning back around, the sting of defeat rising like bile to the back of her throat.

This is not over, she told herself. *Far from it. I will get back at Fenian before this journey is over.*

The tension between them was a tangible thing—a thing she wanted to rip off of her back and throw to the forest floor and feel it crunch beneath Eolas's hooves. They continued until the sun reddened. Aisla could feel the air shifting as they neared the Samhradh border. She could have sworn it was beginning to feel warmer with each step they took.

The trees were a more and more brilliant green as they trekked on. The air smelled of fertile soil, and the forest thinned out, growing sparser as they entered more open land, where the sun burned on Aisla's shoulders beneath her cloak. The grass was vibrant, and she found all the bright colors renewed her energy. They passed yellow daffodils and pink tulips that danced in the evening breeze. There were so many plants she recognized from back home, and some she didn't. She wished to gather them to take home to her bedside collection, but knew she did not have the time. She also did not want to explain herself to Fenian. Aisla took it all in, noted all the flora and fauna that she could not wait to tell Eire about. She found her heart yearning for her friend.

And then she thought of Ruairi, how he was meant to be here with her. This was meant to be *their* journey full of memories they could make and bring back to Eire together.

Aisla's hands moved to the necklace at her throat at the thought of her friends, even though they never really left her mind. She ran her fingers absently along a smooth fragment of wyvern tooth. Eire was always there. Eire was there to guide her and pave the path laid out before Aisla's feet. This was all for her gentle best friend that did not deserve what was happening to her.

"What is that necklace?" Fenian spoke up and Aisla's eyes burned as she blinked away memories of Eire. "I haven't seen anything like it."

"My best friend back home made it," Aisla said. Not a lie. "She found a stag antler near my house on my ninth naming day. It's a good omen to see a stag. And while we did not have the fortune of seeing it, the timing felt too special to ignore. She carved the antler into these pieces and crafted the necklace for me." A lie.

"What's her name?"

"Mona," Aisla replied, quickly pulling the name of the elf meant to be here now, traveling with Ruairi.

"Mmm," he replied with disinterest. "Did you hear that?"

"No." Aisla paused, but strained her ears to listen.

She only heard the rhythmic clopping of Eolas's hooves and the rustle of the grass.

"We're stopping for a meal," Fenian decided, and Aisla looked eastwards to see a fallen tree that could serve as a bench to sit on. Aisla remained cautious while Fenian led Eolas to the fallen tree before jerking his reins to a halt. He dismounted in a smooth movement, and Aisla noted how he did not offer her a hand down for her to dismount like any decent male would, especially considering she had never dismounted a horse before. But she supposed Fenian was no decent male. She only regretted not having the opportunity to reject his offer of help as she swung herself off the tall horse. She landed hard on her knees and they stung with the shock of it, but she kept any reaction off her face so Fenian would not see.

"Real smooth," he snarked, and Aisla looked up to see him looking at her, the judgment clear on his face as she straightened herself.

"Piss off," she grumbled and sat down on the log.

23

AISLA

Fenian wordlessly held out cheese and bread to her from his pack before he sat down.

She took them, feeling shame at her own lack of resources. If she was not stuck with him, she would have already stopped in a village to restock on the supplies Ruairi had left her with. She had not realized how hungry she was until she touched the cheese to her tongue and her mouth watered. It was an effort not to scarf down the rest of it in one mouthful. The bread was slightly stale, but she was still grateful for it. She chased it down with water from Fenian's flask. Her eyelids fell shut as she savored every flavor. She didn't care what Fenian thought.

She kept her eyes to herself, not bothering to look up to see if he was watching her.

The lack of foliage around them made Aisla feel bare and vulnerable compared to the comfort she had felt those last sunrises traveling beneath the cover of the forest. She had yet to come across ash trees in any of the wooded areas. Despite it, she still felt her esos alive and restless.

Aisla made note of the way the ring deep within her pocket had fallen cold, almost silent, where it used to feel like a faint buzz. She didn't allow herself the temptation of running her fingers along its round, silver edge. She knew there was no risk worth drawing even the slightest amount of attention to it. Aisla needed her pockets to seem empty. To give Fenian no reason to feel as though she had something to steal.

There was something about this male. His power, his arrogance, his ease of tongue, and his pure strength were as clear as the sun in the sky without him having to flaunt it. She knew she had to be on her guard around him. There was no room for risks or errors when it came to her alias. She did not trust him, especially the way he refused to let her leave. It made no sense, but she could not help but wonder if he felt as drawn to her as she did to him—an attraction that promised pain and teased peril.

"How far from the capital now?" Aisla spoke up, desperate to get out of her head where her own fears threatened to drive her mad.

It was deafening to feel so alone. To feel like she'd lost everyone she had depended on, and she had no one to blame but herself.

"Roughly four sunrises if we keep up the pace as we have been," Fenian responded.

She tensed under his gaze. "It cannot come soon enough," she grumbled to herself.

"Eager for your initial beating, are you?" he sneered.

"Eager to rid myself of your rotten presence is more like it."

"Me, rotten?" He shook his head in disbelief. "If only you could smell yourself."

Aisla snorted and rolled her eyes, refusing to give in to his bait and biting her tongue. It was not her fault that baths were far and few between when one was a refugee on a foreign continent.

"Were you originally planning to walk this whole way on foot?" Fenian asked, and there was a gleam in his eyes that said he was suspicious of something.

"I was," she replied coolly, carefully. "It was to be a self-journey of sorts, seeing as I have never ridden a horse before, I did not consider it in my travel plans."

"You would not have made it very far on foot if barghests caught you as early on as they did," he scolded. "You seem to be in quite the hurry now for someone who previously did not have a timeline."

"The sooner my journey with you is over, the better."

"Fair enough."

"Speaking of which," she said. "Why do you *insist* on dragging me along with you?"

"I already told you that—it's a matter of honor, *Ellora*. Besides, we're going to the same place, and you would evidently not survive without me," Fenian replied with disinterest. "I was raised a gentleman, and I would not let a lady in danger travel alone, especially if it is no inconvenience to me to escort her."

"Gentlemen let ladies go when they wish to be left alone," she snarked back.

"I was raised a gentleman, which does not mean I am one," he said with an irritating shrug. "And above being a gentleman, I am a male who does not take no for an answer."

"I have noticed."

"Rather than berating me for escorting you to safety," he said. "You could thank me for my services."

"In your dreams," she said with a dramatic roll of her eyes.

"Mmm. You wish you had the privilege of partaking in my dreams."

"Actually, you're right. I would like to stay as far from that realm as possible."

"Keep telling yourself that."

Aisla had half a mind to tell him just where he could put his presumptions and his opinions. But instead, she inhaled a long breath and made her way towards the sound of nearby running water to refill her flask. She clenched her teeth as her emotions once again reminded her of the power she could so easily lose her grip on. This fragile thing which others could wield with such grace was a liability in her possession, and she had to constantly remind herself of that or risk losing control altogether. It whispered to her as it swirled about. It whispered the promise of her strength and power that could be the greatest the nine realms had ever seen, if only she could master it.

She found the small stream and knelt down beside it. She dipped her hand in the cool water, allowing the steady current to slip between her fingers and bring a sense of peace to her. Aisla looked at the gray stones under the current, the way they held fast and stayed in place as the water rushed through and around them. She admired their resistance and consistency—something she longed for more of.

With a sigh, Aisla dunked her flask into the stream, allowing the current to fill it up, then she screwed the cap back on. She blinked slowly and stood, smoothing down the front of her dirty, wrinkled linen pants.

Something in the air stilled as she walked toward the log where she had left Fenian. Aisla paused and strained her ears, hearing nothing but the sound of birds in the sky and wind whistling through the grass. She closed her eyes, listening for a trace of Fenian shuffling around or Eolas moving her hooves, but she heard nothing. A feeling of foreboding settled in her gut as her hand moved to rest on the hilt of *Oidhe*. There was a sudden thud and a loud whinny from Eolas.

Aisla's heart pounded, and she wished she'd brought her pack with her to the water's edge. If she had, she could carry on, run and avoid whatever situation had caused Eolas's panic. But she'd left it behind and it contained the letter, so Aisla dropped into a crouch and drew her blade, approaching with soft footsteps.

"*Fenian,*" she hissed when she was close enough to see the log and he was not sitting atop it.

Her heart thrummed as she picked up her pace to close the distance between her and the fallen tree, glancing side to side, clutching her dagger.

What she saw next was the last thing she had been expecting.

Fenian's unconscious body lay splayed out in the green grass under the setting sun. His arm was bent at an odd angle and his legs were crossed as though he had fallen forward off of the log. She dropped down beside him, shaking his shoulder with her free hand, while she kept her other on *Oidhe*.

When he did not respond, she rose and whirled around the clearing. She grabbed her pack from the ground where she had left it, leaning against the fallen tree. Her ears filled with thunder and her palms sweat. Then she noticed Eolas was missing. There was no sign of the mare. And the grass had dried enough since the storm to not leave any imprints of her hooves behind.

"Show yourself," Aisla boomed with a confidence that she didn't feel as she turned in a slow circle.

Her pack weighed heavily on her back when she looked down upon Fenian once again. She bit the inside of her lip as she made to leave. She inhaled and took one step away from the log, away from *him*. A sharp pain knocked her to her knees before she could turn on the attacker that had come from nowhere.

A second pain came next. And that second pain was followed by darkness as her head hit the soft grass with a thud, and her vision faded to black.

24

RUAIRI

There was a feeling deep within Ruairi's chest that he could not put into words as he neared Castle Eagla. The castle he had only ever seen drawings of in books from his world-telling courses in scoil.

The journey had been long.

He was exhausted to the point of near hallucination, despite the horse beneath him. His feet ached so badly he dreaded the moment he would walk on them again. He was always hungry, and always craving cool water. He could never have enough and would never take for granted the precious life-giving liquid.

And he was so tired. He had hardly slept since joining his new company.

Ruairi could not shake the haunting feeling that tugged on him with each trot of the horse. Each moment of the journey brought him closer to what was surely his doom. He would not wish this dread, this fear and suspense, upon anyone else. He was only thankful Aisla had not ended up here with him, enduring this, too. All the same, he yearned for her presence in a way that was near maddening when combined with all the other conditions of this journey.

Ruairi had accepted his fate to some degree. He had come to terms with the probability he would never again see the shores of Eilean. He would never see his family or his students. He would never again ride atop Gaotha. He would become a memory for Fire.

And the hardest reality to accept was the one where he would never again hold Aisla Iarkis.

Every step closer to the Udar made Ruairi more and more aware of all that was at stake. He spent time in the silence with only his own thoughts and remembered everything of the Siege of Arden. Something about traveling with these people, these laochs, reminded him how real it all was. These were real people with hatred in their hearts for the people of Eilean, but mostly for Aisla herself. He wanted to keep her as far away from this place as possible.

He was a fool to ever bring her to this continent, and he felt in some way that his capture was his punishment. Now, she would be forced to return to where she was safe. Where she was far away, and not in this land that made his skin crawl with paranoia.

He had taught himself not to think of her. He drove the image of her from his mind and tried to unlearn the beauty of her name. Ruairi fought to erase the memory of her lips. It was less painful that way, to not have to think of all he was missing.

And he was selfish enough to protect his heart as best as he could.

Ruairi rubbed at the single tear that had slipped down his cheek, and he clenched his fists so tightly his knuckles turned white.

They reached the top of a grassy hill and looked out over the castle at last. They did not pause, eager to deliver him to their master. His stomach knotted as his emotions warred. A part of him was in awe of the beautiful structure, while most of him was absolutely disgusted by the sight of it.

The castle sat on a sandy land littered with desert flora. It was seated near a large bay that fed directly into the Tusnua Sea. It was larger than he could have ever imagined and eerier than he had prepared himself for. He was fighting the fear, and all too aware of Deirdre in front of him and the way she could surely feel whatever emotions he gave off.

Castle Eagla was massive compared to Castle Farraige, where Cliona lived. This castle was more elegant, yet the stonework was simple in its own way. There was a tower at each corner. It appeared to be at least seven stories tall from what Ruairi could see on this side of the gate. The gate was about three stories tall, and he couldn't imagine how anyone could get through or over the wall to lay siege without first being granted entry through the gates.

The tops of the castle were a beautiful gold that gleamed in the setting sun. The westward side of the castle bordered a tall cliff face, and a bridge extended from an upper floor and above the gates to connect to the top of the cliff.

He looked at the stunning mass of masonry and art and knew in his core that the Myrkors did not deserve its elegance. He detested the way they lived while Eilean struggled to find enough food to survive.

The grass turned to sand that sifted beneath the hooves of the horse as they descended the hill towards the castle. Scattered palm trees and green bushes with leaves similar to ferns speckled the base of the wall that surrounded the castle.

They dismounted once Callum gave the hand signal to the guards at the gate. There were three of them, standing with long spears, prepared to turn anyone away, and waiting to welcome back the laochs who had delivered him here.

Ruairi walked towards them, standing just behind Callum Ronan. Of all the Samhradh laochs, it surprised Ruairi to find that the captain was by far the most tolerable. While he kept to himself and came across more standoffish, Ruairi noted the times that

Callum silently passed him extra food at mealtime, or when he dropped a blanket at his feet during the cooler nights. Callum seemed to have morals his companions lacked. And while Ruairi would not go as far as to say that he liked or respected the man, he would prefer his company to anyone else he had met from Samhradh.

"Here we are," Callum murmured under his breath, so that only Ruairi could hear him. "The castle in the south. The house of wolves."

Ruairi held his silence.

"I would suggest cooperation with our Udar," Callum continued to mutter. He inhaled a long breath as if he felt actual concern for Ruairi. "He is not a male of compassion or mercy. Whatever your expectations are, whatever you think you know of him, think lower and prepare yourself for the male you are about to meet."

Ruairi felt a knot forming in his throat. He nodded. He already hated this male that he had never met more than he had ever hated anyone or anything. He could imagine nothing worse than what he had already been mentally preparing himself for. His head felt lighter with each step onwards—his footsteps heavier.

The words of Callum echoed in his head while the laochs he had traveled with spoke with those at the gate. He did not hear them, could not process the words as he kept his gaze emotionless. The gates creaked open ahead of them. Ruairi clenched and unclenched his fists and he took in a deep breath and released it slowly, repeating the movement as he entered inside the walls of the wolves' den.

His legs carried him forward, though he wore numbness like armor. They had given him fresh clothes to change into just this morning, part of his presentation to the Udar he assumed. There was nothing left on his person that was his.

Even his esos seemed like it had retreated far within, as though it was ashamed to be a part of him. He had never felt an absence like this before. The power had gone utterly still and quiet. The strain of disuse was dampening it—like it was suffocating within him.

Ruairi stepped across the castle's threshold. There was no turning back. Ruairi snuck a glance at Callum, who wore a grim expression as if he expected trouble.

The hallways were bright white marble with streaks of gray running through them. He had always imagined it to be dark and gloomy. They passed golden statues of wolves and portraits of various generations of the tyrannical dynasty throughout the hallways. Paintings of the famous beaches of Samhradh and the different mountain scenes hung there as well. Ruairi focused his mind on these details and on the feel of the stone beneath his overworn boots.

After a series of turns and corridors that Ruairi did not bother to commit to memory, they at last stopped outside of a room with dark wooden doors. Callum led the way in. Ruairi was first struck by the maroon and marigold banners that decorated the walls of the massive room. The ornate rugs were patterned in these same colors. Ruairi forced himself to drag his eyes to the center of the room. He would not avoid it or show intimidation.

He looked at the one true throne—the Throne of Arden.

Iarkises had sat upon it until six generations ago—until the Siege of Arden. It was a beautiful throne composed of dark marble and jade—the blessing stone. The crystal assured that whoever sat upon it may have the approval of all nine gods.

It had been a long time since that was the case, Ruairi thought to himself as the green stones shone in the flickering candlelight.

The throne had intricate carvings that wound into the Crann Na Beatha, the tree of life in Talam. To be in the presence of the Arden Throne was a humbling experience. Ruairi felt the urge to drop to his knees at the sheer power radiating from it. *Almost,* but his awe faded into rage as his eyes traveled up to the man who sat upon it.

He did not even have time to imagine Aisla sitting there, on the throne that was hers by blood right.

Ruairi looked at Faolan Myrkor, the male who had been a part of a generations-long mission to destroy everyone and everything Ruairi had ever loved.

Faolan was a slender man with a gaunt face. His dark features were sharp and hollow. His dark brown eyes followed every twitch of Ruairi's muscles with unnerving concentration, and Ruairi made a conscious effort to relax into a feigned confidence.

Faolan had long dreadlocks that stopped at his chest. He wore a maroon cloak and his hand rested upon a golden scepter topped by a carved golden wolf. His legs were spread with such casual arrogance. Everything about the man screamed at Ruairi to turn and run. He radiated a darkness that seeped into Ruairi's skin and threatened to consume him, to make him give up the fight and accept his own demise.

"And who might you be?" His very voice sent a shudder down Ruairi's spine that he fought to suppress.

"My name is Ruairi Vilulf." Ruairi's sore voice scratched along the edges of his throat. He straightened his back, the hairs on his arm standing up on end. He met the Udar's gaze with a ferocity that said he would not back down—he would not be afraid.

"Why do you waste my time with his presence?" The Udar sneered, directing his attention to Callum behind Ruairi.

"We picked him up off the coast nearest Eilean, your grace," Callum's entire voice had changed. Gone was the soft, yet gruff voice he commanded his troops and addressed Ruairi with. Now he sounded like a true captain. His voice was much deeper and each of his syllables enunciated in a clear boom. "An unmarked ship was spotted shooting through our blockade, and we found him not far from where the ship weighed anchor."

"And how big was this ship?" The Udar asked with only vague interest.

"It was a small ship. Small enough to be manned solo or it could comfortably fit two, your grace."

"So, there could be another?" The Udar raised an eyebrow and leaned forward slightly.

Ruairi felt his heart beating so fast he thought his chest would combust. But he could not let it show. This was the one thing he could not let them know, the whole reason for his silence. They could not have any reason to go looking for Aisla, to be suspicious of her presence.

"We scanned the area," Callum said. "We found no sign of another. We found his tent left behind in his haste to escape, which is suspicious in itself, but it appeared he could have been alone, your grace."

"How interesting."

"The words he speaks are true," Ruairi spoke up once he found his voice again. "I come here on behalf of Eilean. Lofa has ravaged our country—a plague which we will not survive on our own. Our leader has reason to believe there is a cure to be found in Samhradh, and I should humbly ask for that cure. We ask for no more and no less. If you give us the cure, I shall return in a fortnight with a gift from our leader."

"And why should I trust you to return?" The Udar mused.

Ruairi swallowed. He was hit with the part of his plan he had not worked out. It had felt essential to leave the parcel with Aisla when he had been taken captive. They could have killed him and taken the parcel for themselves. Then, they would have been left with no cure, no bargaining chip, and he would have been ended for nothing.

"I give you my word," Ruairi stated firmly. "You may send your own men to escort me and the cure back to Eilean and return with me with the parcel if that would be of reassurance."

"I find your terms hardly agreeable. The suffering of your continent seems to be long overdue punishment from the gods, and who am I to interfere?"

Ruairi felt his heart sink as dread and wrath writhed within him. The Udar stroked his dark beard before rising from the Arden Throne and crossing the room towards Ruairi.

Each footstep echoed louder than the last. Ruairi clenched his jaw and watched the male approach through narrowed eyes. Ruairi's hands shook, and he squeezed them behind his back tighter in an attempt to make them stop. His chest tightened and sweat beaded along his brow.

The Udar paused once he had gotten close enough that Ruairi could hear each breath without having to strain his elongated ears. He could smell the stench of mulled wine on the Udar. Ruairi thought he could feel Callum tense beside him.

The Udar's hand shot out and caught Ruairi's chin before anyone had time to react. Not that any of them would. He imagined they might sneer at the outright display of control and disrespect from their master. He tipped Ruairi's chin to force him to look directly into his eyes. Ruairi ground his teeth. It took a great effort not to explode with his aer esos, sending the Udar flying into the wall behind him. He stared directly into his dark eyes that were filled with rage, despite his calm and confident posture.

"On the other hand, you might be of use to me yet," he purred, his voice a deep, guttural sound. Ruairi fought the urge to barf as the Udar's hot, sticky breath fanned across his face. "There is so little known of the lost continent—of the line of the *gheall ceann* that still resides there."

Ruairi refused to break eye contact. He would not crack. He could not look away as the Udar's eyes darted back and forth between his own. The Udar's grip tightened and Ruairi was sure it would leave a bruise.

"I think there is fun to be had with this one yet," the Udar addressed the room, a sadistic grin spreading his lips. "He *will* break. In time."

Before he could stop himself. Before he could think for even a moment. Before he could convince himself not to, Ruairi spat in the Udar's face.

The room froze.

The Udar flung Ruairi's chin, and he stumbled back a step. Faolan's dark eyes danced with terrifying shadows that gleamed in the candlelight.

Faolan ran a hand down his face, slowly wiping the spit away. Every laoch in the room had drawn their weapon and angled their bodies towards Ruairi, ready for the signal at any moment to end him. In a blink, Faolan drew back his fist, swinging so hard at Ruairi that he felt bone crack. Ruairi's body sprawled on the marble floor, his legs giving out beneath him.

A pair of laochs each grabbed an arm and yanked Ruairi to his feet. He fought to pull his arms from their grasp, baring his teeth as he pulled with what little strength he had left. They wrenched his arms behind his back, restraining him and forcing him to turn to the wrathful face of the Udar.

Ruairi's breaths came in heavy, shallow heaves and anger seated within him. An anger that he could hardly control as he felt his esos just below his skin. The sound of wind roared louder and louder the longer he stared into the soulless eyes of that evil male. Ruairi knew he looked wild, like the beast they imagined him to be, as he sneered at them while the Udar only stood there, stone-faced. Blood trickled down Ruairi's face, and he heard the first drop hit the floor, staining the white marble with a deep red. His face throbbed with an aching pain that would not soon disappear. The Udar shook out his hand with mild disinterest.

"Throw him in a cell," the Udar instructed. "This won't be the last we see of each other, *deamhan*."

Demon, Ruairi thought. *I'll show him demon.*

The powerful arms holding him back tightened their grip as they took him to the exit. Ruairi walked with them obediently. He would not allow himself the shame of being dragged from this room.

Ruairi Vilulf walked towards the dungeons of Castle Eagla with his head held high and his hands trembling as a stone of fear settled within his gut.

25
WEYLIN

Weylin's eyes blinked open to a dark room with candlelight flickering against sloped canvas walls.

The last thing he remembered was Ellora storming away from the fallen tree to fill her flask at a nearby brook. He was checking over his map when a pain shot through his head. Before he could react to it, he fell into the grass.

And then he lost consciousness.

He had been left to the will of whoever his attackers had been.

He pushed himself up as he glanced about the puball. The puballs were larger, more permanent versions of the tents laochs carried in their packs when away for overnight journeys. They were common in smaller villages and were a form of living as ancient as the world tellers' books.

An unexpected rush of relief shot through him when he noticed Ellora's unconscious body next to him. He watched the slow, rhythmic rise and fall of her chest long enough to know that she still lived. Her face was so much different like this—when every glance his way was not dagger-sharp or full of spite. She was beautiful in a simple way. Freckles scattered across her nose and cheeks. Her cheekbones sat high on her face and her lips were full.

The way she had not questioned the reasoning of *atruach* to bind her to him alarmed him. The ways of honor-bound duties were a thing of the past, and she had accepted something he had almost offered in jest with little dispute. He did not know what she was up to, but planned to keep her close until he could discover exactly what she was hiding.

He dragged his gaze from her and noted the two elves sitting in chairs near the entrance flaps. Their eyes were trained upon him, watching every slight move of his muscles. They did not look threatening, but curious, cautious even.

Weylin slowly drew himself to his feet, his hands held out in front of him in a way to say that he was not a threat.

"Your name?" the larger of the two men spoke in a deep, booming voice, and they both rose.

"Fenian Daro. This is my companion, Ellora Morlee, and we were headed south before our journey was so rudely and abruptly brought to a halt."

"What beckons you to Samhradh?" the second male spoke in a slightly higher pitch.

He was short and skinny, while the other was tall and bulky. They wore the traditional leathers of ancient laochs that fit more comfortably than modern attire.

"Our families live there," Weylin lied for the both of them. "We were visiting extended family in the north. Helping them get back on their feet and making funeral arrangements."

The men looked at each other. The slimmer of the two nodded and Weylin gathered he held the higher rank of the pair.

"Are you aware that you trespassed on the territory of the Spiorad Tribe?"

"I was not aware, no," Weylin answered honestly. He had seen no indications on his map. He figured they must be small enough to not have a location on common maps. "Our apologies. We will gladly take our leave and get out of your territory immediately."

"It is not safe out there," the larger one shook his head. "Olc spirits wander these woods of late. We brought you here to warn you and offer you a safe resting place while they are out. We've been tracking their patterns for many moons now, and since tonight is the full moon of Braon, and that is when we have learned they run most rampant, we stopped you."

"You've never heard of the simple art of conversation?" Weylin snapped with a dry laugh. He watched as both pairs of eyes narrowed on him. "Maybe you could have communicated with us and allowed us to make our own decisions on the matter. This whole knock-them-on-the-heads thing feels a bit archaic and rather unnecessary," he gestured to Ellora, who was still out cold on the ground next to him.

"We have found that trespassers do not often listen when issued clear guidance. The trees do not lie, and it is not safe out there tonight," the thin one said defensively. "And aside from that, we had every right to pass you and your companion on for wandering into our land. Now, we take you in to keep you out of the claws of the olc spirits, and you have the gall to scold us for it?"

"I am not *superstitious*," Weylin snarled.

"It is not superstitions that lurk in these woods, *boy*." The atmosphere of the puball seemed to shift as the man's tone switched to one of pure foreboding that made Weylin's skin crawl. "You'd be wise to heed our advice and stay in our company until sunrise. We have an extra puball you can rest in, then be on your way tomorrow. But do not be ignorant enough to depart tonight. The skies have already fallen dark."

Weylin clenched his teeth and rolled over their limited options in his mind.

"We require two puballs," he spoke up.

"You will *accept* the generous offer of the one puball," he snapped indignantly. The male took a threatening step towards Weylin, who held his ground. "We have *one* vacancy, and that is more than enough kindness to extend to trespassing strangers. Wouldn't you agree?"

Weylin sneered, but his retort was interrupted when movement caught his eye. Ellora pushed herself up to a sitting position and rubbed at her eyes and stifled a yawn. Weylin had to fight the urge to roll his eyes.

"Where am I?" she mumbled as her hand moved to feel the lump on the back of her head.

"You are in the tribe of the Spiorad people," the man spoke before Weylin could. "I will allow your companion to fill in the gaps for you, as I have other matters to attend to. We look forward to hosting you beneath the trees this sunrise."

Ellora looked up to Weylin with confusion clouding her usually sharp yellow-green eyes.

"Your puball is the vacant one in the southeast corner of the village. Your packs are sitting outside the entrance," the thinner man said. He seemed to have a bit more compassion than his companion. "We have set your mare up in our stables for the night. We have already ensured that she has been fed as well."

Weylin nodded dismissively and wondered how long exactly he had been unconscious. They seemed fairly prepared, but it was not long after sunset now and they stopped for their meal just before the sun was setting. He decided he would not utter a word of appreciation towards these people as Ellora stood. He felt a new urgency to get to their puball as it hit him that all of their belongings were sitting there, out in the open. The way Ellora shifted beside him let him know she was thinking the same thing.

The two males exited the puball, leaving Weylin and Ellora alone.

They faced each other in the same moment, Weylin's face tight with annoyance, his brows furrowed and lips pursed, jaw clenched.

Ellora still looked half-awake and her eyebrows knit together in confusion. A thousand questions swirled in her eyes.

"We're staying *one* sunrise here," Weylin barked at her before she could voice her questions. "They have warned us of olc spirits in these parts, particularly during the full moon in Braon, they say. We've been given a puball for the night, then we will leave first thing in the morning once the peak of the supposed threat has passed."

"They've offered us each our own puball, right?" Ellora asked, eyes widening.

Irritation flared in Weylin's chest. *How was that the only thing Ellora pulled from his entire explanation? If that was truly her greatest concern, perhaps she had not heard the words he spoke,* he thought to himself.

"No," he snapped. "I already pushed for it and was denied. You're welcome to take it up with them if you think you'll have better luck. Otherwise, you can have a place on my floor."

Ellora glared at him indignantly as those yellow-green flames flared to life. She opened her mouth to protest, but he cut her off.

"Don't worry, I do not cuddle," he quipped. "And even if I did, you'd be the last sort of female I would reach for, even in the dark of the night."

He smirked as her cheeks burned red beneath her freckles. He headed towards the exit of the puball.

"Gods *damn* you, Fenian Daro!" she snarled as she followed. "You are the *most* despicable. *Most* arrogant male—"

"Thank you," he interrupted, keeping his eyes trained ahead, searching for his pack as he headed southeast in the village as instructed.

"It wasn't a compliment," she seethed, trotting a few steps to reach his side.

He did not so much as glance at her.

This village was much different from Briseadhceo. Its buildings were all either puball style or smaller wooden structures. He noted the village counter, tavern, and a communal wash area. A small shop where a dwarf was forging iron tools. Bright fabrics of teal, red, marigold, green, and other vibrant shades decorated the unique buildings and homes, standing out against the taupe of the puball canvases. He noted that no particular realm colors stood out to him. It appeared as though they did not hold allegiance to any one realm. The place had a very natural feel to it. The land was untouched compared to the land of Omra and other populous cities.

He finally spotted the dark brown of his pack leaning outside of a small puball. He picked it up, inhaling a deep breath, and prepared for the tight quarters that awaited them on the other side of the tent flap entrance.

It was about as bad as he had expected.

It was crammed and near suffocating compared to the accommodations Weylin was accustomed to. There was a mid-sized bed with a colorful quilt atop and flat pillows. A wooden bench sat at the end of the bed and one wooden end table took up space on the side of the bed furthest from the entrance. Despite not being thrilled by the prospect of this stay, he had to admit it would be better than their bedrolls on the hard earth. Even if he did have to share a bed with this feral female.

With a sigh, he shouldered his pack higher.

"Be right back," he muttered, turning to leave, and heard Aisla sit down on the bed.

Weylin entered one of the private stalls of the wash area he had passed on the way to their puball. He brought his pack into his arms and rummaged through it, anticipation causing his heartbeat to quicken. He searched for the familiar feel of his crown and the Myrkor iron crest he pinned to his clothes for formal events, desperate to know that they had not been found. Gods knew he did not need these people identifying him, especially not knowing where their allegiance lay.

Relief washed through him when he found them. He shoved

them back down to the bottom of the pack, burying them amongst clothes and his thin blanket and rolled up bedroll. It said a lot about these people that they did not go through their things, and that provided him with a small sense of comfort.

He sauntered back to the puball to find Ellora had shoved her own pack under the bed, which she sprawled out on, eyes closed as he watched the rise and fall of her chest.

"I'm not staying here any longer than we *need* to," she grumbled without opening her eyes.

"Agreed," he grimaced, dropping his pack to the ground and kicking it under the bed beside hers.

26

AISLA

Aisla walked around the village nestled between sparse pine trees, kicking stray pebbles and dodging the curious looks of its inhabitants. She could not stay cooped up in that room with that male any longer, or she feared she would lose her mind.

An anxiousness ate its way through her since the moment Fenian told her they had to stay here. It was killing her to sit here while Ruairi could be nearly to the capital by now. Her journey had been halted by beasts, injuries, and now evil spirits apparently. She let out a huff and hugged her injured arm to her chest. She would have scars where the barghest had bitten her—brutal scars that would never fade where its teeth sunk in. But for now, it was a dull throbbing pain that made her arm stiffen even as she made conscious efforts to stretch it out.

The presence of scattered patches of gritty, golden sand throughout the village was a sign that they were nearing the capital. At the beginning of this journey, the thought of nearing Omra would have unnerved her, but now it made her eager. No fears would keep her from Ruairi. The Udar or the prophecy or any number of laochs could not keep her from him.

Her anxiousness mixed with guilt as she continued pacing around the outskirts of the village. She knew they were watching her, curious, hesitant, maybe afraid of the female with unkempt hair and wild eyes. She did not care to socialize here, even though she knew anything that would help her pass this time of waiting would be a blessing, even in some small way.

Aisla turned on her heel and headed to the wash area of the village. She was long overdue for some freshening up, and the stench of blood and grime filled her nose. She just had not cared enough to notice.

Aisla left the bath feeling like she had regained a morsel of herself. Her hair hung wet and loose around her shoulders, and the surrounding air smelled like the lavender soap that had been left for her. She had lost a layer of her skin under the rough scrubbing, peeling it back to find she looked paler without it.

She headed toward the puball, not sure what else to do. She planned to grab some of her funds and find some food. She finally realized how hungry she was, and now that she had, it was all she could think about.

"Aye, miss," a voice called from behind, and Aisla's hand twitched to reach for *Oidhe* as she whirled to face the voice.

"Yes?" Her eyes met those of the heavier set man from the puball earlier.

"The Priomh of Spiorad would like to extend an invitation to you and your companion to join us for our communal dinner tonight. We will begin gathering soon, should you like to attend."

She toyed around with the idea in her head. A free meal was never a bad thing.

"We will talk it over," she said with a curt nod, still not over the fact they thought knocking her out was the best way to offer her aid.

"I hope to see you there." He ducked his own head and walked in the opposite direction.

It was a little early for dinner, but she supposed the sun was setting earlier in the day. Each sunrise extended the daylight ever so slightly until Litha, the celebration of the start of summer.

Aisla crouched through the entrance to the small puball to find Fenian sitting up in the bed, leaning against the headboard, reading a book.

"We've been invited to dinner," she said by way of greeting.

Fenian snorted. "They won't be seeing me in attendance."

At Fenian's immediate, arrogant rejection, Aisla decided she *would* be attending.

"Glad to hear you say it," she grinned. "I was planning on going myself and was just thinking we could use some time apart."

Fenian rolled his eyes before focusing on the pages in his hands.

Aisla sat at the edge of the small and unstable wooden bench at the end of the bed and dragged her pack out from under it. She pulled out a few coins for her meal, then slipped on her deep-green cloak. She would need it now as the cool night settled upon them.

She left the puball without a word and headed toward the grouping of wooden tables she had seen in the village center. Voices grew louder as she neared. Voices that joined in laughter, joy, murmurs of gossip, and grumblings of frustration.

Her nerves heightened, feeling like an outsider as she came into view of the people gathered to share a meal. There were elves, humans, and dwarves, mingling together as one. All different skin tones, hair colors, and ages. Most of the tables were full, but a few remained empty or half-occupied.

"Ah, here is our guest!" A voice boomed from a table in the

center and Aisla's cheeks heated as she debated turning around and running in the other direction. "Come, sit by me."

The male was a dark-skinned elf with long dreadlocks and a kind face. He spoke with authority, and Aisla had the feeling this was the Priomh that the other elf had spoken of. He waved her over with a grin and she forced a smile that she was sure looked uncomfortable to everyone staring at her.

She noticed that Priomh had left two empty seats on his right side, presumably for her and Fenian. The male stood as she approached and bowed from his waist to her. Aisla nearly shook her head and begged him not to do so, as she so often did back in Caillte when people greeted her that way. Instead, she returned the gesture, and they both sat down at the long wooden table.

The elves, humans, and dwarves sitting around the table looked to her expectantly. Some looked suspicious, while others looked friendly.

"My name is Laisren, and I am the Priomh of the Spiorad people," he said, confirming Aisla's suspicions. "And what might I call you?"

"Ellora," she replied with a small smile.

"Can I expect your companion to join us?" He quirked a brow.

"No," Aisla answered quickly, too quickly. "He is tired from our long day of travel."

"That is quite understandable. I am grateful you made the effort to be here," Laisren said. His eyes were soft and warm, and full of knowledge she could not quite explain. "It looks like just about everyone is here."

Aisla looked around at the tables that had filled up, then at the empty seat next to her.

The area grew quiet; an almost expectant silence. And one by one, heads all around her bowed in prayer. It was something not commonly done in Eilean, but something she did whenever she was in the Trygg household. Eire's family kept that old tradition among many others. She bowed her head along with those around her.

"To the gods, we send our gratitude for another day on this soil. To the gods we acknowledge our place at your feet and your strength. To the gods we ask for the return of the roots of ash trees in this world. To the gods we ask to feel the esos in our blood once more. To the gods we plead for mercy for our brothers and sisters across the sea. By the gods we bless this food and this drink!"

Aisla could feel her heartbeat in her throat as she grasped the meaning behind all the words spoken into the still air of the night.

Even the smallest slip of her esos would be damning to her on this continent with no ash trees and no active esos. She swallowed dry air and sent a silent prayer of thanks to the gods for hiding her esos this long.

Then another wave of shock rattled Aisla and great whoops of agreement exploded all around her from the villagers. Shock at the fact that there were still people with sympathy for her and her continent. The ember of hope she had tucked away flared up brightly.

A presence settled into the empty chair beside her. A presence that she did not have to open her eyes to know.

Fenian had apparently changed his mind and appeared midway through Laisren's prayer, settling in with a silence that was unnerving. She noticed the way he tensed during the end of the prayer. His body stilled, and she wondered, not for the first time, what side of this conflict he was on. If he was from a city so close to the Udar, there was a decent chance he would slaughter her on the spot if he knew her true identity. She suppressed a shudder at the thought.

She inhaled before lifting her face. She gave herself a moment longer to conceal her grin, and the single tear that rolled down her cheek as she recovered from the way Laisren's words had touched her—ignited her.

The shouts following the prayer dimmed to friendly chatter and

laughs as Aisla looked over at Fenian. He stared at her with unusu-
ally curious eyes.

"I am glad to see you made it," Laisren interrupted, and Aisla
tore her gaze from Fenian's.

Fenian simply nodded.

"We thank you for choosing to stay here during the time of the
olc spirits. The moons have been warning of them for several
sunrises now. We have already lost two *anamacha* to them, and that
is two too many."

Aisla recognized the Aosta term for *souls*. A heavy silence fell as
the table's occupants listened in. Aisla struggled to find the words of
comfort to reply.

"My condolences for your loss," Fenian spoke up, saving her the
trouble. "Although, I must say there was little choice in the matter
for us."

Aisla's eyebrows shot up, and she kicked Fenian under the table.
He kept his gaze on Laisren, refusing to acknowledge either gesture
from her.

"What I think he meant to say is that your laochs were very,
erm, very insistent that we stay the night. We appreciate the concern
for our safety, but it was almost maybe a bit forceful," Aisla spoke
quickly, fumbling over her words in an attempt to stop Fenian from
burning any more bridges.

"I understand Sean came off a little strong—he tends to—but
he too has lost much to these hauntings," the Priomh spoke carefully, not a hint of hostility in his voice. "He seeks to avoid any more
unnecessary loss."

Aisla nodded, and Fenian remained still beside her. She shifted
her attention to the plate in front of her, and her mouth watered at
the sight of the venison, potatoes, and green beans. It looked better
and fresher than the meals Hilda prepared back home. It was
evident that these people truly lived from and cared for the land.

There was a large and very full goblet by her plate filled with a red liquid that she assumed to be wine. The smell wafted towards her, reminding her of tipsy nights at home with Eire and Ruairi. They used to crowd Eire's baile and pile up in her bed, discussing the adventures they would one day have. They dreamt aloud of places they still wanted to see atop their wyverns, and the stories they would one day have to tell their descendants. In every hope, in every vision for their future they held, it was the three of them together, side by side.

Aisla's appetite fizzled out, despite the food at her fingertips. Sickness filled the pit of her stomach and tears burned her eyes. She felt the sudden urge to get up and run because neither Eire nor Ruairi were there.

Her lungs tightened and her breath caught in her throat as she gripped the edge of the table. She was *alone*. And it hit her all at once in a drowning wave that smelled of sweet, red wine.

A gentle hand tapped her knee under the table as the breath rushed back into her chest. She came back to herself, hearing the cheery voices and smelling the food sitting before her. She turned her attention to the source of the tap.

"You okay?" Fenian mumbled, low enough that no one else would hear. Aisla was thankful no one else had noticed the fear she had disappeared into. "You look like you just saw a ghost."

Aisla wanted to say that she had. In fact, she had just seen two of them, but instead she replied, "I'm fine. Just lost in thought."

Fenian looked at her skeptically, as though he did not believe her. But he also did not have enough interest to push further.

Aisla reached out a shaky hand and lifted her goblet, slowly bringing it to her lips. She took a deep swig and the warm liquid sloshed down her throat. She would not let her memories and grieving own her. She would not let the familiar taste of the wine take away the strength she would need to continue pressing forward. She said her own toast in her mind. A toast to Eire and

Ruairi and to the adventures they would have because she would find a way to save them.

The sound of cutlery clanging against plates filled her ears and her appetite slowly returned. She savored each bite of the meal.

"Where do you hail from?" Laisren's voice spoke up, calling Aisla from her thoughts.

"Samhradh," Fenian spoke before she could. "We're from Cluain, a small city right outside of Omra."

Aisla mentally added that to the many lies she was having to keep up with.

"What brings you this way?"

"We were visiting family in Briongloid," he replied, and she felt as though she had heard it countless times before then.

She took another drink from her goblet as she sat between the two men. The wine was sweet and crisp with floral notes in it and it tasted better than any of the wines she and Eire had shared.

"Briongloid is a wonderful realm," Laisren said. "Much different from Samhradh, though, I would imagine."

"Could not be more different," Fenian grunted.

Aisla finished half of her plate and her entire goblet of wine while the two males continued to engage in small talk about the different realms, the weather, and creatures encountered along the way. She was thankful when Fenian did not bring up the barghest attack that had brought them together and was responsible for the bandage around her arm. The throbbing that never seemed to go away.

Her tongue felt heavy and her mind was fuzzy as everything seemed to become funnier. She wondered when Fenian had grown a sense of humor.

"We've found the seas easier to manage in the—"

Fenian's words were cut off by a loud hiccup that escaped Aisla's mouth and her eyes went wide, but she could not suppress the giggle that followed.

Laisren's eyes glowed with amusement and he glanced over at her now empty goblet.

"Here," he said with a deep chuckle, and he took a vase of the red wine from the other side of him and refilled Aisla's cup nearly all the way to the top. She eagerly picked it up and held it in both hands. "Being stuck with him as a mate, you deserve as much of this as you would like."

"I—we—are not—"

Aisla's cheeks were flaming with embarrassment as she looked back and forth between Fenian and Laisren, searching desperately for the words to correct him.

"We are not mated," Fenian replied with a mild hint of disgust. "Family friends since childhood."

"My mistake," Laisren nodded with a sly grin.

Aisla chugged from her goblet before setting it back down on the table.

"Well, mate or friend or simply traveling companion," Laisren said. "I imagine you could still use it."

"He is quite serious all the time," Aisla spoke, letting loose some of the tension she held in her shoulders. "No fun at all."

"The wine flows, and it becomes gang up on Fenian night, yeah?" Fenian rolled his eyes, but his amusement lingered. Laisren turned from them as someone on his other side called his attention, leaving Aisla and Fenian. Fenian picked up his own cup to drink from. "It's only fair that I join in on the fun, isn't it, Ell?"

Aisla tilted her head when his lips formed the word, *Ell*. She had nearly forgotten that she was Ellora—that no one here really knew her at all.

"I didn't know you knew how to have fun," she teased, and he raised a brow at her.

"You know very little about me."

"Isn't that the truth."

They were leaning closer together now, his gaze unreadable and soft as the presence of him warmed her on the cool spring night.

"What do you want to know?" Fenian asked in a voice barely above a whisper.

"What makes you the way that you are?"

"Pardon?"

"I mean," she paused, trying to find the words to ask what she wanted to know. "Why are you so cold, so cruel? Why do you act as though the entire world owes you something?"

"A bit of a loaded question, don't you think, Ell?" He said the nickname again, but he didn't sound mad or upset, just dismissive. "Give me something a bit lighter than that. I'll think on that one."

Aisla rolled her eyes, knowing he would never answer it.

"Fine. What is your family like?"

She did not miss the way his face fell. The way he quickly recovered with a fake smile.

"I'm closer to my mother. She is kind and safe with a warmth that draws people in. My father is very different. Tougher. Sometimes it's hard to imagine why my mother ever mated with him."

"He sounds more like my grandmother," Aisla murmured. "I bet they'd get along great."

"Well, you have not met my father."

"Fair enough," Aisla said. They both drank from their goblets once again. She knew well that she had passed the point of tipsy and knew that Fenian could not be far behind.

"And yours?" Fenian asked, and Aisla almost forgot the question.

"It's just me and my grandmother," she said.

Not a lie.

She brought up her parents as little as possible. Their passing was still a gaping wound that she was not sure would ever heal.

"What do you miss most about home?" she asked, changing the

subject before the curiosity swirling in the depths of his amber eyes could come to fruition.

"I miss the salty air, I think," he said, and a knot formed in Aisla's throat. "And also my best friend. I miss him."

Aisla realized she could say the same things. She could wish for nothing more than the scent of the coast and Ruairi and Eire at her side. But even with the wine coursing through her, she knew she could not say these things.

Aisla felt Fenian's gaze on her as he looked at her expectantly.

"I'd say that I miss—"

She was saved from having to lie when loud music started to play from a table on the other side of the room. A cheery folk tune erupted from several villagers who both stood on and sat around the table, playing various instruments. A woman belted an old song that told the tale of a boy who happened upon the tree of life only to have a conversation with its inhabitant, Taistealai, the four-tailed squirrel that served as messenger between the worldly and otherly realms.

Here we sing the tale of
   Our young elf, brave and bold,
   With a heart of pure gold.
   Who journeyed to Crann Na Beatha.

O, Crann Na Beatha, the home
   Of the norns who weave fate
   By threads between the realms' gate
   Golden and bonding to passing on.

Our young elf, brave and bold,

Journeyed far and through the tides,
Over mountains tall and rivers wide,
Until he was met with eyes of green.

O, Crann Na Beatha, the home
  Of the norns who weave fate
  By threads between the realms' gate
  Golden and bonding searc.

Our young elf, brave and bold,
  Stepped forward without fear
  For Taistealai was here.
  Messenger of the gods and mortals.

O, Crann Na Beatha, the home
  Of the norns who weave fate
  By threads between the realms' gate
  Golden and bonding of worlds.

Our young elf, brave and bold,
  Spoke with the creature into the night,
  that the words might be worth his plight.
  In his voice and tales of awe and woe,

Our young elf, brave and bold,
  Found a friend in the squirrel,
  Whom named him dragon,
  To change the world.

. . .

O, Crann Na Beatha, the home
Of the norns who weave fate
By threads between the realms' gate
Golden and bonding to await.

The feeling had shifted, and everyone hummed and sang and shouted the words to the song.

Aisla leaned in, closing her eyes as the music flooded through her veins, entwining and caressing her restless esos. Something about it reminded her of Caillte. She had never heard the song before, but the community, the longing—there was home to be found there.

She opened her eyes slowly as they began the next ballad and noticed Fenian's gaze on her.

"What are you looking at?" She asked.

"Just you," he breathed, and Aisla felt her stomach turn and her cheeks redden.

Aisla smiled but rolled her eyes and shifted towards the musicians. She tipped her head back as she swayed gently with the music, letting herself live for the first time in what felt like a very long time.

The next tune was upbeat as it told the story of the first wyvern rider, and everyone in the room clapped along, standing if they were not already. Aisla joined in and noticed Laisren eyed her with a grin of approval. The place was euphoric, and Aisla had never felt such joy in a single space. Even Fenian stood, clapping along, and swaying ever so slightly.

For once, his eyebrows were not scrunched together, and his lips were not turned into a frown.

"I like it better this way," Fenian murmured, leaning in towards her, his breath warming her neck.

"What do you mean?"

"When you don't look as though you desire to end my life."

"Well," Aisla said around her foggy brain. "You're not doing anything that makes me want to pass you on. Right now, at least."

Fenian tipped his head back with a deep laugh, and Aisla realized it was the first she had ever heard the sound. She found herself laughing along with him, unable to suppress it.

The crowd slowly dispersed, but the musicians did not stop. A few of them had switched out over the course of the night. Everyone was joyful through every moment. Elves glided about the room, holding their partners' waists, while humans jumped on the tables, and dwarves stomped their feet to the beat of each new ballad. Everyone stood and clapped, and the wine never stopped flowing.

Aisla stayed until her legs could hardly hold her up, and her eyes drooped shut.

"Ready to go?" Fenian asked as he placed a gentle hand on her elbow to get her attention.

A shudder raced down her spine at his touch, and she simply nodded in response. She allowed him to guide her between tables and drunken people as they finally reached open air again and both took a deep breath.

She clung to his arm on the short walk back to their puball, and as she looked up and saw it sitting along the outskirts of the village, it hit her. *Their* puball.

She faced Fenian with a raised brow and concern clouding her yellow-green eyes.

"I am *not* sleeping on the floor," he growled, as if reading her mind, already shaking his head. "Nope, but you are more than welcome."

Aisla pressed her lips in a tight line, as she genuinely considered that option.

"Ell, I won't bother you. We can sleep as close to our own edges of the bed as possible," Fenian reassured, annoyance in his voice. "Besides, you've been drinking. Sleep will find you as soon as you hit the mattress anyway."

"*We've* been drinking," she corrected.

"Yes, we have. So, surely we'll both be sound asleep before either of us finds the other's presence too unbearable."

Aisla let out a sigh of defeat, as she crawled in after him, pushing through the canvas flaps.

She moved around him to climb under the heavy quilt, easing her body as far to the edge of the bed as she could, exhaustion hitting her like an ocean wave.

She looked over at Fenian and her eyes widened at his audacity as he pulled his shirt over his head. Maybe it wasn't his audacity. Maybe it was the way his torso rippled with muscles that threatened danger. His back was lean, and his arms looked strong enough to take on a barghest without a blade. Just one though, not an entire pack.

"Can I help you?" Fenian said, smirking as he threw his shirt to the ground and got into the bed. The air grew warmer when he slid beneath the covers.

"You—you're going to sleep like *that*?" her voice betrayed her with a crack.

"Is there a problem if I am?" Before Aisla could even reply, he opened his mouth to speak again. "I thought about your question."

He shifted on his side to face her, and Aisla adjusted her position to mimic his, suddenly intrigued. She raised an eyebrow, silently asking him to continue.

"I think fear turned me cold, and as you say, cruel," he spoke softly, and Aisla's insides twisted with guilt at her own words—even though they were deserved. "I fear I do not know enough to do what is expected of me. And if I don't do what is expected of me, I-I know how greatly it would disappoint my father."

His eyes were genuine for once, and Aisla knew he was only saying these things because of the alcohol that laced his breath. She knew this would never happen sober, and she paused a moment to sit in this rare vulnerability as they held each other's gaze.

"I think sometimes we just have to learn to live with what we can come to terms with on our own," she whispered back. "Sometimes, we cannot spend our lives in the eyes of others."

Fenian nodded. "Your turn," he said. "What turned a young female from Fomhar into a soon-to-be laoch who is savage enough to fell the snarling creatures of the woods?"

"My own fear," she replied with a small, sad smile. "I fear I am not enough. Not enough to be what they need, and I don't think I can ever be."

She had felt it for a long time, but had not voiced her fears before. Aisla was afraid of failing. She was afraid not only of failing Ruairi and Eire, but failing Eilean. Aisla feared failing her people and the wyverns—failing a continent that had waited generations for her arrival. The thought made her sick to her stomach and tears stung her eyes. She fought to keep them at bay, but in a matter of moments, they fell.

Slowly and silently.

Fenian's gaze grew soft, and the intensity of it was almost too much to bear.

He reached out a hand, and Aisla did not flinch away from his touch as he wiped the tears from her cheeks. His eyes searched hers, saying more words than he'd ever speak aloud.

"Ellora, you are enough," he murmured. He tucked her hair behind her ear with a softness that sent electricity through her bones. "Do not let anyone tell you otherwise."

She leaned into his scent of oak wood and ocean air that almost smelled like home.

27

AISLA

Her eyes fluttered open to the sunlight filtering in through the canvas of the puball.

Aisla's head pounded. She squinted, pulling herself into a sitting position when she noticed the empty spot on the bed beside her.

A panic rose in her chest at his absence, at this feeling of abandonment. She laid a hand on the spot where he slept and noted how it was still warm. He had not been gone for long.

Loneliness hit her. It was a loneliness that had been growing since Eire fell from her wyvern and when Ruairi ran from her side to confront the strangers in the woods. That loneliness continued to grow as that voice that had once spoken to her in the rain under the branches of an oak tree had fallen silent. And while she detested Fenian Daro, despite whatever truce had fallen upon them last night, the lack of his presence reopened the wound of her loneliness.

She took a deep breath, trying to ignore the throbbing in her head, and lowered her body over the edge of the bed despite the way it intensified the pain. She looked under the bed and a wave of relief washed over her when she noticed his bag was still there. He had not left her.

She leaned her head against the headboard, hoping to quell the nausea and dizziness.

Aisla allowed her muscles to relax and brushed her overreaction off as the result of waking up in a completely foreign place after a drunken night. Despite those moments of vulnerability and connection, Aisla needed to force more distance between herself and Fenian. Her stomach twisted in a guilty knot, which she swallowed down with some effort. She tried not to think of his amber gaze on her or the way his fingers brushed the tears from her cheeks. Aisla pushed away the words they had shared and how she finally fell asleep in his arms. She could still feel them around her, as though he was a ghost while still alive. She tried to forget the way they traded fears like wares at a market.

She would not allow herself to stay there. The guilt, the regret, the confusion—she did not need any of that right now. She pulled herself to her feet and gathered her things to go to the communal washroom again, hoping to wash off some of the grime from the previous night, along with the pulsing in her skull. She winced at the pain as she slipped out of the puball.

Aisla knew their agreement had been to leave as early as possible, but figured if Fenian could disappear, then she ought to have time for her own needs as well. Besides, she did not know how far they had left to travel to Castle Eagla and when she'd next be able to access a bath.

She could not help but wonder what Eire would say about her walk of shame as she scurried past puballs and villagers who eyed her curiously while she clutched her clothes in her arms. But thinking of Eire made her think of Ruairi, whom she had been avoiding thinking about. Guilt resurfaced at the thought of him, which only fueled her motivation to clean up quickly and resume their journey again.

She looked in a puddle that she passed and noted how her light brown hair was matted and dark circles lined her eyes. On top of that, the potent scent of red wine lingered on her breath and in her hair, and on her clothes in a way that made her want to vomit.

"Fancy seeing you here," a familiar voice purred, and Aisla looked up to meet deep, amber eyes.

Fenian was walking away from the washroom and towards her. He was shirtless, and his brown skin glistened in the morning sun, still dewy. Aisla scowled at him and felt her heartbeat quicken.

"If only you had woken earlier, we could have saved water and some time," he said with a devilish smirk.

Aisla fought the urge to spit in his direction. But once the initial repulsion of his words faded, she found herself smiling with relief that they could fall back into their mutual annoyance and banter without any tangible awkwardness or further lingering vulnerability with each other. It was a comfort in its own way.

"You are actually vile," she said, shaking her head. "I'd sooner pass myself on than take part in whatever it is you might be referencing."

"It was only a joke, *banphrionsa*," he said as he brushed past her, his arm grazing her elbow. "Don't flatter yourself."

Aisla clenched her teeth, struggling to find a comeback. She swore he chuckled as he walked away.

Such a pompous ass, she thought to herself.

Aisla and Fenian packed quickly and reunited with Eolas, who had spent the night in a stable with the village horses. Even with each of them taking the time to bathe in the morning, they were ready to go not long after sunrise. The sun was just over the tree line, having chased away Talam's dual moons.

"Ellora!" Laisren's deep voice boomed from behind them.

She turned with a smile as he approached with several of the other villagers that she recognized from dinner. Sean was among them, carrying a pack at his side.

"The Spiorad people would like to give you this as you continue your journey south," Laisren said once they had caught up to them. His brown eyes were bright and filled with warmth as Aisla reached out to take the package from Sean. "It's not much, but we should like to make your journey easier if we are able."

"Thank you," Aisla said for the both of them. "We appreciate your thoughtfulness."

"We packed it with extra food and some herbs for that wound on your arm."

Aisla instinctively reached for the arm, still wrapped in a bandage as he mentioned it. No one had mentioned it during their time here, but she supposed they would have to be blind to miss it.

"And an extra flask of water and one of wine." Laisren finished with a playful, knowing wink, but the urge to vomit returned when Aisla thought of the sweet red liquid. She forced the feeling down and shared a genuine smile with Laisren as they accepted the pack.

"We are grateful for your gesture of kindness," Fenian's voice spoke up behind her.

"Again, thank you," Aisla added. "We are in your debt, and thankful for the hospitality shown to us here."

Aisla felt Fenian's eyes boring a hole in her back when she said the words, but she ignored him. For all they knew, they could have actually been killed by the olc spirits roaming the woods. Although, even as she thought about it, the knot on her head throbbed as it mingled with the aftermath of her drunken night.

Laisren beamed with pride and he reached around Aisla to offer Fenian a hand, which he shook, then repeated the gesture to Aisla.

Warmth radiated from him, and he gripped her hand with a comforting force.

She looked into his eyes, really looked at him, and there was something there that she could not quite read. His brows knit slightly and his lips parted as his expression changed to one of realization.

"Until the norns cross our golden threads once again, *Gheall*," he spoke the last word in a whisper that touched her ears and her ears alone.

The whispered word danced through her hair and dragged her esos to the surface, even as her heart anxiously pounded in her chest.

She recognized the term of old for *promised*. Her throat tightened and words escaped her. All she could think to do was nod.

He knows, she thought, *he knows what I am. Who I am.*

She also knew with a confidence deep in her heart that Laisren didn't have bad intentions, that he even harbored sympathy when it came to the Eilean people. But she had gotten too far, sacrificed too much already, to take any chances. And she would not lose her alias now.

Aisla was suddenly thankful and relieved they were leaving this place behind. No matter what comfort danced in the tips of Laisren's fingers and laced his words in prayers to silent gods, it was past time for Aisla to make her exit. She didn't even know what she could have done to give herself away. She wracked her brain for any missteps or errors on her part.

Aisla nodded again, and a look that mingled sorrow with understanding crossed his face. Aisla fought to wipe any reaction, any of the confusion, awe, fear, as she turned on her heel, heart thumping so loudly she could hear it. Her esos roared to life, pounding against the inside of her skin in the same beat. A rhythm flooded her ears, and she offered a tight smile to Fenian and he made to leave as well.

Fenian's face did not reveal any sign that he had heard any of what Laisren said, and Aisla was thankful for that as she worked to find her voice again and slow her racing heart.

"Let's get out of here," Fenian grumbled, taking Eolas's reins to lead them out of the village where so much had changed.

"I agree," Aisla said softly, although she was sure she was eager to leave for entirely different reasons.

28

WEYLIN

They mounted Eolas, and Weylin's hands held the reins with his arms wrapped around Ellora's waist. The overwhelming scent of her, the traces of iris and sea breeze that clung to her body, consumed him as her hair blew into his face, and he found himself wishing she would have braided it as she usually did. He was thankful, at least, that she did not stink of the red wine from the previous night.

He winced at the thought.

The memory of her closed eyes and alcohol-flushed cheeks as she tilted her chin to the moons. The steady sway of her hips that followed the rhythm of the folk tunes. Her soft hums. The way she seemed to glow from the inside out with a fire that only existed in her yellow-green eyes. She was alive last night.

Ellora was feral, yes, but she was beautiful, too.

Lovely in her own way, with her soft freckles, the stag antler necklace, and sharp edges that made her dangerous to grow close to. Weylin wondered if she was aware of the danger that danced through her, the intimidation her gaze alone could wield. He wondered what esos hid within her veins. He wondered if she yearned for even just a glimpse of it as he did—if she would kill for the renewal of the ash trees on this continent as he would.

He had felt it when he touched her that night.

As he had brushed the tears falling down her cheeks, he felt a power thrumming within her. It was a power that drew him in when he knew it would push others away. That power was the reason he could not let the female out of his sight until he figured out what she was hiding.

She had opened up last night. There was so much she wasn't telling him, and it made him fear her, but it made him pity her, too. He could see that monstrous fear lurking behind her eyes.

She slept so peacefully. And when he had woken up before the sun had risen, her face held a calm that he could almost feel himself falling into. It was a temptation to put his own shields to rest, but he would not. He had already gotten too close and allowed himself to get too comfortable. He had come to this realization and pushed her from him while she slept and removed himself from the puball.

He had to think of Rania and the promises he must keep. A guilt knotted within him and he remembered the purpose of this journey. The cloud-white hair and piercing blue eyes of his betrothed flashed in his mind, and he realized he'd allowed duty to slip from his mind.

He made a vow to himself to redraw the lines. Make it clear in every conversation and every action that they were not friends. He would dump her at the laoch training camps, where he could trust she would be under careful watch, at the earliest opportunity. He would return to Castle Eagla, and Ellora Morlee would never again cross his mind.

If she somehow became a laoch, and if she were ever assigned anywhere near him, he would not so much as cast a glance in her direction.

He took a deep breath and prepared for the last leg of their journey.

"Are you aware that you hand out debts like candies?" Weylin spoke up after a time of silence and they were well outside the Spiorad village.

"What is that supposed to mean?" she quipped.

"Well," he started. "You have owed me since the moment we met, in case you had forgotten. And now, you tell strangers that you have known for no more than a sunrise that you are in their debt? You clearly don't know as much of this world as you claim to."

He emphasized his words with a *tsk*, and he grinned as he felt her tense in front of him.

"They were more than hospitable towards us," she replied, defensiveness lacing her tone. "They fed us, housed us, and even sent us on our way with supplies to finish our journey out. I don't know about you, but I was raised with manners that would say I am, in fact, in their debt."

"So what? A few free goblets of wine can convince you to conveniently forget the methods used to get us to accept their *more than hospitable accommodations*? They owe me a debt for not passing on the man who struck my head while I was unarmed."

"Now, that's a bit excessive, don't you think?"

Weylin wanted to snap that she did not know who he was. Did not know the importance of the man that shared her bed last night and did not know the extent of the crime the Spiorad male had committed when he knocked out the Udar Apparent.

But he could not say those things.

"Not where I'm from," Weylin said.

Close enough to the truth.

Ellora did not reply, but Weylin could practically hear her eyes roll. She tended to do that a lot.

They carried on in silence, yet again, as they grew ever closer to the border between Briongloid and Samhradh, an anxious energy fluttered through his veins. He was sure that his father had already heard the news of his betrothal, and he trusted Rania to be true to her word when she said her family would not spread news of the bad omen that followed.

Weylin himself was not a superstitious man.

He had long stopped believing in the gods that had ripped esos from the world and denied him the power he could almost taste inside his own blood. He cared not for them and knew they cared not for him. The doves had been a coincidence. No more. No less.

He wondered when his father and Brendan Dorcas would arrange for his wedding. Weylin knew both families would push for an extravagance and grandeur that would require moons of planning that Weylin could do without. He did not know Rania well enough to know if she was the sort of female who would find joy in such things. He knew very little about his mate-to-be. Sometimes a mating of convenience was more suitable than a mating derived from emotions. His father had said so, many times in fact, and each time he did, Weylin watched the flicker of hurt that crossed his mother's gaze. Even *searc*, true mates, chosen by the norns long before their births, were not always met in love.

Weylin thought his mother would enjoy the planning of his wedding. She would throw herself into it, especially as he was her only child. She would busy herself with all the mundane tasks that go into such things, and it would be nice to see her active again, something to pour her energy into that she actually enjoyed. Weylin's mother was a powerful female, and no one would ever dare say otherwise, but she was not the same female she had always been. She had withered into a ghost of herself, and Weylin only sometimes caught glimpses of the mother who had raised him as a young child. She wore the fake smile of a politician, and sometimes when she spoke, it felt like she was not there all the way. There were pieces of her that were missing that could not be reclaimed. Weylin often made efforts to spend time with her when he was home, to check in on her as he knew his father never cared to.

Weylin looked over Ellora's head as he escaped from his own

tunnel of thoughts and came back to the present. He recognized the tall line of pine trees that served as a border between the two realms, and he held his head a little higher.

"That's the beginning of Samhradh's territory," Weylin spoke up and felt Ellora startle in front of him at the sound of his voice. "Right on the other side of that tree line."

"That's it?" Ellora asked quickly, and he picked up on the nervousness lacing her voice. "Right there?"

"Indeed."

"I did not realize how close Spiorad was to the border."

"I would say we are three sunrises away from Castle Eagla now. I'll take you as far as the laoch training camps, then I'm off to my own city, and rid of you," Weylin said, as they had never formally discussed how far they would go together.

Even though he had never really given her a choice in the matter.

"Trust me," she growled. "I'm just as ready to rid myself of your company. I never wanted to be stuck with you in the first place. You brought this on yourself."

"Oh, come on, Ell. You would have been a barghest's next meal had I not stepped in. Or maybe you would've been passed on by whatever olc spirits lurk in the forests around your favorite villagers. You could have never made it this far. I think you owe me a thank you, at the very least."

"I was *fine* before you came along. I've survived my entire life without you, and am more skilled than you could ever be. I'll be damned if—"

Weylin snorted.

"You have never seen me when I am trying, *banphrionsa*," he said. "And if you had, I think you'd be more careful of the words you allow your tongue to set loose."

"I could say the same to you," she snarled, tilting her head enough to glare at him from the corner of her eye.

Anger blossomed in Weylin's chest.

Her audacity and complete lack of awareness never failed to stir it within him. He wanted to draw blades with her and have it out, and a part of him craved the look on her face if she ever found out she traveled all this way with the Udar Apparent.

But that was an expression he was afraid he would never have the pleasure of seeing.

"Maybe I should have stood by and watched then," Weylin said in a calm tone he knew would aggravate her more than any angered voice ever would. The calmness would mean she had not gotten the best of him, but as soon as he let his frustration show to her, she would know that she had caused it and she would feel she had won something. He could not have that. "That day I first found you, maybe I should have watched as the great Ellora Morlee felled the final two barghests that sought to have her for a meal," Weylin continued. He leaned forward, close enough that his lips were nearly brushing her ear. "Or rather, watched as they tore the flesh from your bones and listened as your final cry was torn from your lips."

"*I. Hate. You.*" Ellora hissed as she moved to shove Weylin away from her. "Stop this thing. I want off. I want off *now!*"

Weylin smirked to himself as a feeling of victory cooled his rising irritation. He tightened his arms around her waist, making it very clear that he was ignoring her request, as he held onto the reins and prodded Eolas forward.

"Eolas is no *thing,* and your implications quite offend her. Besides, you hardly know me well enough to truly *hate* me," Weylin said. "Although, I am sure if you did, it would only confirm those feelings. And if it did not, then I would clearly be doing something wrong."

"So you want me to hate you?" she seethed, rage still lacing her tone.

Weylin noted the way she was so much worse at concealing her emotions than he was. Anything and everything that she was feeling could be read from the way she held herself in front of him. He could hear it in every word that she spoke and sigh that she made. And he knew that if he were facing her, he would be able to detect it in every flicker of the flames in her yellow-green eyes.

"I only truly care for the opinions of those worthy of a second thought. You, on the other hand, are a nobody from nowhere desperately throwing herself—unprepared might I add—into a life that you know *nothing* about, in hopes of becoming somebody in Samhradh. So, Ell, I feel no obligation to make you do anything but hate me."

His words hit exactly how he intended them to. The insults struck their mark, and he eagerly awaited her next words, wondering how she would choose to fire back at him.

"And who are you, *Fenian Daro*?" she asked after a moment of silence and several deep, shaky breaths. He felt each one she took, refusing to loosen his grip.

Weylin paused, as he had forgotten for a moment that he was meant to be posing as a nobody from a small town in Samhradh. He had let his words get ahead of him, and she had found the loophole through his insults.

In this world, this one he had created temporarily, he was as much of a nobody as she was.

"I have long accepted the life of a nobody," Weylin replied as the words came to him, almost naturally. "I would suggest you do the same."

Ellora responded with a deafening silence.

She did not utter a single word for the rest of the day. They continued their journey, and Weylin refused to be the first to break. Neither one of them even broke to suggest they stop for lunch, so Weylin continued on with a hungry stomach and reached inside his bag to grab crackers to tide him over until they stopped for the night.

In the silence, Weylin wondered what the future had in store for

Ellora Morlee. He wondered where her journey as a laoch would take her, and what sort of tasks she would be assigned to. He wondered where this grit and stubbornness would take her in this world.

He wondered if their threads were meant to one day cross again. He thought then that he did not know why he insisted on traveling with her this long.

He did not enjoy her company—he was sure of that much. Or at least he thought he was. Then he remembered the way she was last night. The way they both removed the armor the outside world had placed upon them, and when their fears had been reduced to whispers beneath the canvas of a puball. He did not hate her then, and he knew even then that he should.

There was a feeling he could not explain when he was in her presence—a loathing that felt nearly instinctual. At the same time, a part of him did not know how he would let her go. He felt drawn to her like a rope was strung between them, and that was why he had not allowed her to go her own way.

He could not come to terms with the idea of never seeing her again, and he knew the moment they separated that would be the case.

29

RUAIRI

Ruairi Vilulf had learned to count the sunrises spent in his cell by the number of times they fed his breakfast tray through the small metal flap at the bottom of the large wooden door.

The sound of the metal clanking against the cement floor as they shoved it through interrupted his thoughts of solitude like a crack of lighting on a quiet night.

His fourth breakfast had just arrived. Dry wheat toast, an apple, and runny eggs. Ruairi had neglected to eat his first two days' worth of meals. He had refused what appeared there until his hunger was a roaring thing within him. It was a ferocious beast that could have become his demise, but Ruari was not ready to pass on.

The laochs had withdrawn the full plates and replaced them with new plates for lunch and dinner, like clockwork. It was wordless and repeating over and over, and it was the same when he emptied the plates as well. It was as maddening as it was comforting to have the consistency.

His cell was so much smaller than his baile back home. There was a small wooden bed with a thin mattress and an old, worn quilt with two flat pillows. A bucket was left in the corner, meant for him to relieve himself. There was a tub for washing in the other corner, and he was thankful for the fresh cup of water brought in with each of his meals.

No one had said a word to him, or even acknowledged that he still existed within the castle walls.

This was the start of his fourth day with no contact with another being. There had been no acknowledgement that he existed, no sunlight, and no fresh air. Ruairi Vilulf was losing his mind, even in the short time. Four days out there was no time at all, but four days in here felt like a lifetime.

A lifetime of waiting for his doom.

Ruairi wondered if a word would ever again leave his lips. He had long accepted that it most likely would not. He had sworn his silence until he was either free or until his gaze met Aisla's.

He missed her with the pain of an aching chest wound that never closed, never healed, never stopped reminding him of his existence with sharp flashes of pain. He missed her with a yearning that had turned into something viscerally painful. They had been apart before, for longer times than this. It was the idea that *he* had brought her here. He had delivered her to the open hands of their enemy, and he was so afraid. He could only hope with every bit of will that she had made it home. That she was back in Caillte.

He wished he could see the world as she would one day mold it. He wished he could see her one last time.

But these were wishes he could no longer torture himself with.

There were many moments when he was so tempted to summon his esos, summon the last bit of it running through his veins, and break down the door to his cell. The thought crossed his mind relentlessly, like an itch that could not be satisfied. But he knew by using esos in a realm where he had yet to see a single ash tree, he would raise many more suspicions. And they would most likely execute him immediately, and that was not a risk he was willing to take. If there was any hope of seeing her again, of losing himself to her yellow-green gaze one last time, that could only happen if he was alive.

His mind wandered to her often, to the way her lips felt on his and the gentle touch of her fingers on his bare skin. He thought of her scent, her smile, and the way she said his name. Her mind and the brilliant way she saw the world, never failing to look for the best in everyone around her. How she found joy in the plants between pressed pages on her nightstand. He would never again take her for granted, and his only regret in all of this brief life was not telling her how he felt sooner. He grieved for all the moments he had missed out on, all the memories they could have shared.

He was thankful that he knew all that he had to live for, and all they had yet to experience.

Eire would surely have a lot to say about it all. And he knew beyond a doubt that her first words about it would be, "*I told you so.*" Eire had been making sly jokes about Ruairi and Aisla getting together for as long as he could recall. He had always wondered how she could see it so clearly, while Aisla never could. He missed Eire and knew if he could see her again, he would be able to release the fear for her well-being that he had been holding on to since they first saw her in the infirmary. But he did not yearn for their reunion the same way that he did for Aisla.

Eire had always been the perfect balance to their friendship. Aisla was headstrong, protective, and fierce, whereas Eire was outgoing, peaceful, and always so filled with joy. Ruairi found himself right in the middle of the two. It was easy to fall into the comfort of the friendship they shared.

It killed him to linger on that image of Eire. Her pale blue eyes alight with joy and hope. The one he had known for nearly his entire life. It was too stark and eerie a contrast to the female he and Aisla had last seen in the infirmary.

Ruairi shook his head, fighting to free his mind from the image that sunk its claws into him like a bird of prey. He stared up at the blank wall, as he often did. His hope was a small spark that flickered out with every tray shoved through. Every moment longer that held a silence and emptiness within it and consumed him like a wild sea.

His eyes fluttered shut, and he tried to ease his mind and allow yet another restless night of sleep to overcome him.

Until a knock sounded at his door.

A knock that made his throat dry up.

A knock that made his heart race. Palms sweat.

A knock that he thought he had imagined.

Until the sound came again.

And Ruairi knew it was real.

30

AISLA

Aisla's eyes adjusted to the dark of the midnight woods, dimly lit by the moons above her.

She walked with a caution she had practiced, while she approached a figure with a feminine build and long black curls. Her head was tilted back, looking to the night sky above. Aisla's heart beat faster and faster as she recognized the beautiful, lilting laugh. She'd known that laugh for as long as she could remember. It was music in her ears and a grin spread across her lips.

"Eire," Aisla released a slow breath when she recognized her best friend standing before her.

She didn't care that she was in Iomlan. She didn't care about anything at all as she picked up her pace, eager to close the distance between them. Her feet carried her with no second thought. Running to Eire was as natural as breathing.

Aisla gently grabbed her arm, turning Eire to face her, but it was not Eire's face that she saw. Not as it was meant to be.

Eire's brilliant blue eyes, so full of life, were now pale and milky. Her irises had disappeared into the white of her eyes and the only color that remained was the muted gray where her pupils should be. Her tawny skin was cracked like dry earth, dark lines running along her skin and joining up with others to form gaping holes into her flesh, her skin peeling away to reveal her insides. The smell of rot and death and decay filled Aisla's nostrils.

It all made her want to run. But she could not do that to Eire, she could not turn away.

Worst of all, half of Eire's once beautiful face had melted. The missing flesh exposed her gray and missing teeth and the white of her jawbone. The sight was so horrific, Aisla grew nauseous, and combining it with the stench radiating through the woods, Aisla had to fight the urge to vomit. Her mind spun, her stomach twisted, and her throat burned with an agony she could not put into words.

Aisla clenched her fists and forced herself to hold Eire's gaze. But there was nothing to hold. Her eyes were empty and unseeing as they gazed at Aisla, seeming to look through her, as if she was not there at all. Aisla's heart ruptured. Her breaths grew heavy and painful. Her eyes burned with tears that she refused to let fall.

"Eire," Aisla said again when she found her voice. She whispered it as though saying her name could summon back her best friend how she had remembered her. "Eire, please." Aisla could barely push the words from her lips. It was an effort to push them out around her constricted throat as every piece of her threatened to break.

The terrifying *thing* before her was a creature straight out of nightmares that resembled Eire just enough to break Aisla's heart. Aisla itched to grab the dagger in her waistband. But she couldn't do it—she could never draw it on Eire.

Aisla walked backwards, stumbling, even though each step between her and Eire wounded her soul like the stab of a knife would wound her flesh. Each step away was a betrayal to her best friend, and each step left wounds that would never heal. The creature advanced. Slowly, but closer all the same.

A shiver crawled down Aisla's spine and the hairs all along her arms stood on end. The urge to grab *Oidhe* ever-present and growing harder to resist as her heartbeat quickened.

Hysteria blossomed inside Aisla's chest. There was no way out of this because she would not hurt her. *She would not.*

You did this. The voice that was so clearly Eire's hissed at her.

Despite all the things that had changed, contorted, and rotted away, her voice was crystal clear as it ran through Aisla's ears, rattling through her skull.

You made me into this.

"I—I didn't," Aisla stuttered as tears burned her eyes. "I swear I didn't."

Your denial only makes it hurt worse, Aisla, the creature cried out and lunged for Aisla, but Aisla threw her body out of the way just in time. *You need to face this—face* me! *It is all your fault!*

Her last words came as a sharp cry, piercing through the winds of the night, and the creature lunged again.

Aisla leapt away again, flinging her hands out in protection as she winced, but green flames erupted from her. Esos she could not control and had not wished to wield. Aisla's stomach lurched at the sight of the flickering flames she had created, her eyes widening in disbelief.

"No, no, no," Aisla mumbled, half to herself, and half to the gods above that had cursed her with such powers and such lack of control.

The creature screamed as it caught fire. It continued to advance, even as the flames melted the already rotting skin from its bones. Aisla whirled and ran like a traitor, a coward, because she did not know what else to do.

The smell of burning hair mingled with the stench of rotting flesh. Aisla fought to hold herself together while silent tears streamed down her cheeks. Panic consumed her like the ocean tide.

And she could not escape as her feet carried her onwards, towards the sound of a rushing river.

The pounding in her ears drowned out the sound of her own thrumming heartbeat. She thought if she could get Eire to follow her there, the water could put out the fire raging across rotting skin. She could save Eire, and then she could figure out what to do next.

With renewed purpose, Aisla sprinted with all the energy she could muster. She flew over patches of green grass and passed trees that were a blur in her peripheral vision. Heavy footsteps closed the distance between them just as the rushing river came into view.

Aisla took a deep breath and leapt into the water without another thought or a glance backwards. The cold water closed over her head, instantly dragging her to the silty bottom. She kicked and used her arms to pull herself through the water, opening her eyes to find the surface once again.

Aisla inhaled great gasping breaths when she reached the surface. She let the breaths shudder through her body as she treaded water in a circle, and the current continued to pull her downstream. Her eyes darted around, desperate to find the being she had led here. She couldn't spot her, not even along the bank where she had leapt from. Which meant she had to be in the river somewhere.

Eire had made it to the water. The fire was out. That much, Aisla was sure of. She made one more circle, straining to see anything above the rippling current of the river, before diving back under the water, keeping her eyes open to look for her beneath the surface.

Feel, but still your heart. Think, but ease your mind. Endure, but find your peace.

Aisla clung to the words like a lifeline as she pushed herself through the water, looking for any sign of Eire.

With no luck, Aisla came up for air, taking in as many breaths as she could before diving back down again, frantically searching.

She felt like she was drowning.

Water flooded her eyes. Her nose. Her ears. Her soggy clothes weighed her down. Her lungs filled. Defeat hit her, dragging her under.

She could not give up. Not while Eire was still there.

She pushed away the tears. The sobs that threatened to break and turn her over to the tides. She continued to swim, kicking her feet madly as her arms pulled through the water, determination battling the defeat within her.

She finally saw a figure up ahead, bobbing along with the waves. Weightless.

Relief flooded her. She surged forward, fighting to make her way to Eire as quickly as she could.

She watched as Eire was pulled beneath the surface, just when she was about to reach her. Aisla dove in after her, eyes wide open, searching the murky depths for her friend.

Aisla's heart caught in her throat and her insides dropped when she got close enough to the body to discover it was not Eire at all.

No, the wide-open green eyes that stared right through her were not Eire's.

Ruairi's body bobbed beneath the surface, lifeless.

A silent scream parted Aisla's lips as her arms and legs worked to push her forward. Push her towards him.

Aisla noted the scars that lined his arms and bare chest. The long ones that mirrored a whip's lash, and the short, deep ones where his body had been marred by a blade. Bruises coated his arms and his once beautiful face.

Aisla felt the remaining pieces of her fracturing—fracturing beyond repair as she reached out and took his hand.

His cold. Lifeless. Hand.

He did not react.

He was dead. Ruairi was dead.

Aisla could not breathe. Could not feel as a deep, guttural cry of pain sounded from beneath the surface of the roaring river.

Aisla gave up. The water flooded into her lungs.

Filling them until she choked on a final breath.

31

WEYLIN

Weylin was awoken by the sound of a light rain that rushed down the sides of the tent that he and Ellora shared.

He sighed at the interruption of his sleep. It was still dark outside of the tent, likely sometime in the middle of the night. He lay there a moment and remembered the night before and how different it had been. How cold it felt now that Ellora had given him nothing but her silence after their spat atop Eolas.

He rolled onto his side to face where Ellora had set up her bedroll for the night, as far away from him as possible within the confines of the tent.

His heart dropped as he jolted up with the realization her bedroll was empty. Her blanket was rumpled up in such a way that indicated she had left suddenly, but her pack still sat in the corner behind her bedroll. And he knew she would not have left it entirely.

A cold swept over the tent. An eerie feeling chilled Weylin's spine, and he saw shadows moving just beyond the tent. He pulled *Uamhan* out from under his pack, unsheathing the blade as he rose. He clutched the sword and exited through the tent flaps.

Shadows darted about the clearing. They danced among the sparse pine trees, sending the light flickering along the earth at Weylin's feet. He narrowed his eyes as he fought to make out any distinction of the figures, but they hid in the dark of the night. He strained his ears for any sounds of *her*, but there was only the deafening silence of the woods that met him. The elusive beings were olc spirits, of that much he was sure. Nothing but ill intent breezed around him as he stepped forward cautiously.

He knew Ellora was in danger. And something propelled him forward with an urgency he could not explain.

Weylin contemplated calling out for her, shouting her name into the endless depths of the dark, but he knew he could not draw any more attention to himself as the olc spirits roamed these woods.

His head whipped around as a sudden voice sounded.

We've drowned her! We've drowned her! We've drowned her!

A chorus of feminine voices sang through the trees. Their voices were high and sharp, cutting through Weylin's ears like a knife blade. His stomach dropped, and he felt a renewed sense of alarm coursing through him as he ran forward, ran towards the sound of rushing water. He began putting the pieces together.

Too late! Too late! Too late!

The voices mocked him. They seemed to follow him along the way but made no move to attack him. He knew the sort of olc spirits they were—the mares. Such cowardly children of Ifreann that they only preyed upon those sleeping, never awake. He did not have time to wonder why they had left him alone and gone for Ellora, as each of his muscles twitched with the urge to get there quicker. His heart was pounding now, and his mind focused on one thing.

He had to find Ellora.

He could not believe the words of the singing spirits. He would not allow himself.

Weylin did not feel any of the raindrops that poured down on him as he continued to run.

She's dead! Dead! Dead!

The words hit him like a ton of rocks.

Every moment dragged into an eternity while Weylin worked to close the distance between himself and the rushing river just ahead of him. By the sound of it, the current was strong. Strong enough to pull a female such as Ellora under and away from the shore.

He smelled her on the iris and sea breeze that wafted through the air, and knew she had been this way. He held onto that scent as his feet carried him forward.

A snarl of rage erupted through him as he finally got to the edge of the riverbank. He strained his eyes, scanning the white caps of the river current in the dark. Nothing but the dual moons of Talam and the brilliant night stars there to guide him.

"Ellora!" He shouted because he could not take it anymore. The anticipation skated across his skin.

He ran along the riverside, following the current, and sheathed *Uamhan* in the baldric on his back.

A dark object floating along the waves caught Weylin's eye, and he ran forward to get a better look. It was Ellora's hair. Her light brown hair, turned dark by water, floated around the limp body that was carried along by the rushing current of the river.

Weylin threw his baldric aside and dove into the freezing waters. Within moments, he was engulfed by the waves. He broke the surface, gasping. He looked for her again. She was face down in the water up ahead of the current. He kicked and pulled. At last, his fingers grazed her skin. He pulled her lifeless body against him and wrapped his arm tightly around her waist.

He fought his fears as he dragged her along. He would not believe the song of the mares, yet.

"We're getting you out of here, Ell," he grunted even though he knew she could not hear him. "You're going to be okay."

Desperation coursed through Weylin as he heaved her body onto the riverbank. He pulled himself up beside her. He did not have time to feel the ache in his bones or the strain of his muscles from fighting the current and carrying her dead weight through it.

He hovered over her and checked her pulse. Fear threatened to consume him. He felt no heartbeat. Her body was still. So still. And he feared he might not see the flicker of her yellow-green eyes again.

He would have to act quickly. Weylin pushed on her chest as they had taught him to during the mandatory laoch training as a medic. He tilted her head back and gently pulled her mouth open before blowing air into her mouth while pinching her nose shut. He repeated the process, though his hope petered out with every moment that she did not breathe.

One. Two. Three. Four.

He counted the beats in his head. He fought to concentrate. Fought to not scream to the skies in defeat.

One. Two. Three. Four.

One. Two. Three. Four.

One. Two. Three. Four.

One. Two. Three. Four.

One. Two. Three. Four.

One. Two. Three. Four.

One. Two. Three. Four.

She coughed as he pushed on her chest and he held her head up. He lifted her body off of the cold forest floor and his heart raced with anticipation. He cradled her in his arms, and relief overcame him in a wave of shock as her eyes fluttered open and everything slowed down around him.

"Ru," Ellora mumbled. And Weylin did not care what that meant. Did not care who she thought she was talking to, because her voice was an answered prayer. "I didn't do it. I didn't mean to."

"I know you didn't, Ell," Weylin murmured, gently rocking her trembling frame. "It's okay."

His grip tightened as a sob escaped her lips.

32

AISLA

Aisla opened her eyes, and it was Ruairi before her. For just a moment.

For that moment, her best friend of so many years held her tightly, his face hovering just above hers. His green eyes were alive. *Alive.* Not drowned beneath the surface of the river. Not bruised and marred by torture she could not begin to imagine.

Relief flooded her. She gasped for air as she clung to him. He was her lifeline as she cleared her lungs of the river water that had passed her on. Because she *had* been dead for a minute, that much she was certain of. She had followed Eire. Beautiful Eire, who was no longer herself.

A shudder racked her spine, and she again looked to Ruairi, allowed him to anchor her there as she trembled in her drenched clothes.

"Ru," she breathed out, her throat tightening around the word. "I didn't do it. I didn't mean to."

"I know you didn't, Ell," Ruairi whispered as he gently rocked her. "It's okay."

His grip tightened and the realization hit. Green became

molten amber, and Ruairi's pale freckled skin was now that beautiful brown. And it was not Ruairi at all that held her, but Fenian.

"Fenian?" She phrased his name as a question that she already knew the answer to.

"Yes, Ell. I'm here."

And she realized that was all she needed to hear.

She clung to him all the same, and the sobs racked her body as she felt the rain drizzling down on them. If only because it was all she had left. She worked to sort nightmares from reality while Fenian gently rocked her back and forth, pulling her closer into his chest as his head rested atop hers. She cried like she had not in so long. Let the tears fall down her cheeks without fear of judgment and her soul felt a little freer despite it all. Her esos had settled for once, a calm buzz rather than a deafening roar.

"What happened?" she asked, gently pushing away from him, prying herself from his grasp.

"It was the mares," he explained. "Olc spirits, children of Ifreann. They prey on anyone sleeping. They can only twist and contort the visions they extract from the minds of their prey, but they cannot inflict physical pain. The mares will bring your worst fears to life. Their victims can lose themselves entirely to the illusions. It seems as though you came close."

"It felt so real."

A shudder traveled down from her head to her toes as she fought to keep the images from her mind. The nightmares that they had brought to life. The fears she faced in the middle of the night. Eire's rotting, flaming body flashed through her vision, and the pressure of Ruairi's deadweight still weighed heavy on her. She shook, but she could not stop it.

Fenian took her chin between his warm fingers and tilted her head up towards him. She was forced to meet his intense gaze. In the dark of the night, the dual moons reflected in his eyes.

"It's okay," he breathed out, his hot breath fanning across her face.

She could do nothing but nod in response.

Aisla let his firm grip, and those two simple words soothe her racing heart. She let his steady gaze hold her there. She allowed herself to lean into the comfort as she found her breath once again. The panic subsided, and she was guided back to herself with the smell of oak wood and salty air. Salty air that reminded her of home. Home before all of this. And she was again reminded of how unprepared she was for Iomlan. Her own impulses had led her here. She pushed the guilt away as she breathed in and out, slowly, focusing on nothing but the male before her, who had saved her life twice now.

Aisla allowed Fenian to pull her from her dread as her breaths flowed naturally once more.

The air between them grew tight even as she calmed. She opened her mouth to speak but closed it again as words did not come.

She stopped thinking altogether, leaned forward and pressed her lips to his. She felt his initial shock as she grabbed at his back. Then, his arms wrapped tighter around her as she felt relief in his kiss. Relief that matched her own. The feeling of his lips on hers warmed her frigid bones while chilling her insides with a feeling she could not describe as she arched into him.

She was lost in this male she hardly knew. The tension between them dissipated just as much as it strengthened. It was a solace as much as it was discord. Their kisses grew rushed and greedy, although it felt natural as if they had done this every day of their lives.

Aisla felt her esos brewing beneath her skin, threatening to break at any moment, and fear overtook her. This was wrong. *So wrong.*

Guilt and disgust overcame Aisla, and she shoved her hands

between them and pushed him away with a force that took them both by surprise.

But she had initiated that kiss, and they both knew it.

"I didn't mean to do that," was all she could think to say.

"I've never been accidentally kissed before," he growled.

It took one glance at the look in his amber eyes. His dilated pupils. Before she could stop herself, her hand was moving of its own accord. She pulled back with the full intent to slap him across the face, but his hand caught hers and squeezed it so hard it drew a whimper from her lips. Embarrassment reddened her cheeks, and she bared her teeth at the male.

"Don't be a *fool*," he snapped at her.

The hurt in his eyes quickly morphed to rage as he held her hand, suspended between them. He released so suddenly that she had to throw her arms out to catch herself to keep from falling onto the forest floor.

He stood up and stared down at her, which only irritated her further. A sharp pain shot through her bad arm. She pushed down all the feelings dizzying her already heavy mind and she pushed herself to her own feet.

"That makes *two* times you have found yourself incapable of dealing with creatures of the woods, *banphrionsa*," Fenian sneered. "Yet, you continue to insist you are worthy of becoming a laoch."

Aisla crossed her arms in front of her chest as both embarrassment and irritation filled her. She could push him into that rushing river now and not feel a single regret.

"Then why do you continue to insist on dragging me along with you," she snapped. "If I am such a burden?"

"It's far more amusing than traveling alone. I enjoy watching you prove yourself wrong over and over again," he said, taking a step towards her.

She held her ground.

"Oh, is that what that was? Amusement? You kissed me back."

Before Aisla could react, Fenian had closed the distance between them. He gripped the collar of her soaking-wet shirt and yanked her towards him. He pulled her so hard that she nearly lost her balance, but she held her head higher as he tightened his fist in the fabric, his knuckles pressing against her chest. She glared into his eyes with a defiance that made his breathing deepen.

"Don't read into things when you are the one that started that entire situation, *Ellora*. You are *nothing* more to me than the dirt beneath my boots."

Tense and rigid, she forced the hatred coursing through her veins into her eyes.

He released her shirt with a huff and headed back to their tent.

"The next time I find you in a near-death situation," he spoke with a still sort of calm that chilled her more than his growls did. "I will stand by and watch as that final breath leaves your body. I will not make a single move to save you."

Aisla felt the truth in his words and it made her tongue heavy even as her esos stirred with anger. She would hate him until that final breath.

Shame heated her cheeks as she was forced to follow him back to their tent. If her bag had only contained food and basic supplies, she would have left it with no hesitation. But she couldn't leave *Oidhe* and the letter she still needed to save Ruairi's life with.

"I will be going my own way after I grab my things from camp," she stated as they neared it, even though it should have gone without saying.

"No, you're not."

"What do you mean?" Aisla said, jogging a few steps to come up along his side. "Of course I am. I would rather pass on than travel one more—"

"Shall I lend you my blade, then?" He turned to her with a raised, challenging brow.

Indignation burned through Aisla like a wildfire as she once again struggled with the words to reply.

"*Why?*" It was all she could think to ask.

"I have agreed to deliver you to the laoch training camp as an act of *atruach*, and that is what I intend to do," he responded like a soldier given orders, but she had never ordered this.

Never asked for this.

"You clearly hate me as much as I hate you, so—"

"I never said I hated you," he corrected her as if it was the simplest thing in the world.

As if none of the words he had spat at her just moments ago meant anything.

"You did not have to."

"Do not put words in my mouth," he said with a condescending *tsk*. "Didn't your parents teach you better?"

Rage flared within her at his choice of words. He knew it was just her and her grandmother. She had told him as much at the dinner in Spiorad.

She chose to bite her tongue, to have the dignity that he lacked. Her hands trembled as she pushed all thoughts of Fenian down and away. Instead, she found her mind wandering back to what had led them here.

To this.

Aisla knew the gory memories of Eire and Ruairi could never be erased from her mind. And that fact haunted her with every step.

It had all felt so real. She could still vividly recall the way her power felt when it erupted from her palms and the way it set Eire ablaze. She could feel her fear and the desperation to find her, even still, as Aisla bobbed up and down beneath the waves, fighting a current far stronger than she was. Then there was the way Ruairi's lifeless body had felt weighing down on her. She had reached a moment where she clung to him in her defeat.

In that moment, she had taken that last breath and waited for the water to fill her lungs until she was choking on it.

She'd never had a vision, a dream, whatever those mares had presented her with, as vivid. A feeling of numbness overtook her in the motion of a deep breath as she looked ahead to the moons of Talam. The stars in the sky and the trees above her, as the light rain sprinkled onto her skin.

"What did the spirits show you, Ellora?" he asked. His voice had softened as he noticed the way she had gotten lost in the swirling ghosted images of the night. "What dragged you beneath the waves?"

"It's none of your concern," she snapped and continued to march forward.

"You called someone named *Ru*. You said you didn't do *it*, that you hadn't meant to. What does that mean?"

Anger mingled with fear as Fenian spoke *his* name. Her throat tightened, and it was an effort to fight her reaction away. She felt guilty about having released his name to this stranger. She was only thankful it was *Ru* and not *Ruairi*.

"Piss off," she hissed. "I told you it is none of your business."

"Someone is sensitive," he remarked.

"Maybe if you had just been mentally assaulted by olc spirits of Ifreann and had all of your own deepest fears brought to life so vividly that you could see them—touch them—and those images still lingered . . ." The words poured out faster than Aisla could stop them. "Maybe then, you might understand why I am so *sensitive*. Then again, I don't know if those demons could find anything you care enough about to torture you with, and I imagine that is why they didn't bother tormenting you when they came across us both asleep."

Aisla hoped her words stung. She hoped they hurt, at least enough to make him feel even a fraction of what she was feeling.

His silence felt like victory enough in that moment.

"I need to get to Omra *now*. And if you are not going to treat the rest of this journey with the same urgency, then I am leaving and you will not be able to stop me," Aisla demanded as she forced an authority that she did not feel into her voice.

"I could always find you, *banphrionsa*," Fenian spoke with a confidence that made her stomach clench. "We will make it to Omra in two days. I promise."

33

RUAIRI

Ruairi's hands were bound to the table with thick rope that dug into his skin.

His palms were sweating. Heart racing. Body trembling with fear as he stared up into the cold, gray eyes of a man he had never seen before. The two laochs who had brought him here stood behind him, out of his sight, but he could still feel their presence. He had also not recognized them.

"You can talk," the man crooned with a voice that grated Ruairi's nerves. "Or you can sing as the blade pierces your skin."

Ruairi's stomach tightened. He heard the sharp sound of a blade slowly being unsheathed. His breath became ragged. He squeezed his eyes shut as the metal dragged down the length of his arm. Tauntingly slow and gentle. Blood had not yet spilled.

He found the image of Aisla as he remembered her. Strong. Loving. Fierce. Loyal. Beautiful. Constant.

He remembered all that he fought for by turning himself in. His reasons to stay strong as the blade pushed deeper and Ruairi felt the sting as his skin grew warm with a pain that was only the beginning.

His knees hit the floor first. His knees were weak and could not support him as his body slumped forward until he was crumpled there on the concrete of his small cell. He had become a shell of the man he had once been.

He swore he heard a chuckle from the laochs, who had watched the silent torture that had gone on for an unknown amount of time.

He had not spoken. Not once. Not when they pierced his skin. Not as they marred his body. Not even when they removed his left pinky finger from his hand.

He screamed. Screamed until his throat was raw and tasted of blood. The numbness he had forced into himself was not enough to conceal the shouts of pain that escaped him.

They had not gotten his words, but they had gotten his voice. The screams ripped from him.

He was unsure which they wanted more. Which fed the blood-thirsty gleam of the gray eyes that would haunt him until his final breath. And he would still fight for that final breath with every morsel of energy that he had if it meant even a chance he would make it to Eilean again.

As his head pressed against the cold, hard floor where he lay, he found himself longing for those four days of silence.

As maddening as it was, he would take that over the scars, bruises, slashes, and blood crusted along his wounds without hesitation. He wished he could go back to that place. That place of not existing. Because this existence was unbearable.

Ruairi blinked slowly, his vision blurred. Blood smeared the ground where his body had landed. He dragged his gaze down to his hand, the red marks lining his wrists where he had fought against his restraints, and that place where his pinky had been. If he had anything left to throw up, he knew he would have right then.

He tried to lift his arm. And failed. He closed his bruised and swollen eyes and inhaled a shallow, ragged breath, and pulled his knees into his chest with an effort that made him wince. He groaned, slowly turning onto his side, to face the bed that he could not bring himself to get into.

He could not find the energy to make it as he lay there. Defeated. Utterly battered and worn. His spirit had been broken. *He* had been broken. But he had not given up. He let his eyes fall shut again, pleading for the mercy of sleep to take him away into its arms once more.

His mouth was dry as it gaped open in a silent, unending scream.

34
WEYLIN

Weylin entered the small tent with an itch he could not put into words. There was an energy inside of him bursting from all that had changed when he left this tent, not long ago, clutching *Uamhan* in his search for Ellora. Everything felt different in the surrounding air.

He could still taste her lips. He could still hear the disgust in her voice when she shoved him away. Could still see the fire flaming in her eyes as she made to strike him. Each moment replayed in a whirlwind of images that flashed through his mind.

He was thankful he was traveling under an alias. He was sure Rania would not appreciate his travels alongside Ellora so soon after their betrothal.

The mares had not lied. That much he was certain of. When he had pulled her from the roaring waves and onto the shore, she had not been breathing. Ellora had been dead.

The female had to be either blessed or cursed, or maybe some combination of the two. She attracted death at every corner but managed to evade its clutches each time. Even the fact that her life was potentially saved when they were taken in by the Spiorad tribe felt like no coincidence. Weylin could not help but feel there was so much more to this female and the way her fortune was constantly falling one way or the other, but never in the middle.

He did not know what it all meant. Or what the norns had intended when they wove their golden threads together for this time. He felt his paranoia growing with each passing breath.

Ellora was hiding something, and he was blind to ignore it for this long.

Weylin felt an urge to distance himself, but it did not override the deep and primal feeling that called him closer to her. Something about her drew him in until there was a danger brewing just beneath the surface of his skin. Each time he tried to fight it, it only made him hate her more. Above all, Weylin was a man of his word, because if a man did not have his word, he had nothing. He had agreed to escort Ellora safely to Omra, and the laochs, and that is what he intended to do. He also felt that she might not make it there in one piece if he did not.

Not that it was any of his concern.

He would depart from her far enough from the laoch training grounds that he would not encounter anyone who would recognize him. He could only hope that he would never see her again after that.

He had to do something to shake this energy brewing within him and growing into a creature he could not contain. The power that would forever be dormant itched into a burn that grew into a physical pain. And he was curious to see what this girl who claimed to be a future laoch of Samhradh could really do.

"Grab your blade," he ordered as she ducked into the tent behind him.

"No," she said flatly, looking back at him as if he had grown an extra head.

"I said *grab your blade, banphrionsa,*" he snapped again, his patience wearing thin.

"You are insane," she hissed. "And you lack manners entirely."

"My manners only continue to deteriorate as direct orders are rejected."

"An order?" she scoffed, her brow furrowed and her lips pressed into a straight line. "Who are you to command me?"

"If you truly seek to become a laoch, you should get used to being given orders."

"I never agreed to take them from you," she grumbled and he could hear her defeat setting in. "Why in Hel would you want me to grab my blade anyway?"

"I think it's about time you showed me why you think *you're* worthy of becoming a laoch," he responded smoothly. "Considering how I've saved your life more times than you have saved yourself, I'm eager to see your combat skills for myself. Unless you're afraid you would only embarrass yourself?"

"But we—"

"*But we* will stay on track to Omra, I swear it," he interrupted with impatience. "I know the urgency with which you travel, and I have my own life to return to."

Ellora did not say a word. She scowled at him and mumbled something he could not discern under her breath. She reluctantly reached into her pack and pulled out that beautiful dagger of gold and larimar crystal.

They exited the tent and Weylin faced her, unsheathing *Uamhan* and slipping into a casual and familiar stance. Ellora mimicked his foot placement, her hands unsure as she met his gaze, staring at him through long lashes. She raised her dagger in front of her chest, her bad arm from the barghest wound was pulled protectively inwards, and he narrowed his eyes at her curiously. She tilted her head back with a taunting grimace.

"What are you waiting for?" She sneered as he lunged towards her.

A look of surprise flashed across her face, but she was quick on her feet as he had expected. She stepped to the side and ducked as he swung his sword towards her. She took advantage of the moment to kick his knee and nearly caused him to lose his balance.

She twisted her body to his right and thrust her dagger forward, but he was already moving. He intercepted the movement and knocked her arm, making her drop her blade, but she hardly reacted to the loss. She used his momentary arrogance to twist his arm out and away from him and continued to twist until he dropped his own weapon. She dove backwards before he could retaliate. He met her gaze, flames dancing in her eyes as her forest-green cloak billowed around her small frame. She was the image of ferocity. Of beauty and grace. She looked more in control than he had ever seen her. It was nearly intimidating, but Weylin found the challenge in the lines of her creased brow inviting.

"Hand to hand now, *banphrionsa*," he taunted her as she crouched on the balls of her feet. "Don't expect me to go easy on you."

"I would not dream of it," she snarled, curling her lip back to show her teeth.

Ellora made the first move this time. She swung the closed fist of her good arm towards his right, but he moved out of the way as she struck empty air, but it seemed that had been a part of her plan. She quickly moved in a semi-circle, kicking her leg out as she did, and Weylin was taken off guard as he fell to the ground. Irritation flared through his chest, but Ellora was on top of him with the dagger that he had not even seen her retrieve. She leaned in close to him, a victorious grin on her face as she pressed the blade to his throat, straddling his waist.

"*I win,*" she whispered into his ear.

Weylin roared and wordlessly used his strength to flip her over onto her back. An *oomph* escaped her as the breath was stolen from her lungs. He used the side of his wrist to knock her blade from her hand. She fumbled for her blade, fingers splayed out as she tried to lengthen them.

Weylin knelt over her, adjusting his knee to bear down upon her reaching arm, his hand wrapped around her throat, squeezing gently. He had the power to pass her on right then. He caught her bad arm when she feebly made to swing again, refusing to give in to defeat. Her eyes grew wide with surprise. She opened her mouth as if to speak, but she could not.

"No, Ell," he spoke softly, holding her there. Held her in defeat without breaking a sweat. "It looks like I did."

Weylin released her, and both of her hands flew to her throat as she gasped for air. Weylin pushed himself to his feet and stalked over to retrieve *Uamhan*. He heard her ragged breaths.

"You are insufferable." Ellora seethed from behind him.

"I've been called far worse," he sneered and approached the tent. "I will say you are more skilled than I had anticipated, and that is the closest to a compliment you will get out of me."

"I was not asking for your compliments," she snarled.

"But you wanted them all the same."

"No, actually, I did not."

"Keep telling yourself that, *banphrionsa*."

"I do not for the life of me understand why you act like you know so much about me. We've only just met. I think the real problem is that you think you know everything all the time, so you assume you must know everything about me, too. But if you knew even one thing about me, you would know that I do not need, want, or seek your approval."

"I am very aware of what I do not know. In fact, almost painfully so."

"How could you know what you do not know?" she asked, annoyance lacing her tone.

He paused and turned to look at her. She stopped abruptly, and they were standing close, so close he could smell her as she looked up at him, her irritation visible in every line on her face.

"The wise male knows that he knows nothing. The fool believes that he knows all," Weylin responded, his eyes flicking back and forth between hers. "And I am no fool, Ellora Morlee."

"I do not agree with that statement," she grumbled, but he could hear the way that she was turning his words over in her head through her tone of voice.

———

They hastily packed up their camp to continue their journey south. They both stayed silent for the most part. Grabbing their own things first, then wordlessly working together to take the tent down and fit it back into its small bag. He noticed the way she occasionally looked at him from the corner of her eye.

Always wary. Always distrusting.

Weylin could feel her anticipation and eagerness with each movement of her body. He wondered whether it was nervous or excited energy that drove her forward. He wondered if she would be relieved to arrive at the laoch training camp, or afraid of what might await her there.

If they traveled all day at a decent pace, Weylin figured they could set up camp for the night near Anseo, which was a mid-sized city a half a day's travel from the capital. He had told Ellora as much, and she had agreed with the plan. Although, Weylin knew he had left her with little choice in the matter.

Ellora mounted Eolas with ease, and Weylin remembered how she had never ridden a horse before that first day together. He hoisted himself into place behind her and used the reins to nudge Eolas onwards to begin this last leg of their journey.

A sort of finality settled over Weylin as he neared Castle Eagla. Every step brought him closer to his father and all that would encompass. He knew this journey to Briongloid and back had changed the course of his life in many ways. It had changed the future of the world of Talam in many ways, too.

He was now betrothed and soon to be mated to Rania, the Gem of Dreams. She would rule the worldly realms by his side once he was no longer the Udar Apparent, but the Udar himself. They were to be the future of the world, leading through this unknown time of the ninth generation. And Weylin had sealed her fate with his proposal.

Then there was Ellora Morlee, who he might not have encountered were it not for the storm that slowed his travel. Despite it all, she was not someone that he would soon forget, even if the norns never again crossed their threads.

35

AISLA

alerian. The herb she had slipped into Fenian Daro's flask before they entered the tent for the night.

The plan had begun to form when she saw the tall stocks of pale purple flowers along their route here. More patches of it had popped up and her mind had been made.

Aisla lay awake in the dark night inside the Samhradh border. Her heartbeat thundered in her throat.

She rested her palms at her sides, allowing them to kiss the bottom of the tent, the only thing separating them from the cool earth. She inhaled the post-rain air and the fragrance of the pine trees around them then released her breath as she worked to release her fears.

The night was warmer than any of the other nights on her journey this far. But the spring air was still crisp and cool enough. She lay there awaiting the steady, long breaths of sleep from Fenian. She kept her own breathing slow to mimic sleep.

Fenian was not who he said he was.

It had been building in the back of her mind since that very first time they met among the blood of barghests with his knife to her throat. But she *knew* it to be true after their spar, when his ego prevented him from hiding a lifetime of training.

Aisla had fought back with enough effort to come across as an elf seeking laoch training, but she held back her full skill set, full power to avoid suspicion. He had given it so much more than that, and she carefully watched his every movement. The way he read her like only Ruairi ever could. The way he was quick and capable and knew when to use each hesitant moment she so carefully planted to his advantage. She had used it to plant her own trap, and he had caught himself in it.

Fenian Daro was not a nobody from a small village outside of the capital. That much she was certain of.

When the fact had settled within her, she felt a familiar crack along her innermost being reopen and it ached like a festering wound. She did not care for him in the way she cared for Ruairi. For Eire. But she knew she did not hate him the way she had told him she did. She could not hate him, and even felt a pull towards him as she planned her departure.

She felt the loss of Eire. The loss when Ruairi had been yanked out of her grasp. And now she was so far from home. She was so far from Muinin and her grandmother—from the salty breeze of Caillte that carried through the ash trees. She had learned to find a peace in the way Fenian smelled of home when the wind carried his scent towards her. A feeling that had become a familiarity if nothing else. And no matter what way she looked at it, this was yet another loss. Another way to say goodbye.

They had shared moments of fear and vulnerability. Moments of grief and anger. Moments of rage and joy. It might have all been a lie, bits of a story that had never been real, but to Aisla, it was real. Each one of those feelings had been tangible on her tongue as she carried her own secrets down the coast of Iomlan.

And she was exhausted from all the loss.

Aisla did not know who Fenian was, or what he was doing here, or why he had lied. She did not know if he was already a step ahead of her. If he knew who she was, and maybe that was why he refused to let her go as they headed towards the capital—towards the Udar.

Or maybe he was as blind as she had been.

All that she knew now was she had to get ahead of him. She had to take control if she had lost it or maintain it wherever she could.

But curious thoughts pushed away her fears as she lay awake that night.

When she was sure the sleeping herb had done the job, she crept over to where his pack lay. She carefully pulled it to her chest before settling back down with it.

Her palms sweat as she reached down into it. She did not know what she expected to find within the pack, but she had to know *who* he was. The need gnawed at her even as she felt the increasing urgency to take off into the night.

She shifted through the soft fabric of his clothes. She dug deeper and the tips of her fingers brushed against something cold and hard. Her fingers ran over the ridges and caught on gems embedded into metal. It was a circular shape. A shape that could not be mistaken even as her shaking hands continued to process it.

Her breath caught in her throat, and she struggled to find the next one.

She pulled the item to the top of the bag, and unease churned within her. Each hair along her arms stood on end as she held in her hands the crown of the Myrkor dynasty. It was iron with stones of amber and she had seen an illustrated version of it in the teachings of the world tellers in Caillte. Each family of power in the seven worldly realms had their own crown. And this was the worst one she could have found.

But it could not be mistaken.

Aisla held the crown of her enemies.

This was the crown the Udar Apparent would wear until he took over the stolen throne, *her* stolen throne, and traded this iron crown for the crown of skies. The crown of skies was a replica forged by dwarves following the siege of Arden, meant to imitate the crown of stars, the Iarkis crown. It had been the one thing they had not managed to steal.

Her hands shook violently.

She dropped the crown back into the bag and scrambled away from it. Her hand flew to cover her mouth to hold in the scream, building from her toes to her tongue. Her body felt numb. Terror coursed through her veins. Her esos was so still, so quiet. As though it too had fallen silent with fear.

At worst, she had expected to find he was a laoch for the Udar himself. She never would have expected the possibility that she had traveled all this time with the Udar Apparent—one of the two people that hated her most in this world.

Why was he traveling alone? What was he doing in Briongloid? Did he know who she was?

Questions flew through her brain at a maddening speed. She so desperately wanted to put the pieces together.

She had shared meals with him. Learned to ride a horse by his hand. She had shared a bed with the enemy of her people.

Her fear turned to disgust, then to a rage that burned so fiercely that her skin warmed and her palms stung with the threat of her esos.

She needed to get out. Needed to get out before she awoke the sleeping prince of terrors.

She took a deep breath and grabbed her pack from her side of the tent. Each inhale was harder to come by as she crouched and silently left through the canvas flaps of the tent.

Every slight sound echoed like a roar in the quiet night.

Aisla stood there, head held high as she looked back at the tent that contained a sleeping Myrkor. Her teeth chattered and her hands trembled with so many emotions, she could not even begin to parse through them.

Not now. Not here.

She worked to slow her heart, to draw herself in through her core. The wind whisked through her hair and she swore she felt the ring in her pocket warming.

She allowed the restless spirits of her ancestors to fuel her, rile her esos to the tips of her fingers, pulling it to that circle of her palm where she could still feel Ruairi's gentle circles.

She stumbled back a few steps.

The surrounding trees danced side to side. Taunting her. Challenging her. Luring her in as she raised her shaking hands in front of her.

Her esos greeted her with an eagerness that sent a chill down her spine. That familiar feeling of being so out of control threatened to break her, but it could not. Not this time.

The power rushed to the surface of her skin with a whispered cry she could feel in every nerve.

The power to end him was right at her fingertips. Aisla could feel it. Her esos spoke of seductions, stirring within her, but her mind lingered on the male that whispered his deepest fears under cold moons in a village not far away.

Tears stung her eyes as she shook her hands out.

Aisla allowed her shoulders to drop, and she exhaled, pushing the esos back down. She swallowed her fears and squeezed her eyes shut. She could not do it.

She had to walk away from this clearing.

One foot in front of the other, they moved of their own accord. Carrying her to Eolas, even as she felt heavier with each step.

She had to push forward.

She had enough supplies to make it on her own to Omra. She could push forward with all the urgency that the Udar Apparent had lacked, and she could make it there on her own. Aisla would reach the contact that Ruairi had marked on the map.

She would craft a new alias and continue on as though she had never met Fenian Daro.

As she thought back on all that meeting him had brought her, it felt like a lifetime had passed.

Aisla went to Eolas. She was thankful when the horse remained silent. She held her hand out to her, praying to the gods the mare would accept her. She petted her mane and felt the beast lean into her. A good sign. She gently took her reins and mounted Eolas as he had taught her how to, and pulled her cloak over her head. She urged the horse forward, and after a moment of hesitation, the mare responded with a low *huff*.

She just had to make it to Omra before the Udar's son did.

It made her sick to think of him that way. Sick to her stomach. But she could not call him Fenian, because Fenian Daro had never existed.

Fresh tears fell as Eolas sprinted through the trees at her encouragement. Her throat ached with a cry of pain that she could not release.

If she could just make it to Omra, she could see Ruairi again.

She knew if she could just meet his gaze again, if she could touch his skin, they would find their way out of this. This hope and yearning was the only thing pushing Aisla Iarkis forward despite the weight bearing down on her that wanted to hold her in place.

The heaviness of it seemed to grow larger upon her, and there was only so much she could bear before she would be forced to cave to the pressure. But she was grasping to her hope still. To the memories of a home that she needed to protect.

And *he* would not be the one to break her.

PART THREE
REVELATIONS OF HAVOC

36

EIRE

"It's getting worse, Edi. The ones who have given up fighting, the ones whose bodies are not strong enough, they are *unrecognizable*," Eire heard a familiar voice hiss the words with urgency lacing the tone.

Eire recognized the name *Edi* to be the name of the primary medic. The one she most often saw armed with a syringe. She tried to turn onto her side, but her body would not move. Her body rarely responded to her will. She was tired. So tired.

Her throat had long dried up and her skin felt scaly and rough, no matter what salves the menders applied and the abundance of medicinal herbs she had been fed.

The silence of the gods weighed upon her chest like a physical thing as Eire murmured her prayers to them once more. She had not given up. Could not when they were her only hope.

That night, Eire had dreamt of squirrels. She dreamt of them as big as elves were, and they could speak to her too. Only, they spoke the ancient tongue, Aosta, but so did she. She dreamt her bed was floating on great waves in the ocean, sending her tumbling as she rode the current, never falling off.

She dreamt Aisla and Ruairi were there with her atop her bed in the middle of the ocean. She clung to the memory of them like a lifeline, of the meals they had shared and the adventures they had yet to embark on. She clung to Aisla's warm smile and the way that she had loved her friends with a fierceness. Eire clung to Ruairi's laugh and the way he always leaned in when he was listening to her speak. She held tight to her sheets, clutched between her icy fingers, and allowed herself to imagine she was holding their hands.

Eire had heard hushed whispers of their disappearance.

She heard that the two of them had disappeared into the dark of the night, against direct orders of the Mathair. Eire could only imagine how Aisla's grandmother would take the news. Her anger and rage. She heard of a ship gone missing off the coast of Caillte and knew that her friends were off on an adventure.

At first, she was hurt by the news. So hurt that they would leave her here, but now she could only be thankful that they had both escaped *this*. Because Eire knew that none of them were getting out of this unaffected.

Eire turned her chin towards the door, wondering if Edi would come in now.

Her eyes were drooping closed, but not for lack of sleep. She felt all she did now was sleep.

Movement caught her eye from the corner of the room. Her eyes strained to get a better look. Eire heard her heart beating in her throat. She felt her fingers twitch as shadows swirled about the room, inching ever closer. She watched them slip under the door. A black mass of air whistled and whirled around the walls, taunting her. She watched, helpless, in wide-eyed horror while they twined around her cot and licked at her bare skin. The feeling was icy cold and nearly burned her. A scream caught in her throat as she held her breath, hoping, praying, they would leave her alone.

She just wanted to be *left alone*.

The shadows danced in her hair, slithered up her spine, until one wrapped around her throat and gently squeezed. A whisper of a threat.

Eire lost it.

She screamed a high-pitched scream, and the shadows fell away, retreating in a raging tornado that swept her room into chaos. She flailed in her bed, screaming for help, tears streaming down her cheeks at the vulnerability of it all.

Edi burst in through the door, her eyes wide with fear as she looked about the room that now appeared untouched. Eire shook her head frantically—wanting to explain—*needing* her to understand. But the words did not come as Eire's tongue grew heavy, and her mind grew cloudy. She let her head fall back against the cot in defeat.

Edi dropped to Eire's side while Eire struggled to regulate her breathing. She took several shaky, deep breaths before pulling herself into a sitting position with considerable effort, as Edi gently pried her hand from the sheets she still held in her grip and wove her own fingers in between Eire's. A gesture of comfort. She squeezed gently, as she always did when this happened. When Eire had these *episodes,* as they referred to them here.

"It's okay, Eire," she said softly. Her voice was tired and drained, weary and weak. "You're okay. You're still here."

She said the words as though they should provide consolation. But Eire only felt dread.

Eire closed her eyes. She inhaled great gulps of air, recounting the prayers that brought her more peace than the words of the menders ever did. Her body was hot and sweaty, but chilled with the cold of her ever-present fever. She trembled, and every part of her body ached as it had for all the days that Eire had long given up counting.

"Thank you," Eire croaked out in a scratchy voice that she hardly recognized as her own. She felt the tears drying on her cheeks. "I'm okay," she muttered, half to Edi and half to herself. "I'm here."

"You're doing so well, my dear," Edi whispered, her eyes shining with pain. "You're fighting it, and that's the best we could hope for."

Eire nodded back.

"Can I get out of my room for a bit?" Eire asked, desperately needing to rid herself of these four walls that never stopped pressing in on her.

"Sure, Eire," Edi nodded her head slowly, as if she understood her need for escape, but Eire knew she could not understand. She would not understand until it was her lying on the cot dealing with this disease that plagued her. "You're welcome to visit any of the common areas."

Eire nodded her thanks.

The menders had elected to block off a wing of the infirmary for anyone with lofa. There were a few common areas they could venture into, as the solitude was vexing. Eire had not seen her family or her friends in so, so long. It hurt like a wound. It was maddening, this place. This disease. This mind she found herself trapped inside of. Day in and day out. She could scream at the top of her lungs and not stop until it was her very last breath.

She felt her pulse quicken as the anxiety threatened to take hold of her. Threatened to break her, as it often did. She needed out of this room.

Eire pushed herself up on shaky legs that bowed beneath the weight of her, despite the fact she weighed significantly less than she did before her admittance to the infirmary. Edi stood and pushed the wooden walker Eire had been using towards her. Eire leaned forward as she gripped onto it, having gotten used to the need for one.

Edi walked ahead of her to open the door and allow her to pass through. Eire made her way past, the wood in her hands a comfort as she could feel the vibrations as it scraped along the stone hallways of the infirmary.

There were no windows in the hallway, just like there were none in her room.

Her soul felt weary and dark. She saw shadows that danced in the torchlights along the walls, guiding her passage until she came across the door to the main common area the diseased all shared. She opened the door to the large room, which was full of windows and natural light as the rays of the setting sun poured in, providing the glimmer of warmth that she needed to keep on pushing through.

Her eyes darted about as she noted the few bodies sitting at the different wooden tables. Some played children's games while others sat in silence. There was an elderly human woman with skin that was decaying worse than Eire's. It peeled away in gray patches, revealing dark red flesh. Eire averted her gaze, thanking the gods above that she had long become accustomed to the smell of it. It no longer plagued her in the long nights when it prevented her from finding sleep. She had long steeled her stomach to the sight of it as well, no longer feeling the urge to losing her meals to such grotesque sights.

She did not recognize the human. She must be new. But Eire had already seen the patterns. The disease seemed to attack those of an older age much more quickly than its younger victims.

A middle-aged elf male caught her attention on the other side of the room. He sat with his back towards her, and she could not see his face to tell if she knew him or not. From what she could see, he looked less damaged than most of them. But his skin was sickly green, as Eire's had been in her early stages. She had noticed the way that each of them appeared to show different symptoms at different times, but there were always commonalities amongst them.

Finally, Eire felt her eyes soften as her gaze fell upon dark blonde hair. *Fiona*. A breath that had been stuck in her chest since she had last seen the female escaped through her lips. Fear and a thrumming heart quickly replaced her moment of relief. She began to shake. Her lower lip trembled. But she smiled. Smiled as she approached the female she had learned to love before this disease had ever entered their village.

Fiona had not been fighting. The evidence became clearer with every push of her walker closer.

Fiona had taken it all so much worse than Eire. Losing her will so early on. Slipping away. Further and further. A leaf on a windy day just out of reach. No will to stay.

It killed Eire to watch. But she did.

There were sunrises when Eire never ran into Fiona in the common areas. There was no proper way to go about planning their run-ins, but Eire pushed her way down the torchlit halls as often as she could, hoping to meet her dulling brown-eyed gaze.

Eire approached cautiously as Fiona slowly turned in her direction. A child-like smile lit up her face. She clapped her hands together and Eire slowly lowered herself into the seat beside her.

"Eire!" she exclaimed with an empty glee.

Flakes of her skin dropped with the movement. Her jaw hung low and loose. Eire's insides lurched.

"Hey Fi," she said through a pained grimace. "How are you holding up?"

"Not good," Fiona answered. "I'm tired. So tired."

Her smile was a direct contradiction to her answer. Eire raised a brow in question and leaned closer towards her. She tried to remember her scent before all of this. The memories they shared under starlight. Nights at pubs and morning walks along the shore. So much she had not even told Aisla yet.

Because Aisla had been so stressed.

Her nineteenth naming day was approaching, and she would enter adulthood with still no grasp on the esos within herself. Eire did not want to bother her with such trivial things, but she was sure it had been love. It was still love. Fiona had brought out something in her she had never known possible—a new light to life, and a beautiful way to look at the world around them. She believed in the gods too, despite it all.

"I know," Eire said softly. Tears burned her eyes. "I'm so proud of you."

Fiona shifted away from her. Her vacant eyes fell.

"Eire," she sucked in a sharp breath. "What if I just stopped fighting? Would you forgive me?"

Fiona looked back towards her again. Her eyes were glazed over and a chill traveled down Eire's spine. Her stomach twisted in knots and a lump formed in her throat. It was suffocating as the grief blossomed in her chest. Swallowed her whole.

"There's so much left to fight for," Eire managed to get out.

She ignored the question. Because she knew her answer. She knew she would forgive her in a heartbeat, because there were days when she asked herself the same question.

Over and over again.

She reached out and slowly cupped Fiona's hands in her own trembling hands. Fiona's were still. Cold. Hard to hold on to.

Eire swallowed her fears as she willed her warmth into Fiona's hands. Anything she could do to make it better, she would. A silent tear fell down her cheek.

"I don't think any of it could be worth this," Fiona whimpered.

Eire felt her heart breaking. Again and again. In the span of a moment, it shattered and tore and cracked. She knew she had lost her. There was no more she could say. And she was not willing to push.

Fiona slowly pulled her hands away. She held out her arms, turning them over to show all those places where her flesh was now visible. The ways her bone was showing in some of the patches. She was fading away before Eire's eyes and she could not stop it.

Eire had not been affected as badly. She had a patch on her right ear and one over her left eye. But Fiona was coated in sporadic holes that ate into her flesh.

Holes that made her something she was not.

"I—I'm so sorry, Fiona," she murmured.

The only words she could think of in that moment.

Eire ran a gentle finger across the largest of the affected areas, wishing the menders could use their esos to take it all away. She would give her life to see this plague removed from every body on this continent.

"Do you hear the monsters at night?" Fiona spoke low enough only for Eire to hear.

She pulled her arms back into her chest. Away from Eire.

"What monsters, Fi?" Eire asked gently, settling her hands in her lap.

A sort of acceptance settled within her—an acceptance that ached and groaned. Fiona would not have much longer, and Eire knew what she was doing here.

Eire had never seen the bodies of the deceased. There were no funerals or burials, but she had noticed victims go missing.

She saw rooms go empty that others filled. They mourned in their own ways here. Some private in the late nights of these haunting hallways. Others mourned loudly and painfully in the open areas when the realization hit.

"I hear them," Fiona called her from her thoughts. She nodded madly as if to convince Eire of what she was saying. "I hear them each night before the sunrise. They moan and groan. Their voices feel like gravel on my skin. Like an army of dead. Their pain, I can feel it, Eire. And sometimes, they speak my name in the wind. Sometimes, they call out for me."

Eire's concern grew as she looked back and forth between her ghostly eyes. Trying to find remnants of her love in them.

"I think they're waiting for me," Fiona whispered into the silence between them.

Eire shook her head. Lost for the words to say.

She had not been prepared for this.

She had spent her life training in so, so many areas. She had mastered her esos and her books. The sword and archery. Any blade thrown her way. But no one had ever trained her for this.

No one had ever taught her how to watch the one she loved disappear before her eyes.

She was forced to sit there, speechless, and unable to help as Fiona was lost to some other world. Fiona was lost to the grip of a plague that was coming for every soul on Eilean.

Eire was not prepared as dark, ruby blood dribbled from the corner of Fiona's mouth. Then her nose. Fiona held her gaze the whole time. A soft smile resting on her lips and her expression did not falter.

She had planned this. She had come here to be with Eire while she passed on.

Eire wanted to scream. She wanted to shake her.

Instead, she could only sit there, motionless and helpless.

Eire was not prepared as the closest mender dashed towards Fiona, carefully pulling her convulsing body into her arms as another came from behind her. A cot was pushed towards them.

Eire watched as they pushed Fiona from the room. Her last glimpse at her once silky blonde hair while memories flashed by in an instant.

Silent tears poured down. Her throat bobbed.

Eire had not trained for the feeling of loss that sank into her. Her head dropped as she was forced to look at her shaking, sweaty hands.

Helpless hands.

37

RUAIRI

Ruairi clutched the sides of the table, willing himself to disappear. His wrists ached from the ropes that bound him down and subjected him to their will.

He panted in pain as the tip of the blade was withdrawn from his skin. His body barely reacted to the absence of it. There was no rush of relief or feeling of reprieve, because this was not the end. He would suffer again and again because he would not use his voice. Not for them.

"The more you refrain from talking," said the deep voice that would haunt his nightmares for whatever life he had left. Ruairi did not open his eyes. "The more fun I get to have."

Ruairi's breaths came ragged and shallow. Each one raked down his throat like sandpaper as his body weighed heavily upon the table. He was not himself. He had not been himself since the first time that he had entered this room.

Ruairi laid there, helpless and pathetic as the ropes were cut from his hands. Then his feet. He wiggled his nine fingers, ensuring the rest were still there. He tended to numb himself, to *try* to numb himself during these sessions. Ruairi tried not to notice the things they did, the parts of him they stole and maimed.

Rough arms grabbed him under the armpits and hauled him to his feet. He did not have the will to support himself as the laochs whose faces no longer registered shoved his limp body through the door and into the dimly lit hallway.

Ruairi's eyes fluttered open and closed. He did not know whether he was falling into sleep or out of it. The laochs turned, and he realized they were not going the way that they had before. The sound of their footsteps echoed through new halls as fresh blood dripped from above Ruairi's eye onto the cement floors.

His vision was cloudy and tinted red as they shoved open a door. He had to squeeze his eyes shut against the glaring light of the sun.

He was outside. *Outside*.

He had not been outside since he'd arrived at the castle. The sunlight was warm on his skin and blinding to his eyes that could not adjust. His feet dragged through lush grass as the laochs led him around the courtyard.

Then it hit him. This was mental torture.

They were taking him outside so he could inhale the fresh, salty air of a realm so near the coast it was a reminder of what he could have if he spoke—a reminder of home.

Ruairi wanted to go back. He wanted to return to the darkness of his cell where hope was so much harder to grasp. Because hope would ultimately be the death of his soul. It was not fair to hope in a position such as his.

He struggled in their grasp. Tried to dig his heels into the earth, silently begging them to take him inside. But his body did not respond, and he knew it would not matter to them even if he had.

The cool air kissed his skin and opened his lungs wider. He breathed in through his clogged nostrils. Allowed the air to fill him, even as he hated every moment of it.

This torture was nearly as bad as the physical kind.

They continued their steady march around the castle until they walked past a tall stone wall on the south side. He could not see over the wall, even if he had been standing on his own two feet, but as he got closer, a chill traveled down his spine.

The sounds coming from beyond that wall were bloodcurdling. There were gargles and shouts. They were not human nor elven. It sounded like an army of the dead. There were so many voices, he thought he had imagined them. His ears strained to make out words, but only heard pained sounds.

The laochs continued to drag him onwards, not pausing for even a beat. He got the feeling that the intent of this walk of torture did not lie beyond the wall. That it was the glowing sun and the fresh air they intended to torture him with, but he could not help but feel terror at the mysteries beyond that wall. They were the sounds of something so otherworldly it burned his ears to listen to them. They were sounds it would take an eternity to erase from his mind.

He wished he could ask about it, if only to put a name to the fears he would now have.

But instead, he hung his head and closed his eyes as they approached an alternate entrance to Castle Eagla.

The door swung open, and darkness welcomed him. He allowed himself to be dragged into it, finding comfort in its return.

38
WEYLIN

Weylin was awoken by the sun filtering in through the canvas of the tent.

His eyelids were heavy, and he had to work to get himself to sit upright. He had never slept so soundly before, and sleep still tore at the corners of his mind.

"Ell," Weylin breathed, turning his head to look at her.

She was not there. He was sure that he would have heard her pack her things and leave in the middle of the night.

"*Ellora,*" he bellowed, standing and walking out through the tent flap.

No response came.

How had he let this happen?

Weylin ducked back into the tent and glanced at her empty side of the tent where her pack and all of her things were also missing. Weylin furrowed his brow when he noticed his pack lying open in the corner of the tent. His fingers curled into a clenched fist when he noticed his crown lying atop his pack. She had to have gone through his stuff, to find it where it had been wrapped between cloth at the very bottom.

If she had reason to flee upon discovering his identity, he had reason to find her.

He grabbed his flask from the ground of the tent. He pulled the lid off and sniffed the liquid inside. It smelled wrong. He cursed himself for not noticing it sooner. While he had always known something was off about Ellora, he had trusted her to some degree. And that trust had come back to bite him.

A growl escaped his throat as he hastily packed his things and left the tent again. He could not help but wonder what Ellora really wanted in Samhradh. Whatever it was, he knew he would need to warn his father. He would need to make sure she never got into the laoch training camp or anywhere near his castle.

He did not have *time*.

The clearing felt awfully still and empty as Weylin tried to understand what had happened. Then it dawned on him that Eolas was also missing. His fists clenched at his sides.

Selfish, selfish banphrionsa.

Weylin did not have time to feel the betrayal that bubbled in the bit of his stomach. He did not have time to note the way his heart had fractured along the familiar cracks. He never should have left it vulnerable. There was no time to feel the hurt mingled amongst his rage and shock.

Weylin saw red as he pushed forward.

His body still felt slow and groggy from the effects of whatever herb she had used to poison him.

Ellora, whoever she really was, could not be trusted.

———

Mouths dropped and eyes widened as Weylin Myrkor stormed into the nearest village.

He wore his laoch uniform with the Myrkor crest pinned to his chest. His iron crown sat atop his head as he prepared for his homecoming.

"Your Udar Apparent requires your fastest horse, *immediately*," Weylin's voice boomed with the authority that he had not wielded in so long.

It was a comforting feeling to watch fear flicker through their eyes while they tried to put together why he would be here, in their village. He felt a sort of ease as he settled into the male he was destined to be. The sort that commands an audience and causes a chill in the heart of his listeners.

No one moved, and Weylin narrowed his eyes.

"Aye," a man spoke up from his right-hand side, drawing his attention. "I will escort you to our stables, my lord."

The middle-aged man with dark brown hair and a long, unkempt beard bowed. Weylin gave a small nod of approval as the man stood and led Weylin to their horses. Every wasted moment here itched. He had to beat *her* there. He knew where she would be headed, knew it in his gut that her intent was to get to his castle—his father.

But he would get there first, to warn his father of the elf that possessed a power he could not name. They would warn the laochs heading the training camps as well.

Weylin heard hushed whispers follow his footsteps as he stalked onwards across the sandy, worn path between puballs and small wooden structures. Their frightened voices caressed him with the familiar warmth of the power.

They came upon a fenced pasture with wooden stables on its south side. He noted several horses grazing. The animals paid him no mind, flicking their tails and chewing on dry grass.

"She is our fastest, my lord," the man gestured to a stunning, gray speckled mare that stood along the fence nearest them. "Her name is Luas, and she will get you wherever you need to go."

Weylin sized up the beast before him. She was taller than most of the other horses in the pasture that Weylin could see. She would make a fine horse until Weylin could reunite with Eolas.

"Should I find I have been fooled and given an inadequate horse," Weylin sneered, staring down at the man until he looked away from the pressure building in his gaze. "I will remember this village and put it on my personal agenda to make another visit. On far less pleasant terms."

"Yes, my lord." The man looked down at Weylin's feet as he spoke. "I can vouch for her. She will not let you down."

The mare eyed him with suspicion when their eyes met. She was still and quiet. And her suspicion was not defiance, which was enough for him.

Weylin led her towards the edge of the village in silence. He did not look back at the man who had just lost his best horse.

Weylin swung his legs over the mare and mounted her with ease.

He trotted her forward, getting a feel for the way she would take to his handling. Once they reached a level of comfort with each other that Weylin deemed to be enough, he gathered her reins firmly in his grasp.

"*Teigh!*" Weylin shouted the command that urged her forward.

She surged forward with a speed that caught Weylin off guard. He clutched her reins tighter as he grinned to himself.

The wind howled in his ears like a song, calling him home as it rustled through Luas's silver mane.

Weylin raced with Luas to Castle Eagla—to his father's front door.

39

AISLA

Exhaustion had become a familiar feeling for Aisla.

She could hardly remember a time her muscles did not ache and her mind was not so slow and groggy. It was draining in a way that she had never experienced back on Eilean. Her loneliness settled with every step that Eolas trudged towards Castle Eagla.

Her failures ate at her mind like a parasite. At every turn, she had failed her people—her friends and her family—Ruairi and Eire.

She could not help but wonder what would have happened if she'd remained on her island as she was meant to.

Would he be free now?

Not now, young elf. These thoughts will lead to nowhere good. Aisla nearly jumped out of her skin at the familiar female voice that came from inside her own head.

She had not heard it since before she had joined paths with the Udar Apparent. The hairs along her arms stood on end. The ring nestled deep within her pants pocket warmed her skin through the fabric. It had been cold for so long that Aisla had nearly forgotten about the strange caged esos within it.

Again, she wondered why her grandmother would want to give the dainty ring to the Udar, along with the letter laying at the bottom of her pack that she could not translate on her own.

"How am I meant to do this alone? How can I save Ru, and Eire, and my home?" she asked the voice aloud.

No reply came. The answering silence flared the anger that rested within her chest.

"Curse them all," Aisla snarled. "Curse all the damned gods that watch the injustices of this world, while they sit by, doing *nothing*!"

Eolas let out a soft huff, as if agreeing with her. But the rest of the barren earth around them remained silent.

Aisla found her fingers dancing along the edges of a carved wyvern tooth resting against her neck. She wished Eire was here with her, readying themselves to rescue their best friend. Eire always knew the right words to say. She yearned to talk to Eire about it all, about each of the events that had forever changed Aisla since landing ashore on the cursed continent.

She would tell her of the undine in the depths of the ocean. That would lead to the kiss Aisla shared with Ruairi, nestled in their tent under a rainy night. Then, she would have to speak of his capture and how she knew she should have fought harder to stop him.

Aisla would tell her of a male named Fenian Daro, traveling home to Cluain from a family funeral. The male who saved her life not once, but twice. He had breathed life into her unconscious body just two sunrises ago. The male who was the sworn enemy of her family, her ancestors, and her kingdom. She could only thank the norns that she had gotten ahead of him, because she still did not know how much he had known.

A chill traveled down her spine at the thought.

She had evaded death by his hands in more ways than one.

It was not that she particularly valued her own life, but she had so many others depending on her fate. The pressure weighed upon her, and it grew heavier with each passing moment. It became so heavy, it nearly broke her down, and she struggled to breathe when she found herself lost in the throes of it.

She could never share this burden, nor would she want to, but she knew that if Eire was on this journey beside her, it would all feel so much lighter, so much more bearable. She might be able to breathe again.

Aisla let out a long sigh, and the sound of Eolas's hooves steadied her. The constant of it gave her a place, a reality to focus on. She noted the few trees they passed and the frequent patches of sand that slid beneath Eolas's hooves. The air smelled of the coast, of something so familiar but so foreign at the same time.

Aisla set her pack between her legs so she could rummage through it. She retrieved the map and some tree nuts she had packed. Eolas kept a steady pace as she spread out the map, gripping her thighs to remain stable. She felt a slight guilt despite it all for taking Eolas from *him*. The mare had only known one master.

She found their current location on the map and used her finger to trace a path along the worn parchment that felt soft on her rough skin. That path would lead her to their final contact. They weren't far now. They could arrive before sundown if they managed to hold this pace.

She released a long breath as she shoved the map back into her pack. She made an effort to think of each step as a step closer to Ruairi—not to the Udar.

She had yet to formulate a plan beyond reaching the contact. The contact was supposed to grant her audience with the Udar, but once she got to him, she did not know how to begin. Each time she tried, a panic engulfed her she did not have the time to work through. She still had the ring and the letter—the bargaining chips that her grandmother had all but guaranteed would win them the cure for Eire and all the others that had fallen ill. Still, something in her gut hesitated at the idea of handing them over to her enemy. There was power within both that he did not deserve to hold.

She did not have anything else working in her favor, though.

Aisla had not encountered a source for esos on Iomlan, and she was not trained enough to recognize how much of her supply was left for her to wield. Even then, she did not trust herself enough to control it.

She had nothing else, besides the Udar Apparent's horse, which she could hardly imagine being a hostage of any true value, not when it came down to the layers of animosity between families, between realms.

Aisla breathed out a sigh of defeat that echoed in her ears. If she could just get to Ruairi, if she could just see him, he would know what to do. He could decide what to do with the ring and the letter.

Time dragged on until Aisla found herself atop a grassy hill. Eolas climbed with some strain after their long day of travel. Aisla had shared her snacks with the mare as they traveled to keep her motivated and strong enough to continue on.

At the top of the hill, there was an overlook that looked out upon Castle Eagla and the city of Omra. It might have been beautiful under different circumstances.

The land around the castle stretched into a sunlit field that faded away into golden grains of sand. There were gardens around the base of the marble-white castle. The four towers reached up into copper domes that gleamed with hues of red. The pre-dusk light highlighted all the beautiful features of Eagla that she had only seen in books in scoil.

None of the pictures did the stunning kingdom castle justice, even as it made her throat burn.

It was massive. The stonework was pristine and detailed. A tall iron wall surrounded the castle's perimeter, but from this height, she could see over it and into the castle's north facing courtyard. She could not imagine Castle Farraige ever looking so beautiful, but she knew it once had been. That was a different time, under different leaders.

Jealousy surged through her as she admired the castle before her. She knew her people deserved this, too.

Aisla gently closed her eyes and blinked them open as fear of the unknown threatened to consume her. She breathed in a steady pattern while she imagined meeting Ruairi's brilliant green gaze once again. She felt Eolas twitch beneath her as she sensed her emotional distress. Aisla allowed herself to stay there for a moment, until she felt she had the strength to take one more step forward.

A journey of endless sunrises begins with the very first step.

Aisla allowed the familiar words of Ruairi to comfort her and cradle her cheek as she leaned into them. She counted on them to help her take those last steps into the capital.

A calm washed over her like a cool wind as her heartbeat slowed, and she felt a renewed sense of purpose. She was here for a reason. And she would not allow herself to forget that reason. Or any of them.

Get Ruairi. Get the cure. Get Ruairi. Get the cure. Get Ruairi.

Those reasons played on a loop in her mind. She would not leave Iomlan without both in her possession, no matter what it took.

Aisla nudged Eolas into the city.

40

RUAIRI

Ruairi would forever be changed by those first six sunrises in Castle Eagla. *If* he made it out.

He found himself longing for those first four sunrises of unending silence. If he had thought their neglect was torturous, it was a dream compared to the last two sunrises.

The scars had left their marks. Physically. Emotionally. Mentally.

Ruairi would never again be that same male who sailed away from his home aboard *Stoirme*.

Bruises lined his arms and his torso. There were cuts that traced patterns along his arms. Some had left permanent marks, where others were just a temporary reminder of their cruelty. His eye was swollen shut and blood had crusted over his upper lip.

All he could smell was the metallic stench of blood. It flooded his nostrils until he felt as though he could drown in it. Everything looked bleaker now, and he had not seen the sun since the laochs dragged him past the strange wall beyond, hiding some manner of nightmarish monsters.

Ruairi still had not uttered a word. His anger was a pent-up beast raging inside of him. His rage was the only thing giving him the little strength he had left.

The only eyes that looked upon him with a morsel of regret were those of Callum Ronan. Sometimes, when Ruairi was led through the maze of halls and taken to the room where they tied him down, Ruairi would catch the eye of the laoch, and he saw sympathy there. Sometimes, he could have sworn that the laoch would look upon his own comrades with disgust.

He had entered Ruairi's room once, last night. And it was not to haul him away to be tortured, but to hand-deliver his meal. He said there had been a feast in the castle, and that Ruairi deserved to partake while he was there within their walls.

Rather than the cold slop of mashed rice and mysterious meat, Callum brought him a tray of smoked ham, mashed potatoes, and green beans with a goblet of red wine.

Ruairi had only narrowed his eyes, doubting Callum's kindness. He watched, mouth watering, as Callum laid the tray down upon the small table. Callum gave him one small nod and a pained look of sympathy before disappearing through the wooden door.

Ruairi waited a moment, as long as he could hold himself back, before devouring the food on the tray. He savored each bite and allowed the tastes to refuel him.

While Ruairi did not respect Callum Ronan, he was thankful someone looked upon him with kindness in their eyes.

To feel real again.

After he had licked every last crumb from the tray, Ruairi allowed his body to fall back onto the bed. He pulled his legs to his chest and curled onto his side as he awaited the knock that would inevitably rip him from the small comfort he had found within his cell. He waited for it like a flood that he could not escape.

He was losing his mind moment by moment—bit by bit.

Throughout the night, sounds echoed from beyond his cell reflecting the noises he heard outside of the castle. There were snarls and roars and growls and groans. Some sounded almost human, but not quite. They were guttural and terrifying, and Ruairi could only hope that he would never have to face whatever monsters emitted them. Each passing moment, they seemed to grow ever closer, and Ruairi wished he could crawl out of his own skin.

If he had known what was to come from that first step he and Aisla took aboard the *Stoirme*, he would have kept her there. He would have held her on the coast of Eilean and never let her go. He would have begged and pleaded with her not to set sail, to stay with him. Ruairi would have stayed and built a home with her. They could have had a family and a life that he feared he would now only catch glimpses of in the dark of the night when he was stolen away into sleep.

Curse the prophecy. And the gods. And above all, the Myrkor dynasty.

Knock. Knock.

Ruairi sucked in a ragged breath as his fingers dug into the blanket at his side. He breathed out.

He stopped trying to resist the inevitable pain as he sat up, ignoring every aching muscle and every tender bruise of his flesh.

A female entered his room. She was petite, with short black hair and deep brown eyes. Her skin was pale and her smile was bright and unnerving. She looked to be around his own age.

"Hello, elf of the abandoned ship," she said in a silky voice that traveled through the room with a softness that Ruairi had not felt in a long time. He was immediately suspicious of her as he stood to his shaky feet to tower above her. "I have heard much about you."

Ruairi remained silent. He stared down at her through narrowed eyes.

"I see what they say about your silence to be true," she murmured. Her eyes scanned him from head to toe, lingering longer than he would like. "You are not helping anyone here by refusing to speak, but least of all yourself."

Ruairi blinked slowly at her, as if to say, *I have already heard these words phrased countless different ways.*

"My name is Orla," she continued to speak, and Ruairi looked over her head to the two laochs that usually escorted him to the secondary location. His stomach twisted with foreboding. He looked down to meet her gaze again. "It seems as though we will be spending some time together today, and in the future. If you would, please follow me."

She moved towards the open doorway. Ruairi noted her long, black robes that dragged behind her. He followed, his legs heavy and resistant, and the laochs fell into step behind him.

Their footsteps echoed through the halls, and in Ruairi's head as she led them down several long hallways.

At last, they entered a mid-sized room with a wooden table in its center and a chair on either side, so they were facing each other.

Ruairi looked towards the female, Orla, and tried to keep his hands from trembling as she gestured for him to sit down in the chair further from the door. She sat in the one opposite him and met his gaze with an unnerving calm. Ruairi worked to keep his fear from showing, forcing a blank expression as he waited for whatever came next.

She held out her hands, palms up, across the table, never breaking eye contact. Ruairi looked down at them, then back up at her.

"Take my hands," she instructed in her high-pitched voice.

Everything within Ruairi screamed at him not to, everything felt wrong about it, but the laochs took a step forward in unison at his hesitation, hands on their weapons. So, Ruairi took Orla's hands and a pit settled deep within him.

A dread rose within him as his vision went black upon the contact of their skin. He fought to pull away, but her grip was iron-like. The darkness was followed by a searing pain that surged through his body. Frigid wisps of air entangled his limbs and torso, holding him in place like chains that hurt to move against. He fought back a scream as he writhed uncontrollably with the invisible pain. The sound of wind echoed through his ears.

It was his esos. His own esos was holding him in place, and she had used the power of his own mind to do it.

This was no weapon. This was not like the other times he had been taken to rooms within the castle. This was a new form of torture, one that could be far more dangerous. This female was a pryer, just as Cliona was.

She wielded the esos that could meld and break one's mind.

Ruairi gasped for air. His head throbbed. His heart pounded in his ears above the searing scream of the blinding pain.

Amidst it all, Ruairi fought to anchor himself in his body, so as not to be lost within the darkness. He focused on the firm grip of her hands. The skin to skin contact. Anything of this world.

He imagined those walls they had been taught to build in scoil —ones he rarely had use for. He built them up tall and strong in his mind, working up a mental fortitude to keep this female out. He could feel her tearing them down as they were constructed. They were battling for his mind, tugging against one another. Ruairi gritted his teeth.

Then, she released him. His winds vanished. His vision came back slowly, in inky blotches until he could see the whole room again. His breaths came in pants, forcing the air back into his lungs, as the shadows retreated from the corners of his vision.

There was esos on Iomlan.

It came as a relief, first. There had to be a source out there for him to rely on for replenishing his own. It was possible.

Then, it was fear. Fear of the way these people would use their esos. What it meant that the source seemed so scarce here, and he had yet to see any of the other elves wielding their own esos.

His brain began to sort through the facts, but they came in muddled waves through the remnants of the pain. He could hardly see straight when he met her unflinching gaze. She looked at him expectantly, waiting for a reaction.

Questions hovered on the tip of his tongue, just out of reach. But he would not speak. He would not give her that victory or that satisfaction.

"I take it you've never felt a power like mine before," she mused, almost gently. Her voice reached out to soothe the wounds that she had inflicted, and he continued building up that mental shield to block the calming effect. "You are hiding something from us, from my Udar. Or else you would not continue to hold onto this foolish silence—that much is evident. My Udar is determined to figure out what is so important for you to hide. So, if you continue to hold your tongue, I will weed through your mind myself. As you can see, it will not be pleasant. Only you have the power to stop it. You have been given a choice."

She finished with a lilting laugh.

Ruairi clenched his hands at his side, so hard his fingernails dug into his skin, but he did not feel the pain. He felt so powerless, so vulnerable and naked before them.

He could lie, but any lie not properly thought through would incriminate him.

Ruairi breathed. He worked to erase any memory or hint of Aisla as far down in his mind as he could. He released the grip he had held onto her with. He let go of his anchor, his hope, thinking it would be the only way to save her—to save his home.

They seldom practiced training against pryers in Eilean. It was an unspoken law not to use that invasive esos on others. Violations of the mind would not be tolerated.

Orla's hand shot across the table and wrapped around his throat. A sinister smile crept across her lips just before Ruairi stopped seeing at all. He clawed at her hands, gasping, as the white-hot scalding pain returned.

Whatever he had felt moments ago was just the warm-up to

whatever this was. It was a pain he could not even process, he could only feel it, be consumed by it. His arms fell limp at his side.

He was dying.

He was sure of it, but that thought felt like relief for the first time. Passing on would be a reprieve compared to this.

He wished to rip his soul from his body to not feel this pain a moment longer. He might have been screaming. He might have been crying. He could have vomited.

He did not know. He could not tell.

The walls were getting harder and harder to build while she continued to break them. Ruairi pushed with all of his might inside of his mind to block her out. He felt the push and pull inside, but did not give up pushing. He fought to make his shield thicker, all the while she was shredding them like paper.

All he knew was the feeling of the pressure inside of his skull that built and built until he felt he might explode from the inside out. Through that pain, there was a rhythmic prodding like a needle inside of his own mind. He felt himself cracking under the pressure. His mind was splintering open. He could see it coming apart, his own undoing and he was nearly helpless to stop it.

A pair of yellow-green eyes flashed through his mind and fear consumed him. He could only hope she had not seen as he continued to work against the cruel female while pushing Aisla deeper and deeper down beyond his walls.

Help me. Help me. Help me.

He pleaded to anyone who was listening.

Help. Help. Help.

And then there was nothing.

His eyes blinked open, and he felt his feet drag across the stone floor.

Rough hands gripped his arms so tightly, he knew they would bruise. He could hardly feel it. The light of the dim torches burned through him.

His mouth was dry. His nose was clotted with the stench of his own blood. His body was numb.

His mind was shattered.

Ruairi was a limp weight between the two laochs, unable to stand on his own two feet. His body ached and he could not find the strength to lift his head. His breathing came ragged. He assessed the shadows moving across the floor in the flickering, warm light, and guessed there were two other laochs behind him and the ones on either side of him. He heard footsteps approaching from the opposite direction.

"Captain Ronan," the voice ahead of him spoke, and Ruairi figured that Callum must be one of the laochs behind him because he knew that he was not holding his arm.

"Yes?" the captain spoke sharply, authority packed into that singular word.

"The Young Wolf has returned," the man said, and Ruairi felt a foreboding sink into his chest. "He has been searching for you. He, erm, warns of a young elf approaching. Apparently she has the potential to be an enemy to the crown. He seems rather frantic, captain."

The man lowered his voice towards the end.

Ruairi could feel the tension brewing in the air. He could not piece it together. His broken mind was not strong enough to process. He could not think through all that those few short sentences had meant. Something about them felt familiar, and almost comforting.

"Take me to him," Callum Ronan stepped around the laochs holding Ruairi.

Ruairi watched the captain's boots disappear while Ruairi and the three remaining laochs carried forward in silence. Their steps were more hurried now, as if eager to get away from their current duty and find out more about their Udar Apparent's return.

Eventually, the door to Ruairi's cell was thrown open and they tossed him inside with no hint of gentleness. Ruairi let his body crumple to the floor, long past the shame of it all.

Once he heard the click of the door that meant it had fallen shut, he pulled himself to his knees with a grunt of effort. He stared up at the ceiling as tears that could not fall stung the corners of his eyes.

He wondered what Orla could have pulled from his mind and how damning it could be to his home.

Someone was coming for him.

It was terrifying, but selfishly, there was a relief tugging at Ruairi that felt like a weight lifted from his aching chest. It was as though he could breathe again after sunrises spent below the surface of water.

"Aisla," he spoke the name to himself in the dark of his cell where no one else could hear.

It was gravel on his throat, and he barely recognized the sound of his own voice.

Her name aroused something in him he could not place. The syllables felt foreign and far away—as though someone else spoke them from another time.

He collapsed back onto the floor.

He could taste her name, feel her presence. He could not remember what she looked like.

His chest heaved as he smiled to himself even as it reopened wounds that had begun to heal.

Her name lingered on his lips. He allowed his eyes to fall closed.

41
AISLA

Aisla pulled her cloak over her head as she entered Omra alone.

She left Eolas tied to a tree outside of the city perimeter, afraid of someone recognizing the Udar Apparent's mare, even while the guilt gnawed at her stomach at the anxious look in her dark eyes when Aisla walked away.

She shouldered her pack higher, noting the laoch standing at the gate looking her up and down. Her pulse quickened and sweat beaded along her brow with anticipation as she neared the man.

To her surprise, he gave her a curt nod, allowing her to pass into the capital of Samhradh. She nodded back as she held her breath.

Her feet skidded along the sand while she looked about the bustling city. Everyone appeared to be in a rush. Laochs stood at every corner, blades at their hips. Humans chattered about as they pushed past her. Dwarves argued around a bend.

Aisla kept her attention forward as her esos stirred, and she knew that her number one priority had to be keeping it at bay. She could not expose herself. She glanced again at the map gripped tightly between her fingers. The walk to the house marked on the map was not far. She would get something to eat, and then meet the last contact before facing the Udar and begging for the cure while ensuring Ruairi's safe arrival home. She knew she would need strength for whatever she was about to face. Aisla hadn't had a decent night's sleep since back on Eilean, and it showed. She could feel mats in her hair, and the way her stomach had begun to cave in. Her skin was pale and her lips cracked in the crisp air that came with winter's end and spring's arrival.

Aisla was weak. Weaker than she had ever been. The version of herself that approached her enemy was nothing but an echo of who Aisla could be.

Aisla's heart thundered as she wondered what the contact would make of her arriving on his doorstep. She assumed Cliona had told him of Ruairi's red hair and piercing green gaze to watch for, but had she had time the time to give them Aisla's description as well? Aisla did not resemble Mona, who had blonde hair and deep brown eyes. She could only hope they would accept her as who she said she was.

The first tavern she came across was a brick building larger than the village counter back in Caillte. She pushed through the wooden door and approached the large, burly man at the register.

"Serving deer steak and potatoes at the moment, miss," the man grunted as way of greeting.

"How much?" Aisla asked, pulling out her coin pouch from her pack.

The man named his price and she handed him the funds.

Aisla left with her meal in a bag. She found a small wooden table outside. Aisla hunched over the food and pulled her cloak tighter around her. She tore into the food with a savageness that would have brought shame to her grandmother.

Aisla could not imagine Cliona's reaction if she knew how close her granddaughter was to their enemy now. She only knew that Cliona would be disappointed and angry. She remembered their conversation from the night that Aisla had shown up at Ruairi's baile with the high hopes that had led them here.

She wondered if that conversation would be their last.

"Did you hear the orders from the Udar?" A man spoke from a table next to her, and Aisla peaked her ears to listen in.

"Not since he posted that useless guard outside after they took in that elf," another man grumbled back.

"Well, now they're not letting anyone new in the city. I heard his son returned. Something about a female following him," he spoke in a rushed voice. "I just got out here with Deirdre. She was sent to go take over at the gate and lock it down."

Aisla's appetite disappeared even as she forced down the food she knew she would need. She tried to keep listening to the men's conversation, but her mind buzzed with all that she had already heard.

She was relieved to be in the right place, knowing that they had captured an elf and that elf had to be Ruairi. But she felt fear thanks to the confirmation that he was in the hands of their enemy. She wondered how the Udar Apparent could have possibly gotten here so soon. Above all of that, she felt thankful she had made it moments before the guard switched. Moments before Omra would close its gates to the outside world.

She stared down at her nearly empty plate before she crumpled up her bag and threw it in the nearest waste bin.

Aisla's face set with determination as she strolled past the men who could never recognize her. She nearly sneered at the irony. The cobblestone street passed under her boots and she carried onward.

The map led her away from the bustle of the city center and towards a cluster of bailes just outside. They were a variety of sizes, most larger than her own back in Eilean. She sucked in a breath as she turned the last corner to the house marked on the map from her grandmother. She walked up the worn path to the front door and tightened her shaking hand into a fist before lightly rapping on the wood.

The silence roared around her as her palms itched with her esos.

The door creaked open, slowly, and a male peered back at her with wrinkled olive skin, long brown hair, and dark eyes through the crack in the door. The male looked her up and down so slowly she felt violated. She began to feel self-conscious of her ragged state. The worn look in her eyes and the layer of grime coating her skin. At last, he met her gaze with an intensity that almost made Aisla look away. *Almost.*

Aisla opened her mouth to speak, but could not find the words.

"I take it you come from the lost island?" the male spoke in a gruff voice.

Aisla nodded.

"You took longer than expected." His eyes darted beyond her.

Foreboding crept under Aisla's skin, and the hairs of her arm stood on end. He still had not fully opened the door.

"The journey was more complicated than expected," she replied.

If only he knew the truth behind that statement.

"You should have known, *gheall ceann.*"

The moment the words left the male's lips, Aisla's stomach sunk. She made to flee, but his hand gripped her arm with a force that dragged a yelp from her.

"Let go," she snarled.

She whirled on him as she withdrew her blade from her waistband. He did not have time to react before she wrapped her arm around his neck and pressed *Oidhe* to his neck, drawing a thin line of red blood along his throat.

"I would be careful," another male voice spoke from behind them. Aisla turned them around to face the man clad in laoch leathers. There were four more standing by him. They had been waiting for her here. Someone had betrayed them. "We have someone whose life you would not put at risk. It would be such a shame if something were to happen to him now, after you had made it this far, only to never see him again. But it will not come to that unless you force our hand."

Aisla froze, her blood coursed in her ears. She narrowed her eyes at the laoch working to assess her limited options.

But there was only one to Aisla.

Her arms fell limp, and she took a step back from the male who was meant to be their ally. A numbness crept in with her realization of helplessness—of defeat. She had walked into a trap. A trap she should have predicted.

The Udar was a step ahead of her, even if his son had not been. Or maybe he had been all along.

"The Udar has been expecting you, *Aisling Iarkis.*" The sound of her voice on the laoch's lips made her flinch.

The words knocked a blow to her.

They spelled her doom before her eyes.

42

WEYLIN

Weylin Myrkor strode into his castle with his head held high as his cloak billowed behind him in the night wind.

Luas had been left at the castle gates, and his laochs had scrambled to assist him with taking her to the stables. They alerted his father and the captain of his personal guard, his closest friend.

A visit with his father would be the first order of business, the most pertinent, and Callum would understand that. Weylin knew Callum would be expecting him after, ready to catch up on all the sunrises past since they last convened.

Weylin made his way to his father's office. He passed through the familiar marble hallways lit by torchlight until he was standing outside his doorway. Weylin took a deep breath before turning the doorknob and pushing his way into the room.

His father's deep brown eyes looked up to meet his. There was an intensity there that never failed to make Weylin lose some of his own confidence, but he straightened his shoulders and tilted his chin up, refusing to allow his father to see him falter.

Faolan Myrkor looked worn and tired, but there was a faint

glow in his eyes that Weylin could not read. Weylin brushed it away. His father's eyes tracked his every movement until he was sitting in front of him, neither of them speaking a word of greeting.

"My journey was a success." Weylin started with the simpler things, the things he could still understand as he sat before the Udar. "Rania Dorcas is to be my mate. She accepted, and her father approved as well."

"I heard," was all his father replied.

Weylin nodded. He fought a growing irritation.

"I have something else I need to share with you," he said cautiously.

This was unfamiliar territory. This was where Weylin did not know what to expect.

"Go on," his father growled. He sat up straighter and looked at Weylin through narrowed eyes.

Weylin paused as he thought of the way to start. He thought of how to summarize his sunrises with *Ellora Morlee*—of how exactly he could describe the danger he felt was approaching without sharing the friendship that had formed between them.

"There is a threat on the way," Weylin decided to share what was necessary for his realm and no more. "I was traveling with a female elf that sought to become a laoch here in Samhradh. When she realized who I was, she drugged me and fled. I do not know her intentions, but we should be prepared. Especially during this time."

Faolan's eyes flickered with something that was not the surprise that Weylin had been expecting. His father had always been good at disguising his emotions, but Weylin had thought this at least would catch him off guard.

"How do you know?" Faolan asked.

Weylin nearly stormed out at that. The fact that his father's first instinct was to question him rather than trust him.

"I saw it with my own eyes, but believe what you will," Weylin snarled, leaning closer to his father across the desk scattered with papers and plans that Weylin had long stopped trying to keep up with.

Faolan's nostrils flared at his son's tone. His eyes sent a warning that Weylin chose to ignore.

"Her name is Aisling," Faolan spoke up and Weylin could not hide his own confusion. *How could his father know that?* "Aisling Iarkis."

Aisling Iarkis. Iarkis.

Weylin slumped back in his chair as that single word hit him like a blow. His breath caught in his throat. Her name seared through the swirling chaos of his mind. He had traveled with her, the one who had caused all of this. The *gheall ceann.*

And he had somehow been blind to it—blind to her.

He could not force out a reply, even if he had wanted to. He felt shock and fear and more things than he could begin to sort through. Weylin realized how lucky he was to be alive, how lucky he was that she had not killed him if she had known who he was.

Then, he cursed himself as he also realized whose life he had saved on more than one occasion. He could have left the enemy of his family, the enemy of the worldly realms, to die and this could all be in the past.

His body burned. Burned so hot, he wanted to run from the room.

"My ears on that damned island warned me a few days ago. I was going to alert you upon your arrival, but you took far longer than I expected," his father said and sat back in his maroon velvet chair.

"I will not sit here and defend my whereabouts to you," Weylin snapped. "What is to be done with the *mallaithe*?"

"She will arrive to this castle, and we will gather what information we can. Then we will end her and be rid of the threat that she poses forever," Faolan said with confidence, and Weylin felt his insides turn. "And we can finally rebuild the seven worldly realms as they were always meant to be, united."

Weylin nodded. He knew his input would not matter, and he did not know if he had any to give.

"Do you have any other updates for me?" Faolan asked with a raised brow.

"No, my lord," Weylin spoke with an icy tone as he met his father's gaze once again.

"Good," Faolan said with a sigh. "Your mother will begin planning your wedding to the Dorcas female. I imagine you shall be wed within the next three moons in Sneachta."

Weylin nodded.

"You don't seem very concerned with the Iarkis female," Weylin said and watched his father's face darken.

"What do I have to be concerned about?"

"If what we know of the prophecy is true," Weylin spoke in a low voice. "You should be preparing every laoch in the area. We should not be sitting here, in your office, talking it over."

"My ears have assured me she has not come into her power. She is as useless with it as we are here with no source. The laochs we have in the castle will be more than we need to put her down," Faolan responded, smoothly. "Bold of you to question me. I would suggest you do not do it again. I will not always have such patience for a boy who thinks himself to be more than he is."

Weylin stood so quickly he knocked his chair over. The power in his veins riled, and his fists clenched at his sides as his throat burned with anger.

A thousand words danced on the tip of his tongue. Curses, insults, sneers, but Weylin said nothing as he turned and stormed from the room with *her* words from sunrises ago echoing in his ears.

The way she spoke it with a confidence that nearly frightened him at the time, and it frightened him even more now as her yellow-green eyes bore into his memories.

Don't underestimate me, Fenian. Not for a moment.

———

Callum Ronan sat across from Weylin Myrkor as they met to share a drink in the castle's small pub.

It had been a relief to see his best friend again. Greeting Callum was like seeing a brother.

"Congratulations again on your betrothal," Callum spoke. He lifted his mug to clink against Weylin's in celebration. "Rania is a lucky lady. I look forward to meeting her, and I wish I could have gone with you on your journey."

"Trust me," Weylin said with a sigh before he sipped the amber liquid. "I do too."

Weylin was asked to recount his journey. How could he summarize it all and look past all his own blind spots? He had not been able to come to terms with them himself, so how could he expect someone else to? He shifted and looked down at the wooden grain of the worn table in this familiar place that felt suddenly less familiar to him. He knew if there was anyone he could talk to, it would be Callum.

"Have you heard about the new prisoner?" Callum asked before he could speak up.

"No?" Weylin posed the word as a question.

"There's a male they found fleeing a ship that ran our blockade off Briongloid. The ship was unmarked and off the coast closest to Eilean, so of course there are questions surrounding his sudden appearance," Callum spoke softly. His eyes looked around the room for any listening ears. "We've been trying to get him to speak since they took him as prisoner. He demanded some cure, but when he didn't receive it he took a silence, and he's held that silence since then."

Weylin met Callum's eyes wearily. He wondered why his father had not mentioned the male to him.

"What do you think he's hiding?"

"No, not hiding," Callum shook his head. "I think he's protecting someone."

Weylin felt his throat tighten and his stomach sink as he nodded his head slowly.

"*Aisling?*" Weylin asked around the lump in his throat. The puzzle pieces lay scattered before him on the floor of his mind.

"Who?" Callum furrowed his brows.

"The Iarkis female."

"*Iarkis?*" Callum hissed in surprise. "What are you talking about?"

"My father just informed me that his ears in Eilean told him that their ninth generation heir is on our continent. Her name is Aisling Iarkis, and—and I met her. Why would my father not tell you this?"

"I had no idea," Callum shook his head. "Although, I suppose it makes sense why we are keeping that male around rather than executing him. Your father's men find amusement in the etching of his skin."

"I cannot say I blame them given who he could be protecting," Weylin snapped. "Or are you finding sympathy for our enemy?"

"No, my lord," Callum used his formal title as he looked behind Weylin at the wall. "That is not what I meant."

Weylin grunted and took another swig.

"You said you met her?" Callum asked, cautiously.

"Yes," Weylin paused, and it was his turn to avert his gaze as he looked down into the liquid in his mug. "And saved her life, *twice*. I did not know it was her. She was using an alias, just as I was. I found her first trapped by a pack of barghests, and if I had known . . . if I had known what I know now, I would have left her there. I would have continued on my way home and our realm would be saved from the havoc she could wreak."

Callum remained silent, and Weylin did not blame him.

"I messed up," Weylin whispered the words that he could only ever admit to Callum. "I could have let her pass on. I had opportunities, and I missed them all."

"You did not know," Callum said, and Weylin looked up to see him shaking his head. "You did not know. And there are greater forces at play that will have their way in these games."

Weylin nodded silently.

"What is your father's plan for her arrival? How far away is she?"

The captain in Callum was now present. Calculating and planning. Exactly as Weylin would expect.

"He says his ears in Eilean have assured him she is no real threat," Weylin said. "She has not learned to use the power she has been gifted. He says the laochs within these walls will be enough."

"And what if he is wrong?"

"He is our Udar," Weylin spoke instinctively on the need to defend his father's decisions even to Callum. "He will not be wrong."

43

AISLA

Aisla's hands shook and her body trembled. Her mouth grew dry, and she forced herself to maintain eye contact with the laoch who spoke the words that rattled her to her core. She ignored the other pairs of eyes that assessed her and bore into her.

How could they know she was here?

Her heart pounded, and she wondered if Ruairi had given her name. She knew her grandmother would never let word spread that she was on Iomlan. She wondered what it had taken to get him there, and her insides turned.

"How do you know my name?" she snarled with a ferocity that came from deep within and surprised her.

Red tinted her vision. Her mind and body went into a full panic. She held onto her composure by a fraying thread as she thought not of herself, or Ruairi, or Eire, or Cliona, but of all the realms that her life impacted and how out of her hands it all was. She had caused this. She had brought herself to her enemy with no semblance of a plan besides protecting the ones she loved.

"Watch your tone," the man sneered and took a threatening step towards her.

Aisla pressed her lips into a thin line and she sheathed *Oidhe*.

"Eh eh," the man scolded her like a dog and held out his hand. "You have quickly proven that we cannot let you keep that blade. Hand it over."

Aisla nearly dropped the dagger as she withdrew it and placed it in his grubby, outstretched palm. Her hand felt heavier than ever as she pulled it back to her own side.

"There you go, *mallaithe*," the male sneered the term of old for *cursed* like it was bile on his tongue. "You may have your audience with the Udar now. I would advise you to caution your tongue and your hands once you are in his presence. He is not a man known for his mercy nor his patience."

Aisla balled her hands into tight fists, willing them to stop shaking, praying to the nine gods for any semblance of composure and strength. Her esos brewed beneath her skin, almost in reminder. It whispered an offering that she could not yet accept if she wished to see Ruairi alive again.

"How do you know my name?" she asked again, more controlled this time. She tilted her head up to meet the gaze of the laoch.

"Save your questions for the Udar," he replied dryly. "Where is the Young Wolf's mare?"

Aisla glared at the man.

"Maybe I'd answer your questions if you bothered to answer mine."

"You would do best not to forget who has the upper hand here, *mallaithe*," he snapped. "You are in our lands now. At *our* mercy."

Aisla bit her tongue to stop herself from retorting. Her fingernails dug into her palms. She stilled as the male who was meant to give her an updated map and arrange a cordial meeting with the

Udar bound her wrists behind her back, pulling the rope tightly as she gritted her teeth.

He leaned forward and his hot breath tickled her ear. "Cliona should reconsider who she trusts," he whispered so softly she nearly missed it.

They pushed her out of the front door, and Aisla's heartbeat grew more and more rapid with each step they took forward. Her palms burned. Ringing sounded in her ears with the rush of wind. She pushed it all down—deep down—while she continued to glare straight ahead where the laochs in front guided her to Castle Eagla.

She looked at the looming towers of the castle as they made their way towards them with a heavy, anxious heart.

Her feet shuffled through the sandy earth. Her mouth was dry as she tasted the salty sea air that breezed towards her. The body of water that bordered the east side of Castle Eagla led to the south end of Iomlan and into the Tusnua Sea.

Soon, the wooden gates to Castle Eagla towered before her, casting shadows across the earth. She had hoped that at the pace she had traveled, she would have beaten the Udar Apparent here. But considering the laochs were more concerned about the whereabouts of his mare than the Udar Apparent himself, she knew she had failed.

She took several deep breaths and tried not to think of all that weighed upon her shoulders. It was enough to make her break, to make her fall to her knees before she even made it to the Udar.

But she would not.

She was Aisla Iarkis, and she was more than words on paper. She was more than the nine forms of esos buried deep within her.

And she would be enough.

The laochs lead her down two corridors and then into the largest room Aisla had ever been in. She noted the banners of the Myrkor dynasty.

Rage stirred in her chest, and she clenched her jaw.

Her eyes dragged from the colors on the wall to the smug male sitting on a throne in the center of the room.

Her blood boiled, and her trembles of fear became tremors of anger. Everything within her threatened to explode. She realized she was holding her breath as she slowly breathed in and out to calm herself and regain the control that she could not afford to lose.

The male was a near mirror image to his son. They had the same light brown skin and black hair. The same stony gaze. Her throat tightened as she was reminded of the male she had been working to forget.

The sight of him nearly sent a shudder down her spine, but she steeled herself against the reaction. Against what the Udar surely wanted to see. Instead, she set her shoulders straighter and her chin higher.

Aisla knew that the throne he sat upon was the Arden Throne, made of marble and jade. She knew it had been ripped from her family's castle all those generations ago. Aisla could feel its presence, she could sense the way it called to her, even yearned for her in a way that tore at her very heart. She felt it, but she refused to look at it. She refused to break eye contact with Faolan. She feared that looking upon the throne and all that had been stolen from Eilean and the Iarkises would be too much to bear.

She could not risk it for a glance at what should have been.

Faolan was dressed in a maroon cloak, his arms hung casually over the sides of the throne. This man had come from the line that had taken everything and ruined centuries of peace. He had destroyed her future and the future of too many others to count. Eire was dying, and this man had the cure. So many others were surely at risk as well since Aisla had left. She could not let herself think of them now.

"*Aisling Iarkis*," Faolan's voice grated against her like gravel. He said her name like a weapon. He knew by holding that alone, he had more than she had intended to give him. "I have yet to meet an

Iarkis in the flesh, and here you bring yourself into my hall—into *my* throne room. I suppose I should thank you for this opportunity. The opportunity to look upon the face of the female meant to set ruin to the realms."

Aisla bristled at his words. Found a voice screaming inside of her mind at the lies that had been presented for far too long.

"You mean *my* throne?" she growled. "I hear you've been keeping it warm for me."

"Ah, I see words come easier to you than they did for your friend," Faolan spoke with condescension.

The mention of Ruairi immediately brought Aisla back to reality and the power dynamic she could not control. Her nostrils flared. She needed to cool herself down for his sake.

"What have you done to him?" she hissed through clenched teeth.

"Now, now," Faolan shook his head with disappointment. "No formalities? One would think you could return the niceties I graciously showed you. Or do they truly raise barbarians in Eilean, as the whispers on the wind say?"

Faolan stood in a painstakingly slow movement. He approached Aisla with footsteps so graceful he appeared to glide across the stone floor.

Aisla could hear her heartbeat in her ears. And then he was so close to her, she could hear his breaths as they left him. In the blink of an eye, Faolan's hand flew to her chin, and he gripped it there, asserting a silent dominance.

Aisla struggled to jerk her head out of his grasp, but he tightened his hold until Aisla's jaw hurt, and she winced with the pain. He tilted her head up to look at him. He towered a head taller than her. She was incapable of doing anything to retaliate that would not potentially cost Ruairi his life.

"You will say my name," he said with an eerie calmness. "You will say *'Thank you, Faolan Myrkor, thank you for welcoming me.'*

Because you should be grateful that I allowed you into this place. That you and your companion are both not already choking on your own blood—that is a favor I have granted you."

"*Never*." Aisla bared her teeth as rage flickered through his all-too-familiar amber gaze.

He looked over her from head to toe and then back down at her with a smile that made her skin crawl.

Aisla heard a door open behind Faolan, but she could not see around his broad frame as he held her in place.

She did not have to see to know.

She heard two sets of footsteps enter the room from the side door, and she knew it had to be Ruairi. She heard him grunt in pain as his footsteps shuffled across the floor.

It was a relief and a danger all at once.

"Would you like to try again, *mallaithe*?" Faolan grinned victoriously.

The pressure in his grip tightened. Aisla frantically searched for options that were not there. She was all too aware of Ruairi's presence in the room and that her actions would have consequences for him.

"I'm waiting," he seethed.

Her body stiffened. She accepted the defeat. Her arms felt heavy and her head spun.

"Thank you, *Faolan Myrkor*."

The words burned down her throat like flames. She did not miss the sick satisfaction in his eyes, which only made her feel sicker. He released his grip on her chin with force, which caused her to stumble backwards.

Shame heated her cheeks as she regained her footing and glared back up at him.

"Very wise of you to concede." He turned on his heel, and his robe billowed behind him as he walked back to his throne, leaving

Aisla a line of sight to Ruairi. A shudder traveled down her back and she nearly fell to her knees.

Whatever she had been expecting—whatever she had been afraid of—this was far worse.

Aisla's hand flew to cover her mouth as a cry of surprise and pain escaped her lips.

This was not the same Ruairi she had left. One of his eyes was swollen shut, and his face was bruised all over. A still-healing slash lined under one of his eyes that was still red from the recency. Another stood out on his neck. His skin was sickly pale, and he stood slumped over. She saw cuts peeking out from under the sleeves of his shirt, and she could only begin to imagine what damage lay beneath it.

She choked down the bile coating her throat. Her fingertips itched for her esos. A yearning to make the Udar pay, to make this family pay, to make each of the realms and each of the nine gods pay consumed her.

Everything in her *burned*.

She met his gaze with a ferocity even as a guilty feeling settled in her. *This was her fault.*

Ruairi's eyes were glazed as he looked to her. They were alarmed and far away and lacking all the warmth she had grown to know and love. Questions brewed in their green depths, and she realized he did not know how much the Udar knew, and he would not risk giving him any more information by making it obvious that he knew her.

Aisla nodded to him slowly, as it was all she could think to do. It was all she could do.

She hoped he understood.

Aisla's gaze dragged to Faolan, who again lounged in the throne of her ancestors. She saw red as she took in the smirk on his face and the way he seemed amused by all of this. The way Ruairi's wounds and Aisla's grief seemed to entertain him.

"What did you do to him?" Aisla asked in a roar that surprised her own ears.

Any hope for diplomacy, any obligation she felt as the Mathair Apparent to broker a peace, disappeared with the sight of him. A ringing sounded in her ears, but she hardly noticed it.

Shock flickered across Faolan's face, but it passed as quickly as it appeared. Shadows danced around her and she realized it was not her words or her tone that caused his reaction, but the way her esos had slipped from her control. The way the darkness of a Shadow flitted about her like a beast on a tight leash. It licked her skin as if asking permission to attack.

She could feel the fear of the two laochs who pressed nearer to her.

"Aisla," she heard Ruairi breathe out in both warning and in awe.

The sound of his voice melted the ice that had formed within her. The rasp and dryness made it sound foreign, but underneath it was still Ruairi.

"Your esos cannot survive here, *mallaithe*," Faolan snarled, dropping his calm and collected facade as his own anger peaked through. "There is no source for it, so I advise you to drop it now before you do something that gets your friend here hurt."

Aisla knew his words to be true, knew she should be cautious with the fragile thing, but she would not take the advice from him.

"I hear there is something you were meant to give me," Faolan said in a stern voice that radiated the authority he wielded like a weapon. "My laochs searched your bags that were brought in and found nothing of value. So, hand it over."

A slight relief filled her chest at the one thing she had managed to do right when she had shoved the letter and the ring deep within her pockets, not trusting them to be anywhere but within her reach.

They seemed to burn through her clothes, as if the inanimate objects knew he was demanding them. She knew she could not give them to him. She knew she needed to keep them in her own possession. But she also needed the cure, and she needed Ruairi and would choose them both if it came down to that.

"I do not have them," she lied through clenched teeth. "Give me the cure for my people and then I will tell you where I hid them."

Then, Faolan smiled. And Aisla felt the world crumbling beneath her. She knew the words before they left his lips.

"Stupid girl, *there is no cure.*"

Her heart sank, but her determination steeled.

"*Liar!*" she shouted and the floor beneath her feet trembled as the shadows surrounding her swirled faster. "Do not lie to me again."

"And who are you to make demands? You have no weapon, no army, no source for your esos. You are nothing but the name you carry." He rose from his chair now and his presence cast a tall shadow that reached for her own.

The tension in the room was thick enough to touch, but the sound of a door being opened cut through it like a blade.

Aisla did not have to turn around to know who had entered the room. Her esos seemed to pull in *his* direction, like a whisper calling out.

She heard *his* heavy footsteps as he approached the center of the room. She felt *his* eyes boring into her back as she stared ahead to Faolan, who watched his son approach. His lips spread into a wider grin as it all came to a head.

Weylin Myrkor strode forward with a confidence that made Aisla's skin prickle. He passed her without so much as a glance and moved to stand at his father's right hand. When he finally turned, when she was finally faced with the amber gaze she had woken up to the last few sunrises, her stomach dropped all the way to the core of the world.

He wore fine clothes in the Myrkor colors that made him look like the Udar Apparent. His once warm amber eyes were set with a steeliness that radiated a chill through Aisla's being. He looked at her with disgust written all over his face.

He had betrayed her, not that she had expected any different, which is why she had left first.

It didn't take away the sting of his betrayal.

With the pure hatred in his eyes, she knew he would hold a grudge for leaving him drugged and without his mare. But she did not feel a drop of guilt as she bared her teeth back at him with equal hatred in her own heart.

"Hello, *banphrionsa*. We meet again."

44

WEYLIN

Aisling's voice had called Weylin from where he was having a meal in his rooms at the other end of the castle. Her presence radiated through the castle, raising the hairs along his arms.

It had not taken long to change into his fine clothes and make his way towards the throne room. He wondered why his father had not alerted him or involved him in her arrival, but he would not sit this one out. Not when he had his own vengeance to claim, outside of any ancestral feud.

What struck him first was that she did not turn to look at him. She did not bother to see who was entering the scene, and he could not help but wonder if she felt him. If she knew he was there without having to look. Then, he noticed the shadows.

The dark esos swirled around her thin frame like a storm as her esos ducked in and out around her in smooth, mesmerizing movements. She radiated a power that he had never felt from her before.

She was a force he had ignored entirely, and one that they would be remiss to underestimate now.

The scent of iris and sea breeze flooded his nostrils.

Aisling Iarkis stood with her shoulders pushed back and her head held high, but he did not miss the quivering of her small, pale hands. She clenched her fists at her side and her hatred radiated. The shadows were a part of her very being and undulated like the steady movement of a river. They cocooned her protectively, and he felt something within them calling out to him, calling him to a depth that he would surely not return from.

Something dormant and ancient inside his own being called back—roared back.

"I hear you've become acquainted with my son, Weylin Myrkor, the Udar Apparent of the seven worldly realms," the Udar's voice boomed with a false pride. "And we have him to thank for ensuring the safe arrival of Aisling Iarkis to Castle Eagla."

Weylin's heart dropped at the name spoken aloud. The way she did not deny it but stood straighter with pride in her birth name, despite all it had cost her.

She was the ninth generation, and she was right here in their grasp. She did not look nearly as afraid as she should be.

Her death would invoke the wrath of certain gods, but it would be in the best interest of his house and the realms. Countless thoughts collided in Weylin's mind. He tried to sort them out, push some away and draw some nearer.

The tension between the eight players in the room was so heavy that Weylin felt it bearing down on him while he became the ninth.

He felt the urge to drive *Uamhan* through Aisling's heart and watch the life leave those fiery eyes. He took slow breaths and his blade felt ever heavier at his side.

End this. End this. End this.

A voice chanted in his head that he could barely hear over the rushing of his blood.

Aisling Iarkis looked so much like the day he had first found her —surrounded by the dead and bloodied barghests—that Weylin felt his breath catch in his throat.

She looked as wild and graceful and untamed and stunning as the female whose life he had saved only for her to stab him in the back. Her face was set with rage, betrayal, revenge. She met his gaze with no fear in her eyes, as though she was challenging him to look away—to look away from the creature who his actions had helped forge.

Her eyes narrowed, and she bared her teeth when he looked to her again.

"Now, what to do?" His father sneered, calling him from his own thoughts. "What to do with all of this? Or perhaps the better question is, *where do we begin?*"

A sadistic sort of glee laced his father's tone and chilled his blood. He saw Aisling's glare falter as she looked behind Weylin, and he did not have to look back to know her worries were with the male behind him. Her concern was for the elf that Callum had escorted here from Briongloid for torture and interrogation. The elf that would not speak in protection of someone. And that someone was *his* Ellora, who had never really been Ellora at all.

He watched her features soften and her desperation deepen, and he realized she cared more for this male's life than her own. He could see it written on the lines of her face. Despite all the weight upon her shoulders, her priority lay with the male behind him and ensuring his safety.

Weylin stiffened, and his hand moved to rest on the hilt of his blade. Chest pounding, he felt the power beneath the surface of his skin howling like a wolf.

It would never see its full potential thanks to this female before him, he reminded himself.

"I say we begin with her male," Weylin spoke, and she whipped her head towards him, violence dancing in her eyes.

That would dig deeper than any pain we could inflict upon her.

He watched while she debated speaking up. Wondered if

fighting for him, showing her concern would further seal the male's fate.

"Has he not suffered enough?" she snarled. Her front was faltering as pain seeped into her words. "Have you no morals? I am the one you want. I am the one you have always wanted."

Her pleas confirmed all of his suspicions. He clenched his knuckles and whirled around without a second thought. In a blink, his hand was around the male's throat. The guard stepped away from them, knowing Weylin had rank to do whatever he pleased with the prisoner.

Energy coursed through his veins as he slammed the male against the back wall and lifted him off of his feet. His grip wrapped so tightly he could feel the breath leaving the male's body. Power soared through him as the male's eyes went wide, his lips opened, but no sound came out. The male hardly fought to free himself, and Weylin realized he did not have the strength to.

He noted the scars creeping out from the neckline of his shirt. His bloodied and swollen lower lip and the blackness that puffed up his right eye. The missing finger on his hand that feebly clawed at Weylin's arm. Weylin noted the sliver of life in his eyes, fighting to remain.

"Stop!" Aisling screeched behind him.

She rushed forward, and then suddenly came to a stop. Weylin assumed the laochs had halted her.

"How did you ever think you could protect her here? What were you thinking bringing her here?" Weylin growled at the male, who could not reply.

He watched guilt cross his face, how even in such a panic, he cared for her. And his anger grew.

A chill exploded throughout the room. Two loud thuds sounded behind him. Weylin released a guttural snarl, dropped the male, and shifted towards the commotion.

Midnight shadows swirled around the entire room now. The

two laochs holding Aisling back lay on the floor. She held her hands at her side, palms towards the ceiling as she glared at him. She was nearly unrecognizable as her power heightened, and her eyes glowed with the flame that was usually caged within.

He did not turn to see his father's reaction, but he could imagine his anger well enough.

"Whatever heroic act you think you are capable of pulling off, drop it now before you do something that could forever change the future," his father's voice boomed with authority.

His shadow fell amongst the moving ones radiating from Aisling.

Before anyone could move, there was a flash of silver, and Weylin realized she had a hidden dagger in her boot.

In an otherworldly, quick movement, she turned and felled one laoch before he could react, then she moved to the other, whose weapon was drawn.

Weylin held back, awaiting his father's command. They watched as she knocked the second laoch unconscious. His father gave the silent hand signal to advance.

Weylin took a step forward but tripped over an invisible force. He fell hard but held tightly to his blade, refusing to let it out of his grasp. He quickly rose as the red-haired male approached, renewed determination in his eyes.

A thud sounded behind him as Aisling withdrew her blood-coated dagger from the heart of a laoch. The realization hit Weylin that her male was a zephys, wielder of the esos of winds.

Weylin lunged towards the male, but the laoch in charge of the prisoner nodded behind him, indicating Aisling, the bigger and more pressing problem, as he drew his own weapon. It was a silent assurance that he could handle the male and allow Weylin to give his attention elsewhere. Towards Aisling Iarkis.

He turned to find her sights were not upon him, but upon his father, who looked down on her. Weylin wielded *Uamhan* and darted forward, blocking her path to the Udar.

He closed the distance between them, and she turned her head at the last moment. Her small blade clashed against his as she slashed madly, yet artfully. She made to disarm him or to kill him. He did not think she cared which it was.

His father was the only thing on her mind, and he was merely in her way. He fought back with all the skill he had grown up perfecting, but she was a powerful match. He realized just how much she had been hiding who she was—what she was. The wounded female seeking training that he had thought needed his protection was already a fierce laoch that had skills to rival his own.

His father stood back. Allowed them to face each other as laochs should—one to one, with no interference. He would not step in, no matter what. To do so would go against the code of laochs, as ancient as the runic language.

A renewed energy surged through him. He pushed back harder, and her feet stumbled as she nearly lost her footing. Their eyes met, and he no longer saw any part of his Ellora. She had been buried beneath this feral creature, who moved with the grace of a thousand gods and the determination of ten thousand laochs.

One of her hands dropped as she tossed the blade to her other hand. Before he could process what she was doing, her palm shot towards him and her fingers tightened together. Suddenly, his lungs were empty.

His breath was gone, and he was choking for air as her eyes bore into his.

He stumbled forward. He felt the pressure building in his head, building to the point of pain as she wielded her esos to cut his air supply. His blade clattered against the cement.

His knees hit the floor. His hands clawed at his own throat. He could not see his father's face as Aisling stepped forward. Looking first to the Udar, then she looked down upon him.

Something flickered in her yellow-green eyes he could not completely read. Something of regret. Something of sorrow. Something of rage. Something of victory. Then she became a blur of colors before his eyes.

"It's just you and me now," she hissed. "We can continue on this way, or you can let *him go free.*"

Weylin heard his father's booming laugh echoing in his head.

It vibrated through his skull as his head fell back onto the floor.

Everything faded to black.

And all of the pain disappeared.

45
AISLA

Aisla met the Udar's steely gaze. He showed no reaction as his son lay unconscious before him. Her rage only grew as she stepped forward.

Ruairi had somehow handled the laoch nearest him, whether he was merely unconscious or in Hel, she did not know or care.

Ruairi rushed to her side, palms up and determination in his weary gaze. She could tell his esos was depleting. And with no source in sight, he would not be able to help her for much longer, and he was in no shape for hand-to-hand combat. His presence brought her strength as relief filled her, but they both knew he could do no more than that. There would be time to embrace later. She had to convince herself of that much if she was to continue to fight.

She racked her brain for a way out. She was so far out of control in the situation, and her helplessness was eating at her motivation like a parasite.

An idea crossed her mind.

One that she knew would change the future of every being in all the realms, worldly and otherly, but it could be the only way to save *his* future, and that was all that mattered in that moment.

She gave Ruairi a quick, apologetic look, because she did not know if he would forgive her for what she was about to do. She shoved him to the ground before she lunged for the Udar, her small dagger raised, a reminder that she needed to retrieve *Oidhe* as soon as she could—*if* she could.

The Udar opened his mouth to speak as she neared, but Aisla beat him to it.

"Muinin!" she screamed at the top of her lungs.

It was an unforgivable call—a call that would wreak havoc far and wide. It would be a call written in the books of world tellers—a call that began a war. It was not a call Ruairi would have ever made, but her hands were tied and Aisla could not think of any other way out.

Her voice scraped her throat like gravel. She knew in her core no matter if she whispered it or shouted it, Muinin would feel it in his blood and he would respond.

In the waiting, Aisla had to stall.

It had come down to herself and the Udar and Ruairi. She knew she could not take the Udar, could not kill him.

She just needed to stall.

She darted forward and swung her dagger towards the Udar, who had drawn *Anam Marbh*, the ancient blade of the Myrkor dynasty, from long before the prophecy was ever spoken.

Before the Arden Throne was ever stolen.

The blades sparked as they clashed together, and she felt her own crack under the power of his, but she braced herself with a sharp inhale. She prayed to the gods that Muinin would arrive quickly.

Faolan Myrkor's eyes narrowed, and he smirked down at her.

There was something so sadistic in the lines of his face that Aisla's blood boiled as she fought for control of her esos. She knew

she should not still be able to access it—she should have long
burned out of her source, but it was still there and she would take
advantage of any tool that she could use. She still was not confident
in her control of her esos enough to rely on it in battle, so she relied
on her blade as she always had, and there was comfort there, even if
it was not *Oidhe*.

"You can't keep this up forever," the Udar sneered, and she
knew there was truth in his words.

She knew it with each passing breath.

Suddenly, Faolan was flying backwards and Aisla stumbled
forward from the relief of his pressure.

She whirled around to see Ruairi, still lying on the ground, with
his palms out and aimed for Faolan. He had wielded esos that he was
not meant to wield. The pain written all over his face said he was
pulling from a nearly depleted source, as if he was not physically
weak enough already. He was walking that fine line he had warned
her against.

He was hurting himself. She could not let him do any more
damage.

Despair racked her body, and Aisla dropped to her knees on the
floor beside him, silent tears stinging the corners of her eyes.

"Stop, stop, stop," she pleaded and took his hands in her own.

He looked at her with heavy-lidded eyes full of pain and sorrow,
but a small flicker of determination persisted.

"You'll pass yourself on," Aisla choked the words out, and then
she heard the footsteps approaching her from behind.

She flew to her feet to face Faolan, who had regained his footing,
and was two steps ahead of her. He lashed out before she had the
chance to dodge properly. She lurched away as his blade cut clean
across her chest. Her top ripped open, and blood pooled along the
cut. Pain seared through her flesh. She gritted her teeth to hold in
the yelp of pain.

She jumped to the side and gripped her small blade, taking a defensive stance. Aisla vaguely heard the familiar beating of large wings outside, and she knew he could make it. She could get him out alive, if only he would listen.

"Ruairi, *go!*" She yelled, refusing to look away from the Udar. "Go now, to Muinin. She will not leave here without you."

Aisla did not hear footsteps. Only silence echoed back to her and the moments of it were nearly deafening. She accepted her fate, but she could not bring herself to accept his. She lunged for Faolan and gritted her teeth, willing her strength to return.

With her desperation came a silent plea that made her skin crawl. A whispered plea of release tickled her ear and ribboned through her hair. Her restless esos had only begun to show its full force, but she did not know what that could mean. She did not feel drained.

Faolan dodged her attack with ease, and as though controlled by an external force, she flicked her palms out and great, green flames erupted from her, lurching for the Udar. She watched the brief gleam of fear reflect in the bright light of his eyes as he jumped away from the raging flames.

She charged forward, dodging her green fire. Caught in a trance, her shadows writhed around the Udar, entwining his throat and pinning him against the back wall.

"Give me the cure," she roared one last time, an ultimate act of desperation as it all came to a head.

"I told you, *mallaithe*," he said with a laugh that curdled her blood. "There is *no* cure."

As if on cue, Aisla heard the footsteps of laochs as they charged in through the door at the back of the room. There were shouts and footsteps and gasps of shock as they entered the fray.

"Now, Aisla."

A hand wrapped around her arm, but she felt a desperate urge to end this now, to end him now.

She wondered if the Udar would let the flames consume the

still-breathing body of his son, just a few sword lengths away. Rage
rushed through her and the grip on her arm tightened.

She whirled around with a primal snarl to face Ruairi. There
was a plea in his eyes, a plea to leave, even though she'd rather stay
and finish this, even if it finished her as well.

"*Now,*" he commanded in an authoritative tone she had never
heard from him.

She yanked her arm from his grasp. She wanted to turn around
and face them all, but she knew it could not end well. At last, she
followed Ruairi as they sprinted for the exit on the opposite wall,
while the laochs struggled to make their way through her flames left
behind. Her small blade was at the ready.

"Go to Muinin," Aisla instructed through clenched teeth.
"There's something I need to do."

Then, she darted down the corridor, where she felt *Oidhe*
calling to her. She could not leave this place without the blade that
had gotten her so far and through so much.

She felt the protest in Ruairi, but was thankful when he trusted
her. She knew if he did not, he would put up a fight that he would
lose.

She found her pack lying haphazardly on the ground, as if
someone dropped it in a rush to get somewhere. Aisla could not
begin to imagine what preparations were going on in Castle Eagla.
She raced the last few paces when footsteps approached.

A figure rounded the corner who looked to be about her age.
He was tall and lean, with dark brown hair and green eyes. She flung
her blade at him without a second thought, and too soon to see him
calmly raise his hands in surrender. Her blade was already slicing
through the air.

It struck him in the shoulder and forced him backwards a few
steps. She was impressed that the man did not lose his footing all
together.

She did not waste time as she scooped her pack and shifted to sprint towards her waiting wyvern. Towards Ruairi.

"Tell him I'm sorry," the man whom her blade had pierced called behind her. "I am glad you came for him."

She held on to those words but did not let them stall her. She could not think too long on them as she broke through into the blinding sun.

Chaos was the only way to describe the scene that awaited her outside of Castle Eagla.

Her heart thudded in her ears as she saw the laochs surrounding Muinin. Ruairi had somehow made it to her wyvern, and Muinin was shielding him beneath his large scaled wings. He roared and several laochs backed away, while others shot arrows into his side.

Aisla's anger grew and her eyes narrowed.

Muinin turned his head, and his great golden eyes met Aisla's, and Aisla had never felt such love for anything. She dashed for her beast, dashing for the safety only he could provide, no matter the risk it had taken to get here.

Her lungs screamed. She forced her legs to push harder, faster. She could hardly force the breath into them. Ruairi's eyes were full of fear and dread. She quickly looked away.

Aisla heard him calling her name, screaming it, but the sound barely registered. Several laochs averted their attention from Muinin to herself, and she had the feeling they were under strict orders to bring her in alive, or she would already be dead.

She sent up empty prayers with every step, not knowing what else she could possibly do. She was already at her last resort.

A searing pain pierced through her, turning her blood cold as a cry escaped her lips. She stumbled a couple of steps as the source of the pain registered. Something had lodged in her right calf, she could barely keep the leg moving. She willed herself forward.

She reached down, blindly grabbing at the source of the pain until her hand found a wooden arrow. Aisla snapped the long shaft protruding from her skin, but knew better than to yank it out. She gritted her teeth as the blood rushed down her leg and onto the ground.

Every moment seemed to be an eternity as she limped on in a half jog. She could nearly touch Muinin, who Ruairi was mounting. The second Ruairi was settled atop him, Muinin rushed forward to meet Aisla.

None of the weapons flying at him slowed him.

Aisla laid her hand upon Muinin as she clung to a fraying thread of hope. The feeling of his rough scales beneath Aisla's shaking fingertips was enough to yank a sob of relief and comfort from her. Muinin let out a long, low groan of pain as he consumed all the feelings of her journey through that touch. He had been feeling them through their connection, all these sunrises apart.

"I'm so sorry," Aisla choked out and moved to mount her wyvern.

Aisla selfishly snuck one last glance behind her.

And as she looked back at the castle where it had all gone awry, her only regret was that she had not set flames to the camp of the sleeping wolf.

She jerked her chin away as she felt a renewed fury stirring within her.

Ruairi was already in position to help her up. Muinin used his wings to shield them from the flying arrows. He let out a great roar of flames and screams erupted from the laochs below. Aisla did not look over to see how many lived and how many were killed as the smell of burning flesh filled her nostrils. Aisla clamored into place in front of Ruairi, and his arms wrapped around her trembling body. He held her in place, and she finally allowed herself to lean into him, squeezing her eyes shut.

Aisla's insides turned as they were suddenly airborne. Muinin's great wings beat harder and harder as he took them further and further from the gods damned castle.

They were still breathing, and they were headed home. Aisla reminded herself of these things as she felt an ever-present panic building in her chest.

"*Aisla. Aisla. Aisla,*" he murmured her name in her ear as though he could not believe it.

And she hardly could either.

His breath tickled her ear. Tears fell down her cheeks. She fought to slow her racing heart. She fought for breath. Aisla fought to open her eyes. Her chest was so tight, and she could not stop the trembling. Everything felt so far away and out of her reach. Her failure weighed heavily upon her, so heavy.

"I failed, Ru. I failed Eire, and my grandmother, and all of Eilean. Their blood will be on my hands." The words flowed in a voice Aisla could hardly recognize as her own. She could not stop them in the same way she could not stop the fears beginning to consume her. "I cannot go back. I cannot face it. I cannot—"

"Ash, shhhh," Ruairi interrupted her, rocking her back and forth.

"You don't understand." Aisla shook her head in frustration.

"You are right," he murmured gently. "I never could. But we are alive, and the rest we can figure out."

Aisla moved to face him, to look into his eyes, and she saw his silent tears.

She had failed. And she had no one to blame but herself.

46

AISLA

Aisla spent a long while in silence. Ruairi's arms remained wrapped around her, pulling her into him. The presence of Muinin beneath her and the steady beat of his wings were a comfort. Foreign smells still lingered on Ruairi, and the metallic stench of blood—his own blood.

She needed a few moments to process and grieve her failures surrounding the cure before she could face all that had happened to Ruairi. She found her mind coming back to the countless questions she had surrounding the cure. But one stood out above the rest.

Had it ever existed?

She wondered if this quest that had nearly cost Ruairi's life, and her own, had ever meant anything at all. Her throat constricted and pressure built inside of her chest when she thought too hard about it all. She felt so naive. She was ignorant for sailing away for something that had not even existed unless they had been lied to, which she still considered a strong possibility. But when she went too far down that road, she cursed herself for leaving without it.

There was no right answer. Nothing that could bring any

semblance of peace as she left Iomlan behind with more questions than answers.

More nightmares than dreams.

She looked down at Ruairi's hands, where they clasped his elbows around her chest. She forced herself to look at the evidence of his sunrises in the south that she could not ignore. The place where his finger had been taken—removed from his hand, what was left behind was a bandage stained red and black with his lifeblood. Aisla tried not to think about how it would look underneath the bandage that had surely remained on for far too long.

Her rage battled with her grief in a storm that stirred her esos to near action. She choked it down. Sobs racked her body, and she knew she could not remain in her silence forever, but was thankful that Ruairi had not yet broken it.

"I-I'm sorry, Ru," Aisla's voice came out cracked and broken around her tears.

She did not turn around. Could not bring herself to face him again, no matter how badly she had missed his gentle, green eyes.

"You did nothing wrong, Ash," his response was rough and gravelly. His grip tightened on her. "Please do not add any more weight to that which you were already born into."

Aisla could not find the words to reply.

"Born into nineteen years ago today, might I add," Ruairi said lightly.

Aisla had forgotten what day it was. Her nineteenth naming day, not that it would have mattered if she had remembered. She had never been one for celebrations and attention anyway, let alone with everything else that was a far higher priority.

"I think this can go in the world tellers' books for the very worst naming day," she muttered back and leaned further into him.

"I cannot argue with that," Ruairi said grimly.

"Are you—are you okay?" Aisla asked at last, not sure how else she could even begin the conversation.

It was the first time she had ever struggled to talk to Ruairi. What once was so natural felt like walking around broken glass. She was afraid to poke at the boy who had already been broken, but she would not leave him alone. She would be there to support him in whatever capacity he would invite her in.

"I'm okay," he lied. "I will be."

Aisla nodded as Ruairi rested his chin on her shoulder.

"You're going to need to see a mender for that leg."

Aisla looked down at the splintered wood protruding from a puncture wound leaking blood on her calf. She winced as bringing attention to it caused the faint throbbing to increase.

"It's nothing," she replied. "Nothing compared to everything else. To *you*."

She whispered the last part, afraid to acknowledge it as though ignoring it would allow the scars time to disappear on their own.

"I'm okay," he repeated, even less convincingly this time. "Really, Ash, it looks worse than it was."

Ruairi had always been a terrible liar.

She knew he was trying to protect her from the truths that he could not hide—the pain and torture he should not have had to endure.

"Whenever you're ready," Aisla said, "just know that I am here."

She felt Ruairi nod, and he sucked in a deep breath. "Thank you."

His tone made it clear he would not speak of it now, and Aisla wondered if she would ever know what went on in those castle walls. Wondered if she would even want to. Wondered if she would be able to stop herself from flying back to that castle and burning it *all* to the ground if he were to share those details with her.

Bile burned the back of her throat.

She fumbled to find his icy hand—the one without the bandage. She interlaced her fingers through his and held on so tightly, it might have hurt. But she was so afraid. She could not lose him again, and she had learned through all of this that a life without Ruairi Vilulf was not one that she was interested in experiencing. She squeezed his hand gently, to silently tell him this, and she hoped he understood as he squeezed back.

She turned to him.

His eyes had hardened in their time apart. He was the same, but also not. And that frightened her because now more than ever, she needed her best friend.

One of his eyes was purple, and yellow bruises lined his chin. He looked tired—exhausted. He was broken and battered and the evidence littered his skin in fresh red cuts and pale pink scars.

All of it unnecessary. All of it unbearable.

Ruairi's eyes met hers, and she knew he understood how she was feeling in that moment. He gave her space to feel the rage, the grief, the sorrow, and defeat.

"I won't lose you again," Ruairi said, and Aisla watched the way his chapped lips formed the words.

"I was the one that lost you," she breathed out.

"I told you to. Do not blame yourself," he shook his head. "And I also told you to leave—to go home. You promised me you would."

"No. I never promised. I would never break a promise to you, so I knew that was one I could never make."

"You should have gone home."

"I was not leaving without you, and I hope you knew that," Aisla said. "And I had to try—try to get the cure."

A silence weighed heavy between them, following her words. Following their unspoken fears and the reality that they were returning without their primary objective.

"What do we do?" Aisla spoke up first.

"We go home. Then, we figure out what to do next. We can work with the menders. We will continue our research and do whatever we can. Who knows, they may have found a solution while we were away. And, we will have to tell them that the Udar told us there was no cure."

Aisla nodded and again faced the sky. She looked out over Muinin's head into the puffs of white cloud.

"What of the package from Cliona?" Ruairi asked after several moments of quiet as the wind ruffled their hair and whistled through their ears.

"I have it," she replied. Thankful to at least be able to share that good news with him. "I opened it when you left. Maybe I should not have, but it was getting drenched, and I was so, so angry, and I needed to know what she had felt was so great that he would listen to us after all of these years, all of these decades. I will take the blame once she realizes. She will not be as mad at me as she would be with you, and besides, it was my fault."

"What was in it?" Ruairi asked, ignoring the rest.

"There was a letter written in the runic language, so I could not read a word of it. But I would like to get it translated, or at least ask her what it says. There is something about it that I do not trust. It feels weird in my hands, almost like it burns."

Aisla felt Ruairi nod in agreement as his chin again rested on her shoulder.

"Then there was this," Aisla spoke softly. She pulled the small, silver ring out from the depths of her pocket.

Ruairi leaned in closer for a better look at the odd, yet beautiful, piece of jewelry. He put his hand out and she dropped it in his palm. He turned it over in his fingers and she felt her weakened esos pulling against her skin towards the object. Something about it calling out to the power in her veins. She wondered if he could feel it, too.

He dropped it back into her hand, and Aisla found herself anxiously awaiting his response in the silence.

"Something is not right with it."

His reply aroused a feeling of disappointment within Aisla, but she could not put a finger on why. She tucked the ring back into her pocket.

"Why do you say that?" She questioned, keeping her tone disinterested.

"You can't tell me you don't feel that, too. There is esos within it, and objects are not meant to hold such power," Ruairi replied, and she did not know how she had not thought of that herself.

"What kind of esos?"

"I cannot tell," Ruairi replied, thoughtfully. "But I do not trust it."

"How do you suppose the Mathair will react when she discovers I did not give it to the Udar?"

A silence passed between them, and she did not know if it was because Ruairi was thinking of an answer, or if he was trying to filter his answer for her.

"I would hope that it would not matter, because no matter what, the cure does not exist," Ruairi spoke carefully, and Aisla felt that familiar grief, familiar defeat as she nodded. "But, if I were you, I would hold on to them. I would not return them."

"You are suggesting I lie to her?"

"I did not say that," he corrected. "Only that if I were in your position, that is what I would do."

Aisla remained silent while she thought on his words.

"Ash, why would Cli—our Mathair think the Udar had a cure? Where did she get this idea? Why would she send two of our own across the seas to their deaths? If it had not been you and your powers, if it had been me and Mona . . . we would never have made it home."

Aisla's lips parted. The urge to defend her grandmother rested on the tip of her tongue, but no words left her mouth. Because each word had been true. Aisla ultimately saved them, and had Ruairi and Mona marched into his castle, had they been the ones demanding a nonexistent cure, Aisla could not bear to think what would happen then.

"She thought there was no other way," Aisla whispered under her breath.

"I know," Ruairi said, but Aisla knew he did not believe those words.

She knew he had distrusted their Mathair for a long, long time now, and this would further drive the wedge between them. Selfishly, Aisla wanted to repair it because Cliona was all she had left. She was her only remaining kin, and she knew Ruairi was not leaving her life anytime soon.

"I will not give her the items, but I will not lie either. I will figure it out, but I promise to keep them," Aisla said. She felt her head beginning to spin from exhaustion. "*If* you swear not to voice your suspicions. They will only increase the discord that is growing in the ninth generation. And I can only imagine that it worsened during our time away, as Iofa undoubtedly spread."

Ruairi paused, and Aisla could hear his every breath.

"Please," she said and moved to look at him once again.

His eyes were clouded with all the doubts he didn't dare voice.

"Okay," he said and nodded slowly. "Okay, I promise that I will not speak of them. If you promise to be careful."

She instinctively bristled in defense. She knew what he was implying, but she could not bring herself to sort through it. Her insides twisted in knots. She again faced the clouds that raced towards them around Muinin's scaled body.

"Can I ask you a question?" Ruairi spoke up, and Aisla felt weary as she replied.

"Of course."

"What did the Udar mean when he said that his son was responsible for getting you to the castle?"

A ringing sounded in Aisla's ears at the mention of the Young Wolf.

Her heart twisted when she thought of her traveling companion. The lies, the betrayal, the moments of trust, and the secrets traded on a drunken night. He had pieces of herself she had never shared, even with Ruairi. And she thought, even now, there were pieces of Weylin that she held. She had not begun to sort through her emotions about Weylin Myrkor. She thought she preferred it when there was only one singular emotion of hatred before their threads had crossed.

But now he was more than his last name, and she could never go back to how it was before.

She knew Ruairi would have countless questions regarding that singular statement from the Udar, and she still did as well. They would have many moons to ask and answer questions of their time apart.

The questions that she was afraid, neither of them were prepared to answer. The wounds still remained fresh and tender.

In time, she hoped he would talk to her of his time in Castle Eagla, at least the parts he felt comfortable sharing. And in time, she would share the stories of her journey to find him, of her nights under cold moons with Weylin Myrkor when she was able to process them without her eyes stinging and her hands shaking.

"A story for another day," Aisla spoke around a tight throat.

She could sense his disappointment, but he accepted her answer.

"I understand."

There was a strange tension between them she did not like. She knew there was frustration on both of their sides. She wanted to push, to ask why create this distance when they had worked so hard to find each other again, but she could not find the energy to. She let the tension linger, let it grow between them until her exhaustion was a throbbing pain in her head.

"I am ready to see her," Aisla spoke up.

She had not allowed herself to think of Eire for fear of drowning in her shame and her failures, but as the coast of Eilean came into view, she could no longer avoid it. Despite her fears of what she would find, Aisla was ready to see her again. In whatever condition she would find her, she would still be Eire.

And they would figure this out.

"Me too, Ash. Me too."

47

AISLA

When Eilean finally came into view, Aisla's heart swelled with an emotion she had never felt before.

A deep relief fought past her unsettling fears, and she felt a rush in her veins as her esos rose to the call of the ash trees below. The hairs along her arms stood on end, and everything around her seemed to slow with Muinin's steady descent.

She saw the sandy shores that outlined her small continent. She watched the tops of the tall pines fly beneath her as they soared overhead of the Eilean cities and villages, and she had never felt such love for a place—her home.

She was home.

Ruairi's arms tightened around her, holding her close, despite the tension between them when he had asked her about the Young Wolf. She knew he, too, was feeling these emotions. Of both peace and unease. She found comfort in his touch, as she always had.

It was a beautiful thing, to return to a place she had known her whole life. Eilean was as much a part of her family as another elf could be. All of the strange, uncomfortable, cold, and lonely nights slipped from her hunched shoulders as Muinin coasted towards the land just outside of Caillte.

Aisla could see the tops of the towers of Castle Farraige, and her hands sweat when she thought about her grandmother.

Aisla pushed away the thoughts and allowed her mind to linger on Eire. The closer they got towards landing, the more she mentally prepared for whatever state she would find her best friend in. She thought briefly of that nightmare the night before she had parted ways with the Udar Apparent. A shudder traveled down her spine as she recalled Eire's decaying skin and her once beautiful face that turned gruesome. She could still smell the burning flesh after her esos had burst from her palms out of her own control.

Her breath caught in her throat and Aisla found herself praying to the nine gods, that Eire still believed in, that she would be okay. That she would still hang on, knowing that Aisla and Ruairi would never leave her. They might not have the answers that they had hoped for, but they would never abandon her.

"She will be okay, Ash," Ruairi spoke as if reading her thoughts. "She has to be. We would have felt it if she wasn't. We will figure the rest out."

Aisla merely nodded.

Everything had changed as they prepared to re-enter their familiar lives, and they both knew it. That was why Ruairi's voice did not sound the same, and why his comfort did not feel the same. The looming problem that could not stay at bay forever, even as they both refused to acknowledge it.

It all boiled down to that single moment when Aisla had seen no other solution. When the only thing she could think to do was cry out for her wyvern to rescue Ruairi, and Muinin had ended up saving her too.

But in doing so, she had declared war with all the realms of Iomlan. And there was no undoing it.

It was a war that Eilean was not equipped to partake in. A war that her people would not be able to survive in their current state. Soon, Aisla feared that this plague would be the least of the problems facing them. She knew Ruairi had already thought of this, but he had not questioned her.

He had trusted her, as Ruairi always did.

Her decision had been gnawing at the back of her mind despite everything else that kept coming up. She knew she must be the one to deliver the news to Cliona, if she had not already realized it when she saw Muinin fly from Eilean, and that thought alone was enough to make her nauseous.

She fought down her rising hysteria. A thud rumbled through her body as Muinin landed, and suddenly they were on solid ground once again.

Ruairi dismounted first, pulling his legs out from behind her with a grunt of pain as he slid down the side of the wyvern's large body. He shifted to offer a hand to Aisla.

Pain jolted through her as she landed on the ankle that had been pierced by an arrow, and Aisla fell to her knees. Shame heated her cheeks. Ruairi knelt beside her and threw his arm around her shoulders to support her weight. Aisla knew she should be the one helping him after all that he had been through, and she felt guilty as she allowed him to help her into the city, towards the infirmary.

"You'll need to get that looked at as soon as possible," he instructed, ever the protector.

"It is not my top priority," she grunted back.

She noticed the way her boot was stained with blood before turning her gaze to the path ahead of them. Towards the eerily quiet village that awaited them.

"It should be," he said, and Aisla heard the frown in his tone.

Despite it all, Aisla found a soft smile at the familiar light scold of Ruairi. She knew there would be a time to work through his feelings about Cliona, to address the frustrations tightening between them.

But right now, Aisla had to find a thread to hold on to that showed a light in the distance. And she could not count the number of times Ruairi had felt the need to correct her priorities in their many, many moons of friendship. She felt a hope that things would one day return to how they were. No matter how distant that future might be.

"I missed you."

Ruairi turned to her with a surprised look at those three simple words.

He paused a moment before pulling her into a tight embrace. The first moment they had been able to share on the land without enemies watching their every move. She wrapped her arms around his back and held on to him with all the strength she could muster. She burrowed her face into his chest and inhaled his fading scent of ash wood and mint leaves. His arms around her were rejuvenating, and she felt herself healing in small ways that made the biggest of differences.

She took a deep breath as Ruairi Vilulf brought her back to life as only he could know how to. He rested his chin atop her head, as he always did, and Aisla closed her eyes for a brief moment, before pulling away enough to meet his gaze. She looked into those eyes that had seen her long before anyone else had and found herself being pulled in closer.

"Eire," Aisla whispered because she could only find it in herself to say one word.

Ruairi nodded. His grip loosened, but he kept his arm around her shoulders in support.

Aisla looked at Muinin, who watched them with wary, but relieved eyes. Aisla knew he was almost as thankful for their reunion as she was.

"Thank you," she said to her wyvern, who gave a low chuff in response before taking off back towards the wyvern caves.

Without wasting another moment, Aisla and Ruairi headed towards the infirmary as fast as they could manage with her injured leg.

The moment that they entered the village square, Aisla could feel the eyes on her back.

She heard the rumble of whispers. The gasps of surprise. The people leaving their bailes to gawk at the returned *Gheall Ceann*, wondering if she had what they needed to be saved.

Several people moved forward to speak with them, but Aisla ignored the words of greeting and the steps taken towards her that would only slow her down. She could not bear to be away from Eire any longer. Ruairi's grip around her lower back tightened, and they trudged onwards. Her heart beat ever faster and her palms sweat. She could only prepare so much for what she was walking into, and none of it would have been enough.

They walked the familiar paths of their home. Their worn shoes brushed along pebbles and grass as the pines once again towered above them, looming into the cloudy dusk sky above. Aisla kept her gaze straight ahead until the door to the infirmary was in sight. Each breath was an effort to force out.

Aisla's panic rose, and she thought of the last time she saw those doors.

A shudder traveled down her spine. She inhaled deeply, preparing for the worst as her dream returned to haunt her with a muddle of horrifying images. Ruairi stroked his thumb on the side where he held her—a silent, soft reassurance that he understood her fears.

They were in this together.

They pushed through the wooden door, which felt heavier now.

Inside, the infirmary was eerily quiet. The silence hanging in the

364   LE VAN VEEN

air was enough to tighten Aisla's throat. She looked around the entryway where there was usually so much movement as nurses and menders bustled about.

A mender sat at the desk. Her skin was pale, her eyes tired, and dark circles lined them. Still, they widened at the sight of Aisla and Ruairi and the state that they were in.

She gave a small bow as she stood, and Aisla felt uncomfortable. Aisla itched to run down the hallway, but she knew she would not be able to find Eire's room on her own.

"Our Mathair Apparent," she murmured, her voice laced with evident disbelief. "We can take you right away to get that looked at."

The mender's eyes dropped to the wound in her ankle, but Aisla shook her head.

"I need to see her," she spoke with the little authority she could muster, needing to brush aside any concern for her own wellbeing.

The mender nodded with visible reservation, but she knew exactly who Aisla was referring to. Anyone here would. Eire was as much a part of her as Ruairi was.

The look on the medic's face sent a sense of foreboding through Aisla that made her stomach turn, but she forced the feeling down as deep as she could as the mender led them down a series of corridors.

With each step, Aisla could feel her esos anxiously wrestling in her veins. She could feel its return to life with her own return to Eilean.

Aisla could no longer hear the sound of her feet padding across the cement floors as the sound of her heart thudding in her ears drowned everything else out until the mender finally stopped outside of a room. It was not the same room Eire had been in the last time they saw her—it was much deeper into the maze that was the infirmary.

"I should...I should warn you that your friend is not the same as when you last saw her," the mender spoke gently. "She is alive, and that is more than most in her state can say. She is fighting, still, and sometimes she even speaks of the two of you. I think that hope gave her what the others lacked. But, just because she still breathes does not mean she is the same. We have managed to configure restraints for her esos, so she is not a danger to you as she once would have been. Just, try to remember we are thankful she is still fighting, and right now that is enough."

Aisla nodded. A numbness settled within her that had become all too familiar. The mender's words echoed through her head, hollow and distant. Her voice sounded as though it had come from somewhere else—somewhere far away and farther still with each syllable that left her lips. Aisla refused to meet her eyes. She already knew what she would find there.

And pity was not something that she could handle in that moment.

She just wanted to get inside. To see her friend again.

"Thank you," Ruairi said with the strength that Aisla could not find within herself.

The mender pushed the door open.

"Eire, your friends have returned," she said softly and Aisla craned her neck, trying to see around the mender for a glimpse of her best friend. "They have come to see you."

The mender stepped out of the way, and Aisla's heart plummeted down.

Down. Down. Down.

Her breath caught in her throat and the corners of her eyes burned like the rage in her veins.

There were parts of Eire that were not as gruesome as Aisla's nightmare had been. There was no hole in her cheek that revealed decaying teeth. There were no threats and accusations rushing from her lips.

But there were parts that were worse.

She lay there in the hospital bed, and her head slowly turned to face them.

Her eyes were even emptier than Aisla's dream. They were moon-white and foggy in an unsettling way. Her skin had lost all of its beautiful color and was now a gray littered with scaly patches. Her flesh was indeed rotting in places that were deep, exposing the dark red flesh beneath.

The smell was just as bad as in her nightmare.

Haunting. And this time, fully real.

No longer to be blamed on olc creatures of unfamiliar woods.

For a moment, Aisla wondered how the mares could have provided her with a nearly accurate portrayal of Eire's state.

But her thoughts did not linger long as she took a cautious step towards her. She untangled from Ruairi's support and gritted her teeth through the pain as she gently allowed her weight to fall onto her injured leg. She needed to be strong for Eire.

It was all such a harsh contrast to the way Aisla had imagined herself sprinting towards Eire with open arms. She wished to embrace her with tears of joy for the cure that they had journeyed to find.

But that was a fool's dream.

There was no excitement in the air. Aisla could barely walk on her own. Eire was in no state to be embraced.

There was no cure.

"Hey, Eire," Ruairi spoke first, and for that, Aisla was grateful. He spoke gently, carefully, and stepped around Aisla to get closer to their friend. He knew she could not handle it, and the guilt heated Aisla's cheeks. "We've missed you."

Eire crooked her head to the side.

"Too much power. Too much here," she shook her head frantically.

Her voice was hoarse and high-pitched. Aisla hardly recognized it, as her grief heightened.

"It's just us, Eire," Ruairi took another step, to which Eire did not react. "You know us—it's Ru and Ash."

Eire sat up and moved to the edge of her cot. The names seemed to trigger something in her.

"I think I knew you once, many, many moons ago. Before the Arden Throne," her eyes locked onto Aisla's. Aisla fought to hold her gaze. Her grief threatened to break her. Her words were nonsensical, and Aisla could not even begin to form a response. "But now, now there are strangers in my walls. *And too much power.* Shattered glass in my room. The menders would not permit it."

Aisla looked back, but the mender had already left them, given them their privacy. Aisla wished that she had not. When she turned around, Eire was standing and her blank gaze had again found Ruairi.

"I'm sorry," Ruairi mumbled, and Aisla could hear his own grief. She could hear the tears in his voice. "I'm sorry I let you down."

Eire looked up at the ceiling. Aisla followed her gaze, but there was nothing there. Nothing for her empty eyes to fixate on.

"You cannot let me down if I do not know you," Eire spoke with cool indifference in that unfamiliar voice. "I think you have me mistaken."

"No," Aisla spoke up. Ruairi looked to her over his shoulder with sorrow in his eyes. "No, you are Eire Trygg, and you are exactly who we have been looking for. Every night, every moment we spent across the sea, we pushed to make it back to you. We do not have you mistaken, and I need you to hear me."

Aisla spoke with conviction, spoke with urgency, hoping to somehow get her best friend back. She hoped for anything at all that could bring her back to them. If she could remember them, even briefly, Aisla was sure it could be enough to anchor her there, to remind her to keep fighting.

Eire shook her head slowly. She continued to stare up into that space on the ceiling.

"You have me mistaken," she repeated.

Aisla's grief was replaced with anger the longer they sat in silence. She was angry at the gods for allowing this to happen. Angry at the Udar's laochs for taking Ruairi from her. Angry at Weylin Myrkor for wasting her time. Angry at the lies they had been fed about the cure, no matter the source.

But above all, she was angry at herself for not being able to stop any of it. She had not been able to protect the people she loved the most. She was meant to be able to.

"You are Eire Trygg. He is Ruairi Vilulf. I am Aisla Iarkis," Aisla stated firmly, moving around Ruairi to walk towards Eire. "You know us. We are going to get through this."

"It is too late," Eire said with a finality that made Aisla's head spin.

"No." Aisla shook her head. She closed the distance between them. "No, it is not." Aisla placed her hands on Eire's shoulders, trying to get her to look her in the eyes, anywhere but that cursed ceiling, but Eire's eyes remained fixed above her head. "No, it's not! You are Eire Trygg. And *we* will get through this."

Eire's skin was cold and clammy beneath the fabric of the thin infirmary gown. The silence of the room echoed through Aisla's skull as it pounded.

"You are Eire Trygg," Aisla hissed again as she felt her palms heating. "*We will get through this.*"

Ruairi's arms wrapped around her body, dragging her away as the fabric at Eire's shoulder melted. That familiar stench of burning flesh jolted through Aisla's nose as she fought against Ruairi's grip. She kicked and shouted words that were unclear, as Eire did not even flinch as Aisla's flames burned her, but she shifted her attention at last to Aisla.

Her milk-white eyes showed nothing when they locked onto

Aisla, who continued to struggle as Ruairi pulled her through the open doorway.

Those eyes bored into her mind. Tattooed themselves onto her eyelids, to haunt her with every damned blink, as the door fell shut between them.

Aisla Iarkis let out a shaky breath as she felt the fight leaving her body.

48

RUAIRI

Ruairi was alone when he approached Edi, their primary mender.

He had managed to get Aisla into her baile and lying down in bed after the chaos that unfolded in Eire's hospital room. A mender was to meet her there to deal with her wound. He could not let her stay in the infirmary any longer.

He still saw Aisla's hands gripped onto Eire as the green flames slithered from her palms to burn the cloth at Eire's shoulders.

The way she had lost her control—let her emotions rule her— was something he had not seen from her before, not that intensely. A shudder traveled down his spine at the memory.

And that wasn't even the worst of it.

He could hardly bring himself to relive the moments he stood across from Eire in her infirmary room. Her glazed, vacant eyes. The decay and rot ate into her flesh, and he feared the stench would haunt him forever. The voice that was not the voice he had grown up hearing. The way he could feel her blank gaze following him well beyond the confines of her room.

The way he had lost her.

Ruairi blinked away the tears threatening to break. His body ached. He had yet to face the scars that would stare back at him when he looked in a mirror. It terrified him to see the male he had become in those sunrises spent in a cell. He feared where the memories would drag him to.

There were moments he could not bring himself to relive. He would prefer to move on as if it had never happened at all.

He could still vividly remember the hurried moments spent burying Aisla deep in his mind when Orla dug through his memories. She had been buried so deeply that Ruairi almost did not recognize her when he walked into the Udar's throne room. It had been like being pulled out of a fog—one he was still learning to navigate whenever he was near her.

Edi looked up from the papers at her desk and met his gaze. Ruairi shook his thoughts away.

She looked exasperated and drained. He could not blame her.

Her eyebrows raised when she realized who stood before her, when she realized what it could mean. Guilt clenched Ruairi's insides, and not for the first time that day.

"I'm sorry," he said, because there was nothing he could say.

Speaking was still a strange sensation as his voice crawled through his throat. Words felt heavy as they left his tongue.

"We were told there was no cure," Ruairi spoke slowly. He watched Edi's face fall. He chose his words carefully, as he needed answers of his own. Answers that Aisla was not ready to ask for. "It was a fool's errand."

"Was there ever a cure?" Edi whispered.

"That's what I am wondering as well," he responded and took a seat in the chair across from her. "The Udar made no indication of such."

"He could be lying."

"He could be." Ruairi nodded his head, but he saw the doubt flickering through Edi's soft brown eyes.

A tense silence passed between them. Edi looked down at the floor, pulling her brows together.

"Her condition." he cleared his throat. "Will it improve?"

The mender paused and audibly exhaled before replying.

"I cannot answer that. We have yet to see anyone recover from this disease, and we still have yet to discover what caused it. What I can say is that it has stopped spreading, which seems to reject our plague theory. It is not contagious. Our menders and world tellers alike are working on it every waking moment, I promise you that, Ruairi." She looked up to meet his gaze. "There are more questions than answers right now, and I cannot tell when that will change. Eire will need a miracle, but she has held out longer than anyone else. Something is keeping her here, on this side of life. She is fighting, whether or not you could see it when you visited with her, she is fighting."

Ruairi took this information in slowly. He worked to parse through her words for any answers to his own questions.

"And those that were not able to keep fighting . . . have they passed on?"

Edi grimaced. She slipped her hands into her pants pocket. She held his gaze with an expression that spoke of untold horrors. In that moment, Ruairi knew whatever was happening to them was worse than passing on.

Worse than what he had seen in Eire.

"Follow me," Edi instructed softly as a lump formed in Ruairi's throat.

Edi led Ruairi outside of the infirmary and towards the west of Caillte, an area he rarely found himself in. She was silent on the walk over, a heaviness resting between them that only increased with each step. Ruairi had remained silent, too. His voice was tired even from the minimal use, and he wanted more than anything to feel his silk sheets in the comfort of his own baile. He longed to get off of his feet and sit in the silence of the room that had been his before everything had changed.

They stopped outside a large building that had been abandoned as supplies on the island ran low and there was less need for the goods it once housed.

In the silence, Ruairi heard low, guttural sounds coming from beyond the wooden door to the building. Sounds that drove a chill down his spine and filled him with the urge to turn around and refuse to face whatever lurked beyond the door. But he stayed, his feet rooted in place, while Edi used a small silver key to unlock the door.

The click of the lock echoed in Ruairi's ear, and the door creaked open.

Edi slipped in through the doorway and held it open so Ruairi could follow in behind her.

The sounds grew louder, with the door open. They crawled through his skull and scratched at the edges of his mind. He felt himself being dragged somewhere. Somewhere he could not yet place.

The inside of the building was overwhelmed with noise, but there was nothing to see. There were several rooms along different corridors, and Ruairi could hear the groans and growls coming from all different directions. Edi made her way towards the nearest room and opened another door, and suddenly the sounds were impossible to ignore as the barriers were removed between them.

Thud. Thud. Thud.

Ruairi's heart pounded and his ears rang, drowning out the animalistic sounds.

Ruairi peered into the room and saw they had built a cell of thick, iron bars. Behind those bars, there were five creatures. Creatures that were humanoid, but not. Their skin was gray and wrinkled, sagging over bones that stood out as the outline of a skeletal frame. Wispy, white hair protruded from their scalps, some had more than others. Their eyes were white orbs nestled deep into empty sockets. Their lips pulled up and away from rotted, gray teeth. They smelled like Eire did—like rotting flesh. There were holes in their bodies like doors to the rotten skin beneath.

Chills racked through Ruairi's body. Terror overcame him, and he continued to stare at the one nearest him. The one that vaguely resembled a male he had gone to scoil with.

And that made it all the more real.

These were not simply monsters. No, they were monsters created from Caillte's people.

"How did this happen?" Ruairi breathed out, shaking his head back and forth in disbelief. He begged himself to wake up from this nightmare.

"It happens when the disease overcomes them. When there is no more fight to be fought," Edi replied as she looked out at them. Her lack of disgust startled Ruairi. The way this had become so normal for her that it no longer phased her. "Sometimes, their loved ones beg us to end their lives. It's too hard to watch, and no soul should be forced to live like this. In those cases, we give them a dose of nimhebas, so that they may pass peacefully, with no more pain. Others, they refuse to let go. They hope for a cure or a miraculous recovery of sorts. But I am afraid that the ones who are in this way are too far gone for any cure, even if there had been one to find. But, we respect those wishes and we keep them alive—in this state at least. We created this facility to secure them, and we are running out of room, but we are doing what we can."

Ruairi's mouth dried and his hands shook uncontrollably.

Anger coursed through him—an insatiable rage. But above that anger, came a deep fear. A terror as the sounds finally dragged him back to that place—the place he could not forget no matter how hard he tried.

To that wall outside of Castle Eagla where the laochs had once dragged him beneath the sunlight of day.

The sounds were undeniably the same. The memories echoed in his ears until they matched the sounds surrounding him. They were one and the same and it was no coincidence. And something about the dark nature here—something in the air made him recall the feeling of the silver ring in his hand. The dark power radiating from it could be felt here within the cell. Ruairi could hardly breathe.

He had no words to give Edi as the realization hit him like a wall.

With the war Aisla had declared on the horizon, Faolan Myrkor was leaps and bounds ahead of them.

49

WEYLIN

Blood was everywhere when the Young Wolf's eyes opened.
On the floor, on the walls, beneath his body, under his fingernails, in his throat.

The metallic smell burned his nostrils. He pushed his palms against the cool cement floor. He grunted with effort as he lifted himself from the ground. His father was no longer present. Five corpses were scattered around the throne room where the laochs had fallen in their attempt to stop Aisling.

Aside from them, Weylin was alone.

The silence weighed heavily on his chest. His father's laugh echoed through his throbbing head.

And Aisling's last words felt engraved on his brain *"Let* him *go free."*

The desperation in her voice that had become so familiar scratched his skin.

Weylin was well aware Aisling could have ended him. She could have used her shadows to steal all the air from his lungs, but she had spared his life. She had left him unconscious, but still breathing, at the feet of his father.

He squeezed his eyes shut, and he stood, but yellow-green eyes bored into his eyelids and his eyes blinked open again. He took a step forward and felt the strain of exhaustion. Another step and his blood was roaring. One more and he felt his energy coming back, slowly and painfully.

Another step brought the roar of a beast outside of his castle that rattled the walls.

Another and he was panting with the effort it took to move.

And then he was running. Running towards the sound of the beast.

The sunlight caught Weylin's eye as he flung open the doors to the castle entrance. He heard the shouting of the laochs, the beating of wings, and arrows flying through the air before clattering to the ground.

Weylin followed the massive shadow that covered the ground at his feet, dragging his gaze upward.

The beast before him was greater than any illustration could depict. It let out a roar as the laochs failed to pierce it with their arrows. Its emerald scales acted as protective armor against their feeble attempts.

It was larger than he had imagined wyverns to be. Its head was long and narrow and its golden eyes squinted into slits. Faint tendrils of smoke emitted from its nostrils. Its claws were the size of Weylin's hand.

Its wings beat furiously, sending sand flying everywhere. Weylin raised his arm to shield his eyes. He continued to watch the beast gather the wind beneath its wings to take off with the two figures seated atop it.

With one last roar that rattled through Weylin's whole body, it took off into the sky, aiming for the east.

Weylin did not look away as the wyvern of nightmares carried Aisling Iarkis further and further from him.

He could feel his laochs standing by in fear, wondering what their punishment would be for allowing her to escape. But Weylin did not know what to say. No one could have prepared for this.

Infinite thoughts raced through Weylin's mind in the moments it took for the wyvern to become a speck in the sky. He continued to watch until the wyvern was out of sight completely, a great pressure building with every passing beat.

An animalistic growl ripped from his throat. He could not find the words to shout at his men.

He stormed into the castle, head pounding with such pain that he felt the urge to pull his hair out at the root. The pain was so loud he could no longer hear himself think.

Aisling Iarkis had single-handedly declared war with Iomlan.

And if war was what she wanted, *he would deliver.*

TAISTEALAI

I t was a cold, late winter night when Taistealai scrambled up
Crann Na Beatha.

He dug his claws into the rough bark that was damp after
days of rain, pulling himself up the ancient tree as old as the first
humans. He panted, dodging around protruding branches,
hurrying with the thrill of the news he was finally permitted to
bring to the gods.

It was a secret he had held onto since the night of the betrayal of
the norns. Since the night he was indicted as messenger between the
mortals of the worldly realms and the gods of the otherly realms.

The night that Sionna had made the deal with the norns that
could doom them all. That cursed night, nine generations ago.

But now, as the young elf had at last reached her nineteenth
year, Taistealai was to be released of his heavy burden. He had
already shared the words of the norns with the dragon on his way
up to the gods, but his reaction had been predictable—as calm and
stoic as ever. A simple nod and a turn of his heels. But Taistealai had
not missed the pity in his eyes. The sympathy that came from the

immortal male when he thought of what was to come—what was in store for the young elf and her small, failing continent.

At last, Taistealai reached the top of the tallest tree in the realms. The tree that no being besides that two-tailed, four-eyed squirrel could succeed at scaling. Anyone or anything else who tried would have suffocated from lack of oxygen long before they reached the top of Talam's tree of life.

Cool air rushed through Taistealai's rust colored fur, and he flung himself from the top of the tree into the realm of Albios.

The heavens of the world. The home of the nine gods and goddesses.

He burst into the land above the clouds, and the bright light stung his eyes as they adjusted from the night on the worldly realms.

The entrance to Albios from *Crann Na Beatha* put Taistealai in the middle of a dense pine forest by the name of Deithe.

Albios was far larger than the seven worldly realms combined. It extended further than Taistealai's eyes could see, and he had yet to explore every part of it, even in his immortal life.

Taistealai breathed in the honey scent of the beautiful realm before taking off towards the city, Hallamor, home to the mother goddess, Eabha, and her mate, the god of love, Cion.

Their six children all lived elsewhere in Albios in palaces of their own, some grander than others, while their grandson, Ifreann, ruled in the underworld, Hel, the realm of the dark elves and olc spirits.

Along with being home to Eabha and Cion, Hallamor served as the meeting place for the nine gods for occasions such as this.

Taistealai sprinted as fast as his four short legs would carry him until he felt the cool marble stairs that led to the palace of Eabha beneath his paws. He padded up them and caught his breath, before slipping in through the small door built for him.

He walked into the room where all nine gods had already

convened, and although he had been expecting it, he still felt the urge to shrink away from the power surrounding him.

This would be the first time all nine gods shared the same space since the impact of the *Cogadh do Shliocts*, the War for Descendants.

Eabha spotted him first. She turned her empty eye sockets on him. The sight used to send a chill down his spine, but he had long grown used to the peculiar look of the mother goddess. Her white hair fell down her back, constantly waving as if there was a breeze surrounding her and her alone. She carried a wisdom that no one else had ever achieved, and it showed in each wrinkled line on her skin. Her face held an unreadable expression as Taistealai bowed his head to her.

She was meant to be the voice of reason in the conflicts both worldly and otherly. She was to never choose a side.

But Taistealai had heard whispers of the doves that interrupted the betrothal of the Young Wolf. Of the doves that saved the young elf's life as she crossed the Tusnua Sea.

Eabha gave him the smallest of nods. The room quieted, and the other gods broke from their conversation to turn their heads in his direction.

"It is good to see you, little friend," Cion said. He grinned from the lounge chair in the corner of the room.

The god of love had dark skin, long silver dreadlocks, and a calm and inviting look in his bright blue eyes. He exuded an air of peace and tranquility that could become addicting if you spent enough time around him.

"And you, Cion the Kind," Taistealai replied with a dip of his head. His voice came out smaller than he intended it to.

Taistealai ignored the other eyes that tracked his every move as he scrambled atop the granite table in the center of the room and sat back on his hind legs to face them. A gulp of air was the only sign of his fears that he allowed to show.

"Been a long time since I have seen you here," Muir of the ocean's voice boomed from Taistealai's left.

Muir tended to be a reserved god, keeping to himself as much as he could, until his quick tongue would get him involved in situations he had little to do with. So different from his twin sister, Leighis of the harvest and healing, who was so gentle and fair. They looked alike with their tan skin and bright blue eyes inherited from their father, but that was where the similarities ended.

"I have been here," Taistealai replied with an air of confidence. "It is you who seldom visits the hall of your mother."

"Fair enough," came Muir's reply with a deep chuckle.

Taistealai had yet to face the gaze that bored a hole through him. He did not have to look to know that it was Sionna, goddess of war and mischief. Her piercing green gaze pinned him there even as he ignored her presence altogether.

"I assume we can all guess the reason for your visit on this day, my friend?" Taran of the skies spoke up.

Taistealai shifted to look at the blonde goddess with eyes the color of burning fire. Taran was by far Taistealai's favorite of the gods. Her essence was that of comfort and justice, everything the opposite of what Sionna was, and the two oldest children of Eabha and Cion often butted heads. The tension between them was palpable even now.

"It is time," Taistealai said with a grim smile.

For as much as it was a relief of his burden to bear, it was also a heavy load to bring to the home of his friends.

This was the moment he would confirm their suspicions of the young elf, and reveal more than they were perhaps ready to hear. But it was time. Taistealai knew in their own ways they were as eager as he was. Once the words entered the air, there would be no going back. The norns had already set the course, and the events of the past few sunrises were only the beginning of what was to come.

Taistealai could practically feel the protest resting on Sionna's tongue. He could practically feel the way all the energy in the room seemed to shift to her. This had all been her doing, all those generations ago. Her boredom led to a bribe of the norns that would change the course of all nine realms, and the future of the gods.

Taistealai turned to her now, facing her glowing green eyes before he unveiled the one and true prophecy from the threads of the norns. The one that had never before been shared with the immortals outside of the norns, Taistealai, and Sionna.

Sionna should feel lucky that not all truths would unfold tonight—should be thankful for the rules of the norns that kept him from unveiling secrets that would turn all the other eight gods on her in a single breath.

At last, Taistealai returned his gaze to Taran before speaking. He found a confidence in the familiar eyes that gave him the breath to recite the words of truth that had been embedded in his mind:

Under cold moons, the worldly realms will see an ember rise amidst blood already rife with power. An elf will be gifted with the esos of all nine gods to rise from the rubble and dust of circumstance and cruel winters.

The day the winds show their true force, a union or a dissolution of power will chart the course of vanished stars. A shattered glass will bring in a new age of esos and usher in the Mor War.

On the day that air turns to fire, children of darkness shall mark the downfall of an empire and a revival of wyverns to sunken earth. The dusk of the ancients will fall to the power of the blessed as fate hangs in the balance.

THANK YOU FOR READING UNDER COLD MOONS

Share your feedback on social media using #CrownsOfTalam. I would love to hear your voice! Connect with me on Instagram and TikTok @levanveen. To keep in touch and be the first to hear news about the second book in *The Crowns of Talam* series, scan the QR code to visit my website and scroll to the bottom to join my email list! You will also receive a curated chapter by chapter Spotify playlist for Under Cold Moons when you sign up.

If you enjoyed *Under Cold Moons*, please consider leaving an honest review on Goodreads, Amazon, or any platform of your choosing. Your feedback is so important to me and helps indie authors reach a larger audience!

storied stars

PRONUNCIATION GUIDE + GLOSSARY

World Lore:

Airgead [*air • eh • gid*] — currency of Talam

Atruach [*ah • tru • uh*] —an honor binding agreement

Anamacha [*on • om • ah • huh*] — souls

Anamarbh [*on • om • arb*] — Faolan's sword

Aosta [*ee • sta*] — the ancient tongue

Arden [*are • den*] — the true throne

Baile [*ball • luh*] — houses in cities

Banphrionsa [*bon • frin • suh*] – term of old for princess

Barghest [*bar • guest*] — wolf-like beast; malicious children of Ifreann

Braon [*breen*] — one of the dual moons of Talam

Crann Na Beatha [*cron, nuh, bah • ha*] — the tree of life

Dioluine [*dee • loo • nay*] — immunity herb

Eitilt Go Maith [*eh • tilt, go, ma*] — term of old for "fly well"

Esos [*ess • ohs*] — magic

Fior [*fee • er*] — Ruairi's sword

Gheall Ceann [*gal, kee • own*] — the promised one

Laoch [*lee • ock*] — warrior

Litha [*lee • tha*] — summer solstice

Lofa [*loff • uh*] — disease plaguing Eilean

Mallaithe [*mall • uh • hey*] — term of old for cursed

Mathair [*mo • her*] — ruler of Eilean

Nimhebas [*neeve • bas*] — death poison

Norns [*norns*] — ancient beings who name and prophesy the fate of each elf upon birth; they also know the fate of all beings, mortal and immortal

Nua [*new • ah*] — the common tongue

Oidhe [*oy • de • hey*] — Aisla's dagger given to her by Ruairi

Priomh [*preeve*] — a chief in a tribal community

Puball [*puh • bull*] — tent structures, often found in villages

Realta [*rell • tah*] — the crown of stars; the Mathair's crown

Scoil [*scoll*] — school for elves

Searc [*shark*] — true mates

Sneachta [*sh • knock • tuh*] — one of the dual moons of Talam

Speartha [*spare • tha*] — the crown of skies; the Udar's crown

Stoirme [*ster • rum*] — Aisla and Ruairi's ship

Teigh [*chay*] — used to urge a horse forward

Uamhan [*oo • on*] — Weylin's sword

Udar [*oo • der*] — ruler of all seven worldly realms

Undine [*un • deen*] — sirens that live in deep waters; malicious children of Muir

Valerian [*val • air • ee • in*] — herb that causes drowsiness

Names:

Aisling (Aisla) Iarkis [*ash • ling, (ash • la), ee • ark • iss*] — the promised one

Brendan Dorcas [*bren • den, door • cass*] — Lord of Briongloid

Brigid Dorcas [*bridge • id, door • cass*] — Lady of Briongloid

Callum Ronan [*cal • um, roan • in*] — captain of the Udar Apparent's personal guard

Cliona Iarkis [*clee • own • uh, ee • ark • iss*] — Mathair of Eilean

Comhbha [*co • wa*] — Eire's wyvern

Eire Trygg [*air • uh, trig*] — Aisla's best friend

Eolas [*o • liss*] — one of Weylin's horses

Faolan Myrkor [*fay • lan, mur • core*] — Udar of the seven worldly realms

Gaotha [*gwee • ha*] — Ruairi's wyvern

Intinn [*in • chin*] — one of Eabha's doves

Laisren [*lays • rin*] — Priomh of Spiorad

Luas [*loo • iss*] — one of Weylin's horses

Muinin [*mun • een*] — Aisla's wyvern

Oisin Dorcas [*oh • sheen, door • cass*] — heir to the seat in Briongloid

Rania Dorcas [*ruh • knee • uh, door • cass*] — daughter of the Lord of Briongloid

Ruairi Vilulf [*roo • ree, vill • ulf*] — Aisla's best friend

Sinead Bracken [*shin • aid, brack • en*] — bartender in Briseadhceo

Smaoinigh [*smwe • chee*] — one of Eabha's doves

Taistealai [*tash • tuh • lee*] — messenger between the worldly realms and the otherly realms

Weylin Myrkor [*way • lynn, mur • core*] — Udar Apparent of the seven worldly realms

Gods/Goddesses:

Airdeall [*are • dull*] — goddess of the heavens; protector of the gods

Cion [*key • un*] — god of beauty, love, and fate

Eabha [*ay • va*] — goddess of wisdom, mother of the gods

Ifreann [*if • run*] — god of death and Hel

Leighis [*lay • sh*] — goddess of healing, harvest, and hunt

Muir [*moor*] — god of waters

Realta [*ray • all • ta*] — goddess of the sun, moons, and stars

Sionna [*see • on • uh*] — goddess of mischief and war

Taran [*tear • in*] — goddess of thunder and justice; protector of humanity

Locations:

Albios [*all • bee • oss*] — the heavens; one of the two otherly realms

Anseo [*ann • show*] — mid-sized city in Samhradh

Bitu [*bite • oo*] — northeastern worldly realm

Blathriel [*blath • ree • ell*] — capital of Earrach

Briongloid [*bring • loyd*] — southwestern worldly realm

Briseadhceo [*brish • oo • cho*] — mid-sized city in Briongloid

Caillte [*call • chuh*] — capital of Eilean

Cluain [*clu • en*] — small city outside of Omra

Cruthu [*cruh • who*] — castle in Bitu

Deithe [*day • thuh*] — dense forest at the top of Crann Na Beatha in Albios

Eagla [*ogg • luh*] — castle in Samhradh

Earrach [*are • rah*] — southeastern worldly realm

Eilean [*eye • lee • an*] — an island to the southwest of Iomlan; in exile following the War for Descendants; one of the seven worldly realms

Farraige [*far • uh • gay*] — castle in Eilean

Fas [*foss*] — castle in Earrach

Fomhar [*fove • err*] — northwestern worldly realm

Fuar [*for*] — capital of Geimhrigh

Geimhrigh [*gev • ree*] — northern most worldly realm

Hallamor [*haul • uh • moor*] — the capital of Albios; home of Eabha and Cion; meeting place of the gods

Hel [*hell*] — the underworld; one of the two otherly realms

Iomlan [*um • lawn*] — the main continent

Oighear [*ire*] — castle in Geimhrigh

Omra [*ome • ruh*] — capital of Samhradh

Orga [*ore • gah*] — castle in Fomhar

Samhradh [*sour • rah*] — southernmost worldly realm

Scamall [*scom • ull*] — capital of Briongloid

Scamhog [*ska • wog*] — capital of Bitu

Speir [*spare*] — midsized city in Briongloid

Spiorad [*spear • id*] — village on Briongloid and Samhradh border

Sruthar [*suh • roo • thar*] — capital of Fomhar

Talam [*tall • um*] — the world that consists of the seven worldly realms and the two otherly realms

Trasnu [*trass • new*] — small coastal city in Briongloid

Tromlui [*trom • ly*] — castle in Briongloid

Tus [*toos*] — forest in Caillte near the northern coast

Tusnua [*toos • new • ah*] — ocean between Eilean and Iomlan

COMING SOON

Don't miss book two in the *Crowns of Talam* series
as Aisla's journey continues in

BLOOD OF EMBER

Coming 2024

ACKNOWLEDGMENTS

I feel obligated to start by thanking Aisla for being a friend to me for many years. She existed long before Talam did, and I find myself in her strengths and her weaknesses. I also see parts of her that began as so foreign to me, and I have had the great joy of uncovering along the way as I stumbled into her story and her world.

I like to think this is the first of many stories I will write and of worlds I will discover, but it will always hold a special place in my heart. Aisla will always be my first fictional friend.

I am so grateful for Eron, my husband who supported me, encouraged me, and listened to me throughout this entire journey. Talam would not exist without him, and I feel so blessed to have a partner who sees my passion and actively encourages it.

Thank you to my mum, who always gave me a space to dream and the courage to pursue the stars. To my grandparents for loving and leading me with grace. To Caeh for being my built-in best friend.

Thank you Yoshi, Obi, and Luna for being my four-legged friends who I find myself talking to far more often than I would like to admit.

Zoe, this novel would not have seen completion without you. Thank you for always being there to bounce all the ideas off of, for holding me accountable, for believing in me, and for sticking with me and my stories through so much.

Jade, thank you for the cards and encouragement, for always being in my corner, for being the best message proofer, and anxiety calmer, and so much more. Thank you, Kat for being the sister I never had, for donating your wrapping skills to the cause, and for being there in more ways than I can list. Thanks to Erica for the pep talks and listening ear throughout the years.

Shout out to Tommy, who was the first to ever read *Under Cold Moons* to completion. Thank you for your dedication and helping grow this novel. Thank you to my beta readers and my writer friends, Victoria, Britton, Beasley, and Taylor. And thank you Ricki and Ireland for endless support. You each inspire me every day.

I will forever be grateful for all of the creative hands that touched this novel and played key roles in bringing it into the world. Thank you Kelly Ritchie, Becky Wallace, Noah Sky, Alyssa Hurlbert, Drew Flanagan, and Veronica O'Neill. I would not have known how to begin this novel without the mentorship I received in undergrad from all of my professors, but namely, Nina de Gramont, Emily Smith, Tim Bass, Bekki Lee, David Gessner, Sayantani Dasgupta, and Michael Ramos.

I am so thankful for my trip to Ireland and Scotland that inspired Talam's nine realms. To Norse and Irish mythology and culture, which is sprinkled throughout the lore of Talam. And to the Irish language which serves as the roots for the language used throughout this novel. I fell in love with the beauty of this language and find inspiration in the lyrics of the pronunciations. I have provided a pronunciation guide that I researched and put together, but for further help regarding pronunciations, I found teannglan. ie/en/fuaim to be a helpful tool to learn more. I would highly encourage you to check it out!

And thank you, *reader*, for giving your time to the voices of Talam.

Finally, above all, I thank my Heavenly Father for guiding me through every step that has lead to this moment.

ABOUT THE AUTHOR

LE Van Veen lives with her husband and three dogs off the coast of North Carolina, although she spends a good deal of time lost in fictional lands. She has enjoyed stories set in different worlds for as long as she can remember and has long dreamed of building her own. After studying Creative Writing at UNC Wilmington, she began work on her debut novel, *Under Cold Moons*, a YA fantasy novel inspired by years spent dreaming.

Made in the USA
Middletown, DE
07 September 2024

59916921R00241